PRAISE FOR RAJNAR VAJRA

"Opening Wonders is filled with marvels and wonders and really fine writing. This book is 'sense of wonder' taken to the Nth degree."

—JERRY WRIGHT

"One of the best science fiction writers of our time."

—ROBERT J. SAWYER

"Rajnar Vajra is the kind of science fiction and fantasy writer whom not many readers know about, but nonetheless is treasured by those who do. His stories have a certain clarity combined with a sense of wonder that's hard to find these days. Read this novel and join a literary cult of intelligence and taste."

—ALLEN STEELE

OPENING WONDERS

OPENING WONDERS
TALES OF THE PAN-COSMOS
BOOK 1

RAJNAR VAJRA

OPENING WONDERS
Copyright © 2023 Rajnar Vajra

All rights reserved. No part of this book may be reproduced or transmitted in any form or by any electronic or mechanical means, including photocopying, recording or by any information storage and retrieval system, without the express written permission of the copyright holder, except where permitted by law. This novel is a work of fiction. Names, characters, places and incidents are either the product of the author's imagination, or, if real, used fictitiously.

The ebook edition of this book is licensed for your personal enjoyment only. The ebook may not be re-sold or given away to other people. If you would like to share the ebook edition with another person, please purchase an additional copy for each recipient. Thank you for respecting the hard work of this author.

EBook ISBN: 978-1-68057-464-7
Trade Paperback ISBN: 978-1-68057-465-4
Library of Congress Control Number: 2023933789
Cover design by Janet McDonald
Cover artwork by Ali Ries
Kevin J. Anderson, Art Director
Vellum layout by CJ Anaya
Published by
WordFire Press, LLC
PO Box 1840
Monument CO 80132
Kevin J. Anderson & Rebecca Moesta, Publishers
WordFire Press eBook Edition 2023
WordFire Press Trade Paperback Edition 2023

Printed in the USA
Join our WordFire Press Readers Group for
sneak previews, updates, new projects, and giveaways.
Sign up at wordfirepress.com

For my beloved wife, DL Ainsworth

CONTENTS

REVELATION ONE SHADOWCASTER

1. Invitation to the Dance — 3
2. An Ocean Outside My Door — 17
3. Sparks and Flashes — 26
4. All Ears — 33

REVELATION TWO THE TWELVE TRAVELERS

5. Quick Roads and Inroads — 39
6. Home Sour Home — 53
7. A Meal That Remembers You — 59
8. Mind over Manners — 67
9. A Suit for All Occasions — 80
10. There but for Grace — 87
11. Shell Games — 97
12. A Malignant Starfish — 106
13. A Private Ocean — 115
14. Fall from Grease — 124
15. A Medium-Rare Dialect — 133
16. Dodge Baal — 139
17. Swan Lake — 152
18. Boxed Set — 159
19. Written in Mountains — 165
20. No Fun and Games — 173

REVELATION THREE MIRRORMAGE

21. Hex Marks — 185
22. The Big Jump — 192
23. Captain Squid — 201
24. Hard-Boiled Eggs — 207
25. I, Ibis — 215
26. Pushing Against the Sky — 234
27. Sibling Revelry — 243
28. Locution, Locution, Locution — 252
29. The Tides That March — 262
30. Less Than Heavy — 270
31. Tricycle Blitz for Two — 282

REVELATION FOUR THE GOLDBERG VARIATIONS

32. A Crooked House	291
33. Crocodile Tier	303
34. Smoke Signals	314
35. Ceremonial	325
36. Ascent	339
Glossary	349
About the Author	353
You Might Also Enjoy ...	355

REVELATION ONE
SHADOWCASTER

"I see nobody on the road," said Alice.

"I only wish I had such eyes to see Nobody! And at such a distance too!"

—LEWIS CARROLL

CHAPTER 1
INVITATION TO THE DANCE

My phone chirped, snatching me from a high-end wish-fulfillment dream in which some shadowy figure seemed ready to give me the Ultimate Answer. I growled at the phone, but at least had the comfort of waking up in my own bed, my Sara lying next to me where she belonged. Then I remembered she was long dead, and the bottom of my heart dropped out.

Chirp. I snatched up the handset, glancing at the time display. "Hello?" I croaked. A call at 5:30 AM can't be good news.

"Professor Goldberg?" A deep, unfamiliar voice.

"Yes? Who *is* this?"

"Sorry if I woke you. I'm Robert Garlen, and I head the UNDS."

"What's the—you're connected with the UN?"

"Security Division. I'd like to meet with you this afternoon."

"Why? What about?"

"I can't tell you on an unsecured line. Will you make yourself available?"

"I suppose so." I visualized today's schedule. "Can we get together at my university office in the late afternoon?"

"Certainly."

"Do you know where my office is?"

He chuckled. "Expect three of us at four. Have a pleasant morning, Professor." He hung up before I thought of asking for a way to confirm his status. Maybe I could get some info on him online....

I tried, heroically wielding the Shining Sword of Research, namely Google, and could only discover that the UN did have a security division.

After that, I couldn't sleep but wouldn't admit it until the alarm buzzed. The December dawn showed up depressed and gray. Why would the head UN security honcho bother with an obscure professor of comparative history?

I worried the question like a dog trying to chew a steel bone during breakfast and while sedating my students with a morning lecture, and it still bugged me after lunch as I lurked in my office grading undergraduate essays—a trying business even without UN assistance.

I'd assigned my students a topic concerning my favorite extraterrestrial mystery: support or refute Warner's theory concerning the fate of the Scome species based on Scome literature we've studied this semester. A crafty way, I'd figured, to boost my own interest level and maybe generate fresh insights.

Several papers were excellent; most weren't. After commenting on each as constructively as possible—I don't subscribe to the Snarky Critique School of Education—I'd glance suspiciously at the remaining stack, which seemed, if anything, to be growing. Could bad essays reproduce through a hitherto unknown scholastic meiosis, exchanging immature notions, using incomplete sentences as genetic building blocks...?

The problem, of course, was me. Four o'clock loomed and I couldn't focus. The next potential masterpiece awaited, but I couldn't force myself to hoist the thing.

Instead, I gazed out my window rubbing the bald spot gradually uncrowning my head. When that failed to soothe, I turned to my treasure shelf. Between the menorah that had been in my family for three generations and a small purple cube (made on Crossroad World!) that would levitate for a few seconds if you tapped it, sat a kinetic sculpture. My Sara had created this pretty toy of curving glass tubes and tinted immiscible fluids set abubble by a heating element. I turned it on, watched colored streaks slowly drifting, and realized a coffee break was overdue.

That cheered me! I could almost taste Zabar's Jamaican Blend dancing on my tongue. According to my trusty, un-smart watch, I'd have time for a leisurely cup before the UN delegation arrived.

I stood up and stretched. The building seemed unusually tranquil for this time of day, nearly silent apart from shreds of Professor Wu's perpetual Mozart leaking through my walls. Which made the sudden *bang* extra startling. *What the hell?*

In the aftermath, the tinkling of small hard things hitting the floor underscored a sickly hush. Then all was quiet. Even Mozart paused mid-sonata.

Easy to identify the perpetrator. My kinetic sculpture had exploded and taken the menorah and my pottery collection along for the ride. I'd collected these treasures for decades, but *Sara* had created ...

The Crossroad-made cube, undamaged, settled to the floor near my feet. For a ghastly moment, the thick wall I'd built around my grief threatened to crumble. My eyes welled up and my knees weakened; I put a hand on my desk for support and a glass splinter promptly stabbed into my palm. The pain brought me back as I plucked out my unappreciated rescuer, blinked useless tears away, put the cube on my desk, and surveyed the damage.

The shelf had become a dripping graveyard of fragments. Glittery bits had embedded themselves in the ceiling, some barely hanging on. At least the explosion hadn't spread far, horizontally. Aside from my palm, I wasn't so much as scratched, but one especially long shard had found a home in my empty chair. Four murderous inches protruded from the padded backrest like an accusing finger.

I visualized angles and whistled. If I'd remained seated, the glass arrow might've pierced my heart. Interesting. Admittedly, odd little accidents had been plaguing me for years—proof there's a bad side to luck's bell curve. But nothing, far as I knew, had ever threatened my life.

After my hands stopped imitating a paint mixer, I wrapped paper towels around my bleeding hand and more around the long shard then cautiously tugged. Took real force to free it, and the far end was needle sharp. I gave it free admission to my recycling bin. In a way, this glass spear was a blessing, distracting me from the pain of losing yet another piece of Sara.

I heard a token thump on my door and Jim Wu stuck his shaggy head through the doorway, not far enough to see the destruction.

"What up, Dave? Break any bones?"

"Not today."

"You sure? I heard one holy thump a minute ago. I got worried you might've fallen. Or ..." one side of his mouth quirked, "finally snapped and shot the latest class clown. If so, you're my new hero."

"I'm fine, Jimmy." I faked a chuckle. "And no student bodies. I just dropped a vase. But thanks for checking."

Jim was too polite to so much as raise a doubting eyebrow. He said he was going home, wished me a "happy whatever," let the door swing shut, and I felt rotten about lying. He deserved better. But describing the accident might unleash feelings I couldn't afford. Accordingly, I wouldn't call Maintenance for a debris-clearing assist.

I unplugged the ex-sculpture and began cleaning, going over each chair thoroughly. The thought of someone leaning back into a glass knife ...

I'd just finished the final chair when someone rapped twice on my door. Around the Massachusetts Institute for Comparative Studies, knocks come in two flavors: students tap, faculty members bang and barge. Ergo, my company was fifteen minutes early.

Damn. The rest of the mop-up would have to wait. My hands still twitched, one remained bloody, the extent of my loss was sinking in, and enough mess remained to be embarrassing. Oh hell, at least I'd finally learn the purpose of this tête-à-tête. I wiped my paw and opened the door. Three visitors as promised.

The woman was petite, but you couldn't say that about the two fellows bracketing her. On her left loomed a distinguished-looking black gentleman with silver eyeglass frames and matching hair. He stood well over six-three, my height when I remember not to slouch. The second male was two inches shorter than me, but wide as a snowplow blade. Each man outweighed me by at least seventy pounds. They weren't overweight; it's just that I'm built like a pencil. Or more accurately, just the lead.

All three agents squinted up and down the hallway. We were alone except for a slim senior citizen with a dignified bearing. Ben DeHut, my friend and frequent lunch companion, stood leafing through layered flyers stapled to Professor Warner's bulletin board. He noticed us noticing him and called out.

"Ah, David, I was about to pop by for a visit, but I see you've got company. Later then." He nodded politely and strode away. I doubted his back deserved such grim attention. When his white hair disappeared around the corner, my guests were free to focus suspicious eyes exclusively on me.

The men wore black overcoats, the woman a long brown jacket and matching briefcase. Stress-white knuckles on the briefcase handle.

The three kept examining me with no sign of approval. Perhaps a faded flannel shirt with faded jeans had become a fashion faux pas. Or maybe they didn't like my face. If so, understandable. Didn't much care for it myself.

"Professor David Goldberg?" asked Silver Frames.

"That's me." He still seemed dubious. "Honest! Come in. I've been dying to find out why you wanted to see me, but first, anyone care for coffee, tea, or cocoa? The coffee's really good."

"Thanks, we're all set," Frames said, not bothering to glance at his companions. "Professor, I've seen holicons of you. In person, you look ... different. Younger."

My insincere welcoming smile turned real. "No one's ever accused me of being photogenic."

My guests entered, the door automatically swung shut, and the shorter man put his hand on the knob. "Will this lock from inside?"

I stared at him. "Our legal department would throw a fit."

"Why?"

I shrugged uncomfortably. "Some teachers can't be trusted locked alone with students and vice versa."

"Would you object if I secure it during our meeting?" He had a faint accent, perhaps Germanic.

"I suppose not. But how?"

Rather than explaining, he withdrew a small mechanism from a coat pocket and jammed it between door and sill.

Silver Frames resumed control. "Did you recognize that man in the hallway?"

I bristled a bit. "Ben DeHut. Technically Sir Benjamin, but the students call him Old Ben."

"He teaches here?"

"No, but he's always around, auditing classes or schmoozing with faculty. He's a good friend. I'll *vouch* for him."

Frames ignored my smartass tone. "Fair enough. Allow me to present my associates. This is Dr. Susan Rilka." The thirtyish blonde's features resembled my grandmother's in old family photos, but with worry lines like Bubbeh in her seventies. She offered her left hand, apparently unwilling to transfer the briefcase. Cold fingers.

"And this is Special Agent Denys Palmer of our Intelligence Branch." Gadget Man nodded as we shook hands. Moist palms this round. Palmer was one of those steely-eyed, square-chinned, Nordic athletes with a hint of nose, and not a broad hint.

Frames pointed at himself. "And my official title is Supervisor Dr. Robert S. Garlen."

The title "Supervisor Doctor" seemed bloated although I suppose that's what comes from having a Secretary-General as your boss. A second case of clammy hands and Garlen over-squeezed.

"Nice to meet you all," I said, failing to mean it. "Can I take your coats?"

"Not necessary."

"Then please make yourselves comfortable but watch out for broken glass. I had a small accident just before you got here. Are you sure no one wants coffee?"

"Again, thanks for the offer, but no." Garlen must have missed the faint pleading tone in my voice.

Being forewarned, I'd imported an extra perch to supplement my two straight-backed chairs. My guests glanced downward perfunctorily then seated themselves before my desk as I sat down behind it. Palmer half-turned to monitor both the entrance and me.

"What can I do for you?" I wondered aloud.

No one replied. Three pairs of eyes failed to meet mine. Rilka was perhaps counting shiny fragments in the ceiling but didn't ask how they got there.

Radiance suddenly blazed through the window behind me, spotlighting three faces sober enough for funeral directors. The sun had made a surprise appearance, but nobody brightened up. It was so quiet I could hear Garlen swallow. Rilka's death grip on her briefcase never loosened. Were those beads of *sweat* on Palmer's forehead? My office was, if anything, chilly. I started feeling sorry for these people, they seemed so damn miserable. The air thickened with an unfortunate blend of cologne, perfume, vinegar from the broken sculpture, and fear.

Rilka's eyes drifted to some framed Eliot Porter prints on the walls.

"Like the pictures?" I asked, my voice creaking like a rusty hinge after so much strained silence.

Before Rilka could commit herself, Palmer turned to face me squarely and made up for lost time. "Speaking of pictures, Professor, we want you to examine one we've brought. You are *officially* ordered to tell no one what you are about to see. Do you understand and agree?"

I nodded, baffled. When I was growing up, the UN had no authority and not much respect in the US. How things have changed!

Susan Rilka rose and placed her briefcase on my desk. She reached to open it, but Garlen practically leaped from his chair to slap a thick hand over the latch.

"What's the matter, Robert?" she snapped.

He raised his free palm. "Let's take just one more minute here."

"Shouldn't we press on with this?" Rilka's lips now matched her white knuckles.

"Not quite yet, Sue. We've been so focused on our ... problem, it just occurred to me that a history teacher might not have the background to understand what we're up against. Would you mind exploring that issue before we proceed?" He wasn't being sarcastic. "No? Good. Professor, I'd appreciate you answering two questions."

"High time I stood on the other side of the questioning game," I said with a nervous smile and was surprised when Garlen tried, not that successfully, to smile back.

"You're all right, Professor. One: What is ultraspace?"

That was unexpected! Were they having a *physics* crisis at the UN? I shrugged internally and slipped into pedantic mode. "That term," I began, "was coined at the Annie J. Cannon Inter—"

Palmer groaned. "For Christ's sake, just answer the question."

I glared at the Special Agent. Then I winced at my own pompousness and started over.

"Okay. According to the Nemes, our entire universe is a kind of ... sliver, one of many, many slivers in a single multidimensional Domain. Right? Supposedly twelve Domains exist, which means millions, maybe billions of slivers. The aggregate of all Domains is what our astrophysicists have named 'ultraspace.'"

"So far, very good," Garlen said hoarsely.

"Personally," I volunteered, "I prefer a word the Nemes use for the whole ball of wax, the one they translate as 'Pan-Cosmos.'"

Garlen pushed his glasses closer to his eyes. "Second question: what would you expect would be different between one universe—I don't care for your 'slivers'—and another?" He took his hand off the briefcase latch and eased back to his seat, as if my response wasn't important to him. His jaw muscles said otherwise.

An obvious trick question. I pretended to take it seriously.

"The Nemes tell us that parallel universes can't exist, that each reality has to have some variation in natural laws to stay discrete. But as to specific differences between non-parallel universes? As you know damn well, they could be anything at all." I glanced at the purple cube on my desk. "Take that incredible place where the Common—"

"Anything at all," Garlen interrupted, dark eyes glinting behind tinted lenses. "Those are the words I wanted to hear. Kindly proceed, Sue."

I didn't know what to think as Dr. Rilka opened her case and pulled out a three-by-five old-style photograph. She held it as she might a live scorpion, and her hand shook as she passed to me. The paper felt oddly heavy and a little greasy. I took one look.

"My God," I whispered.

When I glanced up, she was back in her chair, paler than ever. "What do you make of it, Professor?"

What, indeed. I studied the thing, embarrassed by my shocked reaction. Any specialist in comparative history should be inured to the outré aspects of ultra-aliens and their creations—strange if something from another universe *didn't* appear strange. Hell, my own research partner was a Neme who easily qualified as physically weird. And I'd seen images of other bizarre Pan-Cosmic denizens including the

Common, the species who'd sent Neme diplomats to Earth to be their representatives. But this!

The ... subject of the photo was an upright gargoyle built from the blueprints of dementia with its zigzag claws, whip-like tentacles, and hippo jaws inset with rows of serrated razor blades. The bulging eyes on its anvil of a head blazed like emeralds with a grudge.

So why did I have a crazy sense I'd seen something similar before?

For a moment, my mind whirled in confusion, but I took a deep breath to still the tornado and looked more closely at the details.

I might've mistaken the photo for an un-glamour shot of a particularly grotesque animal from a darker universe than ours. But along with its organic-looking accoutrements, the monster had six metallic arms, and an illuminated video screen in its chest surrounded by colored buttons. Could these mechanical aspects be part of, or tacked onto, a living creature? After all, electronic doodads and steel arms didn't *prove* the gargoyle wasn't alive.

Once upon a simpler time, the idea of a living creature having a video screen as a natural part of its body would've seemed ludicrous. But ten years ago, on October 31, 2052, the day the Nemes arrived, the boundaries of what *might* exist became invisible from the island of common sense.

Still, it seemed reasonable to assume someone had built this monster because of one extra element. Perhaps some non-parallel animal could grow an organic video display, but why would it grow *writing*? Curving blue squiggles were neatly inscribed above the screen, obviously text.

I held the picture closer to focus on those squiggles. For several seconds, my heart seemed to stop. Then I relaxed, gently swiveling my chair from side to side.

"Why the grin?" Palmer demanded.

"I admit you had me going. Damn clever but doable in flat format."

"What are you talking about?"

"It's a fake of course. Or an artist's conception. Or maybe a meme, in which case I can suggest a caption."

Garlen studied my face as if cramming for finals. "What caption?"

"'There ain't no such animal.'" I laughed, but no one joined in. "Come off it, folks! We all know what this machine is supposed to be, but if anyone found such a thing, it'd be news even the UN couldn't sit on."

Garlen passed the buck back to Palmer with a frown. Palmer wiped his forehead with a jacket sleeve. "What," he asked lightly, "tipped you off?"

I beamed at him. "As you know perfectly well, those curving lines above the screen are script. And the language happens to be *Dhu-barot*, which I've been studying for years because the Scome intrigue me, and Dhu-barot was one of their main languages. *Ergo*, our creepy device is supposed to be a Scome machine. And we all know there aren't any."

Looking at the expressions on those three faces, my confidence dribbled away.

"According to your medical records," Garlen said carefully, "you've never had any vision-enhancing surgery."

"Never needed any."

"That's putting it mildly, Professor. Even young Den here can't see that script without a magnifying glass. I brought one for your use."

"Is my good eyesight a problem?"

"For us, yes. We hadn't intended you to see the writing quite yet. Now that you have, perhaps it's time ..." He turned toward Dr. Rilka.

"Professor." If the room were packed with dynamite and words were sparks she couldn't have spoken any softer. "What can you tell us about the Scome?"

I stared at her. "Are you joking? I know I'm being vetted, God knows why, but now you want to see if I have 'sufficient background' again, *in my own field*?" I felt too astonished to be angry.

"You misunderstand," she said firmly. "This time, we're not testing your knowledge. Humor us. Please."

"Sure. Why not?" I didn't like the hint of petulance in my voice.

"This *is* important," Garlen added, his glasses catching a reflection from the window behind me that hid his eyes.

What the hell was going on? I set my mouth on semiautomatic and searched faces for clues. I'm generally good at reading faces, so good my wife had often accused me of being a closet psychic. But this time, all I could see was fear....

"Hard to imagine a bigger mystery," I quoted from one of my own lectures, "than the Scome disappearance as Nemes have described it."

My visitors nodded to each other at this splendid specimen of triteness, as though I'd said something clever.

"Go on," Rilka suggested.

Encouraged despite myself, I continued. "Fine. About sixty Earth years ago, an advanced humanoid species from a non-parallel reality vanished from their home planet. Overnight. No one knows why they left, how they left, or where they went. The Nemes tell us these beings were facing no known threats—no plagues, wars, famines, or natural disasters."

More approving nods. More insanity.

"The vanished ultra-aliens referred to themselves as the *Scome*, which means 'Tool Users' in Dhu-barot. In that language, their planet was named *Muuti*. That's why the mystery of their disappearance has been called—"

"The Muuti Enigma," Garlen finished for me.

I gave him a puzzled smile. "Pretty much covers the basics, right? Oh, and to complete this litany of generic knowledge: before they'd vanished, the Scome had supposedly, God knows why, removed or destroyed every single mechanical device on their planet."

Rilka leaned forward and her eyes grew very intent. "How do you feel about all this?"

"How do I feel?" I stared at her for a moment. "My entire life has ... crystallized around the Enigma. That's what got me involved in comparative history, and why I started translating the surviving Scome manuscripts."

"A large task, I imagine."

"Next door to hopeless at first, Doctor. But then Able Firsthouse showed up. Did you know we've had a Neme scholar lecturing here for the last three years?" A fantastic stroke of luck for me, good for once.

"We knew," she muttered.

"He's my academic partner and my good—"

Garlen cleared his throat. "Professor," he said, "that picture isn't a joke, or an artist's conception."

"But it *has* to be fake. Unless ..."

How could three dissimilar faces hold such identical expressions? What scared these people so much? Admittedly the photo was freaky, but I'd seen scarier things on TV.

"Do you honestly believe," I asked, "someone has found a Scome machine?"

Garlen just nodded.

If so, what I held in my hands should've had us all dancing the hora. A fantastic discovery! What was the problem?

I began doubting my doubt. If the picture was bogus, someone with rare expertise and an even rarer grasp of Dhu-barot must've gone through a heap of trouble. But why would they bother? For a stupid prank? And the machine's appearance *was* consistent with Scome construction. Muuti is rich, overendowed even, with life and the Scome artistic sense reflected this extreme vitality. They'd designed houses, furniture, even bridges to resemble animals, most often predators....

"I'll bite," I said. "What's this all about? Why have me repeat what everyone knows?"

"We're not here to waste your time," Palmer snapped. "This is *vital*. We've been given the final decision on—"

Garlen shouted over him. "That's *enough*, Den! Professor, we had to find out how heavily ... invested you are in 'what everyone knows.' You've come through for us every time."

"How?"

"By reminding us over and over that everything we know about the Pan-Cosmos and the Scome we learned secondhand. From Nemes."

I shook my head. "Not quite. You of all people must know that a Common, Ru-ahl-tat, once spoke at the UN, in Mandarin no less. After the speech, some webcaster asked about the Enigma, and Ru backed up the Nemes."

Garlen waved a hand in a brushing motion. "True but irrelevant."

"Are you telling me you distrust—"

"What's important right now," Palmer interrupted, "is that you be objective and stay that way."

"I see." Which I didn't. "At least could someone *please* tell me why you're taking this snapshot seriously?"

"Soon," Garlen promised. "Assume it's genuine and tell us what you can about the picture, um, as a whole."

I frowned. "What do you mean? Obviously, it's not a holicon but an old-fashioned 2D color glossy, what we shutterbugs call a 'flat.' And, speaking as a photography snob, the shot is poorly executed." The mechanical abomination appeared at an odd, but unaesthetic angle. Not that any angle could have rendered such an eyesore attractive.

"He didn't ask for a critique," Palmer growled. "Look harder."

I sniffed, not in disapproval, but because a peculiar but faint odor had finally cut through the stronger smells in the room. I moved the photo closer to my nose. Yuck. I'd found the source all right. Whatever substance made the print feel greasy also stank.

"Just a sec." I put the flat down and sniffed my fingers. As I feared, some of the smell, a mélange of rancid linseed oil and gasoline, had found a new home. "What do you suppose—"

The floor creaked. Palmer spun away from his chair and was suddenly aiming an improbably large gun at the doorway. He used a two-handed grip, and his arms weren't any too steady.

"It's nothing!" I insisted. "Just the building adjusting to temperature changes. Happens all the time."

Palmer caught his associates' eyes as he slipped the weapon back into a jacket pocket and resettled himself. Rilka shuddered, and Garlen patted her hand.

I picked up the picture again to hide how much the incident had rattled me and noticed more details. Behind one side of the ... mechanodile, I spotted a blurred section of what might be a similar device. From what little showed, this one was no improvement. Perhaps other machines stood even farther back. Long oblique lines marked a slice of distant wall, possibly some form of writing; several foreground blurs were unidentifiable.

Then it struck me. Thanks to Able, I probably knew as much as any human about the Scome. If these people needed to consult someone about the print, I wasn't the worst choice. A cheering thought! I'd had a growing feeling of being set up for something truly unpleasant. Still ...

"There's a roomful of these toys somewhere?" I asked, struggling not to duplicate Rilka's shudder.

The woman herself watched me with hooded eyes. "Please examine the writing and translate whatever you can, Professor."

The request seemed harmless, but my visitors visibly braced themselves. Palmer wiped his forehead.

"I can translate what's written on the machine, but if those lines on the wall are letters ..."

"We believe they're intended to be viewed from below. Tilt the photograph backward," she suggested.

I complied and the symbols shortened into familiar shapes. "Huh. The Scome never used *that* script! It's a trade language the Nemes refer to as 'Simple,' supposedly invented by the Common. Now I'm confused. You shouldn't find Simple and Dhu-barot in the same universe let alone the same planet."

I felt a coldness in my belly, a gut intuition that hadn't yet made its way to my brain.

"Before we deal with that," Rilka said, one cheek muscle twitching, "could you translate every word you see for us? That could be very helpful."

I studied her and decided to downplay my competence.

"I know a little *Dhu-barot*, but I'm hardly an expert on Simple. It's too bad my Neme colleague just went on vacation, but Professor Warner may still be around. He's probably the premier—"

"You don't understand." Palmer didn't quite meet my eyes. "We're here today rather than yesterday *because* Professor Firsthouse went on vacation."

That arctic finger in my guts reached up to grip my spine. "You're suspicious of *Able*?"

Palmer frowned and said flatly, "Do the translation, then we'll talk suspicions."

"I'll hold you to that. If you knew my friend, you'd trust him." I reluctantly returned to the photo. "Damn. Looking at the wall first, we're off to a bad start. I've seen those first two symbols before, but have no idea what noises they represent or what they signify. Can any of you help? No? Pity. Next word—hmm. I can transliterate the spelling: M-a-a-n-z-a. Pronounced 'Main-za' ... nope, missed a diacritical. Make that 'May-ahn-za.' Accent probably on the second syllable."

"Which means?" Palmer demanded.

I shrugged. "First letter has a dot above it, which indicates it's a proper name although the dot is much bigger than usual. Next to it is a word I do recognize. *Chamm*. Means 'forbidden' or 'hazardous' and it's repeated three times. Someone means it. That's all I know about the wall writing."

Palmer rolled his eyes, but Garlen cut in diplomatically. "Thank you, Professor, I'm sure you did your best. How about the Dhu-barot?"

Palmer's reaction had gotten under my skin. "Dhu-bar-*oh*," I snapped, "the 't' is silent." Then honesty forced me to backpedal. "Actually, Supervisor, I don't know how the Scome pronounced anything. Able Firsthouse says that humans are better off sticking with our own pronunciations."

From the Neme viewpoint, all humans are linguistic basket cases.

"At least," I said, "I can interpret the message on the machine. It's a compound word: 'Shadowcaster.' Means nothing to me. What *doesn't* cast a shadow under the right conditions ... except shadows?"

No one offered any suggestions.

"That's all I can tell you," I admitted. "I'm sorry you've come so far for so little. Perhaps you should get the picture enlarged?" I wrinkled my nose. "That smell really digs into your sinuses after a while, doesn't it? What kind of oil got on the paper?"

"We don't know," Palmer stated. "As to having the photo blown up, we tried. It won't copy."

I stared at him. "Won't copy?"

"Don't bother asking why, we've no idea, but it's one reason we believe it's the real deal. Scan it, and you only get smudge. Maybe the grease scatters the scanning light. We debated sending it to a lab, but decided we couldn't risk letting it out of our possession."

"Huh. Very strange. If I might ask, who took this picture and where, exactly, was it taken?" As I spoke, I finally thought to flip the paper over.

Instant silence filled the office. In the stillness, voices from outside the building and three stories below resonated with that distinctive pre-finals hysteria.

I had a touch of hysteria myself. Two words, in English, occupied one corner of the backing. The tiny lettering was very faint, precise, and starvation-thin, as if written in old-fashioned silverpoint. The style might've been antiquated, but the words were today's headlines:

Planet Crossroad.

I heard someone gasp, probably me. "*Crossroad*! I'm an idiot! Of course! Where else would you find—"

"Keep your voice *down*," Palmer hissed, his accent suddenly thicker.

Garlen put a lid on him before more steam could escape. "Easy, Den! Give the man time."

I barely heard them. Staring at my purple cube, all I could think about was a world beyond astonishing and just on the border of impossible.

CHAPTER 2
AN OCEAN OUTSIDE MY DOOR

Over the last few years, I'd learned a lot about Crossroad. Obviously, nothing firsthand—no human had been there. But on occasion, when Able Firsthouse and I were together, he'd get into these expansive moods and would talk for hours about the place, sharing details that I suspect no other Neme had revealed to humanity. With one exception, he never asked me to keep any of this to myself, and I did share most of it with colleagues. But otherwise I kept my mouth shut to avoid getting laughed out of academic circles.

Comparing time rates between realities is evidently tricky, but Able estimated that concurrently with Columbus seriously failing to reach India, Common ultraspace explorers chanced upon a huge and uninhabited planet in an especially strange universe. When they discovered this world's unique properties, they named it *Ot-u-klin*, literally "Ways of Meeting."

Ergo "Crossroad" although Nemes for obvious reasons more often call the place "Commonworld."

Able described Crossroad as an ultraspacial hub, a paradox planet, the only known world inhabitable by beings from widely disparate macrocosms. I remember his exact words: "Commonworld, David, is *the* trans-cosmic intersection, permeable to the physics of all non-parallel realities. With appropriate environmental adjustments including gravity, virtually anything alive can survive there. On Commonworld, beings that normally couldn't so much as *perceive* each other can and do interact."

When the Common realized the unique opportunity this offered, they decided to use Crossroad as home base for a staggeringly ambitious project.

First, they developed a means to detect the incredibly subtle effects of consciousness on physical reality. Even with superhuman technology, it took them decades to perfect what some pundit at nytimes.com dubbed the "Intelliscope."

Then, with this splendid new toy to dredge thousands of non-parallel universes at a go, they set out on a mission incredible: locate *every* sentient species among the wrinkles and reaches of ultraspace, contact them, and invite those amenable to participate in a Pan-Cosmic community. Occasionally they encountered species so useful or sympathetic or just plain interesting, the Common offered to set up an Enclave for their kind on Crossroad. In some cases, an entire colony.

Able claimed that since the Common began their quest, Crossroad has become something fantastic, teeming with the eerie and exotic, with hundreds of radically different species, each with unique technologies or exclusive styles of—and here's where he lost me—"magic."

Able refused to define magic but provided me some examples, which gave me the impression it involves influencing reality through mental rather than physical tools. He did say, "Any sufficiently advanced magic is indistinguishable from advanced technology."

What I found frustrating about Able's private lectures is how he tended to gloss over items that intrigued me to focus on details that didn't, and my attempts to steer him otherwise always failed. Just before he went on vacation, he spoke of a museum on Crossroad with art collected from thousands of universes. But then, he barely mentioned the exhibits and blathered on about how cleverly the doors were locked! Alien perspectives, I suppose.

Later that same evening, he seemed ... different than his usual relaxed and confident self. His eyes kept hiding themselves within his body, a sign of Neme distress. I asked him what was wrong, and he didn't answer for so long that I worried I might've offended him in some way.

Finally, he told me that he wanted to share some information, but would only do so if I promised to keep it to myself. At least until "further notice." That was a difficult decision for me, but I agreed.

Practically whispering, he told me that Crossroad's "exuberance" had attracted some unexpected and uninvited residents. And not even the Common, should they care to, have the least idea how to expel those entities he referred to as "gods" and "demons."

A barbed insight popped my thought balloon. This photo was a window into a potential calamity.

Garlen nodded slowly. He saw me putting the pieces together.

According to Nemes and confirmed by the only Common to visit Earth, not a single Scome machine had survived the Scome exodus. If this picture had been taken on Crossroad, our ultra-alien mentors were lying—unless some cabal existed, opening its own wormy bucket. Bottom line: if Nemes and Common were lying about anything, they could be lying about *everything*.

Implications left me shaken and queasy.

The Common had become important to human welfare over the last decade, regulating inter-cosmic trade, determining our place in the Pan-Cosmic community, controlling access to ultra-alien sciences including medical technologies.

Certain exotic technologies would operate in our universe right out of the box, and more could be modified to operate. But who decided which technologies came to Earth? Why, our trusted pals, the Common.

Likewise, Nemes claimed that various intelligent ultra-alien races could visit us with minimal life-support equipment; some wouldn't even need equipment. Yet, so far, the Common had only given their agents, the Nemes, passports. Doubtless, with our best interests at heart.

The Common were renowned as the benevolent protectors of delicate, budding species such as us. We knew that because Nemes had told us so. A tower of cards.

I took a shaky breath. Confirming the origin of this photo was crucial. I wiped sweat off my brow and felt a new empathy for Agent Palmer.

But something didn't add up. Even granting that the machine existed somewhere on Crossroad, why in the name of sanity would the UN involve *me* in this? I was so far out of my depth, I couldn't see any shoreline.

Garlen smiled grimly. "What eyes you have, Professor. I wouldn't have thought anyone our age could see that word let alone read it."

"But is it true? Was this taken—" I had to swallow. "—where it says?"

Palmer winced. "The trillion-dollar question. You asked why we take this seriously." He glanced at Garlen who nodded. "From the color spectrum and resolution, it was almost certainly shot with a human-made, pre-holicon camera. But ... fold the paper in half."

"Fold it?"

"Try." I pushed the tip of one corner over. He snorted. "Good enough. Hurry now! Crease it with your thumbnail. Press hard."

I missed my chance because the glossy had already flattened itself out. "Oh. Some kind of smart material. We have something similar on Earth, don't we?"

"Nothing quite like this. You saw the note on the bottom?"

Feeling numb, I looked again. My thumb had been hiding another miniature message printed in the same emaciated script. This one seemed cryptic: *Hall of Games, 10 square.*

"What does it mean?"

Garlen spread his hands. "What would you guess, Professor? I wonder if you'd come up with the same ideas we've been batting around."

"I have no idea. Give me a moment, please." I laid the photo on my desk, stood up, rudely turned my back to the guests, and gazed outside. A flare of sunlight scalded cloud-edges near the horizon.

Looking down, I watched students navigating asphalt paths, seemingly black against the snow-dusted grass. This year's fad had gained traction: "3D" jackets: overcoats plated with a few microns of memory-crystal. Sky glare washed out the displayed animations, but I glimpsed moving surf, celebrities, antique manga ...

The rushing people suggested blood cells flowing along the capillaries of some gargantuan organism. Beyond them, Mead Tower loomed to the west, its shadow pointing straight at me. From the vantage of my ivoroid tower, humanity appeared serious, vulnerable, and in a tearing hurry.

The single exception, a white-haired island of calm. Ben DeHut stood on a path, gazing up at my office. Convinced he couldn't see me considering distance and the reflections from my window, I waved anyway—and blinked when he waved back.

"I'm sorry to nudge you, Professor," Rilka said, "but are you finished with the print?"

"I suppose so," I said, returning to my seat. "At least I finally understand the problem."

Garlen sighed. "We've more than one problem, Professor. Hang on to that thing a bit longer. If the, uh, label's honest, the picture wasn't taken by a human."

"Oh. Right." The idea of an alien shutterbug struck me as outré. But the alternative, a secret human visit to Crossroad, was downright crazy considering that we didn't know where it was and had no way to get there.

Garlen cleared his throat. "But it suggests a few specifics about the photographer."

"Such as?"

"This ... individual must have a visual sense like ours and some equivalent to fingers—assuming an Earth camera was involved. Might you have anything you can add?" I sensed he was leading somewhere but dragging his feet. How and why would an Earth camera or smartphone wind up on Crossroad?

"Well, I'd suppose our photographer felt rushed."

That earned me a round of puzzled looks. Garlen spoke for the group. "Explain."

"Everything in the picture's crooked. Assuming this image was printed correctly, the camera had to be tilted when the shot was taken. Suggests haste, doesn't it?"

"Perhaps an alien aesthetic."

"Let's be fair, John," Rilka said. "We've had weeks with this and he came up with something we hadn't."

"Something obvious," I had to admit, "to a photographer."

Garlen grimaced. "Professor, nothing about this is obvious. We haven't even determined how that picture came to us. Two weeks ago, the Secretary-General found it sitting on her desk."

I met his eyes. He didn't know who or what wanted humans to have this photo or who *didn't*—a category implied by its stealthy arrival.

"Since it came to us, we've had a few odd ... incidents," he said softly.

I felt a new kind of chill. No wonder my visitors were running scared! Some unheard-of terror could be on Earth right now, hunting them down. Able's hints concerning Crossroad weren't all sugar and sunshine ...

And now I'd seen the damn thing myself! What had I gotten into?

I glared at everyone. "How about some honesty on your end, folks? Surely, you've got in-house specialists for translating Simple and Dhubarot. For all I know, you're all experts yourselves. Why come to Williamstown? For a second opinion?"

The general tension seemed to increase, but to my surprise, Palmer suddenly grinned. "You're *way* off."

"What else could possibly bring you?"

Garlen licked his lips and sat straighter. "We three have been tasked to make the final decision here, and I think we're all agreed. Susan? Den?" They both nodded. "Professor Goldberg," he said formally, "Will you travel to Crossroad on behalf of all humanity? Fair warning: it might prove hazardous."

For a moment, I couldn't speak. "Are you saying the Common have actually invited a *human* to visit? That's huge! And you want *me*? To go to *Crossroad*?"

"No one else."

"Unbelievable! Totally—"

Palmer's face: a study in anxiety. I lifted my hands in surrender. "Sorry I forgot about keeping my voice down, Agent."

Garlen waved my apology away. "Understandable and no harm done, I trust." He ignored Palmer's glower. "I'm sure this opportunity must seem ... exciting to you."

"For once the cliché 'chance of a lifetime' actually fits. But I don't understand. Why me?"

He studied his hands. "The Common sent us a list of qualifications. You proved the only viable candidate."

"What qualifications?"

"Why not tell him?" Rilka suggested.

Garlen seemed to commune with himself for moment. "Feel free, Susan."

"First, no living relatives," she began, ticking off each item with a tap on her briefcase. "They want someone acquainted with Simple, comfortable around Nemes, between the ages of forty and sixty, and ... in peak health."

She glanced over at Garlen before continuing.

Her face became slightly flushed. "That's why we had to review your medical records."

"Why would the Common be so fussy?" Privacy issues didn't bother me as much as the no-living-relatives part.

"There's more. They asked for someone with advanced degrees in both history and psychology, and a solid academic reputation. Then we added a condition of our own: the person must be expert on the Scome —and fairly conversant with Dhu-barot."

"Wow. Sounds like a small group."

"Couldn't be smaller," she admitted. "The runner-up was a woman in China with half the requirements."

For a minute, I stared at everyone. "Unbelievable."

Garlen's hands tried to strangle each other. "Believe it. I regret putting you in such a, uh, precarious position, but if you agree to go, you must—" he chewed his upper lip for a moment "—you must make every effort to determine the whereabouts of that room. We know it's a challenging assignment, but you must realize how important it is."

I nodded and almost couldn't stop nodding. "If the Common aren't playing fair, we're in a hole so deep ... but how could you expect me to locate one room on an entire planet?"

More lip mangling. "We believe the 'Hall of Games' part of the message refers to one specific and important location. We hope that the Common will prove willing to tell you how to get there. In any case, you must find a way to do so and ascertain what's there. Perhaps the other part of the message, 'ten square' will provide a clue for finding the Shadowcaster machine, or lead you to another guiding message."

"And if the Common won't give me a tourist map or won't let me go exploring on my own?"

His face tightened. "We'll be back to a certain square of our own."

Right. Square one. "I've never heard of any Hall of Games on Crossroad."

Rilka stepped in again. "I imagine you'll be in places *no* human has heard of."

True, and that aspect pulled me like a super magnet. But the thought of being physically near that monstrous machine wasn't enticing. And now that the notion had sunk in a bit, the idea of me attempting this mission seemed ludicrous.

I had to put an end to it. "This just won't work. Do I look like a secret agent? I'm fifty-three years old. An academic, for God's sake!"

"Truly, Professor," Palmer said, "you'd make an ideal spy. But it hardly matters. You're the only one we can send."

That struck home, and I groped for a way out. "Doesn't it strike you as a bit fishy, this photo shows up from nowhere and then, *bam*, we get a surprise invite to"—I remembered to lower my voice—"Crossroad?"

"A *bit*?" Palmer pinched his nose as a visual aid. "But that doesn't alter our responsibilities. Or yours."

"Point taken."

"Before you decide," Rilka interjected, "you should know the job might be easier than it sounds."

"Go on. Please."

"Would anyone object if we put that horrid photograph away first?"

She dropped it when I handed it over—probably nerves. I caught it in midair and held on until her grip was secure.

Palmer made a faint gasp of surprise. "You've got *very* quick hands, Professor."

I shrugged. "What could possibly make this job easier?" I asked Rilka as she latched her briefcase.

With the print out of sight, she seemed more composed. "The Common have offered to provide you a tour. Just tell them Professor Firsthouse mentioned a Hall of Games, and I'd think they'd take you there."

"Um. They might have some way to know when I'm lying."

"You wouldn't be lying. Clearly you didn't attend Firsthouse's lecture last week."

"I couldn't, and I haven't gotten around to the transcript. He actually mentioned the Hall?"

"When he spoke about architectural scale on Crossroad, he used the Hall of Games as an example of particularly large structures."

"Oh." The only specific places I remembered him bringing up were Hhoymon City, the "Tower of Art," and "Watergod's Grotto," whatever that was. Suddenly, he'd introduced this Hall of Games? My father used to say coincidence was like peanut butter: too much and it gets hard to swallow.

Rilka ignored my frown. "You see? You may have no difficulty reaching the Hall. Once there, simply look around. We don't expect you to enter that room with the machine should you find it—unless you can do so without attracting attention. But you *must* try to determine what 'ten square' refers to. Presumably, the Common will be inviting other human visitors now that they've opened the door, and we'll need that information to take the next step."

"If ten square isn't an address, what could it be?"

She gave a minimalist sort of shrug. "We've speculated. If this Hall has games as we use the word, one might use ten squares."

"Or ten to the second power," I offered.

Garlen scowled. "I doubt it. Why pass us a note and make it that obscure?"

"I hope to God you're right, Robert," Rilka sighed. "He could have a devil of a time just investigating everything potentially involving the number ten."

I had to force the question out. "A moment ago, were you implying you *want* me to explore the machine's room if I can do so, um, covertly?"

Rilka opened her mouth, but Garlen spoke first. "That would be our ideal scenario. In that event, we'd want you to take a new picture."

"Why?"

He answered quietly. "We've collected enough information on Crossroad to know that it's ... strange. Once there, you might not want to trust your own eyes. The camera you'll bring will be harder to fool."

"Assuming I go."

Rilka rushed in to close the deal. "There's an incentive we haven't mentioned. The Common have offered to assist you in any areas of research you fancy. Wouldn't that be a priceless opportunity for a scholar?"

I swallowed hard and could almost feel the barb catch in my throat. "How long would I get to stay?"

Her faint smile belonged on a con artist who's hooked the sucker for sure. "That will be up to your hosts. Probably no longer than one or two Earth weeks."

"Seems I've got no choice. When do I leave, and where does one catch the bus to another universe?"

All three visitors traded glances of unmistakable relief. Palmer gave me a genuine and surprisingly warm grin. Suddenly, I had more sympathy and respect for these people. They'd had plenty of reasons to feel tense, and I'd been one of them. What would they have done if I'd said no?

The meeting ended two minutes shy of nine, but no one had suggested sending out for pizza. Our remaining conversation covered "details and contingencies," but various items in both categories remained vague because the Common had promised some final instructions, such as where to meet that bus, but hadn't yet sent them.

Palmer visually checked the hallway before anyone risked leaving. He took his time and despite everything, the intensity of his caution struck me as comical. I kept expecting him to announce, "The coast is clear!"

When I was finally alone, things didn't seem so amusing. My own thought came back to haunt me: the agents didn't know who or what had brought that photo to human attention. But the sneaky way it had been delivered suggested that someone or something might not want us to have it. I found myself eyeing the doorway as if it opened onto a dark ocean floor—where something gigantic and deadly might be lurking.

To hell with that, I told myself. *I was going to Crossroad!* Nothing this exciting had ever happened to me! Excepting, of course, the day my wife and I first had coffee together. Wasn't it time to uncork the champagne?

But I had to admit that my bubbly had gone a bit flat. It was late and I was hungry, scared, and with a mess still to clean up. And a heap of papers left to grade.

CHAPTER 3
SPARKS AND FLASHES

I worked like a madman for the next thirteen days, or at best someone seriously disturbed. Must've slept and ate, but don't ask for specifics. Whenever I *had* to take a break I'd heat some cocoa, throw a log on the fireplace embers, flop into my favorite chair, and stare into the flames, basking in the bittersweet illusion my wife was nearby, perhaps refining her latest choreography in her mirrored studio. Then, with my drink only half gone, guilt about lazing off would attack, and so much for R&R.

The university closed on the twenty-second. I barely managed to turn in grades on time. Then I had holiday chores and vacation preparations to complete. But mainly, I combed Scome documents for references to hideous machines, bulked up my knowledge of Simple, and pored over a translated map Rand McNally wouldn't recognize, which the Common had sent in an information packet concerning my visit.

To my relief, I was to be housed among Hhoymon, the amazingly humanoid species Professor Wu had been researching with Able Firsthouse's crucial assistance. I'd seen images of all four Hhoymon races; none appeared intimidating, and the tiny Whites were rather cute. Able had raved about their fabulous museum ... mostly about those damn locks.

The weird map was a flexible holicon of Hhoymon City that magnified any area I bent; studying it felt like playing an accordion. I tried to memorize every detail, recalling my dad's hiking dictum: "He who gets his bearings will not lose his marbles." I intended to arrive on Crossroad with a full bag of Cat's Eyes.

When I asked Jimmy Wu to fill me in on the Hhoymon, I got a

strange earful. According to Able, some quirk of evolution had given the species "internal telepathy," the ability for multiple areas of the Hhoymon brain to directly share information without the delay and bother of having to transmit the information. Perhaps it's pan-universal that brain efficiency and intelligence go together like eggs and shells. Jimmy's summary: "David, Hhoymon are super smart."

Able had claimed that this internal telepathy wouldn't work on Earth, so Hhoymon were unlikely to come knocking, even with Common permission. Apparently, a technological marvel that Able called a "Macro-quantum Reality Suit" could solve that issue, but he doubted any species would willingly put up with the claustrophobic effects of such gear for long.

Jimmy discouraged me from attempting to learn more than a few useful phrases in Primary, the Hhoymon equivalent of Esperanto. He explained that Hhoymon languages are superhumanly economical, with context and implication carrying most of the message. He gave me some examples of Gray Hhoymon poetry with rough translations. If James Joyce had read them, he would've wept into his whiskey from the sheer obscurity.

Fortunately and unfortunately, the Common promised me a full-time Neme translator during my stay. Nemes are linguistic savants, so I'd be able to communicate with my hosts although it would likely be painfully slow compared to their intra-species conversations. This translator would also pose my greatest challenge. How could I search the Hall of Games, assuming I could get there, while chaperoned?

Another interesting question: What do you pack when visiting another universe? I'd been told to bring a suitcase. One.

Palmer and I spent hours together. Den proved a decent sort; my initial impression of the man had been skewed by the circumstances. Born in Holland, he'd spent most of his adulthood in the USA, which he viewed with affectionate cynicism. He'd prepared a list of instructions ten miles long, and we went over them endlessly. He also trained me to use an ordinary-looking camera with a six-digit price tag.

And he relayed a commandment from On High. I was to tell no one anything about anything, but should spread some reasonable-sounding manure on friends and neighbors to explain my absence: supposedly I'd be in Connecticut, supervising repairs on the house I'd inherited after my parents died. The emergency number I'd hand out would connect with a live person using voice-synthesizing software.

I signed a sheaf of papers agreeing that the UN had no responsibility, liability, or culpability for my present, past, or future condition.

If confession is good for the soul, I'd better confess. Part of the reason I kept so busy was to keep fear at bay. My mood cycled through periods of near panic, insecurity, excitement, and plain denial. But fear remained a constant companion. I kept wishing I was already on my way back home.

Too soon, departure day arrived. Coffee at 5:00 AM after a night of scattered catnaps. Going online to pay bills I'd nearly forgotten. According to my Googleplex home page it was Tuesday, December 28, 2062. My horoscope ordered me to remain "down to earth."

Then, in the foggy early morning, with my head even foggier, I stood on the curb blinking at an obsolete Toyota bearing an eroded "hydrogen equipped" sticker. I'd expected something sleek and new but, as I was soon informed, we were keeping a "low profile." Denys Palmer, at the wheel, flashed me a tight grin. "Morning, Dave. You'll ride next to the boss."

I slid into the back seat next to Dr. Supervisor Garlen, who was busy typing on a laptop with a privacy display. I should've called shotgun. Garlen pushed the laptop aside to begin a "briefing" that droned on the entire time it took to reach Dulles International, excepting a bathroom break and one more ... interesting intermission, which happened when we were about fifteen minutes along the New Jersey Zipway.

I'd already been informed about where and how I'd be catching my ride to Crossroad and didn't care for the "how" part, but saw no point in complaining. Still, it added yet another layer to my nervousness, which may be why I practically jumped out of my seat when the car's warning alarm buzzed.

Traffic Control had gone off-line and a thousand startled drivers were suddenly piloting their own vehicles. Den grunted and began steering.

T-C has become so reliable some people take naps despite the heavy fine if they're caught. On those increasingly rare occasions when the super-redundant system crashes, so to speak, there's generally an unholy crop of squealing brakes, panicked drivers, and dents.

Not today. My opinion of humanity soared. But then a passenger-less urban bus drifted our way. Den blasted the horn and swerved into the fast lane when the bus driver kept coming. Now we were penned in; a concrete divider blocked any desperate attempt to risk oncoming traffic. A moment later, the huge vehicle had gotten so close that if my window had been open, I could've reached out and drawn my initials on its dusty paint.

Sensibly, Den accelerated. I felt a wash of relief until I turned to look through the rear window and spotted the bus driver. I wished I hadn't.

The man's face had gone sheet white, and I could tell he was screaming. He appeared to be fighting his steering wheel and losing.

Den roared Dutch obscenities as the coach slowly overtook us, which shouldn't have been possible. From a sudden pounding noise, I knew he was pumping the accelerator, trying to force more hydrogen into the engine. No good. The lumbering monster pulled even with us.

After shouting a warning, Den slammed on the brakes. The shuddering and grinding of the anti-lock system was assault enough. To my horror and disbelief, the bus somehow slowed at the same rate.

Den shouted again and floored the accelerator just as I saw a blue flash. Then a Catherine Wheel of sparks blazed where the bus's left tires had been. The coach began listing like a ship about to capsize, and it swung around with easy grace to hit our rear bumper. A doomsday concussion blasted us forward, a steel ball off an iron bat....

Den fought for control. Scraping along the divider, we raised our own spark shower. I turned around again and found the bus now on its side, rotating—a giant lethal version of spin-the-bottle.

Behind us, wholesale mayhem. Cars streamed around the capsized bus like minnows evading a shark, but three slammed into it while others collided with each other. Only the fortuitous resumption of Traffic Control prevented mass slaughter; every vehicle behind or near the coach juddered to a stop. The rest of us proceeded smoothly on our way.

"Jesus *Christ!*" Den squeaked as we drove on. "Everyone all right?"

"One second," Garlen requested. I'd been vaguely aware of his voice all along. While we'd been polishing the concrete divider, he'd been chatting with someone via sat-phone. He said, "Then find out." I had an upsetting thought. Had UN agents, in another car, shot out those tires?

"Fine piece of driving, Den," Garlen said. "How are you holding up, Professor? You're white as milk."

You think I'm *white?* I thought, trying to shake off the shakes. *You should've seen that driver!*

"I'm fine," I lied, "and damn glad we're alive. But my God, some of those poor—"

"Robert, you get a load of that asshole?" Denys interrupted, his voice still shrill.

"Compose yourself, Agent. You mean the bus operator? I never saw him."

"He must've been crazy!"

"I got a look at him," I volunteered. "I don't think he could control his vehicle."

"Oh?" Den spat out. "*Someone* was steering that damn thing. Otherwise it wouldn't have followed us like it did."

Garlen chewed his lower lip. A near-death experience didn't faze him, but now he looked spooked. "That means this someone gained access to Traffic Control, shutting it down except for maintaining command over the bus."

The agent grunted. "Yeah. You're thinking what I'm thinking: our ... saboteur might not be a local."

"That's my fear. But if it was an attack by some, ah, extraordinary enemy, how could they know we'd be on the road just then?"

"How do *we* know what the fuck aliens can do?" Den snarled.

Garlen banged his fist into a palm. "That doesn't justify losing our heads. Gentlemen, we must all stay calm and keep our eyes wide open."

"How about that blowout," I asked. "Accidental?"

"No one," he said slowly, "on *my* staff was responsible."

He refused to discuss the matter further and the "briefing" resumed until Garlen received a call. No one had died from the zipway fiasco although local ERs were swamped. Even the bus driver was "stable." Our ride became uneventful, but I couldn't begin to relax; the incident had added the cherry to my stress cocktail.

At Dulles, we boarded a helicopter that delivered us to the summit of a steep hill in Tennessee near sunset. The next step was the part of the arrangement I liked least. For no reason that I could imagine, the Common had insisted that I remain alone while waiting for my ride. I hated the idea.

Den shook my hand with a pity-about-your-terminal-disease finality, and Garlen seemed painfully sincere as he wished me luck. I watched the copter fly away, clinging to its fading putter as though the sound were my last link to anything trustworthy.

I've battled loneliness plenty of times in my life. Somehow I'd never quite felt as if I ... fit in with other people. But this seemed a different species of loneliness. My only company, a suitcase and a brown-bag dinner I'd acquired at the airport. To my left, a few stunted bushes snuggled against a narrow, tombstone-like boulder. Otherwise the hilltop was snowy and bare.

I set down my luggage, brushed snow off the rock, sat on it and ate. The ambiguous sandwich was dry, but I managed to wash a bite down with root beer. It didn't help that my throat had clenched like a fist.

The repast included a banana so mushy I decided to conserve it for putting out small fires. I packed the contemptible spotted thing into my suitcase along with the nibbled sandwich. On Crossroad, I might be *grateful* for something inedible stuffed with something unnamable.

The hilltop's western side ended abruptly in a sheer drop. I stood and sidled closer to the edge, gazing out at a series of ridges that seemed to get larger in the misty distance. The sun crushed the horizon.

How could I be this scared yet bored? I felt chilled despite my lined jacket and would've greeted a hot drink, preferably alcoholic, like a lost pal. Except my bladder was already too full.

What to do? Leaving the hilltop to urinate, I might miss my ride or annoy the chauffeur, doubtless a Neme, by being tardy. But if I did my business right here and my limousine materialized? Despite my friendship with Able, I had no idea how a Neme would react to being, well, peed at.

Decisions.

Finally, hydraulics preempted debate, and I headed down the gentle eastern slope. No ultraspaceships or angry post-its awaited me when I returned, but the issue raised uncomfortable thoughts. I'd kept myself so damn busy I hadn't bothered asking some basic questions.

Was Crossroad equipped with toilets humans could use? Might I wander into what I thought was a restroom, spy what I thought was a urinal, and proceed to piss upon some shiny white alien who was sixty times smarter than me? My grin was a brief thing. On Commonworld, I *could* make mistakes that ridiculous! Why hadn't that occurred to me before? Had I recently been driving my *life* asleep at the wheel? Or had my UN handlers finessed me into unquestioning submission?

I replayed conversations with Den and company but only noticed something distasteful about myself. In retrospect, I'd regarded the agents as inferiors, no better than students. Why, from my godlike perch at the pinnacle of human evolution, I'd had to make an *effort* to avoid sounding condescending.

Back up, David! No better than students? When had I gotten so arrogant? In the gathering darkness on the hilltop, I saw myself with distressing clarity.

Long ago, I'd vowed to never become the kind of teacher who confused the ability to hand out grades for intrinsic superiority to those being graded. I'd broken that promise. In fact, I'd performed an impressive tour de force of the ego: not only had I looked down at my students because of my role as teacher and evaluator, I'd managed to feel superior to my fellow professors because of *their* feelings of superiority.

Night swaddled the world, but I wasn't comforted.

Cold thoughts on a frozen hilltop.

I stopped pacing, shivered, and gazed up at stars unfettered by city lights or smog. The constellation Orion caught my eye. Beautiful. Overwhelmed by pre-homesickness, I focused on Rigel, twinkling its definitive blue below the Belt. There'd be no Rigel where I was going. My universe had never seemed so precious, so familiar and homey. I wasn't ready to leave. This mission had turned my life around so fast my brain hadn't stopped spinning.

Pacing had kept me from freezing, but doubts kept crystallizing. My footsteps in the snow represented an expanding road map of worries. This mission was too bizarre, too uncertain, and too damn important. Surely, *someone* more qualified ...

Without so much as a polite flash, the great-grandfather of all thunderclaps shattered the peace, rattling the hilltop. The raw shock of it knocked me to my knees. I couldn't believe a sound could *be* that loud. Ears ringing, I stood up.

A small round light the exact cobalt blue of taxiway edge markers floated in midair, about twenty feet beyond the hill's western edge. It quickly elongated into a glowing cylinder with a back-slash tilt that took to spinning propeller-like, creating the illusion of a ghostly wheel.

My vision blurred, and I had no idea what I was looking at.

Ultra-alien communication? Then the cylinder froze in space parallel to the cliff's edge. Abruptly, it stretched toward me into a glowing flat rectangle, which stretched upward, becoming a garage-size radiant blue box with a closed garage-size door.

The box hovered, steady as if it had been glued to the air. The door began opening. White light blazed through the widening gap.

CHAPTER 4
ALL EARS

I'd secretly hoped Able Firsthouse would be the Neme assigned as my pilot. Right now, I desperately needed a familiar face. But the glare within the box silhouetted a huge figure. What the *hell*!

A Common.

Unbelievable! Now *two* had visited Earth.

This one seemed masculine but the required pronoun, I reminded myself urgently to avoid my first Pan-Cosmic gaffe, was "it." No human knew why.

The brightness hurt. Through watery eyes, I watched the alien take a giant's step to the hilltop, and I took a coward's step backward. It stopped and bent down to scrutinize my suitcase before turning toward me. The oddest moment of my life.

I'd studied videos and holicons. I knew the Common were big, over eight feet tall with feathery head-crests rising another two feet. But I wasn't prepared for so much sheer towering bulk. And the pictures hadn't showed enough. From close-up, whoever had classified these Crossroaders as "humanoid" had needed glasses and/or sobering up.

True, it had two arms and stood on two massive legs, had a reasonably spherical head with eyes, even a mouth of sorts. However, each eye had two close-set lemon-yellow irises with slits for pupils, the "mouth" resembled a shiny white diaphragm, completely sealed, and I saw no ears or nose. I had no idea how it could eat, drink, hear, or even breathe.

But I saw it breathing, probably through some hidden orifice. At least its torso kept expanding and contracting. And the frigid air became increasingly perfumed with a pleasant piney aroma.

The Common's upper body appeared shaggy with leafy

appendages: long brown ovals, tiny and sparse around the thick neck but progressively larger lower down until I could barely glimpse the cinnamon-colored skin of its ... abdomen, assuming equivalent anatomy. It wore baggy blue trousers covered with pockets, a saddlebag-sized backpack, and a belt stuffed with mysterious artifacts. Its feet were large, round, leathery, and bare.

The alien studied me with equal intensity, but I suspected only one of us was scared. "Name me Sun-toch-sew," it declared in a resonant baritone. "Means 'Rider-on-beauty.' I am the guide of you."

I shouldn't have been so surprised; the first Common to visit had spoken fluent Putonghua, standard Mandarin. But Ru-ahl-tat had come to address the entire human race. Surely this Rider hadn't learned English just to speak to *me*? Still, the needle on my stress-o-meter eased back a notch. As a general rule, I feel more comfortable around ogres if they can talk.

Subtle twists and vibrations of the white mouth-diaphragm had produced that rich voice. Interesting case of non-parallel convergent evolution: Nemes have a similar speech mechanism, but three diaphragms.

My turn to make noises. "I'm, uh, honored to meet you ... Sun-toch-sew, was it?" Doubtless, I'd mangled the name beyond repair. "I'm David Goldberg. Um. Welcome to Earth." So far, the Host of the Year Award wouldn't have my name on it. "Wish I could offer you something; you've come so far. Would you—would you care for a banana? It's a bit overripe." I shut up before I could plummet to unheard-of depths of lameness.

"Professor David A. Goldberg?"

"That's me." Could even an ultra-alien suspect that some other David Goldberg might be waiting?

"Can you forebear my slowness to alignment? Top master I am not of what you call ultraspace math, as are others among my kind, but you will find my English already of heroic stature and hardening with rapidness. My peers salute me as lingual top-hound, and why should I dispute?" Rider leaned toward me and spoke as if imparting a confidence. "Common do not have such language-sprinting minds as our little Nemes who help, but enjoyment in understanding will be ours, hope I. As for your kind offer of poisonous alien fruit, I must sadly deny."

I blinked and tried to cudgel my brain into coming up with a response. "I heard a loud noise when your ship appeared," I observed, mostly because I couldn't think of anything better to say.

"Cha-ka-*boom*! Yes? Our worlds spin differently, they space move and hold other energy ... variegations. Some differences we use to power voyage, but usually some force remains. This we must dissipate. Or else! Machine pushes big air, makes din. Scared you terribly, I hope not?"

"I'll survive."

Rider emitted a slurping noise with a staccato rhythm. Then it abruptly fell silent and shook its head hard enough to make its leaves rattle.

"Such is my fondest hope," it said quietly.

"Um." The discussion seemed to have run aground. "Tell me, Sun-toch-sew," I improvised with a notable lack of inspiration, "are there bathrooms on Crossroad?"

"Chybris-ayn! In the presence of a traveler stand I! You are about to behold wonders but ask a question of immense practical! Allow me to provide comfort about comfort station. Rest room assured, rest assured!"

I suppressed a frown in case the Common understood human facial expressions. All this verbal tap-dancing had its charm, I suppose, but it seemed so *forced*.

Well done, I scolded myself. *A great achievement in the sport of jumping to conclusions! You just met your first Common and think you've got some basis for forming opinions.* I looked down to avoid the lemon eyes and noticed the alien's hands had eight tapering fingers or maybe tentacles ending in pea-sized balls.

Rider reached out to gently touch my face. "Did some ineffective predator attack?"

Surprised by so much obvious concern, I touched the same spot on my cold-numbed face with a cold-numbed hand and couldn't feel the healing scar. "I nicked myself, um, shaving yesterday. It's nothing really."

"Nothing" had been an understatement. My old-fashioned, double-bladed razor had suddenly fallen apart, and the bare blade had dug into me before I could react. Just another in my series of freak accidents.

"In such case," Rider said, finger-tentacles curling, "we should move with the haste, while terms remain close. Efficiency is beauty, no? Named as I am, should I not then ride on efficiency? And," the voice again turned confidential, "if power I waste, unjustified talk will ensue at home." The guide of me snatched my suitcase and whirled around. "Jump please."

A four-foot gap separated the hill's edge and the ultraspaceship's door. I leapt across, oblivious to the drop below. Which illustrates my mental state.

Sun-toch-sew glanced about, perhaps confirming we weren't leaving any socks behind, then followed a stray wind-gust into the box. The door slid shut.

When my eyes adjusted to the dazzle, I felt let down: bare walls, no seats or visible machinery, and nary a peephole let alone a window. The pine scent was strong here but not unpleasant. I heard a faint click from behind, but turned and saw nothing but the back wall.

Abruptly, dozens of short lines in crayon colors and at random angles appeared in midair, well above my head. My guide extended three fingers to brush three adjacent orange lines, adjusting their slant; a neighboring blue line immediately twisted several degrees on its own.

"Virtual controls?" I asked. To avoid sounding like a rube, I added, "We use VC systems on Earth, too."

"Virtually incorrect, Professor David A. Goldberg. *Subjective* controls."

I didn't understand the distinction, but got sidetracked by dizziness that increased as line after line reoriented itself.

"Apology," Rider muttered, fingers gently manipulating a magenta line. "Thorny analyticals, and I am not brainal-retentive like Hhoymon and Blenn. But we can rejoice, for I've solved ... alas, not yet. Does this not make your internals squirm?"

"I'll say. What are you trying to do?"

"Solve ... Gordian equation while twelve variables joust. Delicate work. Touch this stripe just so, and we jump backward a molecule. Touch slightly harder and we jump beyond this galaxy. Caress two stripes and we slip to another superspace aspect."

"My God," I said with sudden awe. "We're moving through different universes at this *very moment*, aren't we?"

"Imprecisely. We reached our proper oasis in ultraspace when door shut. All this fuss is for placement, alignment, and motion matching."

That was a stunner as was the strongest wave of vertigo yet. Then everything steadied and my guide cried, "Success! Proudly done in record slow time. Be most welcome to Ot-u-klin, Professor David A. Goldberg. My world is on your feet!"

I faced the closed door and waited.

REVELATION TWO
THE TWELVE TRAVELERS

Above, below, where'er the astonished eye
Turns to behold,
New opening wonders lie.

—EDWARD HICKS

CHAPTER 5
QUICK ROADS AND INROADS

The door opened and I had my first look at wonderland: a kaleidoscopic confusion of train station, cathedral, and rainbow. Immense, glittering, radiant.

"Here is Great Hall Four of Triangle Four," Rider announced. "You might name this 'Common' room. Why do you sway like a wind-caressed fern? Are you dancing? Unwell are you?"

"I'm ... not dancing." Was this superspace jetlag? I couldn't quite find my balance and a glass pane seemed to separate me from reality. Reminded me of floating along on gallons of coffee after pulling an all-nighter. Plus, I had strange little bursts of delight. Hard to describe, but it was as if the only apple I'd ever tasted was a mealy Macintosh and I'd just taken my first bite of a superb Honeycrisp.

Rider bent down until our faces were nearly touching. I stared into double-yoked eyes searching mine. After an uncomfortable moment, gauzy layers of eyelids fluttered—a non-parallel wink?—and the Common straightened up without saying a word.

Too insecure to ask what *that* had been all about and curious as hell, I wobbled forward to get a better view of Great Hall Four, a space seemingly too large to be enclosed.

Our craft levitated just off the edge of a plateau big enough for statehood. I took a deep breath and suddenly felt steadier. Then another mini bout of ecstasy gave me enough courage to grip the doorjamb and lean outwards to gaze straight down. Directly below was empty air for perhaps a quarter mile, then thick pearly mist. A dark, tongue-like limb easily taller than a ten-story building momentarily snaked up from the fog.

I backed away and swallowed hard. "What's down there?"

"Docks for superspace jumpers of sincere expanse and handlers without hands," the Common said. "Hear my advice, Professor David etcetera: drink my world in small sips." I nodded, sipping Great Hall Four.

A wide black strip, where dozens of vehicles resembling our luminous box were parked, bordered the complex topography of its floor. A bright, midmorning quality to the illumination provided a sense of cheer and great energy, yet the glowing ultraspaceships were the only apparent light sources. I tried to coax my overloaded mind to interpret the scene.

It wasn't easy, partly thanks to the scale and novelty of this place, but also because of new distractions. The sides of my head prickled, and I kept glimpsing shimmering lights with something like peripheral vision, only my eyes didn't seem to be involved. My first migraine aura? I concentrated on the shimmer. Big mistake. I clung to the doorjamb until the world stopped tilting.

The Hall snapped into focus again, and I realized the gargantuan space was practically deserted. Couldn't make heads or tails out of those few denizens I *could* see, assuming they had either. Perhaps when they'd built this place, the Common had foreseen future mobs. Or maybe some *really* huge aliens visited on occasion.

I desperately needed a reality interpreter ... and a friend. "Would you happen to know the Neme scholar, Able Firsthouse?" I asked Rider without much hope.

"Surely."

"Really? I don't suppose he's ... in the vicinity?"

"Not in this moment."

So much for any chance for a lifeline.

Despite so few inhabitants, the Hall echoed with random buzzes, booms, and whispers. And each moment brought a new smell wafting by. Some were pleasant, some exotic. One reek made my nose want to wave the white tissue of surrender.

I couldn't get over the size of this place. A hundred airplane hangars wouldn't have filled it! The ornate ceiling seemed cloud-high. In the distant haze, immense hexagonal openings pierced the back wall. I was dying to snap a picture, but Garlen had ordered me to reserve every shot for the Hall of Games ... and only bring the one camera.

"We have arranged Great Hall Four for many styles of visitor," Rider said.

Oh. Right! Suddenly, I understood that I was gazing at a mosaic of habitats: toy glaciers, rivers of varying sizes and colors, bubbling pools, small forests, a wedge of sand dunes, and two columns of turquoise smoke. Several rivers oozed along like thick green oil. Even the celestial ceiling held a patchwork of vines, pipes, inverted towers, and various openings.

The mini-desert grabbed my attention. One dune had begun moving our way. It had passengers. When it drew close enough for me to be sure the three figures perched on top were Nemes, I felt some of my anxiety fade. To misquote Will Rogers, I never met a Neme I didn't like.

Then I remembered my mission, and all that anxiety snapped right back.

I glanced to my left. Near the plateau's edge, thirty feet away, an unfamiliar type of alien stood upright, rocking gently, its one leg terminating in something like a large shallow bowl. Hate to admit to being so ... un-cosmopolitan, but I found its face truly repulsive, particularly the ant-style mouth, garnished with strands of jiggling rusty drool. Two short antennae and random coarse hairs failed to beautify its dark wrinkled skull. Its eyes were unexpectedly mammalian, big and blue. Here, I thought, was a living Bug-Eyed Monster, except for the eyes.

Perhaps it noticed my attention. It leaned far over, then flipped back upright like a plastic clown with a weighted base. Before I could ask my guide how or if I should respond, a foggy ribbon detached itself from one of the turquoise columns, wrapped around the buggy creature, and pulled it smoothly and rapidly off into the distance.

"What the hell," I whispered, "was *that*?"

"Queen's ears," my guide said. "Her agent, you would say."

I was about to beg for clarification when something occurred to me. Where was my welcoming committee? Denys Palmer had relayed a promise from Crossroad authorities that my hosts for this visit, a Gray Hhoymon family, would be greeting me on arrival.

No Hhoymon, not even a tiny White one, to be seen. Puzzling. And disappointing; I'd been eager to meet these super-geniuses.

Fifty feet away, a large shimmering bubble materialized directly on the parking area. It popped, releasing a Common and a second drooling, one-legged alien bug. Rider and the arriving Common exchanged honks. Another turquoise band stretched out to girdle the mismatched pair. This time, it tugged its passengers straight up and through one of the ceiling openings.

"No thunderclap?" I asked.

"How remindful you are! But in this Mind-full Hall, any excess is easily stored."

"Oh." Mindful? "What now?"

Rider reached out to tap on one wall of our vehicle and a purple light flashed twice. "Progress! Crossroad technology has finished adjusting environment around your body; you may walk secured. We needn't postpone."

"Postpone what?"

Rider nudged one of the ship's control lines. "Leaving this nest. Further waiting lacks purpose; dune buggy cannot come much closer since sand is sternly limited."

Sure enough, as our box wafted forward and settled on the landing strip, the Neme-ridden dune stopped several hundred yards away.

"Nemes prefer comfort to rapid," my guide murmured. "Lucky that you and I are rich with patience and can afford time wasted. Come, it is a short walk even for short legs. Can you ascend sandy lump by yourself?"

"If a Neme can climb that, so can I."

I decided that Rider's slurping noise was Common laughter. But I didn't get the joke.

―――

The slope felt steeper than it looked, but I stumbled to the top unaided and the dune began moving again, in reverse, slow and smooth. No risk of sand-sickness.

Physically, the three were typical Nemes: about five feet tall with heads shaped like upright peanuts and lower faces trifurcated, each section with a speaking diaphragm and nostril-slits. Below the neck, they became blow-dried koala bears, yellow fur glittering with embedded specks. Their paw-like hands had six stubby fingers arranged almost in a circle; the furry feet were wide and flat. Two had the narrow shoulders and relatively longer arms of females. The one male was shortest of the three but stood the straightest.

On that Halloween night when Nemes first arrived on Earth, people initially mistook the white diaphragms for eyes. In fact, their three eyes are small, black, button-round, and attached to specialized fibers underlying the "eye-band" around their heads: a narrow protein strip that can quickly soften, permitting the orbs to dive beneath the surface and pop out anywhere along the band—quite disconcerting at first.

That first-contact team had explained how they'd learned human languages prior to making first contact: from human entertainment media. The old cliché about monitoring our radio transmissions had come true. Only in this case, it wasn't radio but radio waves.

Despite my worries, I figured that if even one member of this surprise greeting committee spoke English—and Nemes catch languages the way humans catch colds—the next few minutes promised to be interesting.

I'm considered a gifted linguist, and learning new languages is one of my hobbies. But apparently any Neme, in *minutes*, can learn to converse in any human tongue with the clarity and blandness of the anchorperson of your choice. Instead, most prefer to latch onto some unique speech style and stick with it. Four of the five I'd met on Earth had modeled their voices and vocal behaviors on those of some human but not necessarily well-known actor. But one had sounded exactly like John Wayne....

The furry aliens didn't turn toward me. Instead, three trios of eyes surfaced in my direction. Neme eyes normally twinkle with humor and health, but only the taller female twinkled. Uneasy again, I glanced at Rider who, unlike me, had remembered to bring my suitcase.

"This upstanding human," it announced, pointing, "is titled Professor David A. Goldberg. And these three Neme flowers are titled in English mode Strong Eighthhouse, Swift Thirdhouse, and Kind Thirdhouse." Strong was the taller female and Swift the male. Kind seemed unusually slender for a Neme female. I appreciated Rider using the translated names; no human could produce a convincing triple-tone.

Swift reached out to give me a human-style handshake, but I moved my hand sideways to press its back against the back of Swift's paw—a Neme-style handshake. His eye-band rippled slightly, the equivalent of an appreciative smile. Strong and Kind pressed my hand in turn. Kind's eyes drifted sideways to avoid meeting meet mine at close range.

"Honored to meet you all," I said.

"Honor is ours, but courtesy yours," Swift responded, and I had to choke back a chuckle at his thick Russian accent. "Am history teacher like you." The voice seemed vaguely familiar. Peter Ustinov in some old movie? After my wife died, I watched a *lot* of classic movies....

"You know about me already?"

"Less than we wish, but in fairness I share equivalent data: lovely Strong here is physicist and philosopher. Also skilled poetess. Equally beautiful Kind is my cousin and personal assistant."

I turned toward Strong. "I've wanted to meet a Neme physicist for a long time. I've got a question about Crossroad."

"Later," Rider interrupted. "Our sand has reached its destiny. Now we must navigate floor remnant then take a Glideway to our proper Safe-road. Best to be on this Safe-road as soon as probable. Hence, we leave now."

Glideway? Safe-road?

The dune had brought us near one of the great hexagonal doorways. Rider skied downhill on its big round feet and the Nemes followed, partly sliding and partly stepping, unexpectedly graceful. I didn't trip on the way down, not quite.

When I reached the floor, Strong popped an eye toward Rider. "Guardian, may we all accompany you far as that Safe-road?" I didn't recognize this voice, and felt more curious about that "Guardian," but her accent was cinematic Georgia peach.

"Be the guest of me," Rider replied. "But make those tiny limbs swing fast! Built, I am not, for mincing words *or* legs."

I was about to ask why the rush when I felt a tiny pinprick on the back of my neck. A second later, the spot burned like hell.

"Hey!" I yelped, clamping a palm over the pain. "I think something just stung me! Any ... Crossroad bees around?" The fire was already fading.

"No. Move digitals aside and let me listen," my guide ordered grimly, and I assumed Rider had meant, "let me look."

"Nothing," it said after a close examination. "No punctuations to be heard. Surely random nerve firing, all excited by Great Hall."

My companions exchanged a flurry of hand signals, and I turned my head for a better look. Instantly, all hands froze while the Common's leaves started flapping as though blown by a heavy wind. Rider bent down, gazed into my eyes for the second time today, and asked, "Are you feeling strangely?"

I frowned. "Not sure what you—my neck's much better. Or do you mean something else?"

"Else."

"Guess I'm still a bit woozy. And my, um, temples sort of tingle."

"Is that all?"

"I think so." Except for the weight of a world on my skinny shoulders.

"Then all is well!" Rider declared with palpably phony cheer. "Such feelings are a model for normal. You will climb to acclimated before we know it!

"Here on Ot-u-klin, sense organs from many Roads work as they do in their native Road. You hear? Many, many possible senses exist. Visitors arrive and receive ... sensation supplements, which only few learn to comprehend. Your tinglings are un-familial notes."

Plausible enough, assuming I'd grasped the intended concept, but I had an impression Rider was switching little cups around, hoping I'd lose track of which one covered the ball.

"We shall experiment!" Rider announced. "Clench oculars, please."
I deciphered the instruction and obeyed.

Good *God*! Even with eyes tightly shut, I could *see*. Only, I seemed to be gazing directly through the sides of my head! So much for my cynicism: the cranial fizz *was* input from some extra, visual-like sense. Unbelievable!

This side-sight was dim, grainy, and made everything look weird. Weirder, I mean, and wider too. More stereoscopic. Weirdest of all, something I couldn't pin down about the murky scene was utterly bizarre....

"Anything?" asked the Common.

"Not much," I fibbed impulsively, "I can see a little light."

"Ayn-Seris! You are *most* talented. But unfurl your oculars; we must move, faster than ever. Forward April!"

"Um. You mean forward march?"

"Too late, if I remember your month-order."

The joke, if meant as a joke, failed because Rider sounded so tense. As we walked, the Nemes struggling to keep up, I watched for signals. No finger wiggles, but I still felt that everyone else was in on some big secret.

Nasty word for the hour: conspiracy.

I'd seldom been around more than one Neme at a time. When the three began chatting—nine diaphragms spewing words, imitative sound effects, and occasional musical passages—it reminded me of a gag bouncing around Academia. What do you call a pair of scissors and a Neme? A barbershop quartet. Didn't claim it was a funny gag. I could hear much puffing and huffing, but Neme speaking diaphragms aren't lung powered.

One of Swift's eyes swam over to face me. "You relish novelty, comrade?" He only needed one diaphragm for me; the other two never stopped communicating with his pals.

"If not, I'd better learn how."

Swift chuckled Neme-style with a brief hum, and Rider patted me on a shoulder. With a pang, I realized how much I'd like the Common already if only I could trust it.

I amazed myself. Evidently, I'd become two different people: one having the time of his life, the other terrified by excess strangeness, responsibility, and a growing collection of ominous hints.

An ocean liner could've navigated the monstrous opening before us.

We stepped through into an indefinitely long sky-blue tunnel. Its walls and floor resembled sharkskin.

After a few steps, I realized that this tunnel was Crossroad's version of an airport-style moving walkway, only our feet didn't quite touch the floor. The next few steps taught me the folly of making comparisons to anything on Earth. I hadn't felt any change in speed, but I knew we'd accelerated outrageously from how the walls had become a smooth blur. Terrified, I glanced at my companions, but they all seemed to take this, figuratively and literally, in stride. As for me, it took me another minute to calm down enough to ask questions.

"Now I know what a Glideway is," I said, my voice wobbly. "But why no wind?"

"Air is gliding too," Rider answered. "This is seven-league footwear. And good exercise to boot! We are only stepping slow out of respect for our companions' limb-limits."

Slow? I nearly had to jog to keep up.

I had more questions, but I noticed that Rider's attention had become focused on something overhead, its yellow eyes suddenly quite protuberant. *Telescoped*, I thought, but with an inkling of worry that Rider's verbal games were exerting an undue influence on me.

Naturally, I looked up as well, and my eyes did their own, more modest, bulging. A queue of inverted Nemes hung directly above us on the high flat ceiling, flashing toward the Great Hall. Two-way travel and dual gravity! That meant this tunnel's talented winds were rushing smoothly in *opposite directions*. Neat trick. My airport people-transporter analogy had already crashed, but now it burned.

Rider made a quick gesture. I only noticed because my new sense had stretched my peripheral vision.

Strong immediately asked, "You had a question for me, Professor?"

I studied her profile. Had Rider ordered her to distract me? If so, from what? Still, what an opportunity!

"Right. I've never understood something fundamental about Crossroad, and my Neme academic partner suggested that I consult a Neme physicist. If I could find one."

"Curiosity's a gift," she said. "And now you've gone and shared it. I'm wonderin' what you're wonderin'."

Rider finally eased the pace; perhaps we'd achieved maximum glide speed. Even so, Strong, Kind, and Swift kept panting.

"Curiosity can wait," I offered, "until you rest up."

"I am a mite winded, but a Neme don't gossip pneumatically. What all don't you get?"

"Supposedly, all sorts of non-parallel physical laws operate here?"

OPENING WONDERS

"They surely do."

"How does that work in practical terms? Take light speed. In my universe, light zooms at about 670 million miles per hour. But maybe in yours it limps along at 200 million. So how fast—"

"On Crossroad," Rider put in, "light runs at many speeds in many ways. But we are rich in photons and visitors with oculars seldom complain."

"Fine, forget light. What about a change in laws governing, oh, friction? Let's posit a reality where smooth surfaces give better traction than rough ones."

Rider put on a serious voice. "Warning! Abrasive floor, threat of slippage!" Which, despite myself, made me laugh and conjured up a road sign: Slippery When Dry.

"You got one fer*tile* imagination," Strong commented.

"All right, silly idea, but specifics aren't important. Just pretend such a reality exists. Would a chunk of sandstone on Crossroad feel smooth or rough? See my problem? Doesn't make sense for opposing physical laws to coexist in one place."

"But Crossroad *isn't* purely one place, Professor, not the way you're thinkin'. It's layered."

"Layered?"

"Heaps of realities all squeezed together."

I shook my head. "That, I really don't get."

She hummed a chuckle. "Hardly get it myself. Neme science isn't the end-all in *these* woods! Look here. What I've been told is that long ago, the essence of this world lay scattered throughout all Roads: the one, tiny, fully parallel part of every non-parallel universe. But eventually they merged to precipitate into a reality of their own. But they couldn't precipitate as a unified whole because each part retained attributes from its native Road. The effect is that Crossroad isn't so much *integrated* as laminated."

"Hang on. You mean ... once upon a time, we could've taken a *spaceship* from Earth to some part of Crossroad?"

"Only to your version. Technically, millions of Crossroads exist, but nowadays they're all right here."

I stared at her. "Let me get this straight. You're telling me that Crossroad isn't actually a single planet, but a vast number of them all in the same place?"

"Close enough."

"That's ... confusing. You make this place sound almost, I don't know, artificial."

Two of Strong's eyes sunk partway into her head, and I got the feeling that my statement had upset her although I couldn't imagine why.

Swift waved an arm forcefully. "Artificial," he stated, "is un-Neme concept. Nature engenders intelligent beings, nyet? Therefore, products and acts of intelligent beings must be natural."

That statement put a new spin on the subject. I hadn't meant "artificial" literally, but had shied away from using the word "unnatural" because it might've come across as too negative. But it seemed I'd accidentally pressed some kind of hot button....

"I thought," I said slowly, "the Common discovered this world, not that they more or less created it."

"You thought correctly."

"Then what, exactly, glued all the Crossroads together?"

Swift aimed two eyes on Rider and the other on me. "Circumstance," he said after a long pause.

Strong slipped back in. "Let's talk practicalities, Professor. As I said, Crossroads is layered. When visitors arrive here, each visitor remains crystallized, if you'll excuse a fuzzy little analogy, by their native reality. That determines which aspects of this place affect them."

Smooth way to shift the topic, I thought sarcastically. "Hold on, Strong! You mean I can only experience one tiny slice of Crossroad? That contradicts everything I've heard about this world."

"Dear me. 'Haste wastes work,' as Balanced Clearhouse put it—wouldn't you agree, Guardian? I wasn't fixin' to imply all that. Ot-u-klin's integration allows us all access to a passel of ultraspacial prospects. When you drop in here, you get *broadened* a mite, spread through as many layers as possible."

"How's that done?"

"The process is partly innate; think of this world as a prism and yourself as white light. But the Minds help out, they—"

"Exit approaches," interrupted Rider louder than seemed necessary.

Strong hummed a brief but unconvincing chuckle. "Swift, Kind, and I have pressin' business, Professor. But maybe you and me could resume our chat real soon. For now, just remember: all varieties of physics work here, but not always the same for everyone."

The wall texture reemerged as we slowed to our actual walking pace and settled to the floor. We entered a large octagonal chamber and Rider stopped near the Glideway's exit. The Nemes could finally catch their breaths. Echoes amplified the wheezing in Strong's breathing slits. Rider and Swift traded hand waggles, not bothering to hide them. Swift's gestures seemed angry.

Each wall contained a huge hexagonal opening. Six, including the one behind us, were tunnel entrances. The final pair brimmed with golden light that appeared to thicken after a few yards, obscuring whether they were tunnels or long nooks.

I noticed a new smell, clove-like but mustier. Then six ultra-aliens silently emerged from one passage, joining us in the chamber: khaki-skinned humanoids with fuzzy, fire-engine-red hair on narrow skulls and short red manes waving from muscular necks. Each stood nearly as tall as Rider, but the height was largely from grotesquely long, thin legs. The group rushed by, ignoring us, and didn't stop until they'd reached the entrance to our right.

Each stilt-person touched the dull blue border around the opening, stepped two paces into the tunnel, and stood as if waiting for the midtown bus. I gawked as their legs shrank and hips expanded until they were about Strong's height and wider than the average fertility goddess.

"The Vyre," Rider murmured, "so enjoy a practical center of gravity."

"The Vyre?" First I'd heard of them.

One by one, they wafted into the air to land feet first on the ceiling. Their legs elongated as they began to walk upside down and accelerated out of sight.

"Enigma to us they are, as adaptable to circumstance as to surface and so gentle and cooperative. We have not sensed the faintest echo of competition in their speech or behavior. How could such a mild species survive? For our own instruction we invited these pleasing souls to enclave here. Yet we have learned little. They are reclusive."

So even for Common, Crossroad held mysteries! And I'd found a new one for myself. Glideway technology was ingenious, definitely, but considering the supposed level of local science, why not some form of instant teleportation?

Swift and Strong said farewell while Kind waved shyly. She hadn't spoken a word of English. Before the three disappeared inside a Glideway across the way, one of her eyes scooted to the back of her head to gaze at me.

"Now, for some rapid hustle!" Rider declared.

"Why did those three work so hard to keep up with us if they were headed someplace different?"

"Because you and I are the top best company!" It placed a huge hand on my back, gently steering me toward one of the openings filled with ghosts of apricots past.

If the golden medium around us—could *light* be condensed?—were any thicker, swimming would've been easier than walking. Luckily for me, Rider dawdled and kept glancing backward.

"I like this 'rapid hustle' of yours," I said. "It's helping me recuperate from when you were going slow."

"Some hustling is limb alternatives not alternations. Far enough. Now we ride in comforts! Have you appetite? Soon we will reach selectable nutrition."

"Could eat," I admitted, watching the gilded air turning foggy, especially around our feet.

My guide sat down and gestured for me to do likewise. Tentatively, I lowered myself until an unnaturally supportive fogbank caught me like a soft chair. Rider placed my suitcase and its backpack on a misty shelf behind us, sat beside me in a seat as cloudy as mine but wider, and leaned back. I followed suit. Wow. I'd found the recliner retirees could only dream of. Pity I'd forgotten how to relax.

Misty walls rose around us, curling overhead into a roof high enough for Rider's crest. The surrounding fog eddied as I felt a mild acceleration. All that walking had evidently refreshed my guide; Rider smelled like a newly cut forest.

"We now ride a Safe-road, Professor David A. Goldberg. More intensely fast and fun than a Glideway."

"Fun?"

"Just listen."

Gradually, the fog and our misty car vanished. Then we were seated on nothing, zooming through an underwater paradise with flamboyant fish and fantasy coral stippled in blues and yellows.

"My kind evolved on a world without oceans," Rider offered. "Pangs I feel for all beings denied wet marvels! You find this soothing, I hope?"

Okay. My guide wasn't *entirely* sound-oriented. As to "soothing," Rider seemed to need Valium even more than me. The Common practically dripped anxiety.

"Very pretty," I said. "Where are we?"

"Still on Safe-road, where else? All this is pretend, a recording from Blenn homeworld, neither subjective nor projective. And while we enjoy damp rocketing, we have a significant journey ahead, about seven hundreds of your present heartbeats."

"Doesn't sound like a long—how do you know how fast my heart's beating?"

Rider glanced at me. "You have a smell sense. This I lack. But we

Common *listen*. I hear your stomach digesting, blood squeezing, connective tissues squeaking. You are a busybody!"

Note to myself: two doctorates doesn't make a person quick on the uptake. I'd noticed Rider's leaves frequently shifting angles, but had missed the obvious. Those "leaves" were ears that practically covered my guide.

A school of midsize fish with pink streamers scattered before us, an underwater fireworks chrysanthemum. "How fast are we actually moving?"

Rider hesitated. "Twenty times perhaps the quickness of sound through Crossroad air."

"Good God." And me without a seatbelt.

"Haste is needful on such a fat planet. What thought you of Swift, Kind, and Strong?"

The question so caught me by surprise I responded too candidly. "Swift claimed he's a teacher, but his behavior said soldier. Don't think he liked me much."

"You amaze! In truth he's a warrior's aide, not a warrior, but you herald keen acumen. He is *also* a docent; Nemes seldom lie. Still, his primary role requires more caution than friendliness. But you mistake detachment for hostility." The yellow eyes appeared thoughtful. "Will you speak of Kind and Strong?"

In for a penny, I told myself. "Kind must be terribly shy. And Strong reminded me of a Zen teacher I know—palpably content. Serene." Until I somehow managed to upset her.

"She is a peaceful one. But from your heartbeats, your contents are less peaceful."

Denial was out, which left misdirection. "It's that Mach twenty business." Right now, I was mostly worried about why Rider was worrying. "Who's driving this crate? Some computer?"

"Less or more. As you might say, foolproof."

"Really?" Suddenly my lie had some truth to it. From my experience, nothing is more likely to fail than anything declared "foolproof."

"Your heart pumps faster!"

"Right. I had a nasty reminder today that computer-directed traffic systems aren't entirely dependable. And in this, um, virtual ocean, we can't see what's truly out there. How would we know if we're about to crash? And—silly question, I'm sure—do we even *have* brakes?"

Rider was obviously amused. "At such velocity, senses make little difference! But cease all such cares! This is Safe-road. Is really, honestly safe. Listen, marvel, and learn."

The Common pulled a translucent blade with a green handle from the tool belt, turned it point-down, then plunged it toward my right thigh. While I was in mid-gasp, a wad of yellow cloud materialized, enveloped the knife, and stopped it. I could see Rider's arm straining, but the cloud was stronger.

"Hear? This is *Safe*-road! Designed by Blenn. Where you are safe, secure, and protected. Here, you couldn't have a hearts-attack to save your life!"

"Okay." I tried to sound calm, but doubted I could fool that many ears. "I'm impressed. Who are these Blenn?"

"Engineers and craftsbeings most deafening!"

That one took some chin scratching. "You're saying they're brilliant?"

"So much so, they know how to proof things, even from fools."

"I must admit ... you put on a convincing demo." Also horrifying.

I suddenly felt too drained to talk so I just stared at the passing sea life, trying to appreciate the moment. And postpone worrying about how what I learned here could affect the entire future of my species.

CHAPTER 6
HOME SOUR HOME

So far, I hadn't glimpsed Crossroad's surface. Dreamy speculations involving ultra-alien trees, clouds, and seas filled my head. My eyes began to close on their own recognizance.

Then the Safe-road snapped into visibility, and I got that grumpy feeling of a promising nap interrupted.

"You should take a stand," Rider warned. I struggled to my feet. Our foggy vehicle briefly reappeared then evaporated into the surrounding amber brightness. The Common donned its backpack, grabbed my luggage, and strode from the tunnel. I followed, still groggy. We emerged into another octagonal chamber, and I woke up *fast*.

"Ouch, dammit!" I cried. "It happened again!" When I pulled my hand away from my neck, a drop of blood glistened on my palm. I held it out to show Rider, who froze momentarily then examined the wound for so long I suspected my trusty native guide of playing for time. I wondered why some of the fingers touching my neck felt warmer than others.

"This happens to fresh arrivals, but most seldom," Rider finally said. "Gorged I am with regret. The cause is localized change in air pressure from a small slip of the Mind responsible for staking your territory. But as local Mind adjusts to your form and contortions, errors will shrink. Such missed stakes shouldn't repeat."

"Hope not." The pain had already ebbed, but this round had been worse. "What's this 'mind' you keep mentioning? And what's its connection with air pressure?" I looked around uneasily. Was I unknowingly surrounded by hard vacuum with some form of virtual spacesuit keeping me from exploding?

"Not 'mind,' 'Mind.' Emphasis required. We should tread first and resolve matters over Mind later."

So many things were troubling me now that I'd lost track, but Rider's verbal cleverness was getting a bit on my nerves, mostly because it didn't make sense. Someone using English so awkwardly shouldn't be able to play with and on English words and clichéd phrases so fluidly.

A two-minute walk brought us to a large rectangular gateway with a Simple greeting carved into the arched white lintel above: *Aram-holai,* "Welcome All." Hhoymon City at last?

Hardly. Once through the doorway, the environment suggested a big shopping mall. And the shoppers were stranger than anything I'd encountered on Earth—even during the holiday rush.

"What *is* this place," I muttered, taking in the multi-leveled pandemonium, wide pathways winding between strips of purple and orange shrubbery, and rooms—stores?—filled with shelved artifacts.

"Chean-shee Enclave," announced Rider in a relieved tone.

I wondered if Crossroad had given me a bad case of multiple personalities. The scholar in me was rubbing its hands together, savoring its growing list of Crossroad species. In just the last hour I'd added Blenn, Vyre, and now these Chean-shee. True, I wouldn't know a Blenn if one were standing on my foot, but if there's one thing we academics like to devour, it's raw nomenclature.

Another part of me stood aghast. I didn't come here with many expectations, but enough of them to know that something had gone very wrong.

I looked up at Rider. "Isn't Chean-shee Simple for 'four hands'?"

"You render too exactly. Think of these as Constructors."

"Huh. Right now I'm thinking 'Climbers.'"

The city's alabaster walls were latticed with thin brown tubes. In the glare of pinkish floodlights high overhead, hundreds of ultra-aliens were scrambling up, down, and sideways, swinging with the ease of monkeys, making great leaps between walls. Some were just hanging around.

Chean-shee, with few exceptions, were lovely. Fur that ranged from brassy to black covered their lemur-thin bodies. Their earless heads were raccoon-nouveau, striped in burnt orange, gold, and red. They had two arms, each equipped with big, four-fingered hands, and two legs with four-toed, handlike feet. They averaged maybe seven feet tall and went naked except for crisscrossed shoulder straps holding a variety of objects. No visible sex organs.

"With such tails," Rider conceded, "climbing *is* first and second nature."

The great Neme philosopher Balanced Clearhouse wrote, "The eye sees what experience believes." I'd initially overlooked the Chean-shee's most distinctive feature: each had *two* prehensile tails divided at each tip into a grasping member with two powerful-looking opposable parts.

A few miniature Constructors, presumably babies, were riding adult backs, suckling from thin flaps of skin connected to adult necks. One such pair made a stupendous leap over our heads. A tail brushed my bald spot as if in apology.

"Those with neck-nipples are female," Rider commented.

The crowd exuded vigor and purpose, but the city remained eerily silent except for a susurrant applause from a thousand feet slapping the floor, and as many hands and tails grabbing pipes. An army of simian mimes ...

We stepped farther into the alien mall and the temperature nosedived. A new, bitter odor in the air made my nose sting. "Brrr, good thing I've got this jacket."

Rider spun to face me. "Explain."

"What's to explain? Didn't you feel the sudden chill?" Sotto voce, I added, "Right now, you're *lucky* you're missing the olfactory sense."

Rider ran a hand through its head-crest. "Understanding is mine. The local Mind has eased atmosphere control for you. Mind is still watering your health other ways, but this Enclave has close enough gasses for your kind. All is ideal."

Either my guide was a truly incompetent liar, or I was catching on to Common facial expressions.

"Is this Mind of yours a, um, synthetic intelligence?" I asked, trying to hide my disbelief.

"Less or more."

"So, until now, this Mind was providing me a kind of invisible scuba—"

"Soon, we will discuss. For now, warning and reassurance: the Constructors, as you've named them, release airs unhappy for your lungs, but fear no permanent harm."

"Good."

"Unless you breathe here too long."

I glared at my companion. "I withdraw that 'good.' How long is too long? Maybe your Mind abandoned me prematurely?"

"Do not constrict yourself! You will be well." Rider waved an arm. "A law we have. Conservation of energy."

"Sure. We've got the same law at home: energy can't be created or—"

"Law in a different tone. I meant *statute*."

"Oh."

"Most conserving to home you where conditions are reasonably in tune with your needs than to constantly fiddle atmospherics around your body. Ayn-Binae, I have a loud idea! In the oasis prepared for you here, controlling heat and air will be easy. But beyond your place of apartness, we can adjust your comforts with a skin superior."

"Um. Warmer clothing?"

"Far more. A great surprise!" Rider was overdoing the cheer. "Just wait."

"Hold on! You're not putting me up *here*?"

"Not here."

"Good."

"But within this Enclave."

"What? Aren't I supposed to stay at Hhoymon City?" All those hours poring over maps ...

"All things change, including plans."

"Why this change?"

"No more Hhoymon."

"WHAT?"

"We required them to leave. Later, I will explain. Now we have person to meet. Why keep her waiting?"

As we strolled past sizable and nearly identical rooms, all open in the front, while Rider provided a running commentary on their functions —such as a school, a religious center, and a restaurant—I felt horribly lost. In this sea of uncertainties, I'd been keeping afloat by clinging to what few assurances I'd been offered. Now I was drowning.

The ground-level crowds parted courteously for us, but otherwise paid little attention. No Constructor spoke, but many were obviously deep in conversations, gesturing with both arms and one tail. The other tail, I guessed, was an arboreal safety line. Gravity would deal harshly with tree-dwellers who gesticulated with every limb.

Then I noticed the astonishing beauty of Chean-shee eyes. Ultra-alien irises, frequently changing colors and patterns. Eyes of swirled copper and lapis, translucent golden roses floating in purple waters, glowing rubies set in pearl halos ...

Keeping my own eyes open became a chore. In my head, enchanting dreams beckoned. I couldn't tell if this unnatural drowsiness came from the smell or the cold, the loveliness or the strangeness.

The room appeared dim despite its open doorway and reminiscent of my university office. My right pinky grazed something cold and smooth that moved away with a rolling sound. My eyes adjusted. Close to me, a Chean-shee—female, judging from the skin-flaps—squatted on a tree-like stool behind a curved desk, its glossy surface bare except for three Hhoymon MARBLEs and a MARBLE reader. One MARBLE lay trapped under her left tail.

"Oh, I blurted. Sorry."

She just stared at me, and Rider giggled, if that's what the slurpette was.

"Hear you she cannot, Professor David A. Goldberg."

"You mean ... she's deaf?"

"Yes, they lack that sense."

Of course! What was wrong with me? "So they communicate by gesture."

"Not so, although their gestures and eye dances assist. Useful leftovers. Long ago, Constructors only used limbs and eyes to talk. Then new, faster predators made such speech too slow for warnings. The Chean-shee learned another way."

"Which was?"

"Hear for yourself. This female is Enclave Administrator. Speak to her in English. She can't grasp words, but talk will help you focus on meaning. Imagine that meaning as flowing into her. Then, to your internals, listen intently."

Uh-oh. "They're *telepaths*?"

"Most acute ones. Tell her about yourself."

I'd been warned there might be mind readers on Crossroad. But the only instruction I'd received from my UN handlers concerning telepaths was simple and useless: avoid them.

Sick with fear and trying not to show it, or think it, I turned to the Administrator. "Hello. I'm honored to meet you. My name is David Goldberg. At home, I'm a teacher."

"Continue," Rider suggested.

Why not continue? I thought. I'd already reached the pinnacle of awkwardness.

"Well. My students study various human societies and what little we know about societies outside our species. I ... try to teach my students how history shapes perception and ... vice versa."

Green eyes soft as moonlight regarded me gravely. Suddenly, I was drifting away....

A huge hand steadied me, and Rider said, "Can you hear her yet?"

"No, and for some reason I'm having the damnedest trouble staying awake. Is she actually talking to me?"

"Most certainly. You misinterpret your sensations. Let yourself sleep, but only halfway. Apply deft equilibrium."

Gazing into her eyes, now twin polished abalone shells, I deliberately let go.

I hadn't allowed for Rider's generic use of hearing for sensing. Images appeared in my head. I watched my own bronze-haired, four-fingered hands and one tail engaged in various tasks: using a glowing stick to draw on a flat brown screen, placing tiny magnetic cubes on a complex metal chart....

"Yes?" Rider asked softly.

"Getting it. I think she's describing her job because I tried to describe mine. What a way to converse! Sharing dreams."

And it dawned on me that I wasn't all that drowsy—that effect must've come from a lifelong association between sleep and dreaming. But my fear remained. I'd been trapped within a city of mind readers with vital secrets to conceal.

CHAPTER 7
A MEAL THAT REMEMBERS YOU

In the office, Rider's scent had gradually blocked the general stench. The smell almost knocked me over when we rejoined the crowds outside. Was this Constructor body odor or stink copied from the Chean-shee's native atmosphere? And how could it be this cold yet stuffy? Each breath was a multiple assault.

Worse, the exo-simians were now *too* friendly. Word would spread fast among telepaths, and the latest word must've been: everyone should make Dave Goldberg feel welcome. Visions of humans and Chean-shee embracing kept appearing in my mind; each time I felt obliged to murmur and think, "Pleased to meet you, too." I'd been condemned to a tenth circle of hell, The Endless Cocktail Party.

To cap my anxiety, the smell, arctic cold, glossy white walls, constant mental barrage, plus Rider's bad influence had melded in my subconscious into one mortifying phrase. If puns are the lowest form of humor, this one cracked the bottom of the barrel:

Hush, you muskies!

I could only pray the Chean-shee, like some students, could only follow superficial thoughts. Or they'd be too polite to eavesdrop.

The entire time, I also kept trying like hell to forget all about mystery photos and Scome machines. And doing exactly as well as you'd expect.

By the time we reached a restaurant we'd passed earlier, I was shivering and emotionally numb.

We entered the busy room and a large male Chean-shee with

glowing silver eyes dropped from a high pipe and escorted us to one of perhaps sixty white tables. The Constructors apparently preferred the personal touch to any miracles of automated service. Our table was round with pie-chart sections of adjustable height, suitable for your Pan-Cosmopolitan eatery. The waiter bounded off and returned with a Neme chair for me, and a bench appropriate for Rider.

The instant I sat, images of stuff on white plates began flashing through my mind, four plates at a time. I stared at the waiter. Apparently, he was also the menu.

I turned to Rider for help, but the parade of incomprehensible delicacies faded and our server hurried away.

"Liberties I have taken and ordered for you. All is tried and trued human fare with one exception. You are in moods for adventure, I hope?"

"I'm in the mood," I said, yawning, "for something hot. Preferably non-toxic."

Slurp. "We would not food you rudely! As for me, may the ferns here be fresh! I lack stomach for the stale."

I wrapped my arms around my body for warmth and regarded my dinner companion. "How long have you been studying English, if I may ask?"

Rider gazed back, one transparent eyelid at half-mast. "Curiosity is a blessing. You are cozy with Crossroad terms of duration?"

"Think so." Thanks to Able Firsthouse. "Your year is a 'cycle,' about three of ours, and your day is a 'turn' divided into twenty-two 'twists.' Have I got it straight?"

"Right on pitch. Your day and our turn, by chance, have similar strides. I was given human language lessons in the third twist of this turn."

I felt my jaw sag. "You learned that much in *hours*? Lord! You're as good as a Neme! You may use English a little ... creatively, but you've already got an amazing grip on—"

"*Not* as good!" I couldn't imagine why Rider seemed upset. "In speech, Nemes are innately on key, yet we have force-learning techniques of great rapidness. Projective templates. For me, such erudition always follows the same tune. My cunning brain pounces on connections between words first. Syntaxes are paid later. Confidentially," peevishness soured the baritone voice, "your language I find evocative, but insufficiently robust."

"How so?"

"Meaning collapses or transforms with the most trivial change in stress, order, or pronunciation. 'A trophy' and 'atrophy' should never be siblings!"

I shrugged. "You get used to it. I'd love to know more about your teaching methods. Would they work on Earth?"

"Perhaps."

"What are projective templates?"

"Patience. Hearing for yourself will speak clearer than words. We will arrange a demonstration."

"Good. Thanks. Speaking of words, what does 'ayn' mean?"

"Ayn?"

"You often say 'ayn-something' or 'something-ayn.'"

The Common hesitated. "Before or after certain names, it means 'bless' or 'blessings from.' Only an expression."

Our server reappeared, one tail bearing something rectangular on a plate while his arms held two bowls, one filled with steaming liquid, the larger heaped with rust-red foliage. Luckily, I got the plate, the soup, and a spoon-thingy.

The rectangular object proved to be a peanut butter sandwich, unadulterated by jelly. The bread was high-glycemic soft. I tried a sip of broth and thought it was plain hot water, which seemed symbolic of my situation. Then an aftertaste hit me. Mint. It faded and the flavor of dark chocolate filled my mouth.

"What *is* this?" I asked as the chocolate was replaced by an unfamiliar spiciness then a swift barrage of unrelated tastes.

"Forty Savor Bisque. Gray Hhoymon delicacy, made safe for humans. You enjoy?"

"It's ... interesting." Actually, I felt it had about thirty-nine savors too many. At least the weird liquid was warming.

I sipped and let my eyes wander. Most diners here were Chean-shee, silent save for clicks and scrapes of cutlery and various biological noises. But four Nemes I didn't recognize were in conversational symphony at a far table. Two had darker fur than I'd ever seen on a Neme.

Rider placed a handful of ferns against its abdomen. I tried not to look horrified as the skin split vertically into two thick lips. These stretched, enveloped the plants and drew them smoothly inside. I got a glimpse of tiny grinding teeth and a faint whiff of cut grass mixed with fresh cow manure.

No stomach for the stale. Right.

"Do your, um, ferns taste good?" I asked politely.

"Most satisfying!" Like Nemes, my companion could talk and eat at the same time without upsetting Emily Post. "But 'taste' is a slippery notion, my friend. Remember, Common lack smell sensors. But you humans have very bad taste." Rider slurped a chuckle. "You perceive only five qualities, yes? Briny, savory, spiny, sugary, shiny? No? No matter. My kind have twenty-two tones of taste receptors."

If all they eat are ferns, I figured they'd need every receptor they can get.

I finished my meal and leaned back to indigest. But I couldn't calm down. As my core temperature had risen, anxiety had returned. No way around it. I was going to have to ask the question although it might raise a particularly bright red flag.

"Tell me something, Sun-toch-sew. Do all these Constructors know everything I'm thinking?"

"Seris-ayn! No wonders you sound so sour! Not one can hunt your deep shames unless you desire."

"Because I'm an alien?"

"No. As our guest, you have been granted special protections. Too many top-note thought-hearers on Crossroad, real ease-droppers! You would have no privacies. So, think hard to talk with Chean-shee or they will not apprehend."

Relief spread through me, better even than warmth, until I remembered to doubt Rider's honesty. And I saw a new concern. "What about the Mind?"

"It hears thought-shapes for species recognition, not thoughts themselves. Major Chean-shee irk! They cannot converse mind to Mind."

Brushing aside questions about hearing shapes, how could thoughts *have* shapes? I stifled a sigh and a belch—no saying which flavor would return to haunt me—and glanced around the room. Here, Crossroad Aristology had a gymnastic component. Several of my fellow diners were eating while dangling from pipes, perhaps their equivalent to a standup meal. Our waiter also hung up there, watching us, apparently assigned exclusively to our table. VIP treatment. And since I was nobody, the IP's identity was obvious. Conceivably every O-gen-ai would be similarly honored; it was their planet. Which reminded me, why *would* Rider chaperone an insignificant visitor? Why had a Common picked me up from Earth? Somehow, it seemed rude to ask.

One thing I had to believe or give up my mission: no one could probe my thoughts without my consent. That one I'd just take on faith.

Despite the remarkable soup, I wouldn't have awarded this restaurant a Michelin star. The peanut butter tasted too much like the city smelled, but I felt hungry enough to eat most of it anyway. My dinner companion packed away ferns as if the entire crop would soon rot.

I had a bad moment. When our waiter, without being asked, brought me some water, I caught a glimpse of myself, distorted in his big silver eyes. For no reason, I began to shiver again, and it took a while to stop.

Still gobbling, Rider asked if I'd had a pleasant journey to the Tennessee hilltop. Tough one. It seemed possible that Rider knew what had happened on the zipway. Not wanting to get caught in an outright lie, I described the bus incident.

"A real ear-opener," the Common remarked after I finished.

I studied my guide. "Are you suggesting it wasn't ... a fluke?"

"Who am I to say?" Three snakelike fingers twisted around each other. The Common version of a shrug? "Anything is possible."

Except getting a straight answer from you. "Well, one thing you *can* clear up for me is why you kicked the Hhoymon off Crossroad."

Rider stopped eating. "A sad song. Aside from Blenn, they were our highest engineers and theorists. We rate their technology at pitch eighteen."

"On what scale?"

"Twenty-two hypothetic levels. We O-gen-ai subsist at pitch sixteen."

"And humans?"

"Pitch eight, so far."

Interesting. "You Common are twice as technologically advanced as us?"

"Exponential curvings."

"Oh. So level eighteen is really, um, up there. Okay. Why boot out such valuable allies?"

"We have laws. One is, no spilling of another's vital substances."

I stared at Rider's face, which had become an alien mask. "Bloodshed? How bad was it?"

"Many deaths among Hhoymon. Fraction friction. Civil war, you would name it. We believe only a minor rebel group was blameworthy."

"What a shame! I thought the four Hhoymon races got along beautifully."

Rider didn't seem to hear me. "We *should* have known immediately. Our Minds are always alert. Always."

My uneasiness concerning these Minds jumped a level. Not only did they control personal environments, apparently, they were WATCHING.

"The rebels found a way to hide a *war* from your Minds?"

Rider toyed with the few surviving ferns. "For a full turn! Impossible, I would have sung before the fact. But pitch eighteen technology surpasses the impossible. Still, guess what species designed our Minds?"

"Ah. Not those Blenn you're so fond of, I take it?"

"We only learned of trouble when committee of Gray Hhoymon, in full chagrin, warned us."

"I suppose the Grays identified the criminals?"

"No! Attackers were soundproofed and public records distorted to forestall deductions."

Soundproofed? "You mean *invisible*?"

"Essentially."

"Good Lord. And since you had no way to isolate the rebels ..."

"We required the population entire to exit."

While I chewed on that, Rider remarked, "I regret you could not go to Triangle Ten and stay with nice Hhoymon. Their city fits your kind like a belt!"

"No toxic fumes?"

"And warm as sand in the Mother Of Deserts."

"Sounds lovely. Could I stay in Hhoymon City anyway?"

"Unwise. The area has become alarming."

"Oh? How so?"

"Later, we will discuss. For now, I have errands to walk. Remain seated; I will return most soon." Next I knew, Rider was leaving the restaurant, the breeze of its passage ruffling my remaining hair.

And my suitcase had vanished.

I sat alone, surrounded by ultra-aliens. Time dragged and our waiter took to hovering, wiping already spotless surfaces. Perhaps he wanted my table for future customers or hoped for a tip. Maybe Rider had asked him to keep his silvery eyes on the stupid Earthman. But I'd been told to sit tight and didn't dare mutiny.

This had been one long day and wasn't over. I closed my eyes, just to rest them.

And my surroundings were instantly revealed in a *different* light. With all my concerns, I'd forgotten about my Crossroad-induced talent! The ability had grown. I could see dimly through my forehead now in addition to my enhanced side-vision. And that feeling of perceptual wrongness I'd experienced before was stronger, but I still couldn't spot ...

Yes, I could! Again, experience had blinded me to what was right in front of my ... new eyes.

A color I'd never seen before—no, *two* new colors!—gave the room a freaky, dreamlike ambience. Both were subtle. One appeared only as faint surface-reflections, as if an invisible spotlight radiated that one alien tint. I tentatively dubbed it "ultra-blue" because it looked so cool and pure.

The other stranger was more abundant and obvious. Gossamer tendrils of it drifted through the air and zigzagged like lazy lightning between pipes on the back wall. I decided to call this one "ultra-red" for its somber glow.

Unlike ultra-blue, ultra-red came in assorted shades, but neither color formed hybrids with anything along the prosaic spectrum.

I opened my eyes slowly, trying to maintain both forms of vision simultaneously. No luck. Normal light drowned out the other sense and only my extended peripheral vision proved it was still functioning.

I yawned and my eyes closed by themselves. When would Rider return? I was getting cold again.

How odd. A Neme at a distant table wore translucent antlers in a pale shade of ultra-red. They wriggled.

And the table next to mine wasn't unoccupied, as I'd thought. Five hazy forms were seated on its far side. Dwarves? Leprechauns? I couldn't see them clearly, but all five held slingshots loaded with large ball bearings. Every band had been stretched back and every bearing stayed aimed at my head. I found this mildly upsetting. What had I ever done to them?

I could tell they were eager to release the missiles, but they couldn't. Perhaps, I thought, gazing around in gentle wonder, they're confused like me. The room was ripe with strangeness. The antlered Neme barely made the cut.

Two tables down—how had I missed *her* before? Not a Neme. Couldn't tell *what* she was, her shape feminine but indistinct. I noticed her tiny shoulder-wings and felt sad because they seemed so impractical. Her eyes were made of smoke. One delicate-looking hand casually gripped the hilt of a short sword. The blade, glowing red, rested across her bare legs.

Even weirder eyes were on me. An ultra-alien spider clung to the ceiling and its five-point stare was a tangible pressure. It was bigger than any spider should be. And I had the feeling it was farther away than it looked.

A large hemispherical mirror hung on the back wall. Hadn't noticed that before either. It reflected the restaurant and something extra. I looked back and forth from the mirror to an empty chair across from me. In the mirror only, a birdlike humanoid occupied the chair, shaking its feathered head and long beak in avian disapproval.

The dwarves' arms trembled from exhaustion and palpable fury, but they still couldn't shoot. I was beginning to understand why: they were balked by a vast and compelling power. I could feel it myself now, like standing close to an enormous ... spiritual dynamo, or near the brink of some hidden Niagara Falls of the soul. Although it was clearly protecting me, this terrible power frightened me enough to shatter my groggy calm.

I decided to open my eyes but was distracted by a Neme male watching me from the restaurant's doorway. He stood almost in a wushu stance—feet apart, torso leaning slightly forward—but Nemes aren't built for human martial arts.

Then a huge hand clamped down on his furry shoulder, and the Neme waddled away with obvious reluctance. I felt comforted, recognizing the hand as Rider's.

Without moving my head, I again studied the room. Kids, mirror, and the more peculiar watchers had vanished. The sitting Neme remained, sans cranial adornments. I tried to ask Rider what was happening but couldn't speak.

Now, I was *really* scared. The Common stood before me, studying my face with, perhaps, concern. If not, I worried enough for both of us.

"From slumbers, my friend, dig upward," Rider said quietly, patting me softly on the head.

The physical contact startled me awake. "Thanks," I sputtered. "Had the weirdest dream. Could've *sworn* I was awake."

"Humans sleep better on beds," Rider said. "Even I am the knower of that. Come, your compartment is ready."

CHAPTER 8
MIND OVER MANNERS

Rider led me into the Enclave's residential area, a warren of hallways with abundant crest-room for visiting Common. My watch claimed nine o'clock, but it felt past midnight.

Not a neighborhood for sleepwalkers. Ramps, climbing pipes, and an occasional ladder led both up and down through random openings in the floor and ceiling. No guardrails. The ladder rungs weren't spaced for human anatomy, but we stayed on one level. Our route was complex; by the time we reached my apartment, one of many along a sparsely lit corridor but the only one with a door, I would've needed a map to return.

The peephole and human-style doorknob gave me a hint about the interior.

Sure enough. We entered and my eyes feasted on a generic motel room complete with an antique TV remote control thoughtfully screwed to a nightstand. Someone wanted me to feel at home. Still, it was *warm* and one of the two interior doors surely led to a bathroom. I hoped. Two departures from Earth hostelry traditions: a suitcase already waiting, and the air smelled fresh.

"So that's where my luggage went," I said. "Thanks."

"This space is to your tastes?" Rider asked.

"It's fine."

"Your voice betrays your verbals, my friend. Nemes have stayed in such places. We thought humans liked them."

"I guess some of us, um, prefer unnatural habitats."

"Easy to heal. Mind: Scour."

The flocked wallpaper and paint-by-number artwork vanished. What remained was a mostly bare room with glowing gray walls. Aha, I told myself. The old holodeck cliché. But was this standard for an apartment here, or also copied, like the original décor, from Neme research on Earth?

Some features remained: a wall niche with a scooped back and flat bottom, both inner doors, a rectangular slab I assumed was a bed, a shallow alcove near the front door, and of course my trusty suitcase.

"You hear, Professor David A. Goldberg? Adaptive technology! The Mind knows a sleeping platform belongs in human apartments, but if you wish to alter, move, or remove it, the room will oblige."

I moved near the bed and touched it. "Impressive." I meant it. How could the Mind remove something clearly solid? "I gather the room understands English. Or is 'scour' an O-gen-ai homonym?"

"Mind has been aligned for your convenience."

And sanitized for my protection? Which brought up a creepy notion. "That's ... just a shelf?" I asked, pointing to the niche and hoping it wasn't the toilet.

Rider turned toward the opening and muttered a Simple phrase. With no fanfare, a bowl of blue ferns appeared on the bottom. Apparently, those childhood hours I'd squandered on *Star Trek* reruns weren't a total waste....

"Let me guess," I said. "Behind that nook is a device that turns energy into food."

Two twin-yoked eyes studied me, big head canted to one side. "A counter-digestion engine? An exotic concept, but deafeningly wasteful! Exact numbers I cannot sing, but certainly condensing this one snack would require force enough to power Chean-shee Enclave for cycles of cycles."

"Could be a trifle impractical," I allowed. "How *does* your machine work?"

"Sensibly! Converter re-glues molecules, matter to matter."

"I see." Which I didn't. "Getting back to my tastes, any choices other than Seedy Hotel or Monastery?"

"Just tell Mind your wants—furnishings or embellishments—this space is more adaptable than a Vyre."

"It's that easy? May I try?"

Rider waved an arm. "You are the guest of me."

"Okay. Mind, please display, um, a mountain on this wall I'm facing."

A 3D landscape appeared, featuring a snow-capped, lime green colossus of non-parallel geology. "Not what I meant, but wow. Mind, can you make that an Earth peak, say Mount Hood?"

The animated Oregon dawn included sound. Distant cries from a hawk circling in a topaz sky blended with the wind-rustle of summer grasses. The mountain looked to be about ten miles away. Advanced imaging, absolutely, but not that far beyond human technology.

Rider joined in the fun. A brief mutter summoned a bright underwater vista on the opposite wall. A school of purple and orange creatures swam by, shrouded in diaphanous veils.

"Is it not enchanting?" Rider murmured. "I could hear this for an entire turn, but duties cry. Come, we will test your facilities and then roam separate ways for a time."

"You mean test my *faculties*?"

"Is your restroom a faculty?"

I seconded Rider's slurp with my own laugh. "Before we plumb the plumbing—" good grief, I never talked like that before I met Rider! "—please tell me more about the Minds."

"Aduum-ayn! Experience teaches best. But what would you most relish knowing?"

"Are they machine-based intelligences or living creatures?"

Rider twisted several fingers together. "They squeeze poorly into such categories and have no human equivalent. Sensitive they are, aware but not awake; even Hhoymon lack skill to place consciousness into creations."

"So what are they?"

"Beyond all O-gen-ai. Hhoymon speak of patterns of patterns of patterns, self-compounding, equal to great tasks."

"I assume they have, uh, physical components?"

"Certainly. Energy is physical."

"Hmm. I gather from your term 'Mind of Triangle Four' that specific Minds are attached to specific areas?"

"You gather wisely. Pretend, we do, that Crossroad is divided into twenty ... facets. Those are our Triangles, one Mind assigned to each."

"Identical facets?" A planet-sized icosahedron?

Rider hesitated. "Only in abstraction. World is less or more spherical. Listen, our time together this turn nears finale; later we can discuss—"

"Just one more question. Please." Another hawk had joined the Oregon scene, wheeling above the first, its cries barely audible. "Are your Minds, um, networked?"

Rider's leaves rattled. "This truth depends on how you listen. They share information. To one ear, they are separate, to another, there is but one Mind."

Damn. Any blunders I made would get global coverage.

"Ayn-Khunuum!" Rider continued. "There is but one Mind? I begin to resound as mystic as Strong!"

Despite the bad tidings, I smiled. "Or Balanced Clearhouse." The disciples who'd collected Clearhouse's aphorisms had numbered them, the first being "All is one."

"Come along quickly," Rider snapped, "I am yearned for elsewhere."

The bathroom? A clone of its motel equivalent including towels thick enough to dry one finger and half an elbow. Two deviations: no mirror and the toilet didn't flush. Rider assured me it would simply absorb all waste. What really impressed me was the roll of Earth-style toilet paper; seemed like a difficult thing to suddenly manufacture.

My gaze kept drifting back to the toilet. Rider had said the apartment's automat created food by assembling molecules. Question of the hour: where did it get the molecules? I like the idea of recycling, within limits.

Rider studied the sink and experimentally poked the faucet. "Alas, the Constructors failed to educate me about this alien device. Do you require instruction in its use?"

"I think I can manage."

"Good. Now hurry back to sleeping arena, withdraw some apparel, and I will play for you apparel-storage technique."

In the main room, I opened my suitcase. The shirt on top had been decorated with bits of drying banana. Apparently, the suitcase had suffered somewhere along the line and much of the bag-lunch I'd failed to finish in Tennessee was now unevenly deposited among my clothes.

I pushed the shirt aside. "What should I do with trash?"

"Place in converter. Molecules stored until useful. And fear not, Mind mediates converter. It will not convert living flesh."

"Oh. That's good to know."

I found a clean shirt and handed it to Rider who carried it to the alcove by the entrance and touched it to a horizontal white strip just above my head-level. The garment stuck there, upside down. I tugged gently, then harder, but the damn thing seemed epoxied in place.

Voice command? "Let go!" I ordered and yanked forcefully enough to menace the seams.

"Pull upward to reclaim apparel," Rider suggested. I had to laugh at myself when the shirt easily came free.

"Gotten the hang of it, you have," my guide remarked. "I *must* leave, my friend. Have you needs, ask the Mind to reach me, Strong, or Swift. Your commands conduct your environment. Change it as you will but be dainty with the gravity! I will hear you after sleep period. Be welcome and may your resting provide you refreshment!" With these courteous if peculiar words, Rider departed. I was finally alone on Crossroad.

In fact, this was the first private moment I'd had since early morning. I hung the shirt, sat on the miserably hard bed, and sighed. But not in relief.

I wasn't happy. I'd been here for only a few hours and things had already veered spectacularly off course.

I was still reeling from being parked here, head crammed with magnificently irrelevant details concerning Hhoymon and their city. And Crossroad proved even weirder than I'd expected with its Glideways, Safe-roads, Triangles, Minds, and simian telepaths—plus the damn Blenn, whatever they were. The UN professionals from Denys Palmer on up hadn't told me one useful thing. My two least favorite sentiments, resentment and self-pity, were building on my emotional horizon like storm clouds.

And questions kept buzzing me. Why *had* a Common been my driver? What had Rider and the three Nemes been saying via those hand signals? Why did my guide seem so anxious until we reached this Enclave?

This mission looked to be immeasurably trickier than I'd imagined in my most paranoid moments. I not only had an all-hearing Common keeping tabs on me periodically but an all-sensing Mind doing it full time! How could I shake off attention if my chance came to explore the Hall of Games? I wiped my forehead with a clammy palm and found my forehead clammier.

I remembered something my father had said a few months before he passed away. I'd been complaining to him about a passage in a Scome manuscript I was translating. The individual words were clear, but they didn't make meaningful sentences: "... when moments become stones, hail [salute?] our ancient combined [changed?] ones, altered heroes [martyrs?] who bit [sliced? suffered?] for our survival and thus into our monuments."

"David," Dad had remarked in his quiet voice, "here's my three-part protocol for dealing with the unfamiliar: observe, observe, observe. You can't *force* understanding, you can only invite it." In an aphorism contest, Arthur Goldberg could hold his own, even against Balanced Clearhouse.

Okay. Clenching muscles and pulling out my remaining hair

wouldn't invite anything but ulcers. Time to change tactics. First step: get comfortable.

I used the strange toilet and, as promised, the urine vanished. The sink fixtures worked perfectly, and when I rubbed my hands together under warm running water, lather foamed up then rinsed clean.

Intrigued, I bent down to peer under the sink. No soap dispenser. Also no plumbing. None.

Interesting. If a Mind could control individual environments for *all* sorts of alien visitors, including those with gills or the like, it could presumably send water to any specific location. Likewise, cleaning solvents, which might be vital fluids for some ultra-aliens. I didn't care for my conclusion. If a Mind decided to kill you and wasn't in the mood to use heat, pressure, vacuum, or a poisonous atmosphere, it could always resort to drowning you.

Apparently only their creators, the Hhoymon, knew what made a Mind tick. Why, I wondered, would the Common accept such an arrangement? If the rebel faction, or any criminal Hhoymon element, gained control of these artificial gods, they could've held Crossroad hostage, instantly murdering anyone who complained.

Yet the Common weren't stupid. There had to be guaranteed safeguards in place. But who could've installed such safeguards except Hhoymon? Which meant some Hhoymon might know a way around the guarantees....

Shaking my head in confusion, I reached for a towel then stopped. "Mind, please dry my hands." They were dry as I finished the last syllable. Towels and, I supposed, toilet paper were unneeded courtesies to make me feel secure.

"Kindly put a large mirror on this wall in front of me."

Just like that, the entire surface turned reflective, reminding me of my wife's dance studio. Fear, I noticed, made my face even less attractive. And loneliness squatted behind the fear like a toad. Both emotions were understandable, but I hadn't realized they were so damn visible. A sudden helpless longing for Sara and our life together made my eyes sting; my ugly image blurred, making my reflection even uglier.

Sara had haunted my thoughts since I'd seen my first Constructor. She, too, had constantly moved her hands while talking. An image of those beloved hands cradling her usual blue mug appeared in my mind's eye, clearer and infinitely prettier than my tear-smudged reflection.

I could practically smell the steam wafting from her mug. Cocoa. I'd infected Sara with my fondness for the brew and we were always trying new recipes or tweaking our favorites. Right then, the idea of hot chocolate seemed vastly soothing, a touch of home to savor in Sara's memory.

I chewed my lips. David, I warned myself, you've got enough troubles here and now without dredging the past. Besides, cocoa was a universe away.

Or was it? I left the bathroom and stood before the food converter. "Hot chocolate, please, with whipped cream on top." Seemed worth a shot although I doubted the converter had any such thing in its repertoire.

But a mug of steaming liquid appeared, and it smelled wonderful. Then I tried some. The whipped cream tasted like foamy rot—one of the top ten disappointments of my life. I returned the brew to the niche where it promptly vanished. Damn clever, I mused. It knows the difference between food and garbage even when they're identical.

"Hot cocoa again, Mind, but skip the zombie cream."

The new beverage had a spoiled under-taste. Didn't want *bad* cocoa, so it joined its predecessor in molecule-hood. I walked over to the slab of a bed. Considering my bony frame, I thought, this was a case of between a rack and a hard place.

Really, David? I asked myself. *Are you going to keep making Rider-style jokes from now on?*

But how *was* I supposed to sleep? Or just maybe ...

I stretched myself out on the parody of a mattress. At least my toes didn't hang over.

"Softer," I requested but nothing happened. Had I made the command too vague? Or did I need to address the Mind directly.

"Mind, please make this bed more comfortable." Still nothing. "For me," I amended to patch the ambiguity.

I felt myself rising a few inches. I was floating! "*That's* more like it," I sighed. One problem down, a thousand to go.

With nothing solid to push against, it seemed impossible to sit up. But I tried and some force gently lifted my torso. An accommodating air-mattress indeed.

I regarded Mount Hood, still looming on the wall. The Minds terrified me, but they obviously had their uses. "Mind, show me Crossroad."

The mountain vanished, replaced by a dramatic golden planet hanging in darkness. Spinning slowly but visibly.

"Thanks. Please indicate my exact location on Crossroad."

I expected some form of pointer to appear. Instead, the picture zoomed in to a spot near the southern pole. I got one glimpse of a huge, semi-buried structure. The ground rushed up, the viewpoint plunged beneath the surface, and the apparent motion slowed. I had time to count twenty descending levels of tunnels before they became Cheanshee corridors. Suddenly, I was treated to an overhead view of a seated, balding man. The viewpoint scrolled both downward and forward and froze in an image of me staring back at myself.

Not a reflection. I waved at me, mouthing, "You are here," while the opposite arm waved back. And a bleak suspicion confirmed: I look even worse in real life than in a mirror.

But I had one hell of a research tool! The Mind could pinpoint the Hall of Games and—what was I *thinking*? If I could be watching me right now, so could Rider or anyone authorized to use the Minds. Big Brother, move over. Way, way over.

I heard an ugly clicking. Me, grinding my teeth. I urgently needed information, but didn't dare ask suspicion-arousing questions, yet might raise suspicions by *not* asking suspicious but logical questions.

Here was the gold-standard of folly: sending out an agent with no information, no training, and no talent to an incomprehensibly advanced world on an assignment that could alter the course of human history. But how big a fool was I to accept such a mission?

Truly spooked, I gazed at my un-reversed features. I had to do *something*. For all I knew, ultra-alien psychologists were observing my panic with ripening insight.

Then mild inspiration struck. Perhaps all I needed was patience and a lot of luck to proceed in relative safety. Why not follow that trail human politicians have blazed so well and deal only in vague generalities? *Sneak up on info*, I advised myself, *don't try for the pounce.*

"Show Crossroad again, Mind." My voice shook a little. "And indicate surface geology."

The planet reappeared, still slowly rotating. Color overlays expressed elevation through clever shading. Mountains were yellow, tan implied vast deserts; poles were white. Within chasms of graduated purple, turquoise lines curved and branched. Rivers, I assumed.

Good. Now I could play a geographical Twenty Questions, locating the Hall of Games through progressive winnowing. But I'm a sucker for a mystery and this globe offered one. Unless the tan areas weren't deserts ...

"Intensify the river colors, Mind." The tree-root-like curves brightened. Yep, turquoise meant rivers.

"Now show only oceans." The wall went blank. What the hell? "Um ... add lakes." Still nothing. Ridiculous! Rivers ought to flow downhill and on a world with plentiful rivers, large bodies of water should be making a good living.

But maybe the fluid *wasn't* water. I'd look into that later. Right now, back to business.

"Mind, display Crossroad with its Triangles."

The planet reappeared, divided into deformed violet triangles, which were numbered with arabic numerals in no apparent order.

"On that image, show my route from Great Hall Four to this Enclave." A bright blue line appeared within the polar Triangle labeled "4."

According to Rider, the Safe-road had carried us at Mach 20, about 250 miles per minute on Earth. We'd been on the Safe-road for at least ten minutes. Even allowing for several minutes of Newton-defying acceleration and deceleration, and even if sound was somewhat slower here, we'd traveled over a thousand miles.

Neme visitors to Earth, for no clear reason, had been reluctant to provide more than a little physical information about Crossroad World, but Able Firsthouse had been willing to share some details with me after we'd become close.

"Commonworld," he'd revealed, "is nearly the size of your Jupiter, 262,012 miles at its equator, but almost entirely solid. Why do you look so surprised, David?"

"The gravity must be crushing!"

"Only a trifle more on the surface than here."

"How is that possible?"

Able had chuckled, Neme-style. "That surface is quite distant from the core, and more crucially, my home reality does not obey your inverse square law of attraction."

But it's one thing to know, intellectually, that Crossroad's circumference is around 262,000 miles, and quite another to see a thousand-mile line as a mere dash....

My thoughts snapped back to the latest mystery. "Where does all that water go?" I grumbled.

Wasn't expecting a response, but I got one. "Within the greater sands."

I had to swallow my heart. "Who *said* that?"

"This is the Mind of Triangle Four speaking to you." The soft voice had a Munchkin, helium-breath quality.

"Good God. You can talk. Why wait until now?"

"You were addressed because you were alone and verbalized a question."

"Oh. I would've thought—what did you mean *within* the sands?" As I was speaking, large patches of turquoise appeared on the planet's surface. "Those aren't oceans?"

"Beds of expanded mica trap water without permitting it to move freely."

Vermiculite seas! Could Crossroad be any weirder?

———

I'd planned to request a display of planetary tourist attractions, but hearing the Mind talk had shaken me, made the alien AI seem more real. And a bad feeling, a sense of some terrible danger, put the final chill on my research at least for now.

"Thanks for your help," I said, figuring it couldn't hurt to be civil, even to Big Sibling.

Unsurprisingly, my apartment wasn't soundproofed, and I'd been aware of slapping feet passing in the hallway. Now I heard a rumble accompanied by rhythmic pops, like suction cups releasing. Whatever it was, it was approaching fast.

I hurried to the door and managed to get a glimpse of strangeness before something large, round, and fuzzy with waving limbs vanished into a cross-corridor. I also got stung on the neck again.

I yelped, slammed the door, and darted toward the bathroom and its mirror. Then I had a better idea.

"Mind, display—damn, this hurts!—display the back of my neck." The new image was superimposed over Crossroad, a grotesque combination.

"Show my neck ten times normal size."

A mole, the odd freckle, and a crimson trickle, which I wiped away with a paradoxically minuscule finger. Sophisticated imaging! But it revealed nothing helpful; neither sight nor touch revealed anything but unbroken skin.

On a hunch, I closed my eyes: same middle-aged neck, but with a sullen glow, a non-wound inflamed with ultra-red.

"Clear all pictures from the walls, Mind, and put me in contact with Sun-toch-sew."

Rider appeared instantly. "My friend! It cools me to hear you. Are you well? What is your need?"

"Sorry to bother you, but I just got stung again, same place, and it turns out—um. Sorry again, but I'm having trouble conducting a conversation this way."

"At a distance?"

"That's not—you seem to be sideways."

Rider stood apparently defying gravity, feet pressed to a wall, body horizontal. "Near the equator, I am; to me *you're* the sideways personality! If you find this discordant, ask Mind to rotate my waveform."

I did so, getting the Common upright, but I was puzzled. Surely Rider hadn't been gone long enough to travel a quarter way around *this* globe, not even on a Safe-road. Did Crossroad have teleportation after all?

"I thought you should know about the sting," I continued, "and look." I held out my bloody hand. "More than a drop this time."

The lemon eyes widened and creases around Rider's speaking diaphragm deepened. "I will listen more deeply into these stings immediately."

"Something else. With the Mind's help, I got a good look at my neck. The wound's glowing. In a funny color."

A moment of silence. "Define this tone."

"Sounds crazy, but I've never seen the color on Earth. It's ... energetic. Like red, but not."

"This we must discuss soon. Meanwhile, assure you I do: these pains will be stopped. For now, Professor David A. Goldberg, try not to worry and don't neglect your healthful rest. We have a big turn ahead!"

The wall went blank and not at my request. Rider had hung up on me.

Not in the least reassured, I washed up at the sink, then returned to the main room, put my luggage on the invisible mattress, and started hanging up clothes that instantly became banana-free. So the local Mind had another talent as an effective, literally dry cleaner.

I stuffed my lunch remains into the food converter. *I'll be impressed*, I thought, *if it can turn that sandwich into something edible.*

When I moved some underpants aside to retrieve my toiletry bag, I found something I hadn't packed: a plain white jar with a hexagonal lid. Through the clear lid, I saw some dark brown goop.

Rider had promised a surprise waiting in my apartment and this seemed a likely candidate. I tried turning the lid both ways and attempted a bit of prying, but the jar wouldn't open. I put it aside and searched through the rest of my luggage.

My secret Santa hadn't left any other presents, but I dug up the one picture I'd brought along: a small portrait showing Sara, my brothers, my parents, and the family gargoyle: me. I gazed at it, wondering what I'd be looking at if it showed my *real* parents. For the first time in years, I asked myself the question I'd asked every day of my childhood. Why had my biological parents abandoned me?

This is all hearsay, but I believe it.

It seems that on a June evening not quite fifty-two years ago, the Goldbergs were interrupted in mid-dinner by the doorbell, and Michael, the older twin by a proud two minutes, volunteered to vet the visitor. My parents heard the door open and waited. Nothing but silence. Michael wasn't the quiet type, so both adults jumped up to find out who died.

Instead, they found a skinny baby in a cardboard box on the front porch, wearing soft blankets and a goofy grin. My mother estimated my age at ten months.

Joshua, twin two, upon seeing me for the first time reputedly said, "Whoa! What an ugly kid! Can we keep her?"

After a half-year search to locate my blood-relatives, Arthur and Susan were, in fact, allowed to keep me. Despite my thinness, I seemed to be healthy.

Oddly enough, I grew to resemble a cruder, emaciated version of my adoptive father. Joshua offered a theory that since, according to public wisdom, pets and their owners tend to look more alike over time, the same principle applied.

Our similarities weren't only physical, but no mystery there. Young me was a little sponge, absorbing artistic interests from mom while dad inspired my hobbies: languages, running, crossword puzzles, and studying history.

I adored my parents. It's not that I lacked rebelliousness—at fifteen, I had some run-ins with a teacher who considered me insufficiently patriotic. And I've met parents who would've surely inspired me to be as sullen and disobedient as any teenager. But with my own folks, I found nothing worth rebelling against. They were warm, generous, and understanding.

My fondest early memories: those winter nights we all spent in the study, ensconced in chairs by the fire, reading and sipping hot cocoa. At least the memories have survived.

Exhaustion hit. My normally trusty dumbwatch claimed it was 10:20, an obvious lie. I used the toilet again, washed up, flossed, and brushed my teeth with gel guaranteed to make any smile induce snow-blindness. Performing such ordinary acts here felt both comforting and disorienting.

Back in the bedroom, I donned pajamas, put my watch on the floor, and flopped onto my levitation mattress. The air felt warm enough; I didn't need blankets. "Mind, would you kindly, um, create a pillow for me?"

The area under my head lifted several inches. "Thanks," I yawned, "Not what I meant but this is fine. Please darken the room." A sleepy thought occurred to me. "And show the stars on all surfaces." To sleep floating, surrounded by stars ...

The room grew dim but nothing else happened. Perhaps I hadn't been specific enough. "Stars as seen from my home planet," I said, wanting familiar twinkling lights rather than the steady suns of deep space.

Abruptly, I found that "all surfaces" included my skin and pajamas, but I didn't mind wearing astronomy. I began to fall asleep with Orion's Belt across my waist and the blue gem of Rigel shining on my left shoulder. I remember thinking how nice it was that I'd brought Rigel with me after all.

But underneath my sleepiness and physical comfort a thought kept boiling. What the hell was I doing here?

CHAPTER 9
A SUIT FOR ALL OCCASIONS

A nxious dreams riddled my night. I managed to sleep through them and awoke emblazoned with the star Antares, Scorpio's bloodshot eye, resting on my left foot. Then it dawned on me that my own eyes were still closed. Keeping them closed, I sat up, floating on a mattress made of nothing.

My! The room looked *different.* I had to touch my eyelids to confirm they were indeed shut; my new sense was working that much better. The clarity was astonishing, even through my forehead. And when I opened my eyes—dear God! It was like putting on 4D glasses. Everything appeared so large, so *round.*

"Mind, please turn up the lights, but not very much."

Even with the room rather dim, my visual sense of extra-dimensionality became overwhelming. *Don't freak out*, I begged myself. *You won't have to live like this forever.*

I leaned over to glance at my watch on the floor. The numbers seemed double normal size. Ten o'clock? I'd seriously overslept, which would've seemed unusual if Crossroad hadn't stretched my yardstick for unusual. I'd never needed coffee this much. I hoped the food converter was good at caffeine.

If the Mind could manifest or un-manifest water, soap, mirrors, furniture, and God only knew what else, was the food converter merely a prop?

"Mind, scour," I commanded, repeating Rider's procedure. All stars vanished, the room grew bright, and I fell several inches to the bed's original surface, which wouldn't have hurt so much if I had a decently padded bottom.

"Let's make a deal," I growled. "Whenever I'm on the bed and say

OPENING WONDERS

'scour,' leave the ... flotation effect running." The Mind didn't reply, but I was levitating again.

As Josh used to say: up and atom. I pushed myself off my private cloud, got my feet on the floor, and took a step. Luckily, when I fell, I fell backward onto the un-mattress. All right. I needed practice with my new head.

I stood up again, cautiously, and exercised my depth perception by trying to touch stuff. Everything appeared closer than it was as I stumbled around the apartment with my arms extended like some Hollywood mummy.

Strange learning curve, which wasn't a curve at all. One minute, only proprioception and luck allowed me to maintain any balance, and I didn't walk so much as stagger. The next minute, with no transition, I felt coordinated enough to perform ballet—if I knew any ballet. My expanded vision suddenly felt normal and familiar, enhancing my spatial sense. I grinned with unjustified pride and declared myself, if not ready for anything, at least ready for what my wife used to call "the morning ablutions."

What I saw in the bathroom mirror also surprised me. My face seemed younger despite its sags, bags, and wrinkles.

The shower stall appeared ordinary, but as Supervisor Garlen had told me, appearances on Crossroad can't be trusted. Trying out the shower, my body became a magnet for water while the tiled surfaces remained dry. Even lather vanished on hitting the floor. "This is great!" I announced to the Mind over the gentle hissing. "Back home, our shower-curtain industry would be trembling in its bare feet if it knew about you."

Stepping from the stall, I said. "Mind, please dry my body."

Wet to dry in the blink of an eye. A fellow could get spoiled.

I dressed, slipped my watch on, and got a scare when nothing happened after calling for hot sugared coffee. After some highly motivated thought, I repeated my order, specifying quantities.

Only a fellow addict could appreciate my relief when a large white mug appeared, and even more relief when I found it had been filled with a decent brew. I sipped gratefully but wondered why the Mind hadn't been equally fussy about quantities with last night's cocoa. And something was missing....

"Mind, please provide me a comfortable chair," I said, "slowly."

A section of floor blossomed into a lounger. I tried it out. Invisible padding included at no extra cost. Sitting like an emperor on a throne of air, I enjoyed my coffee and contemplated the blank wall before me.

"Is it daytime outside?" I asked.

"On half the surface of this planet."

"You should've been a lawyer. Display a daytime scene from anywhere on Crossroad."

I instantly faced a long, mountain-lined valley. My view was at ground level, but the land sloped away for hundreds of miles. The mountains seemed overly sharp.

On the ground nearby, rocks varying in size and shape adorned flat sheets of iridescent minerals separated by patches of shining sand. Virtually every stone, pebble to boulder, had some light effect playing across its surface or flickering from within, shimmering or scintillating. If I moved my head, the colors changed. And the rocks reflected each other, bouncing beauty back and forth....

"Why's everything so shiny?"

"This area is abundant in various forms of crystallized feldspar." *Someone,* I thought, *has gone whole hog with the Mind's English vocabulary, and they didn't omit the bristles.*

"It's gorgeous," I admitted. Sara would've loved this view.

I disposed of my empty cup and ordered an English muffin. No luck. But getting a buttered bagel proved no problem. Eating it, however, turned into a big problem. The yellow topping was rancid.

Recalling last night's whipped rot, I wondered if the converter had an issue with milk products. I discarded the bagel and requested another with raspberry jam. It tasted exactly like a bagel with raspberry jam. Why the inconsistency? I admired the wall scene one last time.

"Mind, now show me a Blenn."

"Which Blenn?"

"Oh. Any Blenn will do."

How about that. From glorious to hideous in a single bound. I'd already seen two of these one-legged horrors in Great Hall Four before knowing the importance of this species. Another discovery: my augmented vision could be a mixed blessing. I couldn't avoid noticing details of the Blenn physique that were bound to become fodder for my future nightmares.

Beauty's only chitin deep, I cautioned myself, strictly in the beholder's optical organ. Don't be so damn narrow-minded.

The virtual Blenn un-decorating my wall levered itself along on its big bowl of a foot by twisting from side to side. I forced myself to keep looking. Bronze exoskeleton, four parodies of arms covered with little hooks. Its head was less ant-like than I'd thought. The wrinkled, oversized cranium appeared octopus-soft, judging by the wobbling. The humanoid blue eyes were large and mild. Its mandibles had been arranged horizontally, the mouth studded with tiny teeth resembling sharpened seed pearls.

And like the ones I'd seen before, that mouth was adorned with stalactites of brown drool, gelatinous columns refusing to fall despite constant jiggling. I felt ill.

"Good mornin'," an inauthentic Southern accent announced from outside my door. "Kind and I are keen to see you, Professor. Care for company?"

Just hearing Strong's voice helped settle my stomach. "Absolutely. Come right in."

Two individuals entered. I barely glanced at Kind because of her companion who stopped near me, saying, "Real nice to see you again."

"Good God! Is that *you*, Strong?"

"Surely. The Guardian thought you might be comfier with a human-lookin' escort to show you 'round."

"Human-looking" indeed. She stood slim and elegant in a tunic, skirt, and sandals. I noticed Neme sparkles in her honey-auburn hair, and recognized the beauty of her sculptor's dream of a face and bright green eyes—only a pair now. But I could see a strength behind the beauty that I hadn't seen before. It troubled me that in my eyes, she appeared far more noble than in her natural form because it revealed my own limitations.

"This really wasn't necessary," I said. "But how did you do it?"

"By sweet-talkin' the Mirrormage. You'll meet him eventually. I see you aren't dressed yet."

I blinked stupidly. "I'm not?"

"My fault," she said. "Still gettin' used to movin' all these mouthparts to blab, not mindin' my words. I meant 'dressed' as in wearin' bandages. Guess the Guardian didn't help you apply the microdocs."

I looked over at Kind whose eyes immediately popped away. No help there. "Why would I need bandages? And which dots?"

Strong touched her throat, perhaps confirming its location. "*Docs.* Microdocs is my way of translatin' a Gray Hhoymon term. Sometimes called a 'fourth skin' because the Grays, you know, have three dermal layers. In part, microdocs are livin' bandages." Her head stayed still while her eyes searched the room; underneath, Strong remained a Neme. "Seen a small bottle around, sweetheart?"

I pulled the white jar from my suitcase and handed it over. "Couldn't figure out how to open it."

"The Guardian wouldn't want you to while you were alone. If you don't mind, peel off anythin' you're wearin' made of plant or animal fibers."

I stared at her. "But that's everything! Except for my watch and ring."

"You can keep those; otherwise it's down to your birthday suit."

I'm not overly modest, but ... "Is this, um, important?"

"Sure, unless you want to scrap that nice outfit for good. I hear some humans have a nudity taboo, but darlin', we ain't human. Would it be easier if I shucked my own clothes?"

Honesty barely won out over curiosity. "Not really. Never mind, I'll do it." When in Rome, I told myself, eat linguini. I disrobed and stood there, feeling a bit conspicuous, but not horribly embarrassed. I awarded myself a gold star for adaptability.

"*Thretre*," Strong chanted, "*ek-lataghi*." Her face twisted oddly, which alarmed me until I realized this must be a beginner's version of a grin.

"Security code," she explained. "I asked the Mind to uncork the genie, but this new mouth is sloppy for proper Simple." She tugged on the lid, and it popped off. "What do you know? Mind understood. Now don't you fret!" She passed me the jar. "Put any old finger inside and let what happens happen. It's purely harmless."

Obedient me. I stuck an index finger into the viscous brown slime. Instantly, the slop began crawling up my arm.

"Hey!" I yelled, dropping the container. It landed sideways on the floor, but that didn't even slow the process. Goop kept rising from the jar, flowing up my arm and over my body.

"Easy, sweetheart," said Strong. "Microdocs are entirely helpful."

By now, enough glop had emerged from the little container to smack of some hokey magic trick. I wanted to scream when the stuff covered my head but didn't dare inhale, and it quickly withdrew. Suddenly, I was clothed in a layer of brown softness, like wale-less corduroy. Only my head, neck, and arms were left bare. Shaking, I reached down for the empty jar. Supple brown shoes encased my feet.

"You might've warned me," I accused, fingering the fabric on my chest. "What the hell *is* this stuff?"

"Real sorry, Professor! Never seen it happen so explosively. But now you're rightly dressed in adaptive clothin'. Fits you like a glove, don't it?" Her smile was more successful this time. "You're wearin' a temperature regulator, a personal physician, a portable outhouse, and a lot more."

Dear God. "A flotation device in the event of an emergency?"

"It surely would be if your emergency were a flood."

I shook my head and handed the jar to Strong. For no good reason, I expected her to keep it, but after replacing its lid, she casually threw the jar toward my suitcase where it slowly drifted down until it settled onto my underwear.

"The concept," I said, "isn't entirely, um, alien to me. Back home, we've been developing what we call 'nanotechnology,' microscopic machines that—"

"Microdocs aren't machines. Not the way you mean."

"Oh. Should I be thinking 'nanobiology'?"

"Real close, but human science hasn't barked up the exact tree yet."

I searched Strong's new emerald eyes, looking for ... what? Inclusions of guile?

"Everyone I've met here, including the Mind," I said slowly, "seems to be an expert on humans and our quaint ways."

"What a nice tribute! We do try to be prepared."

Never try to outflank a Neme with words. Now I couldn't probe deeper without feeling like a jerk.

I stifled a sigh. "What, exactly, should I expect from these microdocs?"

"Devotion. They'll team up to protect your body, once they've figured out your systems. The colony will react to your environment and changes in your health. And count on 'em studyin' your brain every which way."

"My *brain*?" Wonderful. More spies, this time internal. I tried not to sound as upset as I was. "Don't remember asking for any ... nanopsychologists."

"It's necessary, Professor. How else could they understand your commands? Or know to take extra care when you're tired or accident-prone."

"Mm. Entirely helpful you said."

Her face lit up. "So very helpful! 'Docs can scoot like the dickens for their size and keep themselves fat and sassy on their host's bacteria and waste products."

I stopped fingering the material. "How small *are* they?"

"Depends, but each can wiggle into your bloodstream through your skin."

"A human body tries to kill off invaders." I was hoping.

Strong made a strange noise that might've been intended as a chuckle, and I might've heard a soft hum from Kind.

"You got no idea," Strong chuckled, "how good this technology is. The 'docs can forge any kind of biological credentials. And their manners are real nice; they'll get along with every useful bug inside you, and you humans have trillions of 'em. Microdocs can even project and boost human thought forms so Minds will know just what you are, even in places on Commonworld where there's a heap of natural interference."

I didn't understand her last sentence but felt my ears heating up. Another thing I'd absorbed from my parents: basic standards of courtesy. "Sorry, my own manners need polishing today. Would either of you care to sit down, and can I get you anything to eat or drink?"

Strong and Kind traded glances. "Thanks," Strong answered, "but the Guardian has invited us *all* to breakfast and we're here to pass along the invite and to steer you to the local diner if you accept."

"Of course, I accept."

"That's settled then. Kind and I are ready to go, how 'bout you?"

I glanced down at myself. "After I put some clothes on over this, um, new outfit. Also, how do I take it off?"

For the first time, Strong eyes avoided mine. "There's no call for more garb, sweetheart, and you won't need to take it off."

I frowned. It was cold outside my door, and I doubted this thin fabric, despite Strong's claims, would be enough. Also, the so-called fourth skin was too damn formfitting. As to wanting it off occasionally, what about showers, using the toilet, and just plain airing-out? It hadn't escaped me the suit could be used *as* a toilet. But the idea lacked charm. Mrs. Goldberg didn't raise her boy to poop in his pants.

I glanced at my Earthly wardrobe. *No way,* I promised myself, *will I appear in public wearing a leotard, high-tech or low!* And I hadn't lugged my clothes incomprehensible distances to just leave them hanging. Besides, why would the Common ask me to bring attire I didn't need?

I reached for a shirt.

"Truly," Strong warned softly, "you'd best rely only on microdocs until you come to an understandin' with them about ... accessories."

"What understanding?"

"Not to eat 'em."

"Oh. I hope you're not going to say I *can't* take this off."

She surprised me by reaching out to gently squeeze my hand. "Nothing to it, but don't try it yet."

"Why not?"

"The 'docs won't understand you yet. Give 'em a while, then just put a finger into the jar and tell 'em to scat."

I stared at her, feeling a little betrayed and a lot tricked. "Okay," I announced in the confident tones of someone who isn't wearing a toilet. "Guess I'm ready after all. Ladies first."

CHAPTER 10
THERE BUT FOR GRACE

Despite my fear of stings, all I got in the hallway was a lesson on how badly I'd underestimated the microdocs. My suit swelled to quadruple thickness; brown fabric rolled down my arms and extended to warm gloves; microdoc shoes became insulated boots. I'd been winterized within five seconds.

The strangest part was finding my wristwatch resting prosaically *over* the fabric on my wrist, my ring similarly exposed.

"Wow."

"I take it," Strong stated with her most convincing smile yet, "you're beginnin' to see the merits of a fourth skin?"

"Just one question. If my apparel gets thicker and covers more when it's cold...?"

"Yes?"

"Are we going anywhere particularly warm today? Seems to me this clothing could have some unfortunate, well, drawbacks."

Strong's laughter sounded almost natural; maybe her humanity was starting to take. "Don't get all bothered. Real soon your 'docs will know you well enough to guard your modesty."

We headed down the hall. Strong waddled slightly despite her elegant new legs. I noticed Kind's eyes roving like sentries in a slow circuit around her head.

Strong touched my arm. "Might I ask somethin', Professor, and you just tell me if it's over-intimate?"

"Please call me David." Which seemed reasonable for anyone who addressed me as "sweetheart."

"I'd like that, David."

"Ask away."

She pointed to my left hand. "Is that what you'd call a weddin' band?"

I looked down in surprise. "Right. My wife made it. Her name was Sarasvati." I held it up to allow Strong a better look. "My Sara had all sorts of talents. See the inlay?"

She stopped, stopping us all. "Kind, I expect you'll want a gander at this."

To my astonishment, Kind moved close and gently pulled my ring-hand near one eye. I kept still, feeling as if some shy wild animal had decided to trust me. The flesh around her eye contracted, warping the orb itself. She released my hand and looked right at me.

"Thy wife was fully skillful."

The voice was predictably quiet and diffident, although I hadn't encountered a Neme speaking imitation Middle English before. But the shocker was her pitch, a basso molto profundo. Or maybe bassa....

"Kind's an expert artisan her own self," Strong explained. "I gather your wife passed away?"

"Four years ago."

"I'm truly sad 'bout that. That inlay—what's it based on?"

I forged a smile. "So you don't know *everything* about my planet." When she'd said "gander," I'd assumed it was a Rider-type joke. "It's a stylized swan, a winged animal adapted for floating."

"This animal meant something special to her?"

And to me. I lowered my hand, wishing for a pocket to hide it in. I'd spotlighted the inlay to show off Sara's workmanship, forgetting Neme fascination with symbolism. "She was named after a Hindu goddess often depicted as riding a swan."

She was studying my face. "Is that all?"

I sighed internally. "The swan represents *prana*, the breath of life. And those particular birds ... mate for life." And Sara knew that every time I see a swan or a picture of one, it moves me although I didn't know why.

Strong looked away. "Your bird reminds me, a tad, of someone very special. David, I'm not partnered up yet, but I can imagine how much it would hurt if I lost my mate."

I couldn't imagine it before the fact.

Kind chimed in again. "Dost humans mate for life?"

"Not necessarily, but it looks like I did."

By unspoken agreement we continued onwards.

In a sense, the microdocs saved me.

We ambled along, Kind trailing by several paces. I worried about getting stung again, and how bad the next sting might hurt since each had gotten progressively worse. I reached up to touch the site of the last injury and encountered something smooth and hard. Microdocs, I guessed, but in a new texture. I tilted my head back and to one side, hoping my expanded vision could get a look at my neck. Of course, that didn't work because too much face stayed in the way, but it aimed the other half of my super-peripheral-eyesight at the ceiling just as it collapsed.

I grabbed Strong and leaped forward. We hit the floor hard. The shockwave, as tons of material crashed down, sent us bouncing. The horrific banging and crunching sounds seem to last for minutes as they echoed through the hallways. Vaguely aware my suit had puffed to absorb some impact, I disentangled myself from Strong, sat up, and looked around.

Massive slabs, debris, and dust choked the corridor; near me, the rubble had formed an improbably straight edge except for one gap. Without that gap, my feet would've been smashed.

"Are you all right?" Strong and I asked simultaneously.

"Guess we are," she said, "thanks to you. My, you're Guardian-quick! Where's Kind? And those two Chean-shee we just passed?"

I stared into the dust cloud, then jumped up and began desperately tugging pieces loose.

"Easy, David! They're all fine; our Minds protect us against sudden pressures." She sounded calm and sure. "And a Mind can clear this mess faster than a passel of Constructors." In a thoughtful tone she added, "But this isn't right. Chean-shee engineering *never* fails."

She burst into rapid-fire Simple. The dust vanished and broken masonry began lifting and floating down the hall, but only a few blocks at a time.

"Why the hell," I snapped, "can't the Mind just remove the whole pile?"

"Everything has limits, sweetheart. There's too much material for it to handle all at once, and its main job is protecting whoever's underneath, so it's moving pieces aside to keep the pile from collapsin' any further."

The blocks were coming off faster now. As they flew along, I noticed an oddity: each took a wide detour around a certain point in the hallway. Despite Strong's assurances, my heart kept hammering.

"There she is!" Strong announced. "Let's ask her ..." Her voice decayed to silence.

Kind's body was crushed and bloody, almost unrecognizable.

Strong cried out and rushed toward what was left of her friend. I followed, the Mind shifting debris from our way. We'd just been talking about grief....

Several big slabs next to Kind drifted away, revealing a dead Cheanshee whose gory upper body was almost flat. Past the corpse, an even larger chunk of wreckage lifted off. The Constructor beneath stood up immediately. Not a scratch on him. He saw his dead comrade and his eyes paled to fish-belly white. He began making a quiet but terrible sound, a hoarse nonstop howl.

Strong reached over to grip his arm then bent over Kind, placed a hand tenderly on the Neme's ruined chest, called out a few words in Simple, and looked up at me. Her eyes were deep, somehow not entirely human despite their human appearance. They seemed to me filled with sorrow and pain, but also an underlying humility and acceptance of life, miseries and all. I felt very small.

"David, if Kind holds even a trickle of vigor, there's beings on Crossroad who might save her. I told the Mind to call for help."

I couldn't summon up hope, the little Neme was too obviously dead and surely Strong knew it too. My face felt frozen, incapable of expression, and I was afraid to speak; I might start howling myself.

Chean-shee crowded the corridor now; more gazed down through the gap overhead. Perhaps they'd been summoned telepathically or had felt the collapse. Didn't take mind reading to know how upset they were. Every eye had switched to the same color: a bright, glowing white. A female with a baby on her back joined the group, saw the dead male, and began moaning. Now there were two Constructors keening and neither could hear the ghastly sounds they were making.

"Can you get on to the restaurant by yourself, David? It's not far."

I managed to nod.

"Pass two corridors, take a left at the third. Pass three more, turn right and turn right again at the wider corridor just ahead."

I nodded again.

"You'll get there. 'We grow by bein', we learn by doin'.'" I recognized Balanced Clearhouse's twelfth aphorism.

I forced words out. "Any way I can help?"

For an instant, something strange seemed to watch me from behind her eyes. "'fraid not, David. And the Guardian's waitin'."

"I'll be ... praying for Kind."

"Hurry now."

Strong returned to her friend, and I pushed my way through the crowd, feeling cold and awkward. Most of the Chean-shee had stopped gesturing and were simply standing around.

I hadn't known Kind long, but had sensed something special and precious in her. And she'd finally been opening up to me, coming out of her shell. I followed Strong's directions like a sleepwalker. Except that I kept watching the ceiling.

Near the final turn, a Munchkin voice spoke at my elbow. "Strong of the Neme Eighth House wishes to converse with you. Do you agree to this?" In addition to its other duties, the Mind was evidently the local phone service.

"Yes. Of course."

Strong's drawl came through instantly. "David, I've been told it's too late for Kind. They'll heal folks here but got a rule against outright resurrections."

"I'm so sorry."

"Compassion becomes you. Bye for now."

Swift, radiating outrage, met me as I emerged into the Enclave's downtown section. "Please to follow," he snapped in his Hollywood Kremlin. "Strong told what happened."

"I'm sorry."

He didn't respond.

"Have you learned why—"

"Save queries for Guardian. You are *cold* in extra skin?"

Hadn't realized I was shivering. "Not really."

"Follow."

The Neme began walking, and I fell in beside him. Kind, I remembered, had been his personal assistant.

The rabbi's words at my wife's funeral came back to me. "Such a heavy loss," he'd said, "reminds us we only exist on loan. If we fail to treasure each other right now and treasure life itself, we may lose our chance forever."

Kind's death had cracked my defenses, reminding me of more losses than I could bear. Couldn't imagine ever feeling happy or at peace again. And Crossroad seemed different, darker, its exuberance only a clown's makeup to hide something deadly.

Then I remembered my mission. I couldn't *afford* grief; my actions here could affect the entire human race. The thought was a slap in my face. As we walked, I pushed my feelings aside, leaving behind numbness and a dull wonder at my own foolishness. Why had I allowed myself to get so involved? An ugly accident, but I'd barely known Kind. And why this nagging sense of guilt? Her death hadn't been my fault. I looked over at Swift. Despite my deliberately contracted consciousness, I couldn't miss the misery in his bearing and homely alien profile.

Every Chean-shee we passed acted ... subdued. Bad news really travels among telepaths. And something was different.

"What happened to the smell?" I whispered, unnecessarily.

"Which smell, comrade?"

"This part of the Enclave had a distinct, um, atmosphere."

He grunted impatiently. "You wear a taur—a fourth skin. It protects."

"Against *body* odors?" Without the pungency, the air was sweet.

"Against harm. Including harmful fumes."

At the restaurant, the same silver-eyed Chean-shee or his twin led us to last night's table and seated us. Rider wasn't there.

"How can I smell food, but not ... our fellow diners?"

"Fourth skin," Swift explained unenthusiastically, "is smart filter. These food aromas must be safe for your kind."

"Wasn't Sun-toch-sew supposed to—"

"Was here. Will return. Please to order if hungry."

The server stepped closer immediately although he couldn't have overheard.

"Nothing for me right now, thanks," I thought at him. He moved away, but not far.

Swift sat so stiffly he might as well have been standing at attention. He didn't even glance my way.

"How many cooks work here?" I asked, hoping to crack the thickening ice. My stomach had begun to ache from the strain of keeping my emotions in check.

"None. Machine in kitchen."

Pity. A six-limbed creature could make an impressive Teppanyaki chef. "Look, I'm afraid we've gotten off on the wrong foot somehow and ..."

I'd lost my audience. Swift's three eyes were aimed at the restaurant's entrance. His sparkling fur puffed out, making him seem bigger.

I heard myself gasp.

The terrifying creature in the doorway most resembled a wolf spider. But its head alone was larger than my body and its maroon abdomen appeared roomy enough to digest an entire horse. Good thing for the monster that the restaurant's ceiling was so high; far above its torso, the middle joints on the spidery legs nearly scraped the overhead beams.

Moving like a Harryhausen animation, this outsized horror marched toward us, straight over intervening tables and customers, occasionally ducking under pipes. It trod on no toes or skulls, and its torso would've easily cleared the heads of even standing Chean-shee. The diners appeared unconcerned, but whenever the monster stepped over one, the Constructor hunched over like someone approaching an idling helicopter.

It stopped several tables away, near our waiter. Perhaps asking for the non-smoking section. So much for me feeling numb.

"What is *that*?" I whispered.

"He is Lord Loaban," Swift spat. "The Apnoti." From Swift's tone, I wasn't sure if "Apnoti" was a species name or some Neme expletive.

"But what is he?"

"Fools call him a god."

"*Really?* Never seen a god before."

"You have made poor first choice. Do not misplace faith on this one." Something else I'd never seen: a furious Neme.

The uber-arachnid moved forward again, but with a slow, stalking deliberateness. If Swift had shown the tiniest sign of fear, I would've been out of there before you could say "out of there."

I kept staring. This refugee from a B horror movie had seven legs, maybe it lost one at some point, and walked on six. The other clutched a short silver wand, which looked toylike in the huge claws.

The so-called god rubbed together its—I guess "chelicerae" is the right word—producing a kind of bass squeak. Simultaneously, a flat soprano voice emanating from nowhere in particular said, "I am here." I looked around, unsure who'd spoken.

Loaban moved nearer to me, *much* too near, and lowered his body. Now, I only needed to look upward a few feet to see five eyes, each of a different hue, boring into mine. Even with the legs mostly folded, the hairy leg-joints towered above us like gargantuan elbows.

Another low squeak. "You are the unfortunate," said the mystery voice.

"Are you ... speaking to me?" I asked the spider, leaning away instinctively.

"Who am I looking at, small person?" Loaban waved his silver wand practically in my face. A translating device?

"Sorry, but—"

Swift made an incredible sound, a three-part adagio of snarls. No human could've followed such an avalanche of noises, but the unseen commentator began droning away, apparently translating both ends of the conversation into English:

"Lord Trapper, I am shocked you have come here. You have failed us this day." The bored-sounding inflection denied the glitter in Swift's eyes.

"I owe no apologizes. She was dead before I could act. Only a Traveler could have saved her."

Was Swift blaming the *god* for Kind's death? Loaban wasn't around when the ceiling fell. Even without my improved vision, I would've noticed a truck-sized spider.

The Neme wasn't finished. "What are you doing, Lord? This is not a sanctioned contact. Do you wish to further betray our plans?"

Swift was braver than I'll ever be, shouting at the giant horror while Loaban's russet head darkened to purple. The god's forehead, beneath the sparse fur, began glowing a dull red, revealing chitin almost lunar with pits or pockmarks surrounded by glistening ribbons suggesting scar tissue. And where he'd worn chelicerae like any self-respecting arachnid, Loaban seemed to be growing fangs.

Then it was fangs rubbing together that produced the god's voice, and the new squeak was appalling, a claw scratching down the blackboard of my spine.

"What am I doing, foolish larva? Following my conscience as is my duty." The soprano voice still carried zero emotion; Loaban might have been discussing last month's weather.

Swift slapped a paw hard on the tabletop. "Foolish god, the Mirrormage warned that our enemies move freely among us. Now, in your arrogance you reveal your role prematurely."

All five eyes blazed. "All arrogance is yours. You worship expectations and blame me when they disappoint. Never forget: you need me while I have no need of you. Who else has time and strength to serve when your mages are away, the Watergod dreams in his private ocean, and the Diplomat merely watches?"

Swift stood up. I'd become focused on the translations, barely aware of his real voices blasting away. "Expectations? Is it too much to expect for one who declares himself a—"

The god, perhaps imitating Swift out of spite, raised a leg and smashed it down on the floor hard enough to rattle plates. "What you lack, tiny soft one, is common sense."

"What I lack is a trustworthy ..."

The translation ended because Swift had glanced at me, then at the wand, and abruptly shut up. His eyes lined up vertically—a Neme sign of distress.

"Extra guests for breakfast?" a familiar voice called out cheerfully in English. "And one with a large appetite. Heat the *big* griddle."

The spider lurched to his full height and turned, revealing Rider standing behind him along with a Blenn. Compared to Loaban, the Blenn was attractive.

"Are you, like your Neme helper, shocked that I am here, Guardian?" the spider asked.

Patting the Blenn between the antennae, Rider said, "Not at all. Found this fine worker, I did, near the Enclave entrance. What Blenn, I asked me, would arrive here without a speechstaff? Therefore, someone had ... borrowed hers. Since few beings in this area would require such aid, your presence disappoints not shocks."

Annoyingly, the wand was translating Rider's English, producing an imperfect and confusing duet with variations in syntax and interpretation. "Speechstaff" was also "render-rod," "Apnoti" was "Trapper."

"But perhaps," Rider continued, reaching high to pluck the wand from Loaban's claws, "you visit only to masticate." The god's only response was a soft hiss.

Swift made some hand signals; Rider shot me a look then twisted something at the wand's base.

"This, doubtless, belongs with you," the Common said to the Blenn. The little horror bowed, accepted the speechstaff, and slid it into a narrow sheath.

If Rider's adjustment was intended to block my comprehension, it failed. But the translating voice was softer as Rider switched to an unfamiliar language. "On the other leg, my dear Apnoti, best it might be for you to dine elsewhere."

"You cannot dismiss me, Guardian. I say it's time to give this one enough information to make an informed choice."

The way Rider glanced at me implied the spider had made a telling point. "More faith you have in our precautions than I, Lord. His native strength may yet overwhelm all protections."

"If so, he already knows too much so why withhold the rest? I shall not let your fears infuse my actions."

Rider's slurp resembled a taunt. "You are a power, too true, but you know who listens over us all. She hears more than even you can imagine. Your willfulness is a sandstorm without wind."

Loaban was shaking, and not from merriment. "If She objects to my appearance here, why does She permit it?"

Pause. "She prefers letting others manifest Her wishes."

"You dare claim to know Her wishes?"

"Only to this extent: She has approved our plans. What has changed to allow you to act independently? You must honor our agreements, Lord."

The spider pounded the floor again and a crunch of breaking glass came from the kitchen. I looked around. Every Chean-shee in the restaurant was watching the confrontation. They all looked as tense as I felt.

"Experience teaches even gods," Rider added. "Our task is not to avoid all mistakes, but to avoid repeating them. I know you mean only well, but matters are more delicately balanced than you may realize."

"And how have you balanced the scraps of your ethics?"

"That is my concern. I am personally responsible for our guest and cannot distribute my duty. Force me not to call upon a stronger name than yours."

"You threaten me? You say She works through others and dream She will interfere in a petty squabble? Is our Diplomat, too, a hypocrite?" The Apnoti pushed himself even higher, turning his body back and forth, including everyone in his fivefold glare.

"So be it," he spat. "Guardian, you are as impudent as you are impotent, but I will conform to my word and commit all tragic results to your soul and Hers." His giant trembling legs began glowing, brightening until the spider seemed to be standing on eight fuzzy lightning bolts. Furious sparks shot off the individual hairs.

I was on my feet, chair pushed aside, heart squeezed between awe and terror. Static electricity made my own hair stand on end and zapped the Constructors and Swift into furry balls. Rider's crest had become a frozen eruption of yellow filaments.

I held my breath, expecting something dreadful. But the god gradually became transparent and then, like MacArthur's old soldier, faded away altogether.

CHAPTER 11
SHELL GAMES

Rider's strength seemed to deflate along with its crest. The Common slumped onto a bench while the Blenn looked around, rocking gently on her disk. Around us, Chean-shee resumed business as usual.

"What h—happened to the spider?" I asked, retrieving my chair and more or less falling into it.

Rider gestured for the Blenn to join us. The bug bowed but stayed put. "To Loaban," Rider sighed, "nothing happened. He merely altered pitch. But be assured, the Trapper is our ally."

"Oh? I'd hate to meet your enemies."

"Truly, you would. Forgive me for muffling the speechstaff, but some things you must not hear. Not yet."

Anger can be contagious. "Frankly," I spat, "I'm damn sick of all these hints!" My mission was already more than I could cope with, and now this ... whatever the hell this was. "*Tell* me what's going on."

"Be at peace, we need for you to know. But this is not the time."

"Don't be so sure. Got news for you: you're not exactly omniscient. Whatever you did to that wand didn't work. I heard the whole conversation. I'm *still* hearing a voice, translating English into English."

As Rider stared at me, Swift's eyes again lined up vertically. "He may have learned much," the Neme admitted, speaking in Simple, "even before you arrived, Guardian. I was careless."

I glared at them both. "Look, I didn't understand everything. But I didn't miss Loaban calling me 'unfortunate' and demanding I be given enough information to make 'an informed choice.' Sounds like a plan from where I sit, and don't pretend he wasn't talking about *me*."

Rider's reaction took me by surprise. The Common burst into loud slurping before saying, "That devil of a god! The speechstaff he ... jinxed so I would betray myself. The old warrior has more cunning than legs. Ayn-Aduum, damage has happened, and we must live or die with it."

Swift wasn't amused. "Guardian, I do not expect to comprehend insects, but should I not understand you? You laugh?"

"At myself, young one. How easily Loaban outmaneuvered me! Still, his motives are most audible. What don't you understand?"

"After forsaking Kind, how dared he break pact?"

"*Because* he failed. Guilt overpowers even the mighty."

Rider turned to me. "Professor David A. Goldberg, your unhappiness I hear, but to limit danger, we truly must limit your knowledge. A trade I will offer: Ask any question Loaban's words engendered, and I will attempt an answer. You will then accept your remaining ignorance for a while longer."

I thought it over. The spider had mentioned some names that I wanted to know about. Able had mentioned a "Watergod" living on Crossroad, and had then, well, clammed up on the subject. But who or what was the Mirrormage and Diplomat?

"Only *one* question?" I sighed, "I've got hundreds."

"I dare risk no more."

Better than nothing. "What I most want to know right now is why Kind died."

The yellow eyes darkened. "We have not yet learned why that ceiling failed but have taken great leaps to insure such a thing will not reoccur."

"Not what I meant. After the cave-in, Strong was sure Kind was safe. What made her wrong?"

Rider's head jerked back as if from a blow. "Perhaps my doing. To prevent more stingings, I had the Mind form a powerful barrier around you against a range of intrusive energies. Wide enough this barricade was to embrace Kind and one Constructor during the collapse." The Common made a strange noise, almost a groan. "My *orders* foiled the Mind's response because its needed protective force could not penetrate its own barrier. If you hadn't avoided the falling material, you and Strong would also have been crushed. I fear that Loaban has reason to doubt my decisions."

Rider's misery burst my anger. And even if they were allowed, further questions stuck in my throat. Two people had died because I'd wanted protection. Against being stung.

The Blenn shook itself like a wet dog and finally wriggled closer to the table. It stopped near Swift, bowed, and emitted an ugly buzzing.

Evidently, holstering the speechstaff didn't stop it from working. The bland voice said, "A thousand apologies, but I am experiencing confusion. And I must include another apology for interrupting so rudely."

"Think nothing over it," Rider said in English.

"You are kinder than I merit, Guardian. My name is (buzzing sound). My Least dispatched me to convey an invitation to an individual visiting from the Rushing Universe whose nature, to my shame, is unfamiliar to me." A pincher waved in my direction. "Could this lovely entity be the personage she begs to visit us in Blenntown?"

Rider stayed silent for a moment, probably digesting the idea of me being lovely. "Surely he is. What has confused you?"

"If anyone could clarify—at a convenient time, of course—how my render-rod came into the possession of that magnificent giant who recently departed, I would be most grateful."

Swift spoke up, also in English. "Am Swift Thirdhouse. Honored to greet you, madam (buzzing sound)."

The Blenn's response was a deeper bow.

"Giant," the Neme continued, "was Lord Loaban."

"I have heard of him, noble Swift Thirdhouse, but he has not blessed us by swimming in our waters."

Swift rolled his eyes—literally. "More likely excrete in waters. Sad to tell, this one's undeserved powers far surpass his language skills. Doubtless, he used former to snatch closest available speechstaff. Apnoti would consider theft divine prerogative. I regret inconvenience to you."

"As do I," Rider said. "Incidentally, this 'lovely entity' your queen wishes to meet is titled Professor David A. Goldberg." The Blenn bowed to me, and I automatically returned the gesture, still seated.

She bowed again. "Then that's how it floats! I thank you all for expending your invaluable time to reduce my confusion. If you'll forgive me for wasting yet more of your precious energy ... I fear my aggressive demands for information may have caused offense. I beg you to excuse any insult, however major."

This ultra-alien might be hideous, but she sure was polite.

"Worry not," Rider offered. "Your actions have been entirely inoffensive. Consider yourself among friends."

If only I could be sure of that myself.

"Will you join us at table, (buzzing sound)," Rider continued, "for nutrition?"

"Joyfully would I ingest among this distinguished group. Alas, I would not care to diminish your pleasure by intruding on your company."

"Your company," Rider replied, "will augment our pleasure."

This time the Blenn bowed so low I was sure she'd fall over. "A wiser being than I would have anticipated your stunning courtesy. I gratefully accept your kindness if I would not be imposing."

Our server suddenly hovered closer. Not being hungry, I visualized a plain omelet cooked in butter, as an experiment. Not that I cared much about the result, but as another distraction to keep myself from thinking about Kind, and the sick fear in the pit of my stomach.

As the Constructor swung off on an overhead pipe, the Blenn lowered her torso to table level by twisting her single leg into an impossibly tight helix. I wondered if she'd spin like a top if she lost control.

The waiter reappeared bearing plates heaped with ... God knows what but presumably food. My breakfast alone showed promise. Using an alien cousin to a fork, I sampled my omelet and awarded it a yuck. The rancid butter suggested that *all* the Enclave's converters were lactose intolerant. Disinclined to continue the autopsy, I pushed the eggs aside.

"Have problem, Professor?" Swift asked.

"Nothing important."

Rider seemed distinctly unhappy. Its leaves were drooping and eyelids fluttering as though blinking back tears.

The Neme waved a hand to recapture my attention. "Tell anyway."

I shrugged and pointed. "The butter's spoiled."

Swift and Rider exchanged glances. "Send it back," Rider suggested. "On your world don't you say: the squeaky wheel gets less grease?"

I forced a chuckle. My guide was grieving, but trying to hide it.

I couldn't help but remember how Kind's admiration for my wife's craftsmanship had warmed me; Sara would've liked the shy Neme. Of course, traditional Hindus and Nemes *should* be compatible. Both groups are vegetarians, use specific hands for certain activities, and revere contemplative disciplines. Both live life in stages, ultimately abandoning possessions and subsisting on public generosity. The Sanskrit word for such wandering mendicants is "sannyasin." The Neme term translates as "Clearhouse."

Nemes even have an analog to India's outlawed yet ongoing caste system: their Houses, the first twenty being royalty and status degenerating from there. In the final life phase, however, a Neme's status disappears. A Clearhouse is supposedly free of even unwritten conventions.

Sara had despised the caste system. She'd been raised in a traditional Hindu family but had claimed it didn't take. Still, aren't we all children of our culture to some degree? Certainly, Hinduism had shaped her perceptions, giving her attitudes an underlying Indian flavor. I suppose

Rider would've said she had the curry of her convictions. Perhaps loving her is one reason I feel so comfortable with Nemes. *Face the truth, David. Kind is as dead as your Sara, and you'll never feel the same way about Crossroad. This place is no garden of unearthly delights. It can kill you.* I had a bad hunch that in my case, it probably would.

Rider wasn't currently making jokes, the big head stayed canted forward, hands closed, oversized triangular knuckles sticking out—natural clubs, edged with spikes. Guess my silence had been infectious so the cure was up to me.

"Tell me something, Sun-toch-sew. What's the Crossroad definition of a god?"

"Perhaps I answer?" Swift interceded after a moment.

"Do," Rider said.

"Professor, beings we name 'gods' have positive intentions, great personal power, uniqueness, and generate awe."

"How interesting!" said the Blenn. "Please forgive my intrusion into your profound conversation. My tragically inflated ego, the shame of my family, demands I add an unnecessary point. From my narrow perspective, a god implies worshippers. Of course, we Blenn are relatively dull beings, and my own thinking is particularly inferior."

I had to smile. This bug's charm had already made her physical form less repulsive to me. But I reminded myself not to underestimate her; Blenn had engineered the Safe-roads.

"Worshippers," Rider observed sourly, "the Apnoti has in abundance. On his home sands, many listen up to him."

"*Look* up to him," Swift corrected.

"So I said."

"What's the name," I asked, "of Loaban's species? Where's he from?" The idea of a giant spider world didn't make me yearn for a ticket.

Rider reached far across the table to pat my hand. "You imagine Apnotis in packs? Be easy! Loaban had outgrown his original form, and I know of none to match him. But unlike the Travelers, he wasn't born a god but became one by applying natural gifts and learning to ... body-build while learning to spirit-build. A self-made deity he is."

I stared at the Common, wishing the speechstaff provided crib notes.

"What," I asked, "is a 'Traveler'?"

Rider abruptly sat up straighter and glanced quickly around the room, stopping, I thought, to focus on something behind me. I felt tempted to turn around, but was fascinated by the way Rider's leaves had begun moving in slow ripples. I thought its lemon eyes seemed wary.

"Professor David A. Goldberg, I am distorted with regret. Clumsy I am with troubles and should not have referenced matters religious."

"Hold on there. Loaban used the term 'Traveler' earlier. The cat's head is already out of the bag; you can't just stuff it back in!"

"Perhaps not." Rider sounded surprised, and I wondered why. Its eyes finally came back to meet mine. "Has Able Firsthouse ever spoken of entities both Nemes and Common worship?"

I nodded, suddenly uneasy. "Nothing specific." This conversation had taken a sharp turn to the weird.

"These entities are the Supernals, the Twelve Travelers. A translation of the Hhoymon term might be 'Spherecerers.'"

"Supernals?"

"Many names each has, but respecting propinquity we employ those coined by Hhoymon: Binae, Maanza," Rider spoke as though reciting a prayer, "Woo-Chybris, Arfaenn, Aduum—"

"Maanza?" I was wearing gooseflesh under my fourth skin. That name was featured in a certain photograph....

"So I spoke. There are seven more whenever you wish to hear the entire roll."

"They're your ... private gods?"

"Not private, and these are gods major. You will learn more presently, my friend. For now, you must honor our agreement and nourish patience."

"I have a choice?"

"No. But to water your waiting, I remind you of a gift we've proffered: whatever research you desire to conduct here, we will assist."

The UN agents had dangled this amazing temptation during our initial interview, but purely academic opportunities seemed almost irrelevant now.

"That's a wonderful offer," I admitted, while thinking something very different: just let me research your damn Hall of Games. Did I dare mention the Hall right now?

"What quests would you follow?"

Lost my nerve. "Well ... naturally, I'd appreciate examining whatever records you have on the Scome." A risky subject, but someone with my academic specialty would be expected to pursue it. "And I'd like to learn more about Hhoymon, Nemes, and if possible, your own people. Oh, and that species with the variable legs, the Vyre."

Wrinkles around Rider's speaking diaphragm smoothed. "Easy as succulents. Soon, you will be buried in documents. Would you wish them transposed to English?"

"You can do that? That'd be perfect." Come on, David, I urged myself. It's a scholar's wet dream. You've got to feel a *little* excited.

"We might even send along a MARBLE reader to spelunk Hhoymon records directly. Anything else you might fancy?"

"Yes. I'd like to learn more about Crossroad itself." I licked my lips. "Maybe do some sightseeing?"

Rider leaned toward me. "Perhaps one special sight you would enjoy."

"Oh?"

"I have received a report on your favorite activities. Supplied by a helpful human titled Doctor Susan Rilka." Rider sounded excessively casual.

"How thoughtful of her."

"The report sings that you spend many moments running. We can supply you lovely chances to indulge."

I blinked. "You mean there's a nice ... trail or something around here?" I couldn't imagine anything less relevant.

"Seris-ayn! We have premier subjective tracks in our Hall of Games, near both Hhoymon City and where our Watergod splashes. Three worthy destinations, all within a circle of trivial radius."

I tried to assemble a poker face.

"You are pleased!" Good thing we weren't playing poker. "Thus, you now have a bloated schedule. This very turn you'll meet a wet god, hear a great city, and run to nowhere. And while you drink such joys, a cross-eyed team of cross-referencers will stumble into action. Blurry, poorly translated documents will soon clutter your domicile."

A free pass to the Hall, and I hadn't had to ask! I pushed all sorrow to the back of my heart—God knows I've had practice. Suddenly I felt better enough to feel a bit hungry. I turned in my seat to think an order at our server who took the omelet away for proper burial and returned with pancakes and syrup. How bad could pancakes be?

―――

A public service announcement: I don't recommend dining with a Blenn, perhaps not even if you happen to be one.

Finding Rider's eating technique disturbing, and Swift's use of

Neme feeding tendrils boring, I watched the final member of our quartet dig into a pile of greenish, shrimp-like critters. The Blenn grabbed each morsel separately then hurled the animalcule past her mandibles into her mouth. Her jaws chewed sideways, and the strands of enduring drool grew progressively greener. Before long, I tried to focus exclusively on Swift but couldn't because of my expanded vision. Talk about bad side effects.

It hardly mattered. Crossroad's pancake recipe apparently included rancid buttermilk, which is supposed to be rancid, but not *that* rancid.

Swift, following Neme custom when finished eating, inverted his bowl. "You know of Watergod, Professor?"

"Until I arrived on Crossroad, I only heard the name 'Watergod's Grotto.' I didn't realize there was an actual god involved."

"If incomprehensible wisdom you seek," Rider put in, "or advice obscure, that one is your fish."

I shrugged. "Between Scome literature and undergraduate essays, I'm used to being puzzled."

"Then a suggestion I have. This up-sitting Neme and I must attend an unhappy event. Meanwhile, if you choose, you could remain here with our enchanting new friend or return to your room. In either case, within this very twist, conduct you I shall to Watergod's Grotto and onwards."

Irrationally, I felt hurt at not being invited to the funeral. "Sounds fine but I'm, um, finished with breakfast. And I'd like to fetch my camera before we go anywhere." I'd been ordered to reserve every picture for my mission, but maybe this Watergod would deserve a small photographic accident.

Rider and Swift stood. The Blenn immediately untwisted, creating a small breeze.

"Ask the Mind," Rider said to me, "for guidance to your compartment if necessary. There, I will meet you. And (buzzing sound), please tell your queen that Professor David A. Goldberg accepts her munificent offer; too humble he is to accept on his own behalf."

The Blenn seemed to beam at me. "I shall deliver this joyous message forthwith unless I may perform some service to replay all your kindnesses? My skills are minuscule, but yours to command."

"May we hold your generous offer in reserve?" Rider asked.

"Until the next instant or until my small life has merged with the endless waters."

"Excellent. I bid you both well faring for now."

Rider and Swift bowed and took off before the Blenn had come out of her return bow.

My turn to stand. The bug's courtesy made me want to be just as courteous, but I wasn't vain enough to believe I could match her humility.

"It's been an honor to meet you," I said.

"You deserve more honor than I can provide."

Imitating my predecessors, I bowed and scooted.

Why would a Blenn queen ask for me? More troubling, why hadn't Strong, earlier, told me the Mind could guide me to the restaurant? Had she been too distracted by Kind's death to think of it? Or had she stopped trusting the Mind? I left the restaurant, my stomach emptier than when I'd arrived. Didn't matter. I'd hidden most of my recent grief in that hollow place where I'd hidden the older griefs, but now fear had murdered my appetite.

It had become agonizingly obvious that I'd been brought to Crossroad for a purpose. And whatever that purpose might be, not only was I being manipulated like an exceptionally stupid puppet, it had made me a target for whoever or whatever opposed it. I had no comforting delusion that the hallway cave-in had been an accident or a coincidence.

Just as troubling in a different way, I *knew* that I'd felt something for a moment in the restaurant and remembered thinking it was the presence of some terrible power, but now I could only remember the thought, not the sensation. I felt sure this was important, but my mind kept sliding away from the topic and even the memory of that thought seemed to be fading.

CHAPTER 12
A MALIGNANT STARFISH

My subconscious, always smarter than me, had already memorized the route, but the hike to my apartment wasn't pleasant. I passed the spot where the ceiling had fallen. Everything had already been repaired, yet misery and pain seemed to linger like a sour smell.

That wasn't the worst part. Widely spaced ceiling lamps illuminated most corridors, making my shadow play tricks as I hurried along, lengthening, shrinking, sometimes rotating around my feet. Then, in one apparently deserted hallway, I glimpsed a blurry shadow that *wasn't* mine.

The high ceiling was too low for the Apnoti, which allowed me to chalk the incident up to nerves. But I didn't dawdle. In fact, I was practically running by the time I reached my door, and very glad to close it behind me.

Strong had claimed the microdocs would soon obey my orders. Hoping "soon" had arrived, I headed for the toilet and mentally commanded the suit to make itself scarce. Sure enough, the material contracted to become a brown, lightweight lump clinging to my chest.

I wrinkled my nose. Not because I smelled bad, but because my body smelled as if I'd just taken a shower despite exertion and a surplus of emotions. In the mirror, I regarded the small lump and dispatched a second experimental message: go where you think best.

Instantly, my head was covered from chin to scalp. I gasped and gasped again because gasping had been so easy despite the seemingly solid mask. The microdoc tide receded, and I got another jolt: my hair was shining and *brushed*. My beard stubble, gone. The 'docs had my number, down to where I wanted hair removed and where I didn't.

The idea of nano-spies inside my brain was distressing. But I had to admit they were useful little spies. Their talents even suggested an interesting possibility. I chewed over the idea while brushing my teeth. Silly me. The gel left them a trifle dirtier.

After leaving the bathroom, my fourth skin returned to clothing duty, I retrieved my camera, slung its strap around my neck, sat on the levitation chair, and hunted for something ... safe to ponder while waiting, something not involving Kind, secret plots, or funerals.

But there I failed. So I glowered at my camera through unwelcome tears and tried to distract myself by thinking of all the spectacular photo ops I'd already wasted.

The problem: storage. Modern cameras and smartphones can automatically upload to any cloud-based system, providing unlimited archiving. At this moment, I would've had to upload to another damn universe. Not exactly an option. And although my fake Nikon, designed to remain sealed until back in authorized hands, had a huge internal memory, almost all of it was hogged by a slew of redundant security features, plus I had a nasty suspicion that it might also be doing a bit of surreptitious recording. In any case, the camera only had room for a pitiful twenty holicons and forty flats. That's why I had strict orders to reserve all photography for my mission. I'd wanted to bring two cameras, but Garlen vetoed the idea, fearing that an extra camera might arouse suspicion.

Now I was glad that I'd decided not to take the camera with me this morning. I'd only been trying to avoid temptation, but how phony would it have looked to leave it dangling beneath my chin after the spider-god showed up? Then again, how phony did it look to be taking no pictures at all?

I pressed the on button, admired the splendidly detailed display, then cut the power although the battery could supposedly last for weeks of continual operation.

I felt terribly frustrated. What a lost, priceless opportunity to take unique photos, video, audio recordings, and maybe even samples of whatever wouldn't complain or try to sample me back! Earth's scientific community would be furious if word of my little jaunt ever leaked. Not to mention reaction among our political and military leaders.

I hoped Rider would arrive before I found more things to worry about. Humanity didn't know it, but it was counting on me to discover the truth here, and that also should be worry enough.

My father, a psychologist specializing in personnel evaluation, had once observed, "Sometimes you get more from an interview by having the subject question *you*. The trick is how you ask for clarifications."

On the third Safe-road of our journey to Watergod's Grotto, I decided to try the technique.

"Do those Blenn rods work through telepathy?" I asked Rider, seated next to me in the latest ghostly vehicle.

"No. A speechstaff requires language coding and speaks by wiggling auditory timpani, or other hearing organs. Just so, the Minds speak without sound."

"Interesting. So some Blenn had to program the speechstaff for English? How'd this programmer even know what language I used?"

"A Mind played the coding. And as I've sung before, our Minds share information."

"I see. What's the Blenn queen's interest in me?" For once I *wanted* to get stonewalled.

"I am unsure."

Just in time, I realized Rider would hear a nervous swallow. "Well, since I'm not yet allowed to ask any ... important questions, maybe you'd care to ask *me* something?"

I thought I'd pulled off the proposal with fair nonchalance. But Rider's glance at me seemed amused. "A most thoughtful offer! As the sands shift, I do thirst for answers. Last turn you spoke of hearing new tones?"

"Colors. Two of them."

"And their characters?"

"Um. I told you about the one I've been calling 'ultra-red,' with the warmth and shimmer. The other, ultra-blue, is clear, steady, and cool. Beyond that, I can't describe them."

"Do you hear either tone this moment?"

I looked around, even studying the passing virtual fish. "No. But there are usually strands of ultra-red drifting through our favorite restaurant. And that's mostly where I've noticed ultra-blue."

"In strands?"

"No, more an indirect glow."

"So," Rider said quietly. "That first tone, Gray Hhoymon title *oradep*. 'Orae' means power in Hhoymon Primary and 'dep' is movement."

"What sort of power?"

"Focused intent." Rider paused. "That tone *I* have heard, but only with my awareness fully extruded. Your senses are acute!"

"Honestly, most of my senses are dull as ever, but Crossroad seems to have opened a new one for me. I'm not seeing these extra colors with my *eyes*."

Rider shifted uneasily. "Then your ultra-blue may be what Hhoymon spirit-teachers title 'manis,' a tone beyond my range."

"But here's what baffles me: on Earth, people born blind whose sight is surgically restored in adulthood never develop much ability to see. By then it's too late to develop crucial brain areas."

"On Earth."

I shrugged. "Point taken, but I still have a human brain with human limitations."

Rider went silent and seemed inclined to stay that way. Guess I'd asked one question too many.

———

Our route took us through Hhoymon City, about the size of downtown Manhattan. Most buildings here were designed to accommodate every Hhoymon race, but a few scaled-down skyscrapers were clearly intended for Whites. Street-signs with glowing symbols helped me align the map in my head with reality; here was one place I could find my own way around.

The city was beautiful if assertively artificial. A pleasant warmth left me in microdoc shorts, sandals with cushioned soles, and a thin tank top. The air smelled of spring in New England, if I ignored the hints of pineapple and cinnamon.

The immense translucent dome covering the entire area glistened like sunshine through milk glass, illuminating tall, sharply tapered buildings with richly colored windows, parks with florid trees and dull flowers. Everything was here except the Hhoymon.

Still, it wasn't deserted. Scores of Nemes wandered the streets, some with ultra-aliens of unfamiliar type in tow. One non-Neme alien caught my eye, and I did a double take.

"Seen that creature before," I muttered. "But I can't think where."

"Which creature?" Rider asked quickly.

"The, um, feathered biped near the fountain."

"You are certain?"

I hesitated. "Not really. I seem to remember silver feathers, not those white and black ones. But that shape is so distinctive—whoops. Looks like a certain avian doesn't appreciate attention." The ultra-alien strutted away like an offended heron.

"I believe his intent was to gain our attention."

"His? You know that bird?"

Rider slurped, gently urged me forward with one giant hand, but didn't answer. Which would've annoyed me if my next step hadn't brought the jewel of the city, its central structure, into view: a graceful skyscraper seemingly encrusted with powdered diamonds. Incredibly tall, it appeared impossibly tall as it glittered in the diffuse light, its final crystal spire melting into the dome's apex, a thousand feet overhead.

The official name translated as 'Collectors Tower,' but Able Firsthouse had preferred its Gray Hhoymon nickname—Chhirr-ai-Arfaenri, meaning Heart of Art. And Able had raved about wonders it contained, treasures from a thousand universes. Hhoymon had been sailing the waves of ultraspace even longer than the Common. The Heart of Art was the ultimate museum.

Rider had gotten ahead of me. I hustled to catch up and asked, "Did the Hhoymon empty their museum when they left?"

"I am uncertain."

"Could we possibly," I begged, "take a small detour and peek inside? I've heard even the lobby is spectacular."

"Maanza-ayn! I suffer sincere regrets, but we dare not enter any city building. The Tower least of all."

"Why?"

Rider waved a finger around. "What quality unites all Hhoymon doors?"

The answer was obvious. "They all seem to be transparent."

"Just so. Hhoymon require clear doors to enter buildings beyond fear of ambush. But their windows muffle everything within. Do you follow my thought? I wish to sing no ill of the absent, but as a species, Hhoymon may be ... overcautious. Despite experience and reassurance, they feared theft or vandalism while they were elsewhere. And they fully expect to return."

Overcautious? They sounded downright paranoid. "You're not saying ... you think the museum might be booby-trapped?"

Rider glanced down at me. "Ashamed I am to confess a rare language gap. Is your 'booby' perhaps a predator imprisoned to spring out at trespassers?"

"No, but you've got the general idea."

"Then it is so trapped, this we know. Hhoymon often infuse their structures with discouraging energies against trespass, but within their tower they have done something unprecedented: unhinged space and time."

"Unhinged?"

"We Common do not understand it, but you and I are not equipped to battle such a booby."

Hhoymon were evidently rock hounds. Huge crystals and exotic mineral specimens lay scattered throughout city parks, some left rough, others polished. With such gorgeous stones just lying about, targets for non-parallel pigeons, I couldn't imagine those displayed in the Heart of Art.

Rider broke a brooding silence when we walked past the Tower. "I would not burden you with unwanted information. Yet there is one arena where sharing knowledge cannot harm. And your alien ears may hear something mine have not."

"Believe me, I'm interested!"

"Seris-ayn. When more hearts do the carrying, troubles feel lighter." The Common patted my head. "Our local Mind can no longer reach into yon museum. Discern, we cannot, what procedure twisted its reality. This presents a threat most pressing."

"How so?"

"The technique might be employed against *us* by Hhoymon rebels."

"But aren't all the Hhoymon gone?"

"Who stops them from secret returning? You hear? We *must* understand the Tower's condition."

I glanced at the museum and shivered. "How about sending in remote-controlled robots with cameras or something? Unless the door's locked?"

"Both controlled and autonomous machines, we dispatched many. None sang for long, but we learned of twisted realities contained a disharmony of atmospheric and gravimetric anomalies."

"Sudden vacuums?"

"And worse. In our urgency, we had two Blenn engineers shielded by macroquantum-stabilized ultraspacesuits enter. They ceased communicating within a hundredth twist *despite* each Blenn carrying a twinned-crystal while technicians outside retained the siblings. Such devices cannot fail. In theory."

Able Firsthouse had mentioned these crystals, describing them as transceiver pairs with a ultraspacial connection. I'd wondered if some form of quantum entanglement was involved, but he'd pleaded ignorance.

"What did the engineers tell you," I asked, "before they lost contact?"

"That the building had grown from the inside and was yet growing. According to their perceptions and instruments, it had ... mirrored itself in many directions."

"Sorry, I'm not following."

"One instance: they claimed the structure now descends below ground as deep as the tower is high." Rider waved a finger up and down a few times.

"I still don't—"

"Are you aware of creatures living in Earth's wet oceans with five or more identical limbs radiating symmetrically?"

"Um. Starfish?"

"Just so! The Tower is become a malignant starfish sprouting extra limbs, perhaps ultimately an entire sphere of limbs. And our explorers sang of the museum's 'legs' growing 'legs' of their own, branch offices you might say. Complained, the Blenn did, of severe disorientations."

"What happened to them?"

"We know not. They never emerged. Earlier this very turn, we petitioned a goddess, S'bek the Lightmage, who possesses absolute directional sense. She agreed to assist."

"What happened to *her*?"

"The Tower she entered and has not been heard since. Before meeting you this turn at your apartment, I begged the Watergod to intercede, but he has offered neither help nor advice."

"Good Lord."

"To my thinking, he could be better."

"I meant—never mind. Do you think this goddess and the scientists are still alive?"

"So we hope. Food converters and water should still be available inside and the Lightmage would be in no physical danger. A missive for counsel we sent to Jaahnim, the Hhoymon home world, but have received no guidance missive in response. I am not blaming; loyalists may be *unable* to respond because Jaahnim has discords of its own.

"For now, everyone must shun the museum. I regret we have nothing equivalent to play for you. We Common," Rider added confidentially, "seldom collect tangibles."

Herds of translucent tricycles in various colors and four distinct sizes were parked between buildings. Clearly the bikes weren't booby-trapped or even locked because many were in use, borrowed by bipedal visitors.

Unfortunately, my companion wouldn't fit on even the largest bike, so it took us over twenty minutes to cross the city. As we walked, my suit periodically spread out over my entire body for a few seconds. Cleaning me, feeding itself, both?

Rider said we were headed for a pair of *strindri*, a Dhu-barot term I didn't recognize that it translated as "float-tubes," just beyond the domed-in area. Float-tubes proved to be Hhoymon elevators: empty vertical shafts accessed through meshwork gates. They came in two colors. According to my guide, green meant up and violet down. Gate signs in twenty languages plus various stylized arrows conveyed the same information. And for the blind, colorblind, insufficiently literate, and graphically challenged souls, the shafts were framed in direction-coded textures.

When we were finally inside one, descending with dreamy languor—after, that is, Rider demonstrated how stepping into a gaping void wasn't necessarily suicidal—I decided the Earth equivalent was far less elegant, but far more practical.

As far as I could tell, float-tubes have only two possible destinations: some floor above or one below. No stopping between. So if a Hhoymon building had multiple stories it needed multiple pairs of float-tubes, unless Hhoymon wished to climb stairs. But Rider mentioned advantages: strindri were supposedly immune to failure and sabotage, passengers being the only moving parts.

A half-hour later, we stood in a long corridor with a ceiling Godzilla couldn't reach, before a stupendous double-door, gray and cold to the touch, stretching fifty feet to either side and up nearly to the celestial ceiling.

"The Watergod's Grotto ahead," Rider explained. "May you find great enjoyment in meeting him. For now, wait right here I shall until your return."

"Uh, you're not coming with me?"

"I am not invited."

Uh-oh. "I take it this god is one of those Twelve Travelers you talked about?"

Rider slurped louder than usual. "If you took it, you should give it back. The Supernals inhabit a *far* higher octave!"

My desire to walk through those doors alone wasn't noticeable. "This god is expecting me?"

"I tell you truly: this one you cannot surprise. He is no Traveler, but his least whisper would drown out the Apnoti's loudest shouts."

"Powerful, I get it. Fine. How do I get in?"

"He will open a way when both of you are ready. Prepare yourself."

I felt like the damn Cowardly Lion. My knees wobbled, my heart thumped like crazy. If only the first god I'd met *hadn't* been a giant spider.

A gap appeared between the doors. One of us, I thought desperately, isn't ready!

You'd expect a titanic doorway to open with slow majesty and so it did, but only far enough to let someone my size in. Proof that Rider wasn't welcome. I stepped into darkness as the gray slabs clicked shut behind me.

CHAPTER 13
A PRIVATE OCEAN

I'd stumbled onto the perfect recipe for sweaty palms and severe shortness of breath: entering the lair of an ultra-alien god for the first time. My eyes could only see darkness, and even my ... x-road vision seemed subdued, only perceiving a faint and steady blue glow.

Still, why was I *this* nervous? Surely, Rider wouldn't have sent me into real danger. My skin tingled with a sense of, I didn't know what. Maybe *presence*, of miracles eager to happen. The idea of a Crossroad deity resurrecting Kind no longer seemed absurd. And beneath my fear, another emotion lurked, which I refused to examine.

According to my ordinary senses, the place was as dark and mysterious as the night side of Pluto, but distinctly hotter. The heavy humidity failed to lubricate my throat, doubtless the driest thing in the Grotto. The sense of raw energy all around became oppressive. Intimidating.

The air smelled of brine.

Then either the illumination increased or my physical eyes adjusted. I could see an enormous cavern around me, all rough stone damp enough to reflect a vague aquamarine light ahead. I seemed to be alone.

I shivered despite the heat. Upset at being so upset, I tried a breathing relaxation technique my wife had taught me. But on my fifth slow exhalation, I realized that I'd started unconsciously matching my breathing to a faint rhythmic sound. Perhaps something in the Grotto was doing its own breathing.

For a moment, I simply listened. I heard it: a slow whoosh and hiss, like surf stroking a distant beach. I advanced two steps and the sound grew louder. Not surf, that is not *only* surf. An eerie voice was talking. In waves.

Whoosh: "Welcome, David." Hiss: "Welcome, David."

Without thinking, I walked forward until the voice became clear. "Welcome, David!"

My augmented vision suddenly returned.

Centered beneath a high domed ceiling stood a gargantuan transparent tank lit from beneath by greenish light, the only source of normal light around. The tank held a lake's worth of water and a green-gray creature the size of an adult blue whale.

This titan floated vertically, taking up most of the tank, an elongated form bobbing up and down as if reacting to gentle waves. The head constantly remained above the waterline.

Mr. Watergod, I presume? Putting it mildly, he wasn't what I'd expected.

At first, I saw him as a tusk-less walrus ... as interpreted by Dr. Seuss. But the longer I gawked, the less my host reminded me of anything from the Odobenidae family except that his face sported curving mustaches, which on him somehow conveyed the idea of a smile.

His eyes were huge even for such a giant, widely spaced, and either green or blue, impossible to tell in this lighting. As if in compensation, he had no visible ears, nostrils, blowhole, gills, or mouth. Did he even *need* air? His flippers stretched the length of a school bus, ending in flat fingers longer than my arms.

One eye winked, and the fishy Poseidon began radiating ultra-red like a sun from another dimension. Meanwhile, rivers of ultra-blue pulsed inside him, bright enough to shine through his skin.

The surf-sound rose to a rhythmic thunder, but the words it formed were diamond-clear. It seemed that a major god could sneer at trifles such as language barriers.

"Welcome to my home."

Despite its dramatic origin, the voice carried an intimate and casual quality. Poseidon spoke as if we'd known each other for years.

"I *have* known you for years, David," he boomed.

Damn. Another telepath. "You're hearing my thoughts?"

"What are thoughts? What I hear is internal conversation. Rest easy. I'll preserve your secrets and trust you to preserve mine."

"Thank you." A wave, one of relief, washed through me. I didn't doubt him, but wished I'd questioned Rider about etiquette here.

"No special etiquette is required, David. And 'Poseidon' is as fine a name as any. Care to take my picture?"

A hundred thoughts went through my head but none of them was no. "If you wouldn't mind."

"Then why not get my best side?"

A flipper wriggled and the god spun partway around. After several more mini-twirls, I got it. Poseidon always looked the same. He was quadrilaterally symmetrical with four eyes evenly spaced around his head, four flippers around the thick torso, and four mustache-sets. Even the god's tail was divided into four parts.

"Which," I muttered, "is your best side?"

"The inside, I hope. But you won't find me photogenic."

I managed to smile. "Then we have something in common."

"Indeed we do, David, but not as you meant it. In my case, the term 'non-photogenic' might apply."

Actually holding the camera, my conscience bit. "I'd better limit myself to one shot."

"Then I suggest a close-up. Just ascend my ramp, won't you? Besides, I'd prefer our eyes nearer."

With the god and tank gripping my attention, I'd barely noticed the ramp. It was steep, sequoia-tall, and terminated in a wide platform set against one side of the tank. The flesh was willing, my courage weak, but I climbed anyway.

The closer I got, the bigger he looked. Maybe Poseidon was larger than a blue whale. But then, I'd never stood near an upright whale of any color. Shallow furrows ran down the length of his body and his scales shimmered with subtle iridescence.

Awe made me awkward, and I don't like heights, but I managed to reach the platform. Even there, the god's head loomed a good ten feet above mine. At close range, the enormous eyes radiated kindness along with power.

"Take your best shot," Poseidon said, and his breaker-voice seemed to chuckle.

I took my time, ensuring my subject was centered, waiting for my hands to steady. No flash because the fake Nikon used photomultipliers in dimness.

"Done," I announced.

"How did it come out?"

I pushed the display button. The tank's upper edge appeared on the screen, but the water contained only an amorphous glow. Admittedly, an impressive glow but still a remarkable unlikeness.

"Is this your, um, true appearance?"

Again, a chuckle of rushing water. "In matters of perception, doesn't reality depends on the perceiver?"

"Well ... the perceiver's reality, I suppose. But why shouldn't an objective reality exist? And when the lens sees something I don't—"

"Ah! You believe your *machine* is objective."

"More so than my eyes, anyway." *Am I really*, I wondered, *discussing Philosophy 101 with a god?*

He lifted a flipper and cascading droplets glowed like emeralds. "Whose eyes interpret its images? But you are not here to debate viewpoints with me this fine turn."

My heart sped up. "What do you mean?"

"You want something from me." The roaring voice had softened.

"Just your picture," I said carefully, "I think." My knees started shaking again, and I was beginning to suspect why. "But maybe you know better."

"David, *these* eyes see dark shapes swimming beneath your thoughts. If you wish, we can bring them to your conscious attention."

I licked my lips; how could they dry out here? "Shapes?"

"Hidden feelings. Perhaps suppressed desires. We won't know more unless you let them surface."

My throat felt too tight. "How ... can I do that?"

"Begin with a single word, any word will do. The initial choice is only a starting place."

"Okay. Fear."

"Good! Now try again. Speak without concern."

Fat chance. Then my mouth seemed to open on its own. "*Injustice.*" I hadn't meant to say that!

Eyes larger than my head regarded me serenely. "Injustice troubles you, David?" The waves were quiet now, the voice gentle.

Somehow the question popped the cork on my personal bottle of horrors, and I remembered too many terrible things: Stalin slaughtering his own supporters; Pol Pot's massacres in Cambodia; the Rwandan genocide; Raoul Wallenberg in Nazi Germany risking his life to rescue every Jew he could, then spending the rest of his life in Soviet jails because the Russians wouldn't admit they'd mistakenly imprisoned him. I heard the hissing of Hitler's gas chambers and fifty million screams from men and women tortured in a hundred countries over a hundred centuries. So much starvation! Babies and children suffering. The long misery in so many parts of the world. Cruelty after cruelty. Slavery! I watched a woman busy at her desk in the World Trade Center engulfed in unendurable flames ...

And riding on vision after vision of historical and current horrors were three private nightmares: the airline crash that killed my brothers, the sudden death of my wife, and most recently, the fate of shy Kind. Everything I saw and heard seemed extravagantly, overwhelmingly *unfair*.

My knees buckled, but some soft force held me upright.

"There is great pain here," Poseidon said. "And there may yet be more. I see another shape striving for release. Let it rise to your throat."

I didn't want to. My cheeks were wet with bitter tears and when I wiped them from my mouth, the palm came off bloody and my lower lip hurt; must've bitten it. My suit began stirring, microdoc tendrils questing upward, but I couldn't stop talking, revealing my most cherished memories and ones I most wanted to forget....

For a year, I'd been a visiting professor at UC Berkeley. In my final semester before returning to New England, I'd offered a graduate-level course in early European history.

In those simpler days, when history had only involved human history, I'd treated each new class to a speech I called my "eye-opener." The theme was perhaps a bit self-serving: American society needs to value education far more. Still, I fancied that my insights would be sure to awaken young minds. I could recite the main points in my sleep:

"It all starts with parents. Anyone raising children is essentially a teacher aside from being a caregiver. Yet such vital work is often regarded as insignificant drudgery. This social contempt infects attitudes toward daycare and kindergarten instructors and continues, with diminishing severity, to the high school level. Only we college professors are afforded due honor. Sometimes." That addition always got a laugh. "If anything, the status should be inverted, with childcare providers receiving the *most* esteem." Blah, blah.

"... and children are therefore ideal students, intensely curious, capable of total concentration, brains biologically primed for learning."

More blah until I'd finally haul out the big gun:

"Now I hope you can see why I believe that the general distain for those who instruct the very young not only nurtures low self-esteem among such teachers, it makes their job unattractive to many who are best qualified, thus leaving the field open to some whose incompetence reinforces public prejudice. Children, of course, can't help but absorb these pervasive negative attitudes and grow up perpetuating the cycle."

After that shot, I'd run out of solid ammo and would usually finish off the oration in ringing phrases containing more ring than metal. But in that Berkeley eye-opener, I outdid myself, gesturing dramatically, pointing out obscure interactions between education and historical events, and adjuring my students to go forth and change the world.

The next day, I found this short note on my podium:

Dear Professor Goldberg,

I'm sure you mean well, and I agree with much of what you said, but you clearly have no children of your own, have never taken care of them, or possibly ever been one yourself.

I have cared for children on three continents and while most have been curious and eager, none have matched the sterling qualities of the ideal child you described.

Your Faithful Student,
Sarasvati Shankar

That note lives in my nightstand drawer.

After first reading it, I scanned the faces of my new students. My eyes froze on a beautiful Indian woman wearing a blue sari, elegantly perched four rows back. Just like that, I was in love.

A complete shock. Not only didn't I know the woman from Eve, I'd never felt anything remotely similar before. In fact, I'd always suspected romantic love doesn't even *exist* in the form our culture seems to adore. I was wrong. And now I faced a dilemma: professors do NOT date students. I'd have to wait until the semester ended to even hint I was interested.

For the next few months, I suffered.

After each morning class, I'd try to follow my pre-Sara routine: walk downhill past the Campanile and library; veer left, and stroll through Sather Gate to Sproul Plaza, where the Student Union and administration buildings glare at each other across a wide walkway. I'd intended to then venture down Telegraph and seek lunch.

Instead, I'd flop down on the Student Union's cement steps and gaze dolefully at an endless procession of people who had someplace worth going to. I dreaded the lonely walk back and tended to loiter until shortly before my office hours officially began.

In class, despite my best intentions, my gaze kept wandering in Sara's direction. She gazed back with the attention you'd expect from an excellent student, nothing more. When she submitted her first paper, which was both brilliant and startlingly creative, I finally responded to her note.

Regarding your message on the second day of class, I scribbled in a margin, *I defer to your greater experience.*

With earned guilt pangs, I looked up her address and phone number in university records. Then I waited, with all the aplomb of an opera singer feeling the onset of strep.

The day my students received their grades, I started calling Sara's apartment between bouts of hyperventilation. After some thirty attempts, and thirty failures to leave a message, I figured she didn't believe in answering phones, or had something better to do than sit around hoping some lovesick professor would call. Probably out on a date.

I was about to give up, for a few hours, when *my* phone rang. It was Sara calling from the Student Union, inviting me to meet her for coffee at an off-campus café. I'm sure we had a nice time although all I remember about it was staring into those lovely, wise eyes. And how I started to ... *recognize* her, as someone who'd always been close to me, but not yet in sight. I can't explain it.

The first evening stars winked at us by the time when we left that place. Dinner, we decided, at a good restaurant was called for and she asked me to accompany her to her apartment so she could "change and primp." I remember exactly what happened next.

When we entered the tiny duplex, I spotted a plane ticket near the door. The cliché "my blood ran cold" suddenly made sense as I imagined her permanently rejoining her family in Sri Lanka. She asked if I was all right, so I suppose my face wasn't behaving itself. I tried to act casual as I inquired about the ticket. She laughed and told me she was leaving California to get married elsewhere in the USA.

I could only form the question in painful slow motion. "Who are you marrying?"

"You. I could only marry you." Then she kissed me. Very softly.

Sara claimed she'd been studying me and researching my life all semester. Around finals, she'd concluded I was *it*. Knowing I'd be headed next to Hampshire College, she'd already arranged a transfer to Smith to complete her MA and be near me. Such confidence and so very justified.

"David," the Watergod said, pulling me back to the present. "I dare not attempt to eliminate injustice." He eased lower in the tank until our eyes were almost level. "Can you guess why I live on Crossroad?"

"Not really. To be near other gods?"

"A clever answer! But my peers remain close wherever I am. I live here to remember humility. I'm not the largest fish in *this* pond. And," a bubbling sort of laugh, "the Blenn offer post-graduate training."

"Gods need humility?"

"Only gods seeking wisdom. Doesn't learning require humility? Pride, I'm afraid, is power's first child. And what god lacks power?"

I gazed into the immense eyes. "What are you saying?"

"I, too, feel deeply troubled by unfairness, David. Often. But whenever I've tried to set matters right, I've caused disasters. Imagine the scale of *my* mistakes. Events, my fellow student of history, have something of an ecological dynamic. Alter one factor and be prepared to swim away fast!"

"I don't—"

"Tell me something. I've just seen your Raoul Wallenberg through the eyes of your heart and share your great admiration. Do you think such a being would stop assisting his fellows, even in a Soviet prison?"

I stared at Poseidon, both appalled and delighted he understood me so intimately. "I ... guess not. No. Someone like that would never stop."

"If I could reach through time—not that time is something one reaches through—and prevent his imprisonment, can you say what good I would undo?"

"No," I whispered.

"Neither can I."

"But what about Kind Thirdhouse? What harm could it do to ... reinstate her?"

"I'm not wise enough to know the consequences. So, I dare only mourn with you over the deaths of Kind and your loved ones, including, to answer your unvoiced question, your wife."

"Oh. I see." I felt as though the bottom had dropped out of my soul.

"But I will risk helping *you*, in a small way." A wet flipper reached from the tank. Balanced on it was something like a conch shell. "Take this cup and drink deeply."

I took it, too numb to disobey. A luminescent clear liquid filled most of it. Tiny waves slowly traversed the surface.

The god chuckled. "I would not offer you aquarium water, David. Drink!"

I lifted the shell and took a sip. It had a pleasant taste. Carbonated lime with a whisper of salt—a fizzy margarita sans alcohol. I suddenly felt thirsty and drank the rest.

The tingle began an inch below my navel, expanding outward as if my stomach was a pool and a boulder had fallen in. Soon, my entire body was vibrating in a kind of cellular exuberance. I didn't share the mood.

"What's in this stuff?"

"Consider it a health tonic."

I wiped my lips with my hand. "Guess it worked," I admitted, fighting a grotesque urge to sulk. "I'd bitten my lip and now it feels fine. Thank you."

"I can't accept credit," Poseidon said. "Your interesting garment is repairing the injury, not my tonic."

"Oh?" I touched the spot with a fingertip; the lip felt oddly smooth. "Then why the nightcap?" The vibration had subsided.

"We shall see."

Wonderful. More secrets.

"Sometimes secrets are necessary."

I glared at my host. "Well, since I don't have any secrets from *you*, can you at least help me with my damn mission?" I hesitated then blurted out, "Yes or no: are any Scome machines on Crossroad?"

The titan rose higher in the water again. "I can only offer you some advice."

I sighed. "Advice couldn't hurt."

A low-pitched, multi-toned hum joined the music of crashing waves —an underwater orchestra of tuning forks. As it swelled, the tank filled with small bubbles and the water's surface sculpted itself into eerie circular ridges.

Amid the racket, I heard voices, snatches of old popular songs, lines from old radio shows and movies:

Hello darkness my old friend ... Who knows what evil lurks in the hearts of men ... Night divides the day ... Me and my shadow, and many more.

The humming faded until only the breaker-roar broke the silence. Clearly, Poseidon had made a special effort to tell me something, but the communication was a bust.

The Watergod's eyes had closed.

"Poseidon?"

Nothing.

"Please. I don't understand."

Roar, swish, and splash. No words. I knew the interview was over.

Confused, miserable, and generally pissed, I descended the ramp and stomped away. The enormous door opened without fuss. I stepped out into the hallway and glanced back as the doors were closing, but saw nothing but darkness, which seemed nothing like an old friend. I turned to face Rider, doubting I'd ever see Poseidon again.

CHAPTER 14
FALL FROM GREASE

"Well," Rider asked. "Was it useful? Inspiring? Fun?"

"None of the above." Honesty made me add, "My fault, I suppose. That god is too damn impressive."

"You grew unrealistic expectations?"

Rider's tone was so sympathetic it pulled the truth from me. "I guess in the back of my mind, I hoped that an impossible being with impossible powers in an impossible place could accomplish, um—"

"The impossible?"

"Yeah."

"Have I not walked those same sands? I say count on fingers not on gods."

I glanced up at the alien face. "How do *you* define a 'god'?"

"Swift Neme sang it well. More requirements I could add: exceedingly long life, also utter self-sufficiency. Do you suppose the Watergod tires of his cistern?"

"Good point. You know, I got an impression that he wasn't actually confined in any way. Hmm. Watergod. I wound up calling him 'Poseidon,' but what's his real name?"

"Like most major gods, he wears many names and none. Brown Hhoymon call him 'Wi-shukary,' which means gift giver. Silver Hhoymon—"

"He didn't offer *me* any gifts ... no, I take that back. He gave me a bizarre beverage, supposedly a 'health tonic.' Also he, um, dispensed some advice that made no sense."

Rider stared at me for a long moment. "A liquid, he offered you?"

"Something wet and weird."

"Did he say why?" The Common seemed excited.

"No."

"Unheard of! As to advice, mine is to take his most seriously." My guide squatted to gaze into my face, putting one huge hand on each of my shoulders.

"Do you know what is said about the Watergod?" Rider asked quietly.

"No. What?"

The Common stared earnestly into my eyes. "It is said he works in mysterious waves."

At first, I just looked back. Then my lips twitched. A second later, we were laughing or slurping like maniacs. The release felt wonderful. Rider straightened up.

"I have to admit," I managed to choke out, wiping tears from my eyes. "Poseidon keeps up on current affairs."

That set us both off again. Maybe, I thought, the divine seltzer had healed my funny bone.

"So," Rider said after we'd settled down. "This is good. I wondered when you would into action spring. What turned the tide?"

"Enough," I begged, but with a smile. My depression had broken and washed away. A heavy heart, I decided, makes lousy ballast.

"Know something?" I asked. "For a while, I thought I'd met my first hundred-ton psychiatrist. Now, I'm wondering about you." Why *was* I suddenly feeling so much better? I'm not normally subject to mood swings. Maybe the god-water was spiked.

"What about me? I do not weigh so many of your tons."

"Ever consider a career as a therapist?"

The Common's leaves shivered. "Often, I believe any other career would be an extensive improvement."

"What *is* your career, exactly?"

"This moment, taking you to the Hall of Games."

Without further comment, Rider led us down the vast, empty hallway.

I respected Poseidon's restraint, which didn't mean I liked it. But my bitterness had vanished, and my body seemed near-bursting with energy. I kept up with Rider easily and wished we were walking faster.

My companion seemed so lost in thought, the question took me by surprise: "How progresses my English skills?"

"Hmm? Good, I guess. Haven't really been paying attention."

Slurp. "You are disinterested in my linguistic prowess? For shame! What kind of teacher are you?"

"The tenured kind. We don't have—" I stopped dead.

"*What is wrong?*" Rider had reacted instantly and stood, turning in place, searching for danger.

"Sorry!" I laughed. "Didn't mean to alarm you. It's just that—this is going to sound silly—it just came to me: I'm *actually here*."

"Here?"

"On Crossroad. In another universe, meeting gods. Sightseeing with a Common!"

"Adumm-ayn! Waking up is not silly, my friend, it is required."

The lemon eyes appeared genuinely warm. I'd never noticed how alive they were, how very conscious. And the big ultra-alien face no longer seemed alien to me. Despite myself, I'd become very attached to Sun-toch-sew.

"Ever since I arrived," I said slowly, "I guess I've been too distracted to come to my senses."

"And which sense have you come to?"

I laughed again. "Mainly, my sense of wonder."

We resumed our journey. And I was the one pushing the pace.

An hour later, on an especially long Glideway with bland and seemingly endless brown walls, my newfound sizzle dwindled, a tired irritability had settled in. "Why the hell do we have to *walk*?" I complained.

"When we could be teleporting in comforts and luxury?"

"You got it."

"If you find strolling choresome, I apologize." Rider sounded a bit stiff. "But ask Strong Neme about difficulties in traversing superspace within layered realities."

"Fine. Then why couldn't we ride one of your superspaceships out of this universe and pop back in at your Hall of Games?"

"Why squander energy without emergency when you and I have such clever feet?"

I could see ahead to where the interminable Glideway finally terminated. "Oh hell. Don't listen to me, I'm just feeling crabby. But I'd think you'd at least have ... cars or something."

"Safe-roads are too slow?"

"Hardly, just too rare."

We stopped before a pair of float-tubes. As we stepped inside one and began wafting upward, Rider said, "You wish to get a rise out of me?"

"Cute. But seriously, what if there *is* an emergency?"

"Then we squander energy. Also, some gods can transport persons by fiat."

"Fiat? So you *do* have cars."

Rider looked at me. "My understanding folds."

"Not important." Even on Crossroad a joke's not funny when you have to explain it.

The tube brought us to a wide corridor. Rider pointed to a glowing animation on the far wall, a rotating ball cycling through the spectrum. "This display sings of a brief slice to the Hall we seek."

Brief slice? "A shortcut?"

"Just so. To visit the Watergod we took a route indirect, and this will compensate. And we are here sooner than I'd expected. Pleasant company smooths time!"

That last phrase startled me. Odd to hear a Common paraphrasing Balanced Clearhouse; but then, Nemes and Common have supposedly worked hand-in-paw for centuries.

We walked across the hall and stood beneath the sign. My guide placed a shovel-sized hand on the wall and a large, circular doorway irised open. A blast of colder air redolent of ozone plus something nastier wafted out. "How well," Rider asked, "do you enjoy heights?"

I stuck my head through the opening and stared down the length of a long ramp that began right in front of us and then descended to the floor far, far below. "I don't."

"So. If you wish, I can carry you."

"No thanks." That prospect wasn't pleasing and neither was the view. The ramp's angle seemed gentle enough, but its surface was narrow, glistened greasily, and had no railing. Easy to estimate the distance to the floor: too far.

"Is it ... safe?" I asked idiotically.

"Be easy, my friend. We Common have gripping feet!" Rider abruptly whirled to face down the hallway and wouldn't respond to my questions.

Then I heard a faint flapping noise. Suddenly, two O-gen-ai came running toward us; I'd had no idea Common could move so fast. The pair stopped in front of us with a whiffling sound of ear-leaves falling into place.

"Professor David A. Goldberg," Rider said hurriedly, "I present two members of my team. This is Collector-of-fine-moments; you'd get a bad throat pronouncing its true name." Collector was clearly ancient;

even its crest had wilted. "And here is the always energetic Doorway-to-wisdom, Ru-ahl-tat, who once visited Earth." Doorway was broader than Rider but stood slumped with exhaustion.

"Honored to meet you both," I said, wondering if either understood English.

Protocol satisfied, the three Common began gesturing and speaking at once; the only words I recognized were Hhoymon words Rider had spoken: Binae, Arfaenn, and good old Maanza. The conference didn't last long. When the newcomers took off, again running, Rider closed both eyes and just stood there.

"What was *that* all about?" I finally asked.

The lemon eyes opened slowly. "A—an important visitor may be coming. One most unexpected. This shouldn't involve you." My companion shook its head, obviously distressed. "And we two have tasks to accomplish. Kindly stand very still for a moment."

"Sure. But why?"

"Later I will explain. Now trail me and tread with care." Rider stepped through the opening and onto the ramp.

I followed and placed one foot tentatively on the glistening surface. Yep, slippery as hell. Damn.

"No way I can get down this thing by myself," I admitted. "Not slowly, anyway."

Rider turned, hoisted me with one arm, and stepped confidently onto the slope. Traction seemed no problem ... until a gale-force wind came out of nowhere and blew us both out into empty space.

Falling. My mind froze up, leaving my stomach to panic alone. Rider yelled "Chamm!" the Simple word for danger, but I didn't need the hint.

This is it, I thought.

But after the first rushing instant, I had a crazy delusion we were slowing down. That's what a brain does, I figured, when it sees its own impending extinction.

Rider had kept an arm around my chest. "Your heart has no need for such haste, Professor David A. Goldberg."

Oh. "We're not ... falling very fast, are we?"

"You can't tell? Safe enough, we are. I am all regrets I couldn't prepare you."

"You were *expecting* this?"

"Expecting something. A fine spot this is for our enemies to be creative!"

"Enemies? What enemies?" No answer.

We abruptly dropped maybe ten feet, while my stomach seemingly went the other way. After a brief pause, we dropped again. And again, and again ...

I looked up and saw nothing supporting me. But when I reached over my head, my hand bumped into something solid, thin, and sticky. Touching an invisible object is *far* scarier than it sounds, although I had a hunch what it was. I groped around but couldn't pinpoint any specific spot where the sticky line stayed attached.

Rider pulled me closer between mini-rappels to whisper directly into my ear. "Speak nothing about it."

When our feet finally touched ground, I reached up again and the invisible line was gone. Rider covered its speaking diaphragm with one hand and started walking. I got the message.

After another considerable hike, we entered a cylindrical tunnel illuminated by an arched florescent ceiling, and followed a pathway bordering a languid river marbled with eddying oil-slick hues, subterranean echoes of those surface minerals the Mind had shown me. The path was slippery and so narrow we had to walk single file. Rider put me in front.

But I was grateful for the narrowness. Surely nothing large, unseeable, and say, seven-legged could follow us. Not that I didn't appreciate being rescued.

Then my merciless imagination generated images of a giant spider clinging miraculously to these curved walls. Or striding upside down on the ceiling directly above me. I tried like hell to throw *those* pictures out of my head.

The tunnel echoed with a bone-deep thrumming. "What's that racket?" I asked. "Some kind of engine?"

"No." Rider hesitated. "We pass near the Hearth, to render it in English. A powerful demon, the Firemage, uses the Hearth as home whenever he haunts this Triangle. Since we hear his voice, the demon is in."

"Um, we don't plan on getting *close* to this Firemage, I hope."

"Only a bit closer."

We crossed the oily river on a porcelain bridge, which cast a pale reflection clothed in greasy rainbows, and headed down another tunnel.

The throb in the air swelled to a roar and my teeth started itching. Talk about hard-to-scratch places.

"This is as near—" Rider never finished that sentence. An incredible flash of ultra-red stunned me; a burst of normal light so intense would've left my retinas smoking. And I heard a tremendous splash from nearby, accompanied by a brief, explosive whistle.

"What was *that*?" I yelled.

"Spell or splash?" Rider sounded grim.

Spell? "Both, I guess."

"A message from the demon: no gods welcome here."

"Oh."

I counted seven peculiar indentations on the river's surface, distinct dimples arranged in a very large ring. They remained in place, defying the lazy flow. Is walking on oil considered a miracle?

Rider waved an arm irritably and the dimples filled in. Seven circular ripples widened....

I had to ask. "I gather we're alone now?"

"To sing it one way, Professor David A. Goldberg, our only support here has become each other."

"You always cheer me up. But let's make a deal. How about just calling me David?"

"May I?" My guide sounded delighted. "In turn, David, would you give me the gift of using Sun? Or Rider, if you prefer?"

I'd been thinking of the Common as Rider practically since we'd met. Surely those amber dabs in the yellow eyes weren't *tears*?

I tried to match the spirit of the moment. "I'd be honored, Rider."

But I wasn't feeling all warm and cozy. I was drowning in worries and mysteries and no one, least of all my dear buddy Rider, seemed willing to throw me a line.

Well, to be fair, one being had thrown me a line literally and had wanted to do so metaphorically. Was a monstrous spider my only real ally? I was sick to death of bewilderment. And I was *really* troubled that Rider had said "our" enemies.

"What's the ... itinerary?" I asked.

The Common studied me. "Our fastest route now is to pass through Vyre Village just ahead. A few steps farther, another Safe-road shall happily whisk us to the Hall of Games."

———

Rider seemed preoccupied, oblivious to our surroundings as the Village entrance came into view. I was fully occupied in worrying. To pile discomfort onto anxiety, my teeth were *still* itching even though we'd left the roaring demon mage far behind.

Obviously, we'd been attacked on the ramp. Why wasn't Rider more concerned? Had Loaban returned to duty? Was something even creepier guarding us?

Something hard and gritty fell onto my tongue. I stopped, spat it into my hand, and stared at the tiny object.

Rider was staring, too. "What is that?"

Sometimes small things can be hugely inconvenient. "Part of a filling, damn it. You don't happen to have dentists on Crossroad, do you? This will be bothering me soon."

"Medical attentions, we can supply. Ayn-Seris, my friend! I sing with joy not to have human fangs!"

"How lucky for you." The sarcasm was lost on my guide who was now staring at my scalp. "What," I snapped, "are you looking at now?"

"Tell me, David. If you need a dentist when you lose fillings, what do you need when you lose hair?"

I sighed. "Yes, I have a bald spot. It's been growing for years. So? Or is this more O-gen-ai humor?"

"Bald spots you grow? I understood you grew hair. *That's* humor. But truly, you have many hairs, but only gray ones are loose. That blank spot you wear on top is resounding with fresh dark filaments."

"What?" I reached up. The area felt fuzzy. Meanwhile, my exploring fingers dislodged a shower of gray follicles, most of which were instantly absorbed by my suit.

"What the hell," I muttered, "is *happening* to me?"

"Hard to sing. I hear many possibilities."

"Such as?"

"Perhaps the god-water regenerates your fur."

I nodded. "Oh! That, at least, would make—yugh!" My tongue was suddenly buried in rubble. I started spewing fragments of dental amalgam like an overfull popcorn maker. Finally, I managed to spit out a word, "Sorry."

"All this you held in your teeth, David? A marvel you could lift your head!"

"Might be harder to hold my head up *now*. So much for dignity." I frowned at the floor. "Seems like a lot of debris considering I only had four fillings. How can I clean this up?" At least the itching was gone.

"The local Mind will clean. Are you in pain?"

"No. But ..." I did some exploring with my tongue. "Odd. Can't feel any gaps."

"Your fur is growing back," Rider pointed out with perfectly reasonable illogic. "Why not your fangs?"

"Because human teeth aren't alive. Not the biting surfaces, anyway. There's nothing that could regenerate."

"On the Crossroad, David, surprised you might be what can regenerate. Come, the Village awaits the passage of our feet."

"Just a second. I'm curious. Are we still in Triangle Ten?"

"Yes, but near the Triangle Three border," Rider answered patiently.

"Really? Why should Three abut Ten?"

"Numbered according to when populated."

"Ah."

Twenty warped triangles could encase Crossroad neatly, but I wondered. The O-gen-ai seemed enamored of the number twenty-two. They'd divided their 'turn' into twenty-two 'twists,' and ranked technology and magic into that many levels, and hadn't Rider said something about twenty-two categories of flavor?

Could a pair of secret Triangles be tucked away somewhere? An icosahedron has flat triangular facets; Crossroad's Triangles were curved. Perhaps some were curved enough to create ... wiggle room.

I don't know what inspired this line of thought, but I decided to keep it to myself.

CHAPTER 15
A MEDIUM-RARE DIALECT

I'm ashamed to confess Vyre Village creeped me out. Granted, the overall gloominess, damp cobbled streets, and heavy black flowers dripping black nectar weren't exactly uplifting. Nor was the mildew reek wafting from gardens of huge dark fungi. And rock-steady green flames sullenly burning in hundreds of scalloped wall-alcoves definitely qualified as spooky.

Subfusc, even Gothic, but why should the place get so deeply under my skin?

Groups of Vyre passed, fiery hair purpled by the dimness, faces a sickly gray. Their extreme body adaptations suggested a town of ogres. The females, Rider whispered, always braided their manes.

The streets were crowded but almost silent. No jostling, no joking. Virtually no conversation.

Even the Vyre huddled together here and there on dark benches seemed to have nothing to talk about. These had adapted their bodies for sitting and would surely have been elected to the Couch Potato Hall of Fame. If couch potatoes ever had the energy to hold an election. And build a hall of fame.

I felt relieved to see that we'd be leaving the Village soon if we kept up our pace. But a male Neme stepped out from a nearby doorway to stand directly in front of us, and we had to stop. Oddly enough, I *recognized* him. Evidently, not everything I'd experienced during last night's catnap in the restaurant had been the stuff of dreams. Here was the oddball Neme who stood like Jet Li.

He was a strange one all right. With their rigid necks, Nemes move their eyes toward whatever they want to see. This fellow turned his entire body to stare at me. I glanced over to get Rider's reaction and wouldn't have cared to be on the receiving end of that glare.

The stranger spoke first, in a language with a tauntingly familiar ring that reminded me of my grandmother's Hungarian. Rider rejoined in kind, much louder, but the Neme wasn't intimidated. He waddled up to me and pulled me in for a hug. Nemes don't hug. I felt at a complete loss.

"Do you speak English?" I asked awkwardly, still in the stranger's embrace. No response. "What's going on here, Rider?"

"This individual is confused, David. Very misguided. Now he will be leaving us." Rider practically shouted something in the unknown language and the Neme released me but kept staring at me intensely. With only two eyes.

"What the hell does he want?" I asked Rider. "And what language have you two been spouting?"

"His wants lack importance, and the dialect is one used by those with certain mental impairments, such as an absence of good judgment."

The stranger gave my arm a last affectionate squeeze, spun around, and waddled away. I watched until he'd disappeared behind a brick wall. Then Rider and I resumed walking.

"Friend of yours?" I asked, intending irony.

"Yes. But most wrong to come here. Some beings are pathologically stubborn. Tell me: on *your* world does the concept 'secret' involve shouting for attention?"

"Um, not usually."

"Ayn-Seris, this turn is passing us by! Ready are you to hear the Hall and go for your stationary run?"

Smooth segue, Rider, I hardly noticed. "Any run will have to be brief. I don't have the right shoes."

Three slurps. "You wear adaptive clothing and worry about footwear?"

"Look, there's an art to making good running shoes."

"Trust your fourth skin."

It would be an astonishing luxury, I thought, *to trust anything on this crazy world.*

"Have ever you noticed," Rider remarked as we approached the marmalade glow of a Safe-road, "how seldom events conform to plans?"

"Seldom? You mean, sometimes they *do*?"

———

Ten minutes later, I had a brief aerial view of a space so tremendous it made Great Hall Four seem like a broom closet. Then my eyes and inner ears began arguing. Eyes insisted we were falling. Ears claimed the long, overly steep Glideway we were descending on was perfectly level. Luckily, the eyes didn't have it.

"Welcome to the Hall of Games," Rider announced.

I'd never thought my mission was going to be *easy*, but now? Dear God!

Clouds scudded below the sky-high amethyst dome. A hot brightness from above, suggesting glare from some giant red sun, shone down evenly except in the Hall's center. There it blazed like a plasma spotlight, making the artifact beneath, an enormous fountain of sorts, appear incandescent.

Either my eyes adjusted, or the light dimmed to a more comfortable level, and I watched the geyser-fountain erupt spectacularly. Its spray momentarily coalesced into a hundred-foot-tall transparent statue of a Hhoymon, which immediately melted, cascading down into a tremendous basin. A few seconds later, it erupted again, this time forming a Blenn.

The Hall seemed overstuffed with bizarre architecture, weird machines, and mysterious structures animate with moving lights, flowing liquids, or both. Beyond the crowded sections, scores of open fields in varying shapes, sizes, and contours waited for, I assumed, ultra-alien competitions. Water features such as pools, white-water rapids, and at least one lake were scattered throughout.

"It's too much," I murmured.

Two-lane Glideways webbed the Hall's floor, half blue, half orange. Directional color-coding? I traced the double line of one Glideway practically to the horizon then tried to rub my eyes in disbelief. I couldn't. Something smooth and hard covered them.

Rider slurped. "I hear that you noticed."

"Microdoc sunglasses? I couldn't even feel them! What *can't* this suit do?"

"Tell you, it can't, why we made the Hall so loud."

The environment was somewhat noisy, but ...

"You mean so bright?"

"Just so. Sunlight is collected above and distributed to power the Hall and domains." We were decelerating now, near ground level.

"Domains?"

"You will hear."

Stepping off our escalator Glideway, I spotted Chean-shee and Hhoymon buildings among the more eye-catching exotica. It dawned on me that I wouldn't recognize Neme or Common architecture if it poked me in said eye.

"Who built this place?"

"Hhoymon and Blenn designed it, David. Chean-shee did all physical work."

"It's not what I expected."

"Which was?"

I felt sheepish. "A Pan-Cosmic theme park."

"It seems my grasp on your world has weaknesses. What is a theme park?"

I wished I'd kept my big mouth shut, because now I couldn't help but air one of my most cherished peeves.

"It's a place humans go to for ... artificial adventures, usually designed around specific topics."

"Sing me an example."

A touch of my earlier lightheartedness returned. "I'll try to give you the flavor of such places. There's one called—let's call it Moneyworld. There, you'll have to pay to park your vehicle, pay to get in, and then pay for each ride."

"Ride?"

"Usually there's something you sit on or sit in, and it carries you through a, um, an experience. But before you leave," I heard my voice darken, "there's a ride where a machine picks you up by your ankles, holds you upside down, and shakes you until your bones rattle. All cash dropping from your pockets is then appropriated by the park."

"This sounds unpleasant," my companion said dubiously. "After these shakings, the machine releases you?"

"Absolutely. For a fee, of course."

"You are blowing sand on my ears!"

I laughed, but uncomfortable because Rider was studying me so intently. "We'd say 'pulling your leg.' I'm not exaggerating *too* much. Anyway, to parachute off my soapbox, for some stupid reason I figured this Hall would be filled with, well, theme park-style entertainment."

"This is not one of your currency-grabbing institutions, my friend! The Hall was built for competitions, education, and joy. Chean-shee and Hhoymon emplaced games from many worlds here. Lately, even some from yours."

"Really?" A ray of hope! "I thought Hhoymon never visited Earth."

"Neme recordings they studied."

We reached a Glideway aimed at a distant wall, and I followed the Common onto the orange half. I remained in an oddly exuberant mood and found it exhilarating to be striding along, the gentlest of breezes cooling my face, watching a strange world rushing by. An empty world.

"Where are the crowds?" I asked. I saw only a few Constructors and Nemes, and several unfamiliar ultra-aliens.

"Until recently, most busy was the Hall because Hhoymon so adored it."

Around the room's circumference, as far as I could see in the misty distance, towering walls were pierced by thousands of ground-level rectangular openings about ten feet tall, ten feet wide, and spaced perhaps thirty feet apart. A few much larger openings appeared to be tunnel entrances.

"What are those holes for?" I asked, pointing. "The smaller ones."

"Entrances to diverse encounters: subjective, projective, and dream domains. Some for training in weapons or sports, some for exercise, some for therapies, others for pleasure."

"So where are we headed?"

"Subjective tracks ahead."

"Are these something like virtual tracks?"

"A similar frequency, David. But subjective reality is customized *individually*. On a subjective track, you will perceive one thing, someone lumbering beside you would perceive something very different."

"So that's it! Then what's a 'projective' domain?"

"Some are close." Rider paused. "Why not try one and learn for yourself?"

"Maybe I will," I said uncertainly.

"You remain interested in Crossroad language-mastering techniques?"

"Definitely."

"Then I will definitely take you to a projective domain."

We left the Glideway near a Chean-shee building. The open doorway revealed three Constructors hunched over around a table. I was more interested in someone lurking in a far corner. Although he immediately looked away, I recognized the oddball Neme. Was Mr. Hugs following us ... from ahead, so to speak? If so, how did he know we were coming here? I glanced at Rider, but the Common was watching a distant, solitary Chean-shee struggling to swim down a waterfall flowing straight up.

We caught another Glideway segment, which followed the wall. From here, the gaps between segments weren't visible; the curving roadway ahead seemed to stretch away like the rings of Saturn.

From outside, the projective domain appeared no different than any other cave opening here, excepting the tunnel entrances. No curtain or anything to block light far as I could tell, but even close-up, I saw only darkness within.

"Here we are," Rider stated. "Listen to the picture above this entrance."

The mile-high wall was a speckled glossy brown and the image above the opening appeared in a lighter shade of brown, as if the architect had wanted nothing to detract from the sight of a surface apparently climbing forever.

I studied the "picture" of something akin to an "L" shape made with a long stick and a shorter one.

"I'll bite," I said. "What am I looking at?"

"This wall-stretch is the Corridor of Arms, David. Every domain here is projective, each scored for training in a specific weapon. Hear how the symbol is embossed not engraved? Therefore, this domain is unoccupied."

"The design up there is based on some weapon? A scythe?"

"No, a Hhoymon 'hurling stick.' A thousand cycles ago, a Brown tribe invented them."

"Hurling stick?"

"Soon, you will master its use! Hurry within so you will have time to run before we take nutrition. May I preserve your camera until you return? It will encumber you."

I handed it over. Reluctantly. Then, after Rider provided some quick instructions, I walked through the opening, trying to ignore a still, small voice of alarm. What was my problem? I wanted to learn how Crossroaders learned, and here was my chance.

How could it hurt?

CHAPTER 16
DODGE BAAL

It was quiet in here, but not peaceful. A feeling of expectancy tautened the atmosphere and I felt ... watched. In this dimness, the entrance should have blazed; instead, the opening was a barely noticeable dull gray rectangle. Something more than shadow obscured the walls. Even using my Crossroad vision, I couldn't guess the room's size or shape.

The hall's rumble had no power here, but I noticed, through my feet, a steady vibration.

As my eyes adjusted, I saw the floor "plate" Rider had described: an octagonal outline in pale blue light. Following instructions, I stomped on it once. Suddenly, I stood outdoors on another planet. The illusion was perfect. A garnet sun smoldered overhead, the sky cloudless and tourmaline pink. Beneath my feet an alien lawn glistened: a field of short, translucent grass glowing in the burgundy sunlight like thin stalks of fire. The floor texture now matched the apparent texture of the lawn.

I wasn't alone.

Facing me from twenty feet away stood a being like nothing I'd ever heard of or imagined. I had a moment to stare before something materialized in my right hand.

The weapon was far more sophisticated than the sign had led me to expect. I now gripped a long, very light staff made of brown plastic or some plastic-like wood, holding it as I would a torch, upright and near the bottom.

Under my thumb, a segmented trigger hooked onto a thin cable running up the staff's length. This cable ended in a nest of three-pronged, metal clamps, one of which grasped the end of a short spear pointed straight ahead. The spear had a sharp triangular tip and feather-like fletching.

My clothing began acting up, becoming thicker, but only along the front of my body. This worried me.

The virtual entity—or was it a projective entity?—waited with the stoicism of a Buckingham Beefeater and it, too, now held an identical weapon. Perhaps, I thought, a generic warrior, one acceptable as a trainer for many different species.

My new friend, only a bit taller than me, vaguely resembled a stunted T. rex painted a dull blue. It had the heavy reptilian tail, but four long arms and Common-like hands. I found the head ... disturbing: featureless and spherical, but as though someone had made a convincing imitation of a globe with very tiny blocks.

Cross a bipedal dinosaur with a multi-armed Hindu deity and you might get something like this, not that you'd want to. But looking closer, I realized that my mind had been playing tricks on my eyes. The creature's body, like its head, was an illusion within this illusion, not unified flesh but a complex construction of small rectangular plates. I wondered how they'd stay together if the thing moved.

And move it did without falling apart. The trainer began transferring its hurling stick from arm to arm to arm to arm. Its myriad plates smoothly shifted like overlapped playing cards being flipped, and I suspected this being could change form more radically than a Vyre.

Then I got a surprise. The globular head lengthened and developed an Etch-a-Sketch rendition of human features—all produced by minute adjustments of the tiny head-plates. The proportions and seagull-wing eyebrows made it a cubist satire of *my* face. Charming. A chip off the old blockhead.

Having gotten my undivided attention, the trainer demonstrated how to use a hurling stick. Targets with bull's-eyes materialized around us at varying distances. Brahmasaurus, tail extended, spun around once then flicked its staff like a fly fisherman making a cast. The spear flew off and pierced the center of a target about a hundred yards away.

So far, I'd been underwhelmed by projective technology—hell, humans were within virtual spitting distance of this.

Then my body, moving without my consent, imitated the spear-casting maneuver I'd just witnessed. As my wrist gave the staff its final snap, my thumb pushed lightly on the trigger. The spear flew off to mortally wound the nearest target.

A running commentary, in English no less, accompanied these actions, explaining what my body was doing and why in a soothing tenor voice. It went on to tell me my staff was called a "lever" while the clamps were "grapples," which could hold as many as six "javelins" to be released simultaneously or individually depending on trigger pressure.

While the voice described how to load a javelin, how to fix a jammed clamp, and how to disarm the hurling stick, my body acted out the instructions. No mention was made about the risk of removing someone's visual organs.

Then Brahmasaurus and I took turns using the hurling sticks like old buddies playing horseshoes. Didn't need to reload; whenever a javelin left my lever, another appeared in its place. After I'd punctured perhaps twenty targets, I gradually resumed muscular control. When I fully commanded my body again, by gum, I'd mastered the weapon.

To put it mildly, I was impressed. It might have taken months or even years to develop such proficiency on my own. To a lesser degree, I was impressed with the hurling stick. Evidently, "primitive" Browns weren't so primitive.

The voice congratulated me on graduating basic training and offered a choice: I could now begin accuracy or combat training.

Accuracy sounded dull. "Combat," I decided, figuring a domain speaking English would understand it.

My suit went crazy, roiling and bubbling like an overheated stew. When it stabilized, I found myself wearing a quilt-like arrangement of blunt triangles. Didn't seem a good sign, but I felt too curious to cancel combat mode quite yet.

The ruddy world and the targets were gone. The trainer and I stood on a flat sandy plain stretching endlessly in every direction; the sky was matte pewter. Next to each of us, a table stood burdened with dozens of javelins.

My staff was unloaded, so I nervously grabbed a spear, placed its end into a grapple, and pushed until it locked in place. Then I studied my trainer. Brahmasaurus had changed; it seemed more alive, more precisely balanced. And some new element had been added, which I couldn't pinpoint.

The trainer had also loaded its lever.

The voice said, "Begin."

Since my opponent wasn't real, I had no problem with trying to hit it. I assumed the game would be fair enough to give me an even chance.

The trainer began to spin. I moved quickly, but a spear was already flashing toward me as I completed my release move. It struck me in the chest, vanished, and I felt a mild shock.

My return spear had been well aimed, but my opponent, in no apparent hurry, leaned aside at the last moment, grabbed a new spear and reloaded as part of the same movement.

"That wasn't so bad," I muttered to my microdocs while inserting a fresh spear of my own. "Why were you making such a fuss?"

"Begin," commanded the voice.

This time the trainer moved faster, and I could've sworn it had suddenly grown a few inches. Once again, I was late in my release.

The shock felt worse this time and Brahmasaurus didn't even glance at the spear flying an inch over its head.

I glared at my opponent. What had Rider gotten me into?

Perhaps I was taking this too seriously. "All right," I drawled. "This town ain't big enough for the both of us. You're goin' to regret the day you was born. Or hatched as the case may be."

When the contest started, I *moved*, throwing the spear immediately and jumping to one side. A javelin hit me in the chest anyway. And I lost my balance, winding up sprawled on the ground, smarting both from the fall and from a shock that was distinctly obnoxious.

While falling, I'd glimpsed Brahmasaurus deflect my spear by slapping it aside with the lever. The trainer now raised an open hand toward me, imitation palm out. I stood up and watched, intrigued.

The generic warrior, undeniably larger now, began spinning its lever around its arms and body. The movements were slow, and the long shaft wobbled as it went, detracting from the performance. The trainer stopped and seemed to stare at me.

"Very interesting," I said. "But you can see the same thing, only better, in every Kung Fu movie ever made. No offense." I hoped I wasn't expected to execute those complex moves myself.

The creature bowed then began the same routine, only faster. Now, the staff whistled through the air and all movement was smooth and sure. Again, the trainer stopped.

I applauded. "You've got it."

Another pause and the performance was repeated with inhuman and accelerating speed. I kept expecting the lever to break as it shrieked along. Soon, I couldn't begin to follow the blurred movements.

Suddenly, I was looking at ribbons and circles of fire. It took me a moment to realize the lever's ends had burst into flame. The trainer stopped showing off and quenched the fire with its big hands.

"Ah! I get you now. It's all about *pace*. Right? For every skill level and weapon there's a proper speed. I've been trying to move too fast for my present ability."

Brahmasaurus bowed again and duplicated my applause, only with an extra set of hands. I smiled.

"Thanks. Didn't know you cared. Tell you what. Now that we're getting chummy, what say we call off the contest?"

Another javelin was headed my way. I hadn't seen the warrior load up and hadn't heard any "begin." This time, it *hurt*.

"Hey! That's enough!" I yelled.

Nothing changed except that my opponent grew again and loaded *two* spears. This could lead to nothing good....

I simply threw myself as fast and far out of the way as possible. The ploy worked ... in part. Only one javelin hit me, and only in my shoulder. But the pain felt anything but virtual.

Something awoke in me, cooler than anger. My thoughts turned clear. No human could win this contest; perhaps Hhoymon were faster, or masochistic, or the domain's programming was corrupted. In any case ...

The devil was larger than Rider now and more commanding, standing like some unstoppable force, as if discipline and authority had been rendered incarnate. Not only that, the bastard was holding *three* spears in its lever.

I pulled the table over on its side and hid behind it. Not very courageous, but I could live with that. In fact, I intended to.

"I give up!" I shouted, desperately searching for any sign of a glowing octagon on the ground. I was supposed to step on it again to end the session. "Stop the game! Rider! Can you hear me? I need *help*!"

A second later, my table illusion was shattered by three javelin illusions. Fortunately, this slowed the spears enough so that when two of them hit me, the pain was bearable.

Still no octagon. But the endless plain, the weapons and tables vanished anyway. I was back in the cave, but not alone. For a long, spooky moment, the warrior gazed at me inscrutably. Then it, too, disappeared.

I trembled with adrenaline and something more. At the last instant, I'd seen ... I don't know what. Brahmasaurus had transfigured. Magnificence had poured into the strange form like water into a vase.

For minutes, I stood there, blinking and repeating, "What the hell?" Finally, I calmed down enough to stagger out of the projective domain. Glare and noise hit my nerves like a forging hammer. Dead ahead, Rider loomed, hands on hips, surrounded by six agitated-looking Common all yelling at once. I glanced at my watch: not even four o'clock yet. And I'd thought yesterday had been a long day.

I suddenly felt very homesick.

―――

Rider's piney fragrance was cloying multiplied sevenfold. Or maybe the intensity of O-gen-ai feelings intensified the odor.

I wasn't the only one watching the argument. Strong, Swift, three Blenn, and an elderly Neme were nearby, inconspicuous next to the flamboyant giants. Also, keeping his or her distance, the birdlike creature I'd seen near the Heart of Art calmly observed the scene. Merely rubbernecking, or was this another player in whatever game Rider seemed to be hosting?

Wait. Didn't I see this bird, or something like it, along with the un-Neme-like Neme in that dream I'd had in the restaurant? The memory had become fuzzy, but my suspicions were sharp as a hurling stick javelin.

If anything, the argument had heated up. But why so *much* racket? Was I standing in some nexus of echoes? I noticed the Blenn stayed attentive, periodically bouncing on their single legs as if nodding agreement to well-made debating points. And each was gripping a speechstaff.

Oh. That explained the excess noise. I'd evidently been receiving running translations, but so many concurrent voices saying different things added up to babble.

Swift kept walking in place, a Neme's way of fidgeting. Strong, still a beautiful woman, noticed me and nudged Swift, who was holding my camera. She waved. I waved back and waited for the tumult and shouting to end.

Finally, the Common seemed to reach some grumpy accord, and fissioned off in various directions leaving only Rider behind. The aged Neme and two of the Blenn stepped onto the nearest Glideway segment and accelerated away. I looked around and didn't see the bird.

The crowd had shrunk to Rider, Strong, Swift, one Blenn, and me. I stepped forward, greeting the Blenn via the translating rod and exchanging hand-touches with both Nemes. Strong and I held our contact longer than courtesy dictated, and I knew we were both remembering Kind. Besides, she was comforting to touch.

"What was that all about?" I asked Rider quietly.

"Surplus leaders and a follower deficit. But to you, not relevant. So. Are you ill, David? Offense not intended, but you sound like your own corpse."

"*Look* like own corpse," Swift growled.

I had to smile. "Thanks, Swift. Makes me feel much better. Rider, why the hell didn't you warn me before sending me into that lion's den?"

"Warn? What happened?"

As I explained, Rider's twin pupils dilated, and its leaves shook. Swift pulled one eye inside his head and kept it there; Strong just watched me. The Blenn buzzed a few times, but I heard no translation.

Thinking all this was a fitting reaction to my story, I milked the harrowing aspects a bit but omitted the interesting behavior of my suit. Maybe microdocs typically respond to approaching danger. But if, say, Poseidon's miracle juice had made some useful ... alterations, keeping this secret might give me some sort of edge. Right then I wanted a truckload of edges.

When I finished talking, Rider studied the dark opening behind me. "David, this is a wrongness. You should have encountered a humanoid trainer. David, *certain* are you it wasn't a humanoid in armors?"

"You bet I'm certain!" The only armor had been mine. What would've happened to me without microdocs?

"Ayn-Seris. Perhaps our 'fuss' *was* germane for you. You, my friend, seem to have encountered an ... embodiment of a certain Supernal."

"What do—wait! You mean one of those Travelers you mentioned at breakfast?"

"I do mean."

"Are you saying these private gods of yours are *real*?" Not my shining hour for tact.

"More real than you or I! And they are yours as much as mine."

I shook my head. "Never even heard of them before today."

"To all beings they belong. But humans have a special connection. For thousands of cycles, Woo-Chybris the Librarian, Spherecerer of History and Records, has lived on Earth."

"What?"

"The White Pyramid rests at the muddy bottom of your ocean Atlantic."

I could tell that everyone was staring at me, but I kept my ordinary eyes on Rider. "That's ... interesting. This Woo-Chybris is another water god?"

"No. Chybris only moved below the waters to protect your kind. Also, Supernals are their own categories." Rider's leaves all rose and fell at once. "Eternal they are, in a sense. Each envelops a particular Sphere —more exactly, each Supernal *is* an aspect of mind."

"Where did they come from?"

"Seris love us! A poor time we share for ontology lessons! What know you concerning Pan-Cosmic cycles?"

"Absolutely nothing."

"So. Know you the origins and fate of your home universe?"

I glanced at Strong, who smiled encouragingly.

"Most human scientists," I said, "believe it began with a massive explosion."

"We name such events an 'Unfurling.'"

"We call it the 'Big Bang.' Supposedly, our universe is expanding, but may eventually collapse into a 'Big Crunch,' then the whole business can start over."

"Many Roads sing this song as does the Pan-Cosmos, in its own mode."

"You mean, someday the *entire Pan-Cosmos* will shrink into—"

"Shrink? What is size, David, with no outside for comparisons?"

"Good point." One I'd made myself on occasion.

Slurp. "Your word 'point' resonates! The Pan-Cosmos has its own cycle of death and birth."

Whoa! I suddenly realized that no other human knew any of this. I begged myself to memorize every word. "How do the Travelers fit in?"

"Last and first. Last to rejoin the Undivided; first to awaken in the Pure Dawn, the unfurling of a refreshed Pan-reality. But for powers of cycles, until conscious life evolves, the Twelve are alone. In this quiet period, they relearn to manifest bodies and to commune with each other. Time enough they have to develop *personalities*. Thus, the Spherecerers are at once diffuse yet maintain discrete locations in ultraspace and ultratime. Why do you smile so loudly?"

"You're finally opening up. And the incredible things you're saying! But what did you mean by 'diffuse'?"

"Arfaenn the Dancer, Supernal of Arts, dances as an example. Whenever any being anywhere has artistic inspiration, She is there. Such is what She is. Yet the Dancer is also a distinct individual and maintains a ... body, although unlike yours or mine."

I rubbed my forehead, perhaps unconsciously trying to press all this new information inside. "My God, Rider! At any given moment, countless beings must be coming down with artistic impulses somewhere. Is this Arfaenn aware of them *all*?"

"Ask that of the Watergod or Mirrormage. They know more of Supernals than I. Perhaps the Dancer is capable of total awareness, but normally is no more conscious of individuals than we are of our body cells."

"You say 'She.' These Travelers have genders?"

Rider blinked with several sets of eyelids. "Why would they? But Nemes and Common honor Hhoymon pronouns when speaking of Supernals. Hhoymon perceive three Travelers as male, three female, three with both attributes, and three possessing neither."

"What makes Hhoymon the authorities?"

"Experience. Earth is not the only planet a Supernal has chosen as a temporary home. But we have become laterally-tracked. Your training in the projective domain was most wrong. Such training is never hurtful or dangerous."

"Tell that to my bruises."

"Why? They will not hear regrets, David. But the domain could not have been at fault. Instead, I suggest we aim blame ... much higher. Your trainer resounds of a typical body manifested by Maanza, Spherecerer of Strength, Warfare, and Protection. Only smaller."

"Smaller, huh? Well, the bastard did keep growing. How big is it normally?"

"When last I heard Him," Rider said, emphasizing the pronoun, "He wore a body five times the height of mine."

"Good Lord!"

"Good and bad are concepts too petty to match the Travelers."

"This Maanza's some kind of super warrior?"

"Far more. His Sphere involves every mode of defense, enveloping aspects of science and medicine. He's nurtured His specialties since the last Great Unfurling, creating technologies beyond dreams of even Hhoymon or Blenn." Rider paused and turned toward the Blenn. "You people do dream, don't you?"

The bug jumped at being addressed but it buzzed promptly. Translation: "If you say we dream, Guardian, who am I to disagree?"

"So. As I was singing," Rider continued, "Maanza created a planet-fortress, Ramdajulad. Seeking competent warriors for His armies, He found us when we were newly on the Roads and has helped us ever since."

"Maanza's a *friend* of yours?"

"You stretch the word. An impersonal nurturer perhaps."

"Fascinating, but why do you suppose He showed up? Why should He try to kill me?"

Rider blasted out a tuba-like squeal. "If He had wished you dead, mourning we would be! I cannot guess His intent. But the timing seems significant, for we are in crisis. Our risks have amplified, and I no longer know how many seats surround the gaming dune, let alone who sits in them."

"Personally," I gritted, "I'd appreciate knowing what the *game* is. At least tell me about this crisis."

The Common's ear-leaves all turned one way and a moment later, I heard a faint rumbling coming from that direction.

"Binae lives here on the Crossroad, David, so other Supernals visit."

"You've lost me already. I've heard the name several times now, but who's this Binae?"

"Supernal of Diplomacy. You must understand, my friend, that while mortals are somewhat inaudible to such vast beings, most Travelers are careful not to harm us. Binae, Maanza, Arfaenn, and, of course Seris, understand our tenderness. But to a few, we scarcely exist. One such Traveler caused grievous harm upon touching our world. Since then, caring Supernals warn us before arriving so that we may apply ... precautions. They alert us either through the Watergod or that demon we passed when—ayn-Seris! As you would sing, speak of the devil!"

The rumble burst into a full-throated roar and Rider spun around. Something incredible was coming.

"Firemage," Rider muttered sourly.

Crossroad was more picaresque than picturesque. This day was one damn encounter after another.

Given a genuine backbone, I would've snatched my camera from Swift. Instead, I was a fawn in the headlights, watching strangeness approach in impossibly huge leaps. I had no idea what a demon should look like, but surely this wasn't it.

The Firemage was an ursine centaur: a joining of bear and stallion. But *this* stallion dwarfed a Percheron, and his head and torso belonged on a Kodiak scaled to match. He landed softly, stopping about twelve feet from me, radiating power and enough body-heat to melt lead. His charcoal skin appeared infested with speedy vermin, small scarlet flames crawling all over him. I had to look twice at his hooves—bright blue cones, points downward—to realize he stood balanced on four growling gas jets.

Strong and Swift scuttled behind Rider while the Blenn courageously hopped to a position behind them all.

Compared to Poseidon, the Firemage was tiny, but he overtopped Rider by five feet and projected no similar aura of kindness or friendliness. *Crossroad*, I told myself, *has too many damn giants. I'm sick of looking up.*

Glowering at Rider, the demon opened a toothless mouth crammed with glowing embers to emit an earthquake roar embellished by sparks, fire, ash, and smoke. The Blenn's staff translated calmly: "We trust you have a satisfactory explanation, Guardian. Shall we enumerate your failings?"

Interesting language. Did the Firemage come from a world with classical dragons? Or garrulous volcanoes? He had plenty more to say and despite the distracting pyrotechnics, I gathered he was inflamed by a breach of protocol.

I began to put it all together.

Apparently, Poseidon and this demon had a deal: if either learned of an impending Supernal visitation, they would instantly inform the other. Each being would then relay the news to other members of their respective sacred or unsacred circle.

This time, the Firemage had learned the Supernal of Art was expected by bumping into Arfaenn Herself in Great Hall Four.

Rider, responding in English, seemed on the verge of ultra-alien apoplexy. "You claim She is *already here*?"

"Feign no ignorance," blasted the demon. "And burn this into your expectations: slights bring reckonings. We will speak no more of this. Move aside, mortals."

With this encouragement, Rider and entourage stepped or hopped to the right and the centaur sprang forward, abruptly standing between the rest of the group and me. For a split second that felt longer, glowing eyes met mine, and a burning hand rested on my shoulder.

The blue-flame hooves howled like a jet engine, lengthening and intensifying, painting the floor with heat-mirages. The Firemage crouched, then jumped more than a hundred yards in one leap. He turned briefly to fire out a final remark then continued leaping until he was out of sight. The roaring faded to rumble then was gone.

We all stared after the hellish being.

Rider turned toward the Nemes. "Beyond speechstaff range he'd been for his parting flame. Did anyone comprehend it?"

Strong shrugged human-style. "He merely screamed at us, Guardian."

"How ideal. As usual, Shahl-venn assumes the worst. The Watergod received no message and only *felt* the Dancer might arrive soon. But there's no squeezing water from dry sand!" Rider faced me. "Hear you the difference between gods and demons, David?"

"I'm not—"

"Demons are gods we don't like."

Soon Rider, both Nemes, the Blenn, and I were zipping across the Hall on a Glideway, with any luck aimed toward food. I'd begged off using the subjective track due to my stomach trying to eat itself.

"What's the story," I asked Rider, "on this Firemage?"

"Once he was ... closely associated with Chybris. Later he lived on Muuti."

Nothing like a shot of intellectual caffeine. "The Scome world!"

"Clan Dhu titled him H'ap Shai."

"Oh! So *he's* the 'Fire-spitter' mentioned in Scome texts! Figured he was mythical."

Rider gave me a strange look. "Here, real and mythical harmonize."

Keep asking questions, I told myself, *before the river of answers dries up again*. "I take it Shahl-venn is his Gray or Brown Hhoymon name?"

"This one you may keep. In English: Firemage. One bad turn he arrived here and never departed. I know little else about him."

"I see. If you're still in a sharing mood, why do you suppose the Dancer didn't warn anyone She was coming?"

"Live for countless cycles, David, and you too might be difficult to comprehend!"

I frowned. "Those two Common who intercepted us earlier? They were warning you about Poseidon's hunch?"

Rider paused before answering. "Yes. I wished not to agitate you with my fears."

"Fears? You said the Dancer is careful around us mortals."

Longer pause. "Arfaenn is no direct danger."

"Then what is?"

My guide fell silent so long I wondered if I'd get an answer. "I hear no compelling need," Rider finally said quietly, "for you to suffer *all* our difficulties. Yet I cannot bear you believing that we do not love and trust Arfaenn."

"I'm listening."

"Her presence, particularly with Maanza's attention focused here, may act as a ... catalyst." Rider raised an arm to forestall interruption. "Listen with intent, David. The full truth you must drink from the bottom upward."

"Fine. So what's lying on the bottom?"

"History. Maanza has often aided other Travelers with His talents, and some are capable of gratitude. Yet how can Supernals repay one of their own?"

"What do you get for the God Who Has Everything?"

"Just so. Urien, Supernal of Insight, once asked the Defender that very question. Maanza's only desire was that other Supernals attempt to destroy His body."

"Good Lord. Why?"

"He has honed His bodies and battle skills throughout countless cycles. Yet, in His personal aspect, He requires challenges to keep developing, just as you and I. By now, only his peers could offer a challenge."

"Ah."

"Thus, Travelers sometimes assay that demolition the Mirrormage titles 'Maanza's Reward.' If a Supernal succeeds in damaging or eliminating the Defender's latest body, He is joyous and sets about creating a superior form immune to such attack."

Weirder and weirder. "So this danger Arfaenn presents involves Maanza's suicidal hobby?"

"Indirectly, through a third party."

"Let me guess: another Traveler."

"Just so. But enough. I will not accelerate your heart with songs of horror."

Back to secrets. And something about Rider's tone raised goose bumps under my microdocs.

"But the dangers cannot stir," Rider continued, "if rendered deaf to Arfaenn's presence. We have means to mute Her radiations, but they require diversion of energies needed elsewhere."

I nodded. "Another guess: that big argument I walked in on concerned diverting those energies?"

"You are insightful this turn! We were debating urgencies."

"And your decision?"

"Meaningless! Arfaenn *already* dances here; we lack sufficient time to prepare. We can only roam about our business and hope for the better. If Maanza hadn't touched you, these worries I would not have laid on your spirit."

"Glad you did. But I'll need to digest all this."

Rider sped up a bit. "Digest! *That* is what my life is missing! I can hear the restaurant from here. After food, would you still wish to go running?"

"No thanks. I've had all the exercise I can stand for today."

CHAPTER 17
SWAN LAKE

This restaurant seemed only moderately crowded, its layout similar to the Enclave's eatery but with tables and chairs in even more sizes and shapes. I was having a sham déjà vu of this morning's breakfast scene, with an extra Neme and a different Blenn. And with luck, the spider-god wouldn't show up and ruin everyone's appetite.

We were seated—in the Blenn's case, squatted—at a round table, waiting to order, and I tried to avoid staring at Strong. She sure *looked* human. More than ever. I wondered about the Mirrormage who'd supposedly altered Strong's appearance and knew more than Rider about the Supernals. I'd seen the Firemage. Perhaps this Mirrormage, whose name kept coming up, was an equally intimidating monster....

Swift touched my microdoc sleeve to attract my attention and then introduced the Blenn as "Helper," explaining that her real name wouldn't convert into English. The Blenn, Strong volunteered, have three sexes and our charming dining companion was a "female-neutral."

After much prompting on my part, Helper admitted that she worked directly for a *Least*, a Blenn queen; and even more reluctantly confessed to being a minor student of Supernal lore. I intended to ask if the Common had drafted her for their squabble because of this special expertise, but then I noticed something peculiar.

A few small dots and swirls of ultra-blue had begun floating in through the restaurant doorway, settling on diners and furniture like soap bubbles or cool sparks. Everyone else seemed oblivious to the phenomenon except for Strong who watched the sparks and exchanged baffled glances with me.

The dots kept getting thicker and brighter, becoming flakes in a mystic horizontal snowstorm. I felt a sudden touch of breeze in this enclosed space, and perhaps others felt it too. Helper abruptly untwisted her leg, spinning and extending to her full height. Rider and both Nemes stood up. Then I was on my feet, facing the doorway, ignoring the blizzard ...

Grace itself had entered the room.

I couldn't focus on Her face or guess Her true size, but I knew exactly what She was. The Supernal seemed to travel by generating a series of bodies, ghostly afterimages of a supremely gifted dancer moving with total elegance through a series of inspired yet formalized postures. She *flowed* from one spot to the next, never bound to any specific place. Her power and beauty were immaculate.

Arfaenn flowed over to our table and flung a thousand sheer veils in a thousand shades of manis in my direction. Suddenly—

I am standing alone on the grassy bank of a large lake, its surface is rippled by a gentle, warm wind. The sky is the richest of all blues and a huge golden sun pours clear soft light like a blessing past and through sparse pale clouds.

The colors are unbelievable. Perhaps matter here is constructed entirely of photons rather than duller particles. Everything around me both reflects and emits light—a world of multicolored rubies. The lake is a million harmonizing hues of teal and turquoise; each little splash drips lambent sapphires.

A fringe of glittering sand borders the water, easing into a wide lawn of tender emerald grass. Past the lawn stands a forest with foliage surpassing any New England fall: astonishing leafy fireworks of red, orange, violet, and yellow that make lake and sky seem that much bluer.

Beyond the forest lie gentle hills covered in exotic spiraling evergreens. And past the hills ... *mountains* soar.

They tower as the Himalayas loom over Nepal's lowlands, glowing white and golden-white in the sunlight, with shadows of blue, blue-green, and violet refining their shapes, making them seem more than solid and more eternal than time.

Textures here are almost painfully profound. The water appears smoother, cleaner, and more flowing than any water I've seen. The mountains are more majestic; the air, perfumed with jasmine whispers, tastes as fresh and life-giving as a breath of pure forgiveness.

I look down at my feet and see three shadows. One appears thick and muscular, one looks emaciated, and the third is ... strange.

Small jewels define the water's edge, blue and white. I reach down and pluck a blue one. The gem in my hand radiates hardness so extreme I sense even diamonds couldn't give it the tiniest scratch.

I carefully replace the stone in its sand bezel and gaze down into the water. Huge golden carp drifting beneath the surface seem more alive than fish should be, every scale shimmering with energy. White and blue lotus blossoms, glowing like flower-shaped suns, float on ...

Wait! The waves die down for a moment. Will I see my reflection? No, the surface remains too agitated. What I see is incomprehensible. Sadness that I don't understand fills me.

Suddenly, I am desperately thirsty. I kneel on velvet grass and velour sand and bend over, cupping my hands under the cool water.

I lift the liquid to my dry lips but feel something warm and soft push my arms down. There comes a whisper, "In Anusar, you must not drink of the soma." Then, almost too quietly to hear, "Not yet, my beloved." I obey, opening my hands although I weep with frustration and loss.

Through my tears, I see a miracle approaching.

At first, I think I recognize my dead wife, seated on a magnificent white swan, playing a long, stringed instrument. But the female figure and Swan keep getting larger and more potent as they get closer. The illusion that the woman is human fades. The bird isn't merely white; deep colors flash in its feathers like the finest of opals; at certain angles, faint images appear.

Now I can name the Goddess. Those jewels in Her hair are stars, the saddle an immense lotus, Her instrument is the vina, and She has four arms. I try but cannot raise my head to look upon Her face. She is my wife's namesake, the Hindu Goddess of learning and music, Sarasvati. My spine turns to frozen electricity as She steps to the shore, bends down from high above, and kisses the top of my head, which ignites painlessly into a cold fiery crown of white light.

As She strides off on some unimaginable errand, I shiver as if in the grip of malaria. I turn to find myself face to face with the Swan. The bird's liquid black eyes are so full of understanding and compassion that again, my tears flow. I feel rather than see the great wings reach out and pull me close.

The Swan's body is warm and supremely comforting, redolent of sandalwood and vanilla.

When my shivering stops, the bird releases me, floats backward a little and speaks. "One name I bear is Hamsa. Would you care to hear a small portion of my story?"

"Please," I say, although I am content simply to be near such a being.

"When I was young and more careless, I fell asleep one summer day. My child had been swimming nearby and when I awoke, he was gone. I searched, but could not find him. Life holds dangers, and I feared he was lost forever.

"Yet we were lucky. Entities of another species found my son and raised him as their own. Still, he was unhappy. His form was unlike that of his new brothers and sisters. He thought he was hideous. Do you understand me?"

Excitement courses within me. "I know that story! I loved it when I was a kid. My mother had this illustrated child's version; she read it to me over and over. I'd always cry and then ask her to read it again. Your son was the Ugly Duckling!"

"Can you recall the pictures?"

As the Swan watches me fondly, I remember how the young swan misunderstood his own nature until his true mother showed up. Hans Christian Andersen had written the original in 1844. Whoever had rewritten it for the very young had added some refinements....

As sudden and illuminating as a bolt of lightning, I remember one scene: The Ugly Duckling's tears of distress had fallen into a lake, distorting his reflection. Seeing the deformed image confirmed his belief that he was ugly.

I hadn't thought about this fable for years. But now, as an adult, I see depths in it I'd never suspected, ideas that touch me on many levels. I am not ready to wrap my new understanding in words.

"You must return now," the Swan murmurs.

"So soon? No! I need ... won't you tell me more of your story? Please?" I am a child unwilling to be put in bed for the night.

"Not yet. Do not fear, dear one. Part of me will remain with you." She lifts her great wings high and lowers them with a stupendous flap that cracks like thunder, half lifting her body from the water. A single opal feather comes loose and lands on my microdoc-covered chest. It glistens for a moment then melts into my fourth skin. I am covered in shining white feathers. Then—

I was standing in the restaurant. Rider, Swift, and Strong were staring at me. Helper, too, kept staring while hopping backward until she bumped into a table. Even the other diners, mostly Chean-shee and Nemes, seemed to find me of paramount interest.

To me, *everything* was interesting. Wherever I looked, intense manis reflected off every surface, especially faces. Strong's eyes were ultra-blue beacons.

"David!" Rider cried. "Where did you *go*?"

"And what," Swift put in, "happened to fourth skin?"

I looked down at my suit. No feathers, but the fabric was now a matte white with flashes of colored fire. And I discovered the source of so much ultra-blue light. It radiated from my chest.

I opened my mouth to ask if I'd really vanished. But my vocal cords had gone on sabbatical. Was I dreaming again, thinking I was awake? I didn't care.

Crossroad should've appeared dull and dark in comparison to the luminous place I'd just visited. Instead, the restaurant seemed homey and warm. It was murkier, true, but everything had an oil-painting richness. I felt a connection to everyone and between everyone unlike anything I'd experienced. Even the Blenn now returning to the table seemed altered. She'd previously looked as attractive to me as a deformed cockroach. Now, she possessed an inexpressible sleekness and symmetry.

My heart was opened to the Nemes, and my distrust of Rider had evaporated. I wanted to tell my dear friends what I'd seen and how I felt, but all I could do was stand and grin.

Rider moved closer. "David? Can you understand me? Ayn-Seris! So much for nutritions. I know not what the Dancer did, but you can all hear the results. Goodbye beautiful fresh ferns, stow you away I will, and you may stale yourselves at your leisure."

The Common turned to Strong, singing more than speaking in some inordinately lush O-gen-ai language. Thanks to the speechstaff I could savor the translation: "Strong, you know much about contemplative states of consciousness. What is your council?"

Swift pointed out, in English, what seemed perfectly obvious. "Expect nothing from poetic Strong, Guardian. Appears we have dual victims." I grinned wider at the notion we were victims.

Strong radiated ecstasy along with a fainter version of the exotic light beaming from my chest and from her eyes. She gazed at me as if I were the single most wonderful thing imaginable.

"Strong?" said Swift, "make effort to respond. Can you walk? Da? Nyet? This is irritating way to manage conversation! Instructions, Guardian?"

Rider answered indirectly. "If grasp my meanings you can, David, I intend to carry you to your apartment. Others will tend to your partner in dysfunction. Is that nice with you? Why bother asking? Listen to him, people! To this one, all the cosmos is nice."

I made a heroic effort to convey that I was fully functional and may have even managed to move my lips. But the tiny movement sent a shiver of energy though me. My body filled with a kind of bubbly electricity, and I lost contact with the outer world....

My ears resumed working first. I heard Rider and Swift talking and knew a speechstaff had to be nearby because they were speaking in Simple, and I was getting a translation. But the discussion seemed nonsensical.

"Upsetting," Swift said, "when you gave Strong credit for most superior spiritual expertise."

"I respect your feelings, but there is no tragedy here."

"You feel no loss, Guardian?"

"Some loss, some gain. Mostly, a difference. When you reach your goal, you no longer reach toward that goal. And I have compensations, my dear friend. Perhaps someday you will make the same choice."

"You had a choice?"

Rider went silent for a moment. "With Binae involved, who knows?"

Then, for an indeterminate time, the world faded in and out like a weak radio station. When everything steadied, we were on a Glideway in a blue-lit tunnel. Rider strode along, carrying me cradled in one arm as if I weighed nothing.

My sense of touch returned, but with enhanced sensitivity. Rider's leaves tickled me right through my fourth skin. I happily stared at my suit, a sleek blue opal in the azure light. Needed some polishing though....

I heard myself chuckle.

"Ayn-Urien!" Rider declared. "It noises! Stand clear, everyone. Professor David A. Goldberg is about to explode into activity!"

The activity was only another chuckle, but my guide must've figured I'd become lucid enough to comprehend simple sentences. "Are you interested, David A., about recent events from my points of hearing?"

"You bet," I whispered.

According to Rider, Arfaenn had danced through the restaurant until one of her projections intersected my body. Then She and I vanished without even the courtesy of a displaced-air pop. An instant later, I'd returned with an overdose-grin and a brighter, whiter suit.

"Still, you are so entranced, sound curdles around your head," Rider finished. "We will let you sleep this away. Will you tread on your own now?"

"Sure."

"Joking I was! With voice so fragile, legs should not be trusted. Enjoy the ride of me. In your condition, enjoyment should be easy."

To disprove Rider's silly idea of my helplessness, I managed a small wriggle. Again, my body filled with bubbly vibration and again, everything else went away.

I surfaced in my apartment, alone, floating on my imaginary mattress. Looked around and smiled. Someone, presumably Rider, must've asked the Mind how I'd set up the décor for sleeping purposes, and misinterpreted the answers. Here were stars that *didn't* twinkle: countless steady points of brilliance in a myriad of actinic colors. Galaxies even. Didn't mind a bit. In fact, the sight felt inspiring and oddly soothing. I stared at it with my eyes closed, for hours.

Finally, as I drifted off, the intense little lights began to seem *related*, reflections of a single incredible star bouncing off innumerable tinted mirrors.

CHAPTER 18
BOXED SET

I awoke with a kind of hangover. No headache or queasiness, but I felt like an old car with a dead battery.

"Scour," I said without thinking. Good thing I'd exempted the mattress.

The light seemed aggressively bright, but both forms of my vision were blurry. I needed a jump-start.

I requested coffee strong enough to rouse the decomposed and a fresh armchair in which to do the rousing. My wristwatch claimed it was eight in the morning. Thursday in New England, God knows what on Commonworld.

There should be a Supernal of Caffeine. Gradually, I summoned enough oomph to reach the bathroom where I glanced into the mirror and froze.

For decades, I've heard loose talk about upcoming anti-senescent miracle treatments, from telomere therapy to tailored hormones to dead-cell-stripping agents to regenerated blood. Some have showed promise. But I doubt any could work like this. Overnight, I'd lost ten years. The fine wrinkles around my eyes were mostly gone as was my bald spot. I turned and studied my profile with x-road vision. The old scar near my right ear was AWOL.

Somehow, this didn't seem right.

And I had mixed feelings about my clean-tasting mouth, gleaming teeth, and just-shampooed-look hair. My suit, still white, had been busy while I'd slept. I rubbed my baby-smooth chin, tucking an interesting notion into the back of my mind.

"Nice work, Jeeves," I admitted. "But I can do some of my own damn housekeeping."

Another problem emerged, or rather didn't, when I tried, strictly out of habit, to use the toilet. Nothing happened. The cause was obvious—I was wearing it—but it gave me another splinter of worry. Having a perpetually empty bladder and unused lower digestive tract could have *nasty* consequences. Excess salt alone could kill me. How well did Jeeves know its business? Was my body similar enough to a Gray Hhoymon's for the system to fully—

Wait. Who ever said 'docs were intended exclusively for Grays? Perhaps this was a one-size-fits-all-Hhoymon garment. If so, just how adaptable would it need to be? How dissimilar, physically, were the four Hhoymon races?

Well, they certainly looked different. The human-sized Grays with their piano-hinge ears, black doggy noses, and concrete-colored skin might not draw a third look in downtown Manhattan. The shorter but wider Browns might not even rate a second glance despite the extra fingers. But the glossy white skin, platinum hair, rectangular irises, and protruding brows of the child-sized Silvers would definitely grab attention. And the even smaller Whites, pallid sprites less than three feet tall, would probably earn coos of "aren't they *adorable*" until said cooers got a close look at their eyes, which are icy, pale as last week's dreams, and transparent enough to reveal underlying capillaries.

All right. Assume microdocs are adaptable. But are they adaptable enough to work perfectly for another *species*?

I gazed down at Jeeves and had a mild epiphany. Hhoymon and humans might be universes apart physiologically, but I had something better than Hhoymon technology to trust: the Swan! She'd transformed the suit, and I was sure *She* knew her business. Whatever it was.

Something else troubled me. I'd always believed that if humans could evolve to be a little smarter, war and lesser forms of violence would disappear. But if the inhumanly brilliant Hhoymon fought among themselves, what chance did *we* have? Had I bought excess stock in sheer intelligence?

I ordered Jeeves to withdraw from most of my body, and took a hot shower simply for the soothing effect. Afterward, I plunked myself into the armchair and faced the wall. I craved comfort food, food that clings to the ribs with both hands. I gave the food converter a glare. Considering its milk-product disasters, I couldn't bear the thought of what it might do to pizza.

Funny, I remembered wondering why the local Mind didn't handle all cooking. Now I wondered why I'd believed the Mind could produce food just because it could manipulate environmental factors.

"Mind, can you display Earth's Pacific Ocean at sunset from any beach in California?"

"There are many such recordings."

"Put a random one on this wall. Oh, and filter out all harmful radiations."

The view was splendid, and my precaution made sun-staring harmless, theoretically. Seagull squeals echoed; briny whiffs tickled my nose. Had a miraculous doorway to Earth opened? I walked over and reached out. Nope, the wall remained as did my problems. Along with a bumper crop of questions:

Why had I been invited to Crossroad? Why had a Common done the fetching?

What was really going on here? Why wouldn't anyone tell me?

How did the Travelers fit into whatever was happening? Likewise, the Apnoti, the Firemage, and the mysterious Mirrormage?

Why had Strong been the only one aside from me zapped by the Dancer? For that matter, why had she been given human form?

Why had the Chean-shee ceiling fallen?

Who was the weird Neme who hugged me?

What had caused those stings? Had they stopped permanently?

Why had Poseidon given me his *eau de dieu*? Why had Maanza—

Me: looking around wildly for my camera, seeing it hanging in the alcove near the door. Me: feeling foolish. A fool with a huge regret. Yesterday, I'd encountered a *Supernal* and missed the photo op of a lifetime! I sighed and sat down again. Okay, back to worrying....

Why had Maanza's avatar attacked me? Why did Arfaenn send me that vision? Why did the Swan transform my suit? Who, exactly, *was* She?

Why's my hair growing back?

How the hell could I accomplish my mission under the Mind's constant scrutiny? And an oldie but goodie: what the hell was a "10 square?"

At least I knew where to start looking for it. Rider had mentioned an area in the Hall of Games devoted to human games and surely that's where any self-respecting clue intended for humans would be hiding.

One bonus question: who was running the show? By Rider's own admission, the Common weren't the most advanced or powerful denizens of this world. Were they truly in charge?

"Howdy in there," drawled a voice through my door. "How're you feelin'?"

"Come in and find out!"

Strong entered, the very picture of beauty and contentment. Her eyes still held a hint of ultra-blue. She took one look at me. "My, haven't you just gotten younger!"

"Yeah. Can't imagine why. But it's the same old me inside." Which wasn't quite true. A transcendent experience should *change* a person and it had, but I'd been too depleted to notice. A small thing perhaps, but big to me: I was no longer terrified, just scared.

Strong walked over to hug me, and I could've sworn she purred. After a while, I felt like purring myself. I gently disentangled from her.

If she noticed my condition it didn't seem to bother her. It sure as hell bothered me. I'm weird, I know, but I hadn't ever felt truly attracted to anyone other than my wife, and Strong remained an *alien*. Sure, she looked lovely, but it hadn't affected me much until now. Was this an aftereffect of our shared high? Had she also shared some of my experience?

"Tell me something, Strong. After Arfaenn appeared, did you see a giant goddess or a swan?"

"That's what you saw? No, sweetheart. Mostly, I felt ... dissolved, like the universe was quiverin' with joy."

"I got that too, later."

"But I was also aware of—I don't know."

I smiled. "A Neme at a loss for words?"

"This one is. I'll tell you what, though. I've been brimmin' with poetry ever since. I'd love to hear what happened to you."

"Oh. I guess we're both at a loss."

Strong hugged me again, briefly. "Not ready to chatter 'bout it?"

"Not yet, anyway. But it all seemed ... symbolic."

"That's fine. You just take your time. But I didn't come around just to be social." Strong grinned. "Brought you a present and it's just outside. Shall I haul it in?"

"What is it? Never mind, guess I'll find out soon enough. I can get it myself if it's heavy."

She laughed exactly like a human with a nice laugh, opened the door, grabbed the carrying strap of a large sky-blue box sitting in the hallway, and threw it in my general direction while closing the door. It landed on the floor, settling as lightly as a butterfly.

"I'll bite," I said. "What's inside?"

Her eyes sparkled. "Why not look for yourself?"

I walked over and touched the cool blue surface. "How's it open?"

She giggled, the most un-Neme-like thing she'd done yet. "Think it open."

OPENING WONDERS

Experimentally, I visualized the top lifting. The lid swung up, revealing a stack of thin brown laths like foot-long sections sawed off a wooden yardstick.

"Whoa! The way you slung this around, I assumed it was almost empty. A little gravity assist from the Mind? What are these slats?"

"What were you expectin', sweetheart? Memory sticks? Disks?"

"Oh. They're *documents*?"

"Monographs, reports, whatevers, all transcribed and translated," she said smugly. "Just what you ordered."

I stared at the pile. "Fantastic! I mean it. But how do I read them?"

"Same way you made that chair behind you. This room is floored in an agreeable 'skin' and the Mind molds it however you say."

She picked out a slat and handed it to me. "That's a Chean-shee 'skin' embedded with words. You can ask the Mind to shape it into a screen, or a scroll, or ... watch! Mind, you turn that codex in David's hands into an Earth-style manuscript."

Suddenly I was holding a thick fanfold of papers. The cover page read, "Journal of Charming Secondhouse." Probably not a Neme version of *Sleeping Beauty*.

"Hey! Can I also get an un-translated copy of this? Never actually seen Neme writing."

She moved close to me to read the title. She even *smelled* good.

"Sure you have, sweetheart. We use Simple. We invented it 'cause we make too many noises to squeeze into a practical alphabet."

"And the Common adopted it? Interesting." I regarded the folded tome in my hands and then looked over at the slat-filled box, realizing the magnitude of this "present." And my resulting responsibility ...

"Strong, thank you for all this and please tell everyone involved how much I appreciate it. Can't wait to dive in."

"Start divin' right now if you like."

"Um. Any way to open these ... codices on Earth?"

Her eyes danced. "You're 'fraid you'll run out of time and miss somethin' important. We're way ahead of you! We're crunchin' all and more into a Hhoymon MARBLE so you can take everythin' home when you go."

"Thank God! I can't imagine even scratching the surface in less than a year. How did you get so many documents translated so fast?"

"A Mind did most of the heavy liftin'. Sorry, but I got me another mission so I best get on with it. You can find your own way to the restaurant now?"

"I think so."

"Ask any Constructor if you need help. Guardian's invited you to breakfast again, and then on a tourist-pleasin' spaceflight. I'll be seein' you real soon." She turned to give me a quick kiss on my cheek. *Not* a Neme gesture.

"Are we gettin' some kind of interspecies thing goin'?" she said, smiling.

I still hadn't found a reply when she stepped through the door.

CHAPTER 19
WRITTEN IN MOUNTAINS

A*sk any Constructor*. Again, Strong hadn't suggested relying on the artificial genus loci. Interesting and disturbing.

I had the Mind return Charming's journal to lath-dom although it was a trial not to take even a peek inside. Strong had, essentially, handed me King Tut's unopened tomb on a platter, and the platter was the Rosetta stone. But I knew myself. One peek would stretch into hours and academic research was caboose on my current priority list. Rider was waiting and one issue had to be addressed *now*.

The Mind was an information cornucopia, a domestic genie, and a vital buffer from destructive environmental conditions. But for me, it was also a pain in the assignment. How could I evade its attention while, at the same time, preserve its protection?

Impossible? Not necessarily. The Mind seemed an overly literal sort of intelligence, and *could* be fooled. Hadn't Hhoymon, inventors of both the Minds and microdocs, concealed a civil war? I had reason to hope 'docs could be programmed to alter the Mind's perceptions.

My first night here, Rider had said the Minds use "thought-shapes" to identify species. And when I'd donned the fourth skin, or it had donned me, Strong had claimed that microdocs could "forge all sorts of biological credentials" and would keep me human in the Minds' eyes, implying they were blocking off my natural radiations. Thought-shapes I knew from nothing, but considering Strong's transformation, Big Sibling couldn't rely on optical identification. Which gave me a fighting chance. If I had the courage.

"Mind," I said hoarsely, "what species am I?"

"Homo sapiens."

"Any other species present in this room?"

"None can be detected."

I rubbed my chin and paced. If microdocs could emit both Hhoymon and human thought forms, why not others?

Strong had also said she'd never seen microdocs jump on anyone so "explosively." Why would she be present when a *Hhoymon* applied a fourth skin? More likely, she'd seen the result on Nemes. I sure hoped so. For my experiment, I needed to choose a species comfortable on Earth. It wouldn't do to fake being, say, a Vyre. For all I knew, Vyre breathed argon.

I glanced at my watch. No time to stall....

I took a deep breath and mentally asked Jeeves to exude as much Neme-ness as possible. Then I chuckled. Suddenly, the idea of clothing obeying such an abstraction seemed the hope of a lunatic.

I stopped chuckling. Was it my imagination, or did the air feel drier? "What species am I?" I asked.

The answer came in three-toned gibberish. Unbelievable. It couldn't possibly be this easy! The little train that didn't think it could had *jumped* over the damn mountain.

"Repeat that in English, please."

"You are a Neme."

I blessed the Hhoymon for creating such splendidly unimaginative devices. Then I remembered the danger. While the Mind, in its present confusion, should be keeping my personal environment suitable for a Neme, the Neme ability to survive Earth conditions wasn't proof I could survive a Neme's native environment.

What a weapon, I thought for the hundredth time, the Minds would make! They could squish you, bake you, suffocate you, freeze you, or kill you in more creative ways if those weren't enough. No wonder the Common were afraid to let any Hhoymon return.

I waited, paying extreme attention to my physical sensations. This experiment was tantamount to landing on an alien planet and stepping outside the spaceship without any testing or protection.

A waste of good adrenaline. I didn't gasp or keel over, the air just tasted dry. Neme-hood suited me.

So now, in theory, I could hide my identity from Big Sibling, go anywhere on Crossroad and a local Mind would keep me comfy. Irony of the hour: my stunt wouldn't fool a primitive video surveillance system. Of course, it wouldn't work here either if any living beings were spying on me. I had Jeeves resume human mode. I'd already kept Rider waiting too long.

Then it hit me. If Nemes could wear 'docs, they surely knew more than me about microdoc abilities. If any criminal with a fourth skin could fool the Mind this easily the Common *must* have countermeasures in place.

My gaze drifted down to the material on my chest. Small flashes of fire reminded me that mine was no longer your standard-issue fourth skin. I had an odd hunch, one I'd check out later.

"Mind," I said while grabbing my camera, "please tell Sun-toch-sew I'm on my way."

Didn't expect an answer, so I didn't wait for one.

Twice, as I hurried through Chean-shee corridors, my suit fluffed a bit then deflated for no apparent reason. Another question to add to my list: was I the only one worried about the stability of these ceilings?

Once in the restaurant I felt safer. Rider greeted me warmly, announced I was in for "treats" in space, and asked how I was feeling.

"I'm fine now."

"Not earlier?"

I shrugged. "Woke up a bit fried. Yesterday, I think someone plugged my nervous system into the wrong outlet. Too much electricity," I added to clarify.

"You were overcharged." The lemon eyes studied me with exceptional intensity. Rider probably wanted to know what the Dancer had done to me, but I didn't want to think about it, let alone talk about it.

To avoid dairy products, and hoping the human menu reflected human census proportions, I ordered a Chinese breakfast: congee and *you tiao*, Chinese crullers. Our usual server brought me sort-of-porridge and some fourth-cousin-twice-removed to breadsticks.

Rider kept staring, so I sighed internally and described yesterday's experience without mentioning the Swan.

I finished and asked, "Does the name Arfaenn mean 'Dancer' in some Hhoymon language?"

"'Time dancer' is nearer."

"Why would She seek me out?"

Rider lifted a shovel-sized hand, turning it back and forth as though proving it was empty. "Beyond me this is."

This time, I sighed out loud. "Okay. Did Her visit cause whatever trouble you were worried about?"

"No, thank Seris! Our sleeping problems slept." Rider pointed at my bowl. "What species of nutrition is that?"

"Rice gruel."

"Consumption thereof is grueling?"

I nodded and gave in to Rider's bad influence. "Gruel and unusual punishment. But—don't tell the chef—it's tasty compared to this cruller."

"So. That must be cruller and more unusual punishment."

It caught me by surprise, and I cracked up. Across the table, Rider's fern-chomping didn't interfere with the slurping.

"Seems strange," I observed when we'd settled down, "that two people from different universes would laugh at the same thing."

Rider just looked at me as my words echoed in my head.

"How the hell," I said, "could I have missed it? Humans, Common, Nemes, Chean-shee, Hhoymon—maybe even the Vyre and Blenn—we're all non-parallel versions of each other!"

"What else? Even here, creatures prefer traveling within close circles of comfort."

"Birds of a feather."

"Just so. Of course, sentients thrive here who are *not* similar to us."

"I wonder ... never mind."

"Why not ask your wonders?"

"All right. What about the Scome? Seems they would've fit nicely into our little circle."

Rider looked away. "Surely. David, why are humans obsessed with the Scome?"

I was glad the yellow eyes were turned away. "Mostly the mystery of their disappearance, I think. And partly the resemblance."

"Resemblance."

I frowned. "In pictures, they appear more human than even Gray Hhoymon—if you ignore skin coloration, lack of body hair, and making *me* look bulky."

I braced myself. "What happened to them?" I asked flatly.

"A question superb," Rider said, swiveling its eyes back toward me.

Suddenly, I was sweating. And fuming. "Well? Did they leave their world voluntarily? Were they all wiped out?"

"Ayn-Khanuum! Hoping were you to surprise me into *confession*?" Rider sounded as angry as me.

"But you have the answer, don't you?"

"If so, are we not *both* hoarding information?"

I felt such a rush of fear my vision darkened. How much did the Common know? Rider had stopped eating, half a fern protruding from the cinnamon abdomen. "Let us agree," it said in a calmer voice, "to leap topic. Can you explain your suit changing tone?"

"No. Not really."

"So," Rider grunted. "How sad to interrupt our festival of ignorance, but Blenn have loaned us a spaceship. And since they mistrust their best technology, they will not swim easy until we have returned with no dents in the jumper or ourselves. Are you fully breakfasted and ready to go sound-hearing?"

Who could turn down an offer like that?

After the Hall of Games, Great Hall Four seemed almost cozy. But today it was busy, and some very strange creatures had emerged from the woodwork, perhaps literally.

The Blenn spaceship proved to be a Glinda the Good bubble. We soared into the sky without noise or discomfort. At Rider's command, the spherical shell around us turned utterly transparent except for a small blot that dimmed Crossroad's sun regardless of the ship's orientation.

Actually being there, floating high above a planetary surface, was infinitely more thrilling than watching even the clearest virtual image.

From ten thousand miles above Earth's atmosphere, if holicons can be trusted, our little planet is a shy beauty, a turquoise marvel with blue-white endcaps, a spherical ocean obscured by cloud and politely interrupted by continents, outlined in space by cobalt fluorescence. Even our clouds are gorgeous: translucent bands or soft wads assembled in flowing rows and elegant spirals. Subtly tinted landmasses support mountains too small to seem three-dimensional. The terminator line, where twilight mediates night and day, is faintly blurred but has a reasonably smooth, precise curve.

From the same height, Crossroad was a bully: a golden giant where size, density, and weak tidal forces conspired to produce geological prodigies. Earth was flat by comparison.

With its high albedo, outrageous mountain ranges, immense chasms and canyons, icecaps just thin enough for the ocher-colored ground beneath to bleed through, and no visible oceans, Crossroad seemed too big, bright, dry, and too damn fancy to be real. Patches of fog drifted mostly around the lowlands, and the relatively few clouds appeared dispirited, as if sulking at being asked to cover too much terrain.

Commonworld glowed, crowned in power and light with its global corona of luminous ultra-red and deep blue. Its terminator, fainter but far wider than Earth's, zigzagged so much in following the exuberant topography it seemed to be spelling out primeval words in some forgotten language of titans.

And despite all this beauty, I kept remembering Strong's smile. What was *wrong* with me?

Our flight was, in both senses, the high point of my day. The forces keeping us aloft also provided a slow, rocking motion, which Blenn, according to Rider, found soothing.

"Have to say," I admitted, "Blenn know how to travel."

"You hear why we are so impressed with them?"

"Definitely. Not only is this one elegant device, I think it's been personalized for humans; even the air smells right. And that *view*!" At the moment we gazed down on a vast amber desert. "Are *you* comfortable?"

"Yes."

"Got one minor worry. How's our oxygen supply?"

Rider slurped. "Adroit the Blenn are at folding things within things. We have sufficient breathables for a most long journey, my friend."

Origami folded space? "Good. Great. So what the hell are we doing here?"

"This is not enjoyable?"

"Very. But you must have better things to do than take me sightseeing."

Finger-tentacles made a brushing motion. "You suspect me of exterior motives."

I snorted. "I wonder why."

Rider searched my face. "Something in you is *different* this turn, David. You are ... stronger. Can you guess why I brought you here?"

"I imagine for the same reason you've been so, um, closed-mouth all along."

"So?"

I pointed to the planet below. "Down there, the Minds hear every word. The ultimate eavesdroppers."

"You believe for privacy we fly?"

"Why else?"

Rider patted my hand. "You make my work easier and harder."

"Thank you. I think."

"Great efforts we've made to muffle your eaves. And while your concerns earn merit, we Common are reasonably sure we retain the Minds' primary loyalty. We believe that without our assent, no one can use them to spy. Still, our enemies seem unaccountably aware of your location. Already, we've blocked fifteen attacks armed at you."

Rider fell silent.

"Okay," I said after a minute, still digesting the fifteen attacks. "That's a lot of hedging you just did. Reasonably sure? We believe? But let's say your beliefs are justified. If the Minds won't help enemies keep tabs on me, could they somehow be used to conceal how someone *is* managing the trick? So up here, away from your synthetic intellects, you might be able to detect ... I don't know. Tracking beams or something."

Rider seemed to light up. "What a joy you are! You are more astute than—WHAT IS THAT?" A long narrow bump bulged the desert sands far below, then vanished.

Small as it had looked, that bump had been *huge*. From this height above Earth, the Great Wall of China isn't even a nubbin.

"An eruption?" I guessed.

"Of grief, I fear. Ayn-Seris! What else can go wrong?"

"Explain. Please."

Rider's leaves quivered. "Soon, David. This I promise. But for you right now, knowledge equals danger."

What could I say? I marinated in frustration while Rider accelerated our craft, gradually moving it through the planet's magenta shadow into ...

I gasped. Rider had turned us to face away from Crossroad and the sky was unbelievable, with a texture closer to a finely quilted comforter than anything astronomical. Untold billions of stars running a wide gamut of intensity and color created the effect. These tiny lights were generally dimmer than Earth's stars, but were arrayed in spectacular profusion. And the distribution seemed *organized*. Suns of similar magnitude in related hues were clumped together into geometrical clusters.

"So many stars," I whispered. "Or maybe some are galaxies? I understood Crossroad's universe was smaller than mine."

"Much smaller. Remember: this world was once attached to every Road. Some light remains transmitted."

Heavens filled with the light of a billion universes.

"Whatever our differences, Rider, I thank you for showing me this."

My guide waved a hand at the starry quilt. "Some things must be shared. It shines best without gasses in the way."

We watched the fantastic sky in silence, but didn't stay long.

Perhaps beauty overheated my brain; it spat out an extraordinary notion while we were descending to ex-terra firma much faster than we'd ascended. Rider seemed tense and impatient.

"Before we land," I said slowly, "I wanted to ask you about that strange Neme who—"

"Stop! Speak not about this, I beg you! Next destiny, we return to Hall of Games where I promised you a running. This time, perhaps no Supernals will interfere."

Rider's obvious sincerity shut me up. Still, I couldn't help speculating. If it doesn't shed water, doesn't fly, and doesn't quack, it's *not* a duck. Something, I thought, is horribly wrong.

CHAPTER 20
NO FUN AND GAMES

After we'd reached the Hall, my guide led me past the Corridor of Arms to a subjective track, its entrance a typical opening in the vast wall.

Rider explained that subjective domains work through "perceptual induction." Once the local Mind determines the user's species and preferences, it generates a customized information stream, which the user's mind interprets as appropriate sensations.

I would've gladly foregone the pleasures of subjective running and gotten down to business, but this was my excuse for being here. And since my previous experience with domains had been such fun, I wasn't thrilled to hand Rider my camera and step into darkness. But after I touched the plate, a human figure appeared, listed my choices, and asked for my druthers—all most civilized despite some baroque options.

I kept the experience as down to earth, so to speak, as possible. No jogging on water or underwater or on clouds, no monsters chasing me for that certain extra incentive. And it felt pleasant enough. My fourth skin converted into the perfect running ensemble including shoes, but the whole thing seemed an idiotic waste of time.

While cooling down, I decided that next time I used this facility I'd include one pursuing monster, a smallish one, just for laughs. Which proves I wasn't any kind of psychic.

Rider was gone by the time I left the domain, but Swift stood at attention, holding my camera at port arms. Thanks to Jeeves, I didn't even need a shower.

We said hello, and I asked for the grand tour. Swift proved willing although hardly eager and we spent hours roaming the vast space, taking a lunch break at the eatery where the Dancer had swept me away. No Supernals showed up to swipe my french fries, even if I could've gotten french fries. Then we resumed touring. I kept my eyes and Crossroad vision peeled for any human-style games, but stayed alert for other possibilities.

Might as well have kept all eyes shut. They spotted nary a baseball diamond, football field, or even a pinball machine, and nothing with ten squares or where the concept "10 squared" seemed relevant. But this Hall was so damn big I could've overlooked the Superdome. I kept squelching an urge to simply ask Swift where the tennis courts were hiding.

And an obvious question finally bit me: even if I found the right place, how the hell could information be hidden there from everyone but me? This was a public area where any kind of secret message could be exposed to entities with all sorts of senses. But I had to keep looking.

After five hours plus, my eyes felt like hard-boiled eggs and my brain like the pot they'd been boiled in. I thanked Swift for his help and companionship although the most companionable thing he'd done was to rush ahead at one point and say, "You wish revisit area?" which saved me from wasting even more time.

When I told him I wished to return to my apartment and have a solitary evening, just me and some documents, he offered to lead the way. Might've heard a hint of sympathy in his voice but it was probably my imagination.

But upon stepping through my door, I gave the box o' slats one sad glance, flopped into bed, and called for darkness. Didn't even have enough oomph to remove my shoes; luckily with Jeeves I didn't need to. At least I had a whole night to recharge.

This comforting thought earned me an advanced degree in anti-precognition.

The first dream came straight from memory. Our usual gang hogged our usual dining table at our usual Williamstown's hangout: Sara of course, white-haired Ben DeHut, and Professors Jimmy Wu, Bill Warner, and Nakeen McClellan.

Bill had introduced a new subject, art, and proceeded to declaim.

"I say it's all in the frame. Place a frame around *anything* and voilà! Art!"

"What about sculpture or an unframed painting?" Jimmy asked seriously.

"A sculpture is its own frame. Likewise a canvas." Bill turned toward my wife. "Sara, you're the artist here. Wouldn't you agree?"

Sara's eyes twinkled. "Sorry, William. It's your word 'anything' I contest. Art without feeling is mere decoration. Framing cannot elevate decoration."

Sara's insight delighted me even more than Bill's dropped jaw, but as I reached to pat my wife's leg under the table, she vanished. A sick feeling of loss swept me into another dream....

I was back home, lying in my own bed, alone. A full moon shone through my thin, summer curtains as they rippled in the occasional warm breeze. Outside, an all-cricket orchestra kept rehearsing.

I'd just let my eyes close up shop for the night when I heard—a footstep? No. Too heavy and, somehow, *damp*. The crickets shut up, leaving their symphony unfinished. I sat up.

For a full minute, nothing. Then, with an aggressively slow cadence, something stomped up the stairs, one at a time. My bedroom door, ghostly in the milky moonlight, wasn't quite closed.

I waited, heart hammering. The moonlight dimmed. As the darkness grew, so did my dread.

When everything became pitch black, I heard the door open with exquisite gentleness. A reek filled the room, worse than rotting meat. Why weren't my microdocs filtering this out?

That thought was so out-of-context, it woke me a little. Wasn't this just a bad dream? I tried like hell to wake up. And couldn't.

A final stomp shook the house and a dim sliver of phosphorescent green glimmered in the doorway. Had no idea what it was, but that sliver was the single most terrifying thing I'd ever seen.

Suddenly, a sword-shaped flame ignited in the blackness. The backspray of light revealed its wielder, yet another figure I recognized from my dream in the Constructor restaurant: the feminine-looking creature with small shoulder-wings. In a dream, dreaming about a dream that hadn't been a dream?

The glow illuminated nothing more, but I felt a horrible, growing pressure and somehow knew that something too enormous to fit through the doorway in one piece was squeezing more and more of itself into my bedroom. The air stank like a cesspool and kept thickening, almost compressing to liquid. I couldn't breathe.

The sword slashed into apparently empty space, leaving a fiery trail behind. I knew it hit *something* from the dull thud and shower of pink sparks, but the pressure only increased.

The tiny wings blurred, producing an eerie whine. My protector held her blade higher and its fire roared, heating to a searing sky-blue. The weapon opened like a flower, the painfully blue flames curling away like pedals, revealing a thinner flame, translucent and violet.

Another sword slash. This time it had an effect.

A bubbling screech scared me half to death. From the sound, something smashed my door and its frame to splinters and then shattered my staircase on its way down.

The air cleared. In the window, moonlight returned.

I remembered my nightstand lamp and reached to flip it on. For just an instant, my guardian seemed to be a nude human woman, except for the wings. Then the illusion fell apart. Her breasts and nipples and pubic hair were only tricky shadows. Even with my lamp on max, her wings were the only part of her I could see clearly.

But now I realized she wasn't exactly *in* my room. Past her were walls in all sorts of colors and at all sorts of crazy angles. Then eyes less defined than smoke met mine. I was sure hers held a message.

Next thing I remember, I was waking up.

Honestly, I'd prefer forgetting the next five days. Friday night, by my watch, I didn't stay up to celebrate New Year. By Saturday evening, I was in even less of a party mood. Ditto for Sunday, Monday, and Tuesday. My mission was shaping up beautifully as a total failure.

Every day had become identical.

After awakening too early, I'd order coffee and a piece of fruit—the converter had a talent for fruit. I'd allow myself one hour to study manuscripts and learned some fascinating things about Hhoymon, but nothing immediately relevant. Those few documents concerning Nemes, Common, or Scome were suspiciously uninformative.

When I belatedly noticed *two* hours had passed, I'd make a frantic dash to the restaurant where I'd apologize to Rider for losing track of time, again. Then we'd eat and talk.

Post breakfast, Swift or Strong would accompany me to my next bout with the Hall of Games, which I'd mentally divided into eight sections. After my obligatory run, I'd search another segment of infinity, which I sneakily justified as research since the nature of the ... diversions here did provide useful information about the abilities and preferences of various ultra-alien species. Every morning, I fully intended to ask my current companion where the human games were located, but never followed through. Could be, I'd acquired a perverse compulsion to find the spot unaided, or I plain didn't *want* to find it. The consequences of both failure and success terrified me.

After at least five hours without spotting a chess-set or luge track, I'd return to the Enclave for dinner with Rider, Swift, and Strong. I'd excuse myself early, go home, study some more, fret about my continuing attraction to Strong, and throw myself into bed for some—ha!—sleep.

Every morning, I looked younger and felt more exhausted. The only bright notes: no stings, cave-ins, Supernal distractions, or potent nightmares.

A break in this stressful monotony occurred on Tuesday, when Rider ferried me to Blenntown. We used an ultra-fast "Super-Safe-road" to reach Triangle Fourteen near Crossroad's equator.

Blenntown: an ultra-alien Venice with liquid streets and briny odors. Colored mists lofted Blenn-kind up the walls of geodesic domes, into doorways hundreds of feet up. In the canals, the Blenn became torpedoes leaving v-shaped wakes. Amphibians *plus*, said Rider. Vestigial wings rattling beneath chitin produced their buzzing voices.

Nemes cruised around on silent boats but, oddly, I saw more Vyre.

Two Blenn towed our raft to the dome-shaped residence of a Least, the local queen. Even the huge, fierce-looking Blenn warriors guarding the entrance were self-deprecating as they let us in. We were expected. Rider warned me not to say "your Highness."

The dome, from inside, proved to be a symphony in stained glass accompanied by smokes rising from golden censors. Couldn't smell a thing, so evidently my microdocs vetoed the smoke. Ribbons of pink mist suspended the faceted censors in midair. Lovely, but my mind was elsewhere.

I'd been on Crossroad a week, had achieved nothing, and my time here was running out. I had to find the human games *today*.

In a wide and shallow pool, a Blenn-shaped giant with a grotesquely distended abdomen floated on her back. I know a queen when I see one. After Rider introduced me, she greeted me via a permanently mounted speechstaff and offered her regrets if I found the environment uncomfortably ostentatious.

In my distraction, I blurted out, "It's beautiful. But I'm surprised someone with your title would live in a palace."

She responded as if my words hadn't set a new benchmark for the concept "ill-considered."

"Perhaps I can clarify, Professor. We Leasts are servants of servants. And since our planets are crowded, we require much soothing water."

Social lubricant?

The Queen paused for a time, perhaps offering me the floor, before continuing. "For a great depth of time, competition among ourselves has been hazardous to us, while cooperation has encouraged our survival. It has become our nature to defer to others."

Another pause, which I filled with a lame, "I've noticed."

"You are a clear observer, Professor. You are probably aware that deference itself can become competitive."

"Oh?"

"Imagine two of us arriving together at a doorway wide enough for only one."

Right. Two Blenn could make Alphonse and Gaston look like amateurs. "How do you work it out?"

"Our solution involves a form of sacrifice. After ages of overcrowding, we have learned to ... taste pride's pressure in members of our own species. When the pair reach the door, the humblest one walks through, putting herself first to allow the other the humility of putting herself last. I hope I have spoken plainly for I have already wasted too much of your precious time and energy."

Reading between the lines, the Queen had more important business and the audience was over. Rider and I thanked her, she thanked us twice as hard, and then a Blenn "wet-nurse"—surely a term meaning something different to amphibians—led us from the throne-less throne room.

On its surface, this meeting had accomplished nothing and there'd been no reason for the Queen's invitation. But I'd gotten the message: the Blenn expected to have dealings with humanity in the future. The Queen wanted us to know the rules.

Back in the Hall, Rider passed the Goldberg baton to Strong. She'd taken to holding my hand as we wandered, and I often felt she was the one leading. I wanted to ask the obvious question but for the umpteenth time, I balked. So I wasted more hours searching the seemingly immeasurable for the seemingly unfindable until my energy bottomed out.

Waking up Wednesday morning, I knew this turn was likely my last and I *had* to act. My heart began pounding. I wasn't hungry, but to establish a ghost of normality, I ordered my usual pre-breakfast breakfast. And, in the same spirit, I pulled out a random slat from the box and stared, without much initial interest, at a long and nearly incomprehensible Hhoymon article about "molecular couriers."

It slowly dawned on me these couriers were microdocs. The specific topic concerned using them for biological "tracing," analogous to our technique of injecting microbubbles or nuclear dyes in medical imaging.

I reread the beginning paragraphs, but couldn't follow the leaps in reasoning so I skimmed the document trying to snag the gist. By the time I left for official breakfast, my head buzzed with ideas.

It was Swift's turn with me in the Hall of Frustration. The moment we arrived he pushed an eye my way. "Have idea, comrade. Care to visit human games in Hall?"

Unbelievable.

But I was more surprised when we arrived at the right spot. No wonder I'd missed it. Its largest feature was a pint-sized basketball court with a hoop set at half-mast. I gawked at the jungle gym, slide, tetherball setup, and other elementary-school paraphernalia.

"What *is* this, Swift?"

For the first time, I heard this Neme hum with amusement. "Even great minds fumble, nyet?"

He explained. After Nemes made first contact with humanity, they'd come home, like all good tourists, laden with videos. The Hhoymon council obtained some of these, as the Common knew they would, so the Common transmitted a warning to Hhoymon City: you must repress any temptation to bypass our current prohibition against visiting Earth; the ambient physics there will reduce any Hhoymon from Homer to Homer Simpson. Admittedly, the warning may have been worded differently.

"Why should Hhoymon," I asked, "be that interested in us?"

"Shape similarity. Mage of mirrors says inclusive spirit between all Hhoymon races due to evolution. Very long warfare. Only tribes embracing *all* Hhoymon forms survived."

"You're saying they're ... instinctively drawn to creatures resembling themselves?"

"Evolutionary urge to combine groups."

"Huh. But that doesn't explain this playground."

"Earth visit impractical for Hhoymon, but they expected Common would invite humans here. They studied visual recordings from Nemes. One showed human youths in schoolyard."

"Oh. They built this for our *kids*."

"No. Hhoymon consider children banausic, not worth recording. Seeing images, they assumed humans, too, have divergent sizes."

"Good Lord. They figured the kids were silver humans! Or white."

"Da."

"Must've been a shock when we fell a little tall of their expectations."

I chuckled. The Hhoymon had installed games they just knew we'd enjoy. Such as hopscotch. But playground or not, the logic remained. Any message in the Hall intended for a human should be here....

"This place," I tried to say smoothly, "brings back my childhood. Mind if I poke around?"

"You are guest, comrade. Do as you wish." Strong appeared stiff as ever, but I sensed he was privately amused.

Fighting an urge to run, I strolled toward the tetherball pole. The sight of it really did bring back childhood. Here was an activity clearly designed by sadists for masochists, a game with options: hurting your hand by hitting the rope or the metal insert where the ball is attached. Or getting your pain fix when the ball slams into your face. A game calculated to maximize aggression.

I examined ball, rope, and pole. Nada.

Then I noticed a four-square court painted on the floor and nearby, for those with lesser motor skills, a bisected rectangle for two-square. At last, games associated with the word "square!" But I saw no message or clue.

Next, the jungle gym....

Twenty minutes later, I squatted on a bench three sizes too small for me and fought despair. *Think, David!* Believe *the clue is here. Narrow the field.*

Hopscotch? Too much hop and too little scotch for my money. For some crazy reason, I envisioned a Blenn jumping back and forth. *Tetherball?* In my mind's eye, two Blenn batted the ball back and forth.

All right, subconscious. Seems you've got your teeth into something. Care to let me in on it? No? Then kindly stop filling my head with garbage. Too damn bad there's no such thing as a ten-square game—

I jumped to my feet.

"You are well, comrade?"

"Perfect."

Binary. Idiotically simple. In binary, "10" means two. The real message was "Hall of Games, two-square!" So obvious, why had the unknown party who'd scribbled the message bothered being cryptic at all?

Still, I felt as if the weight of worlds had fallen off my shoulders.

That glorious feeling lasted almost three minutes as I paced over the twinned squares, scrutinizing every detail while trying to appear introspective. Nothing. This was getting awkward. I glanced over at Swift.

A stroke of luck! That birdlike character I'd noticed several times now had struck up a conversation with Swift, keeping him occupied. No one was watching me.

I dropped to my knees and went over every inch of the small court with eyes, and hands too in case the message was tactile. Periodically, I glanced at my palms. Writing could be the same color as its background and might be designed to transfer. My hands got sore, but not even a palm-reader could've found a secret clue.

I pulled the game's big ball off its stand, studied it, shook it, and bounced it in hopes of a revealing print. No luck.

Back on the court, I tried everything from scraping my feet to crossing my eyes. I'd been so damn sure.

In a last-ditch hope of future revelation, I took a picture of the squares. If I put a printout under my pillow tonight, I thought bitterly, maybe the Truth Fairy will come.

Don't ask about the rest of that day.

The night was no improvement. I lay in bed and endlessly retraced my logic. Someone had gone through great contortions to provide directions to that spot. I should've found *something*. Perhaps my binary idea was wrong. Or I'd been too dense to find the message, or it'd been erased. I felt sorry for my Chean-shee neighbors. I was undoubtedly making a very loud and unpleasant telepathic noise.

Sleep, when it finally came, brought no revelations.

My eyes opened to my latest bedtime decoration: a tropical lagoon at midnight with palm trees and a quarter moon to keep the stars from getting lonely. Felt as if I hadn't slept at all.

"Scour," I muttered. "And the usual." What the hell was I supposed to do now?

I took my coffee to my latest Mind-generated desk and thumbed through the Hhoymon monograph on microdoc tracing techniques.

Suddenly, the room felt like a cage, and I had a nasty sense of someone spying on me though the bars. I started pacing like a trapped tiger, passed my camera, grabbed it, and pressed the display button. Surely, I'd missed *something*.

And there it was.

"Stupid, stupid, stupid ..." With each "stupid" I banged myself in the forehead with my palm, but gently. Clearly, I couldn't afford the loss of even a single brain cell. Jeeves roiled uneasily.

"Now see what you've done, David," I ranted. "You've gone and upset the wardrobe."

In retrospect, it was too damn obvious for words. The photo Rilka had shown me had been taken with a *human* camera. And who else but me would be likely to carry such a device around the Hall of Games?

My eyes stayed glued to the display. Superimposed on the two-square court was an incredibly detailed map leading from the Hall of Games to a specific point in Triangle Six.

I knew where to go and how to get there. My sigh of relief seemed to last forever.

REVELATION THREE
MIRRORMAGE

The fool resents the wise,
The wise accepts the fool;
But who can see them both
As ripples in a pool?

—BALANCED CLEARHOUSE

CHAPTER 21
HEX MARKS

The restaurant seemed unusually crowded and the crowd was unusual: some truly exotic diners were keeping the regulars company. The atmosphere felt different, keyed up. Maybe it was just me.

I noticed, toward the back, a medium-size biped dressed entirely in bright gold with a ship's prow of a head and four arms. He, she, or it kept having little burps of levitation, rising several feet into the air then slowly settling. Probably ordered the beans.

I joined Rider, Strong, and Swift at our official table but wasn't hungry. The Chean-shee kept scraping utensils against plates.

Rider seemed tense, uncharacteristically quiet. Swift and Strong, perhaps compensating, argued about Clearhouse's fifth aphorism, stressing the importance of balance in all things.

"The sage," Strong declared sweetly, "was talkin' an *active* process. Constantly correctin' imbalance, not keepin' some fixed rigidity."

"Have not *claimed* balance equals rigidity! Issue is speed of corrections." Swift made a seesaw motion with one paw. "If cup teeters, is balanced? Your thoughts, Guardian?"

"I think irrelevant philosophy disrupts digestion."

While Rider grumbled, the gold-clad creature passed our table, lumbering along on two short and strangely jointed legs.

"Recant I do," Rider said, watching the colorful figure exit the restaurant, rise several inches, flip upside down, frantically wave all four arms to get upright, then float away like a rogue balloon. "For some, equilibrium is of paramount relevance."

I gathered my nerve. "When, exactly, will I have to return to Earth?"

"Soon," was all Rider would say.

For me, reaction was setting in. I'd found the map. Terrific. But I couldn't imagine anything riskier than following it. And I needed to start right away. I put my hands under the table to hide the shaking.

Swift migrated an eye toward me. "To Game Hall after breakfast, comrade?"

"Not today, Swift. I'd better take a break from running to let my muscles recover." I swallowed hard. "If no one objects, I'd like to spend this whole turn studying those manuscripts Strong brought me." I hoped the speech sounded more natural to ultra-alien ears than to mine.

"As you desire," offered Rider. "Will we hear you at dinner?"

"Maybe. I might get too ... engrossed to take a break. Don't wait for me."

"If your intentions change, let me know."

"Of course."

The Nemes resumed bickering, and I mostly tuned out until Strong dropped an unfamiliar name. "Who's this Koriosae?" I interrupted.

"Spherecerer of Leadership, sweetheart. The ultimate exec."

"Other Hhoymon name is Yoav," Swift volunteered sourly, "'Busy One.'"

"So busy he needs two names?"

He pointed all three eyes toward me. "Hhoymon honor separate Traveler aspects with separate titles. Compassionate Seris is also Quanen the Healer. Urien the Messenger, Supernal of Communication, has many names."

Urien. What had Rider told me? "Isn't Urien the insight Supernal?"

"Da. And in other aspects Reyaenal the Laughing One, Amien the Adventurer, and Hhurm the Hidden."

"What kind of adventures would the Honcho of Insight have?"

When Swift didn't answer Strong took up the slack. "Those involvin' self-discovery, the way I hear it."

Service was slow, probably delayed by the extra customers. I bolted a small breakfast without consulting my taste buds and made my exit ASAP.

I now had to accomplish two impossible tasks: leave the Enclave *secretly* and conceal my absence should anyone peek into my apartment using the Mind. Of course, if anyone other than the Mind had me under continual surveillance, the ball game was over. Couldn't think about that. No matter what, I had to follow the map.

I stepped into my room and got to work. Strong had claimed the Mind could mold the apartment floor into anything I wanted....

"Mind, create a solid, animated image of my body. Seat it at the desk, studying."

Sure, the idea was beyond far-fetched. Yet there he was, a carbon-less copy of me, poring over some manuscript, occasionally rubbing his overly long chin. Perfect. But the sight dropped an icicle down my back, which wasn't due to my tragic resemblance to Ichabod Crane.

"How accurate is this image?" I asked quietly.

"The model is a physical duplicate of your appearance to the useful limit of resolution."

The bathroom mirror hadn't told the whole story. My doppelgänger practically glowed with youthful health. Full head of hair, even. Somehow, it didn't seem wholesome. But right now, I had more pressing issues....

I'd understood precious little of the Hhoymon tract concerning microdocs, but one concept had managed to squeeze through. Given proper instructions, microdocs would leave the host body and sally forth to perform simple tasks.

Turning my back on my anachronistic decoy, I mentally ordered the 'docs to dispatch a Special Ops team to transport themselves to Goldberg Two and, from there, begin emitting human-style thought forms. Should the duplicate vanish, their orders were to retreat to home base.

I asked my remaining microdocs to recreate my Neme disguise. Was the Mind's imagination-vacuum seamless enough for *this*?

"Mind, how many people are in this room? And where are they?"

"Two. A known human sits at the desk; an unknown Neme stands by the bed."

I felt off-balance, as if I'd braced myself to lift a boulder only to find it papier-mâché. I was two for two in experiments only a nut would've believed could work.

But how could the Mind take Fake Me seriously when it itself was generating the physical illusion? Hell, even if it really was that gullible, it was probably recording everything I did and said.

Still, my microdocs kept surpassing reasonable expectations. More proof a certain Cygnus had enhanced them?

Since it might seem a tad suspicious to someone peering into my apartment and counting two of me, I ordered the Mind to eliminate my backup and had Jeeves drop the disguise. Proof of concept, accomplished.

Grabbing my camera, I sat at the desk—giving me a weird kind of déjà vu—and called up the map. In an emergency, I might not have time to consult it, so I needed a cramming session.

I cranked the camera's zoom function. The near-microscopic labels were in English; green stars evidently marked cities or enclaves, color-coded wiggles indicated transportation types. No scale bar. No saying how long the trip would take.

One corner held a directional legend, fancier than any human compass rose including our thirty-two-point nautical version. This flower had sixteen major petals, each subdivided eight times.

According to Balanced Clearhouse, "Function chases form." Crossroad was too damn big for fewer compass points to be useful.

Someone, I told myself, *is procrastinating*.

Rather than attempt to memorize the entire map, I set out to learn the sequence of turns, an orienteering trick I'd learned from my father. A glowing line highlighted the suggested route.

A tunnel at the back of the Hall of Games led to something labeled a "High-Speed Secured Transport" which would carry me to Triangle Six.

Once there, the path was straightforward until, shortly past the spot marked "Oracle Waters," I'd find a float-tube, assuming that's what was meant by a violet dot labeled "Descending Hhoymon Shaft." From there, the map had a new feature: dotted lines in pale turquoise. I caught myself rubbing my chin. When had I developed the habit?

Dotted lines. An underground route? In any case, the path doubled back toward "Oracle Waters" via a maze of hallways so elaborate that here, I'd *have* to depend on the map. Almost directly beneath the "Waters" was a spot marked with a bright red hexagon.

Hex marks the spot.

I put the camera down and wiped my forehead. Me: sweaty despite my fourth skin and panting like a setter in July. I forced myself to take deeper breaths. If I was this scared while still safe in my apartment ... I couldn't afford to finish the thought. *Concentrate, David!*

Okay. I could fool the Minds. One problem solved. And by now, I could get to the Hall on my own. Probably do it in my sleep. Unfortunately, I'd always seen plenty of fellow travelers on the way, and they'd seen me. I needed to keep my trip *secret*. Hell, even if I followed a different route, call it plan beta, I could easily encounter living beings. Then perhaps a disguise? Could microdocs become a camouflage suit? Or better—if the spider-god could do it—could they make me *invisible*?

For once, the little buggers failed. And when I tried to alter its colors, Jeeves refused to deviate from whiteness by so much as a pinstripe.

It was willing to change *shape*, however. After some fiddling, I got Jeeves vaguely formed into a Neme-style pelt, asked the Mind to manifest a mirror, and checked the result. The effect was ideal, I thought, for scaring children and attracting horrified attention. I returned the suit to normal.

My Swan-altered garment seemed far too distinctive so I grabbed some Earth clothes and put on a shirt, which disintegrated so fast I couldn't even save the buttons. Upset, I pulled down another shirt.

"This time, Jeeves," I commanded, "*don't* eat the competition!"

The second shirt also dissolved.

What was this? Wardrobe rivalry? Or did Jeeves sense a safety issue?

Plan beta seemed to be my only choice.

"Mind, display every path from here to the Hall of Games."

I goggled at the posthumous Jackson Pollock. "Um, show only those likely to be deserted in ... thirty terrestrial minutes. Label them in English."

Much better, but the picture remained fearfully complicated and included unfamiliar labels. Safe-roads and Glideways were marked as such, but what the hell was a "Jump-way?" Too many turns to memorize, and I couldn't take *this* map along.

Then a lonely neuron must have fired. "David," I told myself as kindly as possible, "What is the purpose of that rectangular object currently resting on yonder desk?"

I grabbed the camera and ordered the Mind to slowly shrink the wall-image. When it fit the viewer, I took a picture, had the Mind erase the wall, and studied this new map. Which roads would prove less traveled?

I memorized a few starting options, turned off the display, slipped the camera strap over my head, and gulped down some water despite not being thirsty. When would I get another chance? I tried to use the toilet. Nothing doing. Jeeves had been handling waste disposal solo for almost a week.

Suddenly, my legs were as steady as a newborn colt's. *Too much was riding on this!* Whatever courage I'd gained through Arfaenn wasn't enough. I couldn't judge which was larger: my responsibility or the danger. I felt thrown into a horror movie; I *knew* something ghastly was coming, but not what or when. Only one thing was obvious: the intended victim.

Ever since my arrival on Crossroad, I'd been guided, fed, protected, and in general, coddled. Facing this incredible world alone terrified me. I didn't begin to know enough. And Rider had mentioned ... enemies.

But humanity *had* to know if the Common were a pack of liars, and

I was the only human with any chance to find out. I set my watch-alarm to go off in ten minutes; when it did, I'd walk out the door, ready or not. Meanwhile, I needed to pry the suction cups of my mind away from fear. What would make a good distraction?

"Mind," I said slowly. "Can you display images of the Supernals?"

"Some images can be provided, but visual recordings of Spherecerers degrade with time."

"Figures. Show me—" *Who was the one living on Earth?* "—Chybris the Librarian."

I stared, then blinked hard. It didn't help. The creature still had three long necks, each terminating in a different species of head. The left one belonged on a dolphin, the right on a supersized eagle; between those, a human giant's face smiled with palpable sincerity, huge eyes seeming to meet mine....

"Try Binae the Diplomat instead."

An outdoor scene appeared on the wall with a crowd of Common facing a ground-hugging cloud that floated steadily despite gusts mussing head-crests and ear-leaves. It took me a minute to realize the Common were talking, but not with each other. Either they were crazy, or the cloud was Binae.

A moment later, it condensed into a glowing shape resembling a Common but much larger, a transformation that didn't discourage Binae from standing comfortably in midair.

Fascinating, but none of this fed my starving courage. What about fighting fire with heat? One Supernal in particular scared me.

"Replace Binae with Maanza."

My murderous instructor from the projective domain appeared, striding through some Great Hall and He *towered*. My neck hairs rose as the Supernal of Warfare turned and bowed in my direction.

"Scour," I choked out. The desk and chair vanished but the Traveler's image lingered. Maanza lifted one incredible limb as if bidding me farewell, then slowly faded to nothing.

"*Nice* distraction, Dave," I told myself in a shaking voice. "So very relaxing." And another photo op missed. I was *wearing* a camera and hadn't thought to use it! The Travelers were too much. Wasn't even safe to look at their damn pictures.

My alarm beeped. Perfect.

I killed the beeps, ordered the Mind to recreate my decoy, had Jeeves send missionaries to emit human vibes from the decoy while emitting Neme vibes on my behalf, trotted to the hallway, and glanced back into the room. There was me, studying at a recreated desk. I felt jealous as hell. After closing the door, I turned left instead of heading toward the Enclave. Didn't see any giant invisible spiders, but then, one never does.

God above! Had anyone, anywhere, been in so far over their head?

"A thousand-mile-journey," I muttered, "begins with but a single shlep."

CHAPTER 22
THE BIG JUMP

Right away, I felt it. Couldn't pinpoint it, but something more fundamental than humidity had changed for the worse. As I scurried down unfamiliar corridors, I was sure something nasty squatted around the next corner, or the corner behind me. But Jeeves stayed placid, which helped. A little.

On the bright side, I was unbelievably lucky. The only person I saw while sneaking out of the Enclave was that silver-eyed restaurant employee who passed by without a glance.

Two Glideways later, still no company and nothing pounced, but I could almost taste the threat. Then I came to the "Jump-way," which resembled a Safe-road, only the jellied light was greenish-gold. As fog appeared, I began to sit down, SOP for Safe-road travel.

But this time, no foggy chair caught me. The fall jarred my teeth despite impromptu microdoc padding and the cold floor was either vibrating or carrying a mild electric charge. What the hell?

Strong had taught me how to operate Blenn transportation, and I'd done so dozens of times unaided. Nothing to it. You just imagine yourself traveling, and the Safe-road handles the rest.

I stood up and imagined for all I was worth. Nothing happened.

I wondered if the problem involved my mental disguise. Was the Jump-way waiting for instructions in some Neme-specific format? *Damn.* I *had* to take this route or backtrack practically to my apartment, but if I dropped my microdoc mask, the nearest Mind would spot me.

Wait. Could microdocs translate my *visualizations* into Neme? I tried again, asking Jeeves to act as interpreter.

Success! Just not in any way I could've expected. The fog grabbed me and placed me on the vibrating floor, stomach-side down. I began to slide forward.

Two things happened in rapid-fire sequence. My speed increased sharply, and I heard more than felt something small and solid bounce off my neck. I reached up and touched a hard microdoc collar. Then I knew what had changed.

I hadn't sensed the force protecting me from stings, but I'd felt its withdrawal....

I forgot all about stings. With a new, appalling burst of acceleration, I was *moving*. Any friction between my body and the road-surface, and I'd have been eroded to a smear.

Wind blasted my face; by Crossroad standards, this Jump-way was crude stuff. Jeeves thickened and generated a hood with built-in goggles.

The tunnel ended in a cave, but my ride wasn't over. The fog lofted me up toward the stalactite-covered ceiling and through a thin aperture between stony spears.

Then I was outdoors, flying between starlit frost-covered canyon walls at a speed that shamed the word "reckless." At that horrible moment, someone *really* stomped on the accelerator.

Some filtering system kicked in; the wind force remained nasty but constant as I was flung over a canyon wall and hurled thousands of feet upward. My flight leveled and even from this height, the ground below rushed by.

Clearly, some irresponsible daredevil species had perverted Blenn technology to create this damned Jump-way. The ride wasn't even smooth. Patches of turbulence shook me up in every sense, and I felt anything but safe. I put my arms out diver-style and the turbulence eased slightly. Now I was hurtling through the atmosphere like Superman, in a similar body posture even, but with one difference: I could be crushed.

The trip went on far too long.

Whenever I soared into sunlight; my goggles darkened. I appreciated the courtesy, but I grew a new worry. Safe-roads automatically carry the user to a specific destination. Was the same thing true here? Was I suffering in the wrong direction? As if some comptroller found the idea offensive, I abruptly dropped like an unusually aerodynamic stone.

Before I could brace myself, I was hurled at break-everything speed through another narrow opening. A moment later, I stood on trembling legs. Lesson learned. Next time, I'd jump some *other* way.

A brief map-check, and I hopped a Glideway terminating midway through the Hall of Games.

My chances of strolling along the Hall unobserved seemed none to less, so my hopes rested on avoiding anyone who knew me.

At least, I'd lost my sense of horrible pursuit, and my astonishing luck held: didn't see a soul. This end of infinity appeared deserted. Maybe today was some Crossroad holiday and that's why the Enclave restaurant had been packed. But it was a long and nervous trip to my exit point. Which gave me time for second thoughts concerning the mockup in my apartment.

No one had outright forbidden me from roaming Crossroad on my own. If someone found me here, I could try for a plausible excuse. But if anyone discovered my *decoy*, whoops. My behavior would look too fishy for even Rider to enjoy.

And I should've brought along food. At least I wasn't thirsty. Yet.

Chewing only on regrets, I left the Hall via a curving tunnel. I was now, supposedly, at my starting point on the hidden two-square map. I pushed camera buttons to call up that map. Full speed ahead....

To my utter relief, the "High-Speed Secured Transport" was indeed a Super-safe-road. Visions of another sky-jaunt or riding some turbocharged tsunami had been haunting me. And Super-safe-roads are *fast*. I only had fifteen minutes to contemplate how hungry, frightened, and stupid I was. Then I arrived in Triangle Six. Where I made an astounding discovery: I was *smiling*.

Smiling? Fear and stress remained on my payroll, but a crazy exuberance had joined the staff. Had my impossible rejuvenation turned me goofy? Or was it the scholar in me, blindly eager to examine a Scome machine?

Following the marked route, I entered a Glideway that let me off in a corridor halfway between "Learner's Lair" and "Oracle Waters." The environment changes startled me.

Soft, low grass carpeted the floor, bordered in taller grasses and fragrant flowers. I took deep appreciative breaths. Occasional alien gnats darted through the air along with wispy, ribbon-like creatures.

It hit me how sterile Crossroad had seemed until now. Reminded me of a time I'd been visiting an injured friend in the hospital, too worried about her to be conscious of institutional surroundings and medical smells. Upon finally stepping outside, I'd been overwhelmed by fresh air and natural beauty.

Illumination here was strange, but aesthetic. Large lily-like jewels sprouted from the walls, each glowing a single color—sky-blue, emerald, amber, or wine red.

Movement in the grasses edging the floor caught my eye.

I had company. Lots. The taller grass was inhabited or infested with small animals: alien mice with too many legs, alien spiders with too few, and snaky critters with coppery, knobbed skins. Luckily, the fauna kept itself near the walls. I didn't fancy stepping on any, *especially* the arachnoids.

I hurried along, so busy certifying no stragglers were underfoot that I didn't notice the weird odor and open doorway to one side quickly enough. I stared into what might've been a non-parallel tapas bar catering to particularly alien aliens. Here, my luck reached the miraculous.

Surprise and some grotesque condiments held me frozen, but not one bulging eye bulged my way. Finally, it occurred to me that moving on wasn't a bad idea. Appalled by my carelessness, I started jogging.

Running on grass felt comforting. I let my legs cut loose and avoided thinking about spiders. Soon, I heard a rumbling hiss. A waterfall? With luck this should be Oracle Waters.

Beneath my feet, the lawn brightened to neon green, reminiscent of the verdant carpet in my Dancer-induced vision. The walls became garlanded in delicate silver vines with tiny gold and purple flowers. Fewer lily-jewels, but these vines glowed silver-blue.

The tunnel turned misty, and it seemed odd to still breathe the arid Neme air. Jeeves shrank to shorts and a mesh top. Those "condiments" had killed my appetite, but I should've been thirsty. Had to be microdocs, gathering moisture and feeding it into my bloodstream. Apparently, Jeeves could add catheter to its résumé.

I ran until the waterfall bellowed and the ground shivered. Oracle Waters had to be just ahead. But when microdocs suddenly flowed over my arms and legs, I braked to a cautious walk. Everything appeared peaceful. Ahead, the walls grew progressively farther apart, and the ceiling rose steeply.

I kept walking.

A quarter mile later, I came to an enclosed valley bisected with a foamy river rushing away from a tremendous, Niagara-like cascade on my far right. The lawn turned damp and slippery. A translucent amber bridge vaulted the river. Obeying the map, I crossed over and entered a corridor dead ahead. Back to jogging. *False alarm, wardrobe?*

I reached a pair of float-tubes and grinned, relieved that my map-reading abilities hadn't abandoned me. I hopped inside the violet tube and timed the descent. Three minutes. Kept expecting my ears to pop, but the local Mind must have intervened. On the way down, I lost my smile.

From the tube, I stepped onto a partly foggy, partly sunlit meadow. Could've sworn I was outdoors. Rocks littered the mossy ground, which eased down to a small, central pond reflecting the turquoise "sky" and its mild pearly sun. An illusion of far vistas hid the walls except where they were pierced by the entrances to several tunnels. The vegetation glowed from within.

The air was more than fresh; it was *vibrant*. Simply standing and breathing made me feel taller. I heard water dripping and faint, mellow birdsongs. Tiny insects flitted by with metallic shimmers and gentle hums.

More than anything in the Pan-Cosmos, I wanted to lie down under the un-shade of a shining tree and munch a good sandwich. I'd have gladly taken just the lying down.

Instead, I consulted the map, crossed the meadow, stepped into the appropriate tunnel, and began working my way through a labyrinth.

Not the scariest part of the trip, but exhausting. Overhead, bell-shaped tubes cast plenty of light, but illuminated nothing worth seeing. Miles of rectangular corridors, miles of gray walls and gray floors. No vegetation whatsoever. After an hour, I'd have been thrilled to encounter a blade of grass. Might've even tolerated a spider or two. And at every damn intersection, I had to make sure I turned the right way.

My mind grew so numb I felt annoyed to find a tall, closed door blocking my way. Then reality hit. I'd reached my goal.

Now what?

The unfinished-basement illumination failed to shed light on how to open the door, a gray rectangle with a small black circle near my eye-level.

I tried pushing, pulling, twisting, prying, putting my eye and hand against the circle, commanding verbally, commanding mentally, cajoling, sending microdocs, praying, asking very politely, and a large amount of what I'm afraid might be considered yelling.

Finally, I remembered that profound dictum: as a last resort, read the manual. I called up the map, centered the red hexagon, and zoomed in and in and in …

The camera had plenty of zoom. At max magnification, the hexagon was nothing but red pixels and blank gaps between them. But I noticed that the gaps made a complex pattern. On a hunch, I pressed this image to the black circle. The tall door swung open a few inches. Cute. The photograph was a map *and* a barcode key.

Stink wafted through the opening: linseed oil gone very bad, mixed with a soupçon of gasoline, a smell I'd encountered on Earth, on a certain photograph. The idea that Scome machines lurked beyond this door seemed far too plausible. I remembered thinking that the Shadowcaster device, when I'd first seen its image, wasn't nearly as scary as current movie monsters. But then, I'd never been in the same room as an actual monster.

I had a bad feeling about this.

On top of that, or perhaps because of it, I had a disturbing thought. Rider had practically admitted knowing what had become of the Scome, which added another layer to the puzzle. Why would the O-gen-ai, through their Neme agents, fake some big mystery? If they wanted to keep secrets, why bring up the subject at all?

And why would Rider give the show away to me by hinting?

Enough stalling. I shoved, gently, and the portal opened wide. The smell blossomed and the full bouquet had an acridness I'd been lucky enough to miss until now. *Microdocs, are you lazing off?*

I entered cautiously, breathing through my mouth. The mapmaker hadn't shown much imagination; the large room *was* hexagonal.

The hideous machines were here all right. I peeled my eyes off them. Didn't care to go another step without knowing every way out, but I spotted no other doors.

Six beige walls rose about thirty feet to meet a six-facet ceiling, which shed a flicker-free, cold white light. A pervasive hum filled the room. My God, the place stank! The fumes made me grateful my stomach was empty. I ordered Jeeves to wake up and be my gas mask. Nothing changed.

Perhaps two hundred feet of floor separated each wall from its opposite number. Still, the place was large enough to hold a mechanical army. The "soldiers" all faced the wall just to my left. They remained as motionless as parked cars, but I had the creepy feeling they were ... alert.

Each device was built to resemble an animal, an *imaginary* one, I hoped. Each was different, but all were ugly and had the look of extreme deadliness. They stood lined up as if awaiting military inspection. Wouldn't have cared to meet the inspector.

Several walls displayed messages in Simple featuring the words "Maanza" and "chamm." But I already knew the place was dangerous.

Yet where, exactly, *was* the danger? The machines were hulking and beyond repugnant, but fixed in place with bolts thicker than my arms. Besides, Jeeves was placid.

Glossy gray flooring about ten feet wide bordered the room. Narrower strips divided the phalanx of machines into rows and columns. Each machine stood mounted on a thick black slab.

Nine horrors loomed in the first row and the middle horror emulated some grotesque reptile with bizarre appendages and clawed arms. The blue Dhu-barot letters on its scaly chest spelled the word I'd translated as "Shadowcaster."

Camera time, and I'd start with Shadowcaster. I stepped forward, looked up at the machine, and frowned. Unless my memory played tricks, the angles were wrong. The original snapshot must've been taken from a position well above my head. Had *Rider* taken the picture? With an obsolete Earth camera? Whatever, the job had been botched. I'd show the UN agents how photography *should* be done....

Vanity can be hazardous. What I did next was terminally stupid. I stepped closer to my subject and lifted my pseudo-Nikon. Shadowcaster loomed over ten feet tall. From close range, it glistened and stank. A preservative coating? Some kind of ... conductor?

Studying the preview image, I perfected the centering, held very still, and slowly eased the shutter-release—

A posse of mechanical arms flashed toward me. Dozens of telescoping appendages hoisted me high in the air. Something hot or very cold clamped itself to my scalp. Then the machine paused for a few unpleasant seconds before reaching up with the larger arms mounted on its sides.

My super-peripheral vision supplied a terrific view of needle-sharp claw tips approaching the sides of my head. I heard myself making some rather ghastly sounds, but couldn't even wiggle far enough to give myself abrasions.

The claws touched my temples with startling gentleness, and a million tiny lights scintillated somewhere within my forehead.

Dizziness.

Unaware of passing out, I awoke just as the machine was putting me back on my feet. The room spun. I felt sick to my stomach, but I tried to turn around and walk out the door.

My legs went on strike. I fell sideways, landing near the machine to Shadowcaster's right. Which proceeded to grab me and give me a second unrequested treatment.

I woke up *this* time lying on my side, head resting on my extended left arm. The floor felt soft, and I was entranced by a mysterious pattern before my face, vague rounded shapes separated by dark lines. Then my eyes focused. I'd been admiring my own right hand.

But I kept staring. *When did my fingernails get so dirty?* I tried to remember. *Had I been weeding? Or fixing the accursed lawnmower again? Why wasn't Jeeves keeping me clean?*

Then I remembered where I was. Wary of my traitorous legs, I swung the camera around to my back and started crawling. Couldn't smell a thing. Either I'd grown acclimated, or Jeeves had decided I'd had the day's quota of nauseating fumes.

By the time I reached the exit, I was sweating, trembling, and lightheaded. Felt poisoned. Jeeves had let me down and in a big way. I had to rest for a moment. What the hell time was it? According to my watch, I'd been unconscious all night. *Plus* an entire day ...

Good thing you feel ill, I lied to myself. *Otherwise, you'd be ravenous.* At least Jeeves had saved me from dehydration.

It proved a big job getting to my feet. Leaning against the jamb, I took several pictures of the room, quality be damned. When I staggered into the hallway, the door swung closed behind me with an authoritative click. It could've welded itself shut for all I cared.

But I couldn't risk leaving yet. I grabbed the camera and called up the last pictures I'd taken, praying they'd serve. The Shadowcaster photo looked even more amateurish than the version I'd seen in my office. But even Eliot Porter might've bungled a shot while being grabbed....

Like the previous image, the machine appeared at a crazy angle with blurred objects obscuring the corners. Now, lucky me, I knew they were head-clamps. The original photographer had also been grabbed.

I lurched down the hallway. The air smelled sweet as syrup, and as my head cleared I felt a sweet sense of relief. Best of all, despite how impossible and dangerous it had seemed, I'd found and recorded the evidence Earth needed. Victory! Champagne for everyone! Now, I simply needed to return to—

No. My mind grew clear enough to realize that things weren't sweet or simple. I'd now *proved* the Crossroaders were liars. I shuddered, imagining the probable fallout. On a more immediate level, my absence had surely been noticed by now.

Wiping fresh sweat off my forehead, I couldn't tell which was greasier, my hand or my forehead. My whole body had to be oily and reeking from that damn room. Was Jeeves holding out for a raise?

I examined my hand. What the *hell*? Apparently said damn room had given me blood poisoning. Each fingernail had a black line running up the middle; and the quick, which had always been an underappreciated off-white, had become a dark smudge.

Lovely. More to worry about. Speaking of which ...

Why had the Scome built those mechanical nightmares? From the harsh way they'd dealt with me, I suspected they might be medical devices of some alien sort. If so, why make them hideous? More relevantly, if they were medical machines, what kind of treatments had they given me? And for a bonus worry: assuming Shadowcaster had snatched up my predecessor and done its thing, what, exactly, had become of its previous victim?

Was the same thing about to happen to me?

CHAPTER 23
CAPTAIN SQUID

I studied the map and started retracing my steps. Getting my legs swinging and lungs pumping eased my queasiness and allowed my stomach to notice all that excess room.

Still, I should have felt hungrier; this beanpole body isn't equipped for starvation. If microdocs were keeping me hydrated—I glanced down at my garment.

Damn. Jeeves was definitely looking threadbare; microdocs had to be feeding me by sacrificing themselves. The suit seemed thinner by the second. At this rate, I'd soon be starving, unprotected, *and* naked.

I followed the map, my new personal angel.

When the corridor floors finally showed traces of greenery, Jeeves began recovering, so to speak, and I felt stronger myself. Evidently, the microdocs were doing some emergency harvesting.

As my vitality improved, so my mood soared. Perhaps Jeeves was pushing uppers. I croaked out an Archie Fisher tune as I strolled into the half-sunny meadow, enjoying my unjustified bliss.

Jeeves was less pleased. The suit went crazy, foaming over like boiling potatoes, leaving me covered from head to toes in quilted armor except for a small clear plate over each eye.

Still dissatisfied, the microdocs added a second protective layer: reticulated, fibrous bands twisted into bizarre ridges and whorls. And even *that* wasn't enough. In a heartbeat, my garment turned shiny. Now it looked exactly like polished opal and wasn't much more flexible. How practical was this? Both fight and flight had been ruled out.

So much defensive activity scared the joy out of me, but the meadow remained placid. Still placid. Perfectly tranquil ...

I noticed a subtle stirring in one foggy patch. A radiant emerald beam, quite gorgeous, emerged from the fog and played across my chest. My microdoc goggles darkened, otherwise the beam seemed harmless.

Like hell it was harmless! The light bouncing merrily off my armor was vaporizing nearby plants. I watched one shrub become a column of hissing smoke.

A ray of golden topaz joined the party, then two thin lines of violet. A final, thicker ploy in brilliant indigo appeared. The beams traveled up and down my body like searchlights in Hell's grand opening.

Didn't feel a thing, but I shook with fear and anger. Part of my rage was directed toward Jeeves. Someone was trying to *ignite* me, and the best I could do was inch away.

I wasn't the only one with problems. The rays vanished and I heard an eerie howl of frustration.

For a few heartbeats, peace reigned except for the crackling of vegetation. Then I caught a glimpse of something long and flexible whipping out of the fog. Simultaneously, something grabbed my left arm and jerked me high in the air just as a fist-sized stone came flashing my way.

It hit me like a cannon ball, cutting through my camera strap, splintering the armor on my right arm. Shattering my arm from elbow to shoulder. I heard myself make an ugly sound, halfway between grunt and scream, and time seemed to freeze up.

For a long moment, all I felt was the surprising heat of my blood where it flowed over exposed flesh. I stared at the gory pieces of broken bone poking through my skin.

How unusual, I thought in a sick detachment, *to see part of one's own skeleton in cross section*. And blood on white armor made a striking contrast! I savored the aptness of "striking" and wondered, idly, what was gripping my other arm. Whatever it was had just saved my life; that rock had been coming straight at my head. Interesting. But near my injury, ragged pieces of broken armor began melting and joining, which seemed even more interesting.

Then my x-road vision spotted a big silver ball covered in silver flames entering the meadow. It rolled toward the fogbank concealing my attackers. The fog was sucked backward, *fast*, and the chromed fireball followed the mist into a nearby tunnel.

Then the pain hit. Must've blacked out. I seemed to be getting fainting down to an art.

Jeeves looked very different when I revived. The fancy armor had gone, but except for a band around my middle torso, it remained rigid. I could breathe but otherwise couldn't move.

Microdocs were busy on my broken arm. They'd built a fantasyland of spiraling ridges and protuberances resembling oil-derricks. Thousands of tiny threads ran from ridges and derricks to pieces of visible bone.

So many pieces. My arm hadn't been broken so much as *totaled*. Even with surgery, it might never function well. What, I wondered dully, did Jeeves have in mind? I found out the hard way.

The threads began tightening and bone fragments shifted. The pain was unreal. I screamed and sent an emergency-gram to Jeeves: STOP!

The microdocs didn't obey. But a liquid sensation ran through my arm and the agony backed off a trifle. Perhaps the local anesthetic or whatever it was would've worked perfectly on a Hhoymon. For me, it reduced suffering just enough to keep me conscious.

Apparently, the fourth skin was programmed to deal with some injuries despite the host's wishes. Made sense. A wounded person could be irrational. Still, I had fresh insight into the attitudes of torture victims. Clearly, Jeeves worked for my benefit, but pain and helplessness kept my gratitude under control.

I'd stopped bleeding. Bones and bone fragments were smoothly twisted, pushed, and pulled under my skin while my arm was rotated this way and that. Panting, groaning, pleading, and cursing, I watched my arm becoming whole.

After the last bone fragment vanished, the next excruciating sensations came from things moving *inside*. Meanwhile, Jeeves bound my torn skin with microdoc sutures. Finally, the playground on my arm smoothed, merging with the rest of my suit. I could move again but the area covering the damage was a rock-hard, feather-light cast.

The operation had taken less than four minutes. I wouldn't care to repeat any of them.

I tried opening and closing my right hand. I could, but it sure hurt. I wiggled my arm, testing how much motion the cast would allow. From shoulder to hand, one dull ache, a far better result than I could've expected. But the lessened pain allowed me to notice my *left* shoulder yelling about supporting my weight all this time.

I turned my head, expecting to see another microdoc miracle or *not* see spider-god silk. Instead, a black cord thinner than my wrist connected my left hand to a tree limb about twenty feet up. The cord had a strange, rather blurry look, and wrapped around the thick branch but didn't appear to be tied.

"I'll bite," I whispered. "What the hell is it?"

I traced the line downward and got a fresh scare. Close to my fingertips, the dark thing divided into five separate strands, each running under a different fingernail in a Torquemada-approved arrangement. Yet my fingers felt fine. The sensation suggested something evenly gripping the entire hand, wrist, and forearm. The only real complaint came from my shoulder, now burning so much I could practically smell the smoke. How the hell was I supposed to get loose? If only my feet could reach—

The line stretched until I stood on scorched earth. Huh.

Nothing ventured, nothing gleaned, as dad used to say. "Let go," I commanded mentally, as though instructing Jeeves. The cord separated from my fingertips and dangled from the tree, swaying.

I reached out to feel the uncertain material. The free end lifted by itself and seemed to caress my left palm. Before I could react, the entire cord came loose from the tree, shrinking at a fantastic rate until it was gone.

But had it *shrunk*? Or had the blackness ... dived into my body through my palm? The idea of it inside me, coiled like a giant tapeworm, wasn't soothing. Praying the thing was still feeling obedient, I issued one hell of an eviction notice.

Skinny black tubes emerged from the fingertips of *both* hands, extending themselves upward for five feet. They hung in the air, unsupported, waving in the breeze.

"What the ...?" Both horrified and intrigued, I visualized the tubes shortening. They did. Then I ordered one tube to lift a small rock twenty feet away. It stretched far enough, but the line snapped when the stone cleared the ground.

I combined two strands, and neither broke when they picked up the rock, or when I had the doubled tubes throw it a few yards. Within a minute, I had four fist-sized stones hoisted at once.

"Pumping granite," I muttered. "Let's see if these things can handle delicate work."

As I practiced picking up pebbles of various sizes, I began to feel the alien substance within me, soft and fluid. As I pushed it out, more took its place. Gradually, the truth dawned: my body was *manufacturing* the stuff. My subconscious must've caught on to this new resource and acted to save me.

But why had such a weird talent suddenly appeared? Was it a gift, like my x-road vision, of Crossroad's crazy environment? Could the godwater be responsible, or—what was wrong with me? A Scome machine had given me a mystery treatment and, voilà, I'd gained this bizarre ability. *Shadowcaster*. The name actually made sense.

"Look out, Pan-Cosmos," I said. "Seems I've come down with an exotic *power*." I couldn't imagine one less impressive, but then, whoever heard of a Yiddish superhero? Since Samson, anyway.

If Crossroad had such a thing as a Hall of Heroes, perhaps they'd ask me to join. I could bake rugelach for our superhero meetings. And accomplish awesome feats with my new talent. With practice, I might stand on the ground and pluck fruit off tall trees, scratch the very middle of my back, and—who knows?—perhaps even learn to make entertaining shadow-figures with nary a wall or light!

Imagine my induction ceremony: Fellow heroes, please welcome our newest member, Professor Dave Goldberg, who can squirt black stuff from his fingertips. Don't worry, you will not be expected to shake hands. Everyone, say hello to ... Captain Squid? Mr. Inky?

Of all possible powers, to have picked up the ability to squeeze out dark goo ... *Ah well*, I thought, *sludge is life*.

But if my subconscious was so clever, why hadn't it blocked the speeding rock with shadow? Was the stuff simply too fragile? Once thing for sure: it could *move*. That first line had attached itself while the rock was en route.

Curious, I created a short dark rope and ordered it to snap back and forth, faster and faster. In moments, the thing was whistling obnoxiously and whipping up a healthy breeze.

I let all blackness withdraw into my body. Maybe this talent wasn't entirely useless. I could be my own ceiling fan.

A sweat droplet wriggled down my face. I used my good hand to wipe my brow, which felt cold and clammy. That ended my internal standup comedy routine. *You're in shock, idiot. Wake up!*

The meadow jumped into focus. I stood within a large irregular oval of blasted earth, barren except for two small, foot-shaped patches of healthy grass. A wide ring of badly seared plants surrounded the scorched oval.

Where's my camera?

Panicking, I looked around but didn't recognize the poor thing at first. Burned is too mild a word; it'd been slumped. I stared at the black puddle blending so nicely with the blasted soil. My pictures and success were gone.

That damn rock, I thought bitterly, *must've been traveling past Mach 1 to break the tough strap, Jeeves,* and *my arm*. But why had the camera melted? The dancing rays hadn't even singed the strap while I'd been wearing it, and they'd stopped pre-rock.

Obvious answer: the ground had become lava hot. Jeeves, I realized, must be an incredible insulator. Logically, microdocs rather than the local Mind had preserved me from cinder-hood. My attackers wouldn't have used energy weapons without a way around the Mind.

Like a dreamer waking up, starting the day's work, and then really waking up, I finally wondered why the hell I was standing here, gawking around like a tourist except for being shy one camera. Something bizarre even by Crossroad standards had chased my attackers away, but they knew where I was and might already be returning. Couldn't count on that silver ball rescuing me twice. I rushed through the meadow and leaped into the green float-tube.

Seemed to take hours to reach the top. Once there, I headed toward Oracle Waters. Jogging proved tricky with a cast, but it seemed a bad time for a stroll.

Losing the camera was devastating, but my mission wasn't yet a total bust. Not if I could survive, get back to Earth, and spill the beans.

Question: what kind of ultra-alien could've turned a rock into a damn rocket?

Nemes? Nope. Out of contention with their short arms and delicate feeding tubes. And since I'd glimpsed a very long arm or tentacle, Blenn were eliminated. Hell, if the humble bugs had wanted me injured, they would've first apologized profusely and made sure it was a convenient time for me to be hospitalized.

That left a planet-full of suspects. The Common might be capable of the stunt—a horrifying notion. And maybe the Vyre could adapt an arm, or even a leg, for high-speed throwing, but they didn't seem strong enough. Chean-shee tails were powerful, but too short. Most likely, the thrower was something I'd never heard of.

Decision time. Seek help right here or try to reach Triangle Four on my own? Could I use the local Mind to contact Strong or Swift? That would mean confessing I'd snuck away....

"Mind?" I called out experimentally. "Can you hear me?"

No response. Perhaps the local monitor didn't savvy English, despite Rider claiming the Minds shared information. Perhaps my enemies were blocking communications.

One thing for sure: I was on my own.

CHAPTER 24
HARD-BOILED EGGS

Nearly at the river, I noticed a repetitive booming that wasn't part of the waterfall roar. The concussions kept getting louder until they sounded like someone dribbling a ten-ton basketball.

I stopped and spun around.

The thing approaching me stood twice my height, egg-shaped, armless, faceless, and supported by four squat, thick legs. It moved in mighty leaps and rebounds: jumping forward, bouncing off its flexible bottom, and pushing off with its legs. The thump each time it hit sent visible shockwaves along the grass-carpeted floor.

Loops of kelp-like flesh in clown colors—sulfur yellow, green, and red—festooned Dumpty's shell, flapping with each jump. I thought seriously about getting the hell out of its way, but Dumpty stopped about twenty feet from me, bouncing in place until gradually settling down.

What was it? More importantly, was it friendly? Even Jeeves couldn't decide, shifting restlessly from form to form.

"Hello?" I said.

A small hole opened midway in the shell. Figured we were about to have a nice chat, the egg and I. Instead, a thick yellow gob came zipping toward my face. I leaped to one side and my broken arm twinged painfully. Everywhere mucus had landed, the floor was all bubbles and brown smoke.

The egg wasn't friendly.

I tried sidling away, although it's hard to sidle properly when you're terrified. My new problem waited until I traveled a good ten yards down the hall, then caught up in two bounces. The hole reopened, Dumpty quivered with effort, but spewed only droplets. Out of ammo?

Unfortunately, not out of options. A foaming vertical crack suddenly divided the shell, which swung open as if hinged in the back. Fabergé hadn't designed the interior.

The right side was stuffed with yellow goo, plenty of ammo after all. The left half contained a smaller four-legged egg perched on a bulging, transparent organ sack.

Junior hopped out, dribbled itself over to stand to Dumpty's left, and opened to reveal egg *three*, which also bounced to the left until it wound up beside Junior. This runt of the litter box stood no taller than my belly button.

"Wonderful," I groaned. "Nested nightmares."

God only knew what threat these Matryoshka horrors posed—aside from killer spit—but this couldn't be leading up to anything pleasant.

Runt was an individualist, opening to reveal its own sack of greasy organs and gallons of something like tiny golden-brown raisins. The raisins slopped onto the grass. All three eggshells snapped closed, and the Dumptys leaped to new positions with Junior blocking retreat toward the river, Runt guarding the way forward, and Pappa Dumpty to my side, twenty feet away.

I eased backward, toward the nearest wall without quite stepping into the taller grass. Even now, I hadn't forgotten the arachnoids. My heart pounded so violently that everything I saw appeared to vibrate.

Suddenly, dull bands of ultra-red linked all three eggs. These zigzagged across the floor toward me, weaving themselves into a doily-like pattern. Didn't feel anything when the pattern passed under my feet, or when it froze into a semicircle stretching from the Dumptys to the wall behind me. But I sure hated being in the middle of it.

Something hissed. Along the semicircle's outer arc, grass seemed to be vaporizing, the effect working its way inward. I ran forward and leaned over for a closer look.

Insects.

Millions of translucent golden-brown bugs were mowing the lawn down to dirt at a furious clip. These bugs had disproportionately large heads with wide mouths, apparently with built-in Cuisinarts.

I wanted to jump over the insects, dodge eggs, and run like hell, but my gut said it wouldn't be that easy.

I plucked an iridescent flower underfoot and hurled it down the hall. As it sailed over the buggy line, the ultra-red doily stretched upward. The blue flower turned green from a coating of amber insects, instantly devoured in midair. Had a hunch these critters weren't vegetarians.

Experimentally, I extruded a low shadow-wall. It barely slowed the tide; my black stuff wasn't that tough per square inch. And neither was Jeeves as I'd learned the hard way. Microdocs could handle energy beams, but when it came to sticks and stones ...

The invaders had already gobbled their way close to me. I jumped back, jarring my broken arm.

Pain on top of fear, and I lost it. Three black ropes shot from my left hand, whipped through the miniature army, and sent clouds of bugs flying. The glowing doily brightened. Suddenly, my whips only bounced away, inches from the ground. I backed up again; my homestead was shrinking fast.

What to do? Even if I could sprout shadow wings and flutter off like Tinker Bell, I'd wind up bug-covered and eaten. Since I could no longer touch the insects, my only hope lay in dealing with their controllers. I needed a *weapon*.

I generated a shadow-club but couldn't keep it stable enough to crack a real egg. My shadow-bullets disintegrated as they flew. I had to retreat once more, putting me farther from my targets.

New, squeaking noises from up the corridor didn't help my nerves. Then a whooshing joined the orchestra. Tsunami headed this way? Had some Leiningen-like savior released enough water to wash my troubles away?

Ha. The "wave" arrived: thousands of alien spiders, mice, and snakes scrambling or slithering down the hallway edges, crawling and hopping over each other in their haste to escape ... *what*?

Every creature that ran or got pushed into the insect-line was eaten alive. The doomed ones could see the slaughter ahead, but mob-pressure kept forcing them into oblivion. If the bugs consumed grass as fast as meat, they would've reached me already.

How, I wondered, could the little monsters gobble so much flesh so quickly? Weren't they getting full?

Not one critter outside the ultra-red doily managed to join me inside, but the tall grass behind me already housed a respectable population. As the semicircle contracted, my fellow prisoners, the ones with legs, began jumping up and down like popcorn of the damned.

I felt torn between horror, terror, pity, and disgust. The bugs were too damn close again. I *had* to step back and join the border patrol.

Now my playmates surrounded me, some leaping waist-high. I hopped sideways to avoid a particularly large spider and winced at feeling small bodies crunch underfoot.

From my chest down, Jeeves covered itself with opal scalpels in constant motion. What the ... why was I moving while standing still? The spider and mouse brigade had thinned enough so that I could see my microdoc footwear covered in hyperactive scalpels. But the main feature of interest: I stood on a layer of knobby backs, and the snakes were carrying me straight toward the ravening bugs! Before I could jump, my ophidian taxi slammed into reverse. Same thing happened when we neared the insects on the other side. I'd boarded a shuttle to nowhere. With a shrinking route.

Finally, the remaining snakes ran out of maneuvering room and had to stop. In every sense, my back was against the wall. The yellow lines were inches away. And that obnoxious squeaking kept getting louder....

I needed a *real* weapon. *Now.*

I found myself suddenly gripping a shadow hurling stick with a loaded shadow spear. No cable or trigger, but so what? At my command, microdocs flowed to the spear's tip and hardened into an opal spike. I'd been trained to use a hurling stick. But could I do it with my left hand?

My feet turned yellow. Jeeves worked hard to fight the bugs off, but they tore into the microdoc knives like kids chewing rock candy. Lacking room for a proper spin, I flicked the shadow lever forward and gave the release command at what I hoped was the right time. The white-tipped black javelin whistled as it rocketed forward.

Pain! Felt like my toes had caught on fire! Swearing, I tried to shake off bugs and push them away with shadow, but kept my eyes on Papa Dumpty. No chance for a second throw.

BANG. The shell didn't break; it *exploded.* Grotesque chunks rained down. The big organ-sac hit the floor and ruptured, hissing and smoking, releasing a stench so abysmal, I gagged and my eyes watered.

The doily pattern wavered then died out; the insects quit gobbling and scattered. Jeeves flicked off the horde still on me, smoothing out as they wandered off. The smaller eggs seemed frozen in place.

I went all woozy. A second wave of wall-hugging creatures was coming, but this time, there were no bugs to eat them. To avoid the stampede, I stepped forward onto what was now bare topsoil.

Pain blossomed to agony. I fell backward, moaning, staring at my bare, crimson-swabbed feet and ankles. Slowly, as if they too were groggy, microdocs surged into the wounds, generating bow-waves of pink froth, perhaps neutralizing some evil residue.

Jeeves advanced, absorbing and stanching the bleeding, forming a plastic-clear shield over the exposed muscles. From just above my ankles down, my fourth skin had become my only skin, a *Gray's Anatomy* illustration. The pain ebbed. Fighting nausea, I gingerly touched my right foot. The microdoc dressing flexed enough for me to feel the slight pressure.

I sat, waiting for my breathing to slow, clenching handfuls of soil and letting the dirt trickle through my fingers. Then I forced myself to stand and tried a few steps. I could walk, but the soft dirt underfoot burned like live coals. I ordered the shoe sole microdocs to firm up and nothing happened. Perhaps Jeeves, too, had run short on energy.

Conceivably, this wasn't my lucky day. So far, I'd suffered a compound fracture and gotten flayed. How much of me would be left by evening?

Without a map, the only route I knew for returning to the Hall of Games lay dead ahead, where something that panicked oversized tarantulas lurked. Even if I got past that something, I dreaded another Jump-way flight.

Animal refugees kept pouring down the corridor. I gave Runty Dumpty a wide berth and began shuffling upstream. Runty didn't even twitch.

A quarter mile onward, the nerve-twisting noise became deafening, and I still couldn't see its cause. And my feet hurt like hell. Would shadow-crutches help? Better yet, what about padding? I stopped to concentrate. My, the dark stuff sure responded quickly, and I learned something: evidently, I could squeeze shadow not only through my feet but also right through Jeeves.

My homemade padding felt spongy under my soles, already an improvement. Then, to spread my weight over more territory, I added shadow until I seemed to be wearing black snowshoes. Walking turned awkward but reasonably comfortable.

I glanced back and noticed a flicker of green light. Trouble ahead for sure. Trouble behind?

Three narrow passageways leading God-knows-where connected to this corridor section. I hesitated but headed toward the more certain trouble.

Three minutes of shadow-shoeing brought me past a gentle curve in the tunnel. As the fingernails-on-blackboard effect rose to the level of ear torture, I finally knew what had spooked the wildlife. Couldn't guess at the creature's exact size because all I could see was its mouth ... filling the entire corridor. But from the sound, the monster's body scraped the walls as it advanced. It certainly exuded a stink fitting something gigantic.

The long, three-sectioned mouth was crammed with agile tongues or tentacles in graduated sizes, diminishing as they approached a gullet large enough to swallow me without the added insult of mussing my hair. Tongues kept busy snatching vines and lily-lights off the walls. One lashed out to snatch me.

I jumped back and didn't bother listening to my bad arm complain. Two inches from my nose, the tongue quivered and split, revealing three nostril-like holes. Great. My lifetime supply of adrenaline used up in one morning....

Big Mouth roared out the all-time champion belch plus a cloud of putridity. Suddenly, all tongues were dripping saliva and pointed straight at me. The monster lurched forward and the scraping rose in pitch.

Still, my pursuer didn't set any land speed records. This latest abomination was terrifying and needed an ocean of mouthwash, but couldn't harm me if I kept moving backward. But it presented one hell of an obstacle. And if our slow-motion chase continued much longer, we'd reach the river area. How fast could Big Mouth move given elbowroom?

While I was chewing that one over, I glimpsed greenish flashes reflecting off slimy tongues. I whirled around. Maybe a hundred yards off, a glowing lime whirlwind drifted my way. So much for options. I sprinted to the nearest side-passage as fast as my shadow-snowshoes would allow, ducked inside, stopped, and turned. No way any locomotive-size monster could squeeze into this narrow tunnel, but it might be roomy enough for the green threat, whatever it was, to fit.

In an ideal Pan-Cosmos the monster would've kept moving forward, forcing the whirlwind to retreat. Then, when Big Mouth had passed my hiding spot, I could've resumed my journey, whistling.

I suspect the whirlwind followed the script by backing away. But Mouth advanced just enough to block my exit, and then, like a train pulling into a station, squealed to a dead stop. I waited. And I waited. As did the monster. The corridor I needed might as well have been a light-year away. Finally, I gave up and began walking down the tunnel. Without the slightest idea of where I was going.

―――

This passageway wasn't a claustrophobe's paradise. My shoulders often bumped the walls, and I had to keep bobbing my head to avoid ceiling nodules. Occasional Art Nouveau vines made the space even more cramped, and I was deeply grateful for my x-road vision; jewel-flowers were rare here.

Whoever had made this tunnel had never met a straight line they liked, and the hard floor was anything but level. My feet began hurting and it took me far too long to realize that their padding had dissolved. I would've scolded myself, but I was too tired and scared. With a fresh pair of shadow-snowshoes, travel became easier if not much faster.

Two hours passed according to my watch. Then a third seemed well on its way to going down the same toilet. Did this tunnel go *anywhere*? But intuition or cowardice stopped me from heading back. The curving walls made it impossible to see far in either direction, giving my imagination scope. The idea of something pouncing from behind was particularly distressing. Should I leave a plug of shadow in my wake? The stuff wasn't reliable; every few minutes I had to replace my shadow-shoes.

If only it were stronger! Well-placed, razor-thin, black wires might cut pursuers to ribbons ...

That thought brought me to a halt. What had become of that gentle academic, Professor Goldberg? I was in bad shape: gasping for air, dripping with sweat. My hands could've been used to shake paint cans. All of which bought me nothing. I couldn't *afford* to be this scared. Someone or something was out to kill me, and I needed every resource I had.

The downside, I thought, *might even have a sublevel*. Perhaps I'd been ... finessed into this passageway.

Strangely, the notion steadied me, widening my perspective. Ever since enduring Shadowcaster's abuse, I'd been batted around like a mouse between cat paws. A shame, but did I have to be so damn passive about it? I toyed with an idea that might, conceivably, provide Crossroad authorities a means to learn who or what killed me. Why not try it?

I gave Jeeves a long list of instructions, probably too long. Oh well. It would work or it wouldn't. I resoled my shadow-shoes and resumed walking.

An hour later, my terror hadn't exactly worn off, but was wearing thin. I felt overtired, depressed, and exceedingly hungry. Then I saw it. "Hey," I whispered. "There's really a light at the end." A bluish glare tinted the distant walls. I hurried forward.

Within ten minutes, the endless passageway ended. I stepped out into a surprisingly wide hallway floored with yellow-orange sand. The vague blue ceiling seemed blindingly bright until Jeeves manufactured sunglasses.

Ceiling? Hell no. That was *sky*! I now walked outdoors, along the bottom of a deep chasm.

The silence felt intense, broken only by my ragged breathing and soft squeaks every time I took a step. My footwear had dissolved again. I stopped. The glittering cliffs to either side were riddled with openings, many quite large, and some at ground level appeared to be tunnel entrances. Had to gaze almost straight up to locate the cliff tops: broken ridges and jagged pinnacles tall enough to stab the wispy passing clouds.

I'd seen Crossroad's surface before, but never at ground level while standing on my own skinned feet. To my eyes, the robust geology seemed dead wrong, the spires too sharp, rock faces pregnant with overhanging boulders that should have long since fallen. If gravity was weak here, the scene might've made sense. But I didn't feel light. I fed a handful of sand to the air and it fell at the familiar rate. Surely Crossroad's gravity couldn't attenuate rapidly with height?

Why not?

Finally, I *knew* right down to my bones that this wasn't Earth's reality.

"Bravo, David," I said. "You blow your tourist credentials by losing your camera. Then you try for reinstatement by gawking at skyscrapers."

I tried to chuckle, but failed. I stood lost in a place stranger than I'd ever imagined, starving and alone, isolated even from my *universe*. And unknown enemies were surely on their way to murder me.

One bright spot: I had a silver ball for a friend. I'd be sure to look it up the minute I figured out where it was. And what.

Decision time again. Should I explore a different tunnel? Or do the sensible thing: double back to the main corridor? By now, Big Mouth could be gone. Then again, I could stay put and pray for rescue, or continue walking this sandy road to nowhere.

Before I could decide which choice I hated least, fog began pouring from a big triangular opening across the way. *How nice*, I thought sarcastically, *my attackers brought some meadow mist along*.

Thousands of rocks, ideal for throwing, lay scattered near the cliff walls. My entire body seemed to wince in anticipation.

I stumbled and looked down. Jeeves had gone shiny, heavily ridged, and stiff with extra layers protecting my bad arm and skinned feet. It became tricky just to keep my balance and as for running, forget it. Not that running would help; I remembered how fast my hidden enemies could move. I faced the fog and waited.

CHAPTER 25
I, IBIS

Before a single ray, rock, or expletive emerged from the mist, a ball of chromed fire rolled to a stop in front of me. As if sucked by the ultimate Hoover, the fog whooshed back into the passageway.

The ball remained motionless for a moment. Then with a gentle tinkling, it disintegrated, flames and all, leaving behind a passenger: an avian-like biped with twinkling, alert eyes and white body feathers. Its head, heron-like legs, and long back plumes appeared jet black with a blue shimmer. Its bill was thin and aquiline; arms and hands seemed as human as mine. More so since my fingers are unusually elongated.

"Do you know me?" the bird asked in clear English but with a creaking sort of voice.

"I've ... seen you around."

"Indeed."

I pointed to the fog-vacated hole. "What, um, rushed in there just now?"

"If only I knew. Are you well?"

After all I'd been through today, I almost laughed. "Thanks to you."

My rescuer performed a sweeping bow. "Well spoken! I accept your plaudits, which I deserve to an immense degree. Why the frown, dear boy?"

"You sound just like someone I know. Well, you don't *sound* like him, but you talk—"

The avian shape blurred. A white, short-sleeved shirt, and black trousers replaced the feathers. Brown oxfords covered what had been three-toed feet. And the head ...

Sir Benjamin DeHut, friend, campus fixture, and frequent lunch companion—on Earth!—regarded me, shaking his white-haired head.

"You must learn to be more flexible, David." His voice had resumed his usual light baritone. "Save for your jaw, which requires closing."

"*Ben*? What ... how did you *get* here? I thought ..."

"Pray continue. I'm most interested in your thoughts."

"Look, when I saw an alien pop out of a reflective ball, I figured you were that Mirrormage everyone keeps mentioning."

"And so I am."

I grabbed for a straw of sanity. "I get it. You're not really Ben, you're just changing your—"

He raised a hand. "Steady, dear boy. I'm your favorite Benjamin."

"*And* the Mirrormage?"

"I will be candid, David. Discounting your arm, Crossroad has been the very tonic for you; you appear younger than some of your students! But your intellect, ah, that seems to have suffered."

"This is crazy! I've known you for ... what? Eight years? You've been visiting Earth for that long?"

"*This* is where I visit. Earth's my home, don't you know. Born there, lived there for centuries. Quite enjoy the place."

"Centuries?"

"Truly, I'd enjoy nothing more than to stand here and, as young people say, or said four decades ago, chew the fat. I daresay we've a question or two to exchange. But this is scarcely a strategic location; the sooner we depart, the better. And we have an appointment."

"We do?"

"Quite. I've taken the liberty of arranging something rather special. Come along."

Ben started walking and I re-formed my shadow-wear to join him. Didn't know what to say. Hell, I didn't know what to *think*.

After a few steps, Ben glanced downward. "Hang on. What's all this?"

"Oh. Right. I'm starting to take it in stri—take it for granted, but something incredibly weird happened. I've picked up this ability to—"

"Not that, dear boy. I know all about *that*. But why the swaddling?"

"Oh. Okay. Short version: bugs skinned my feet."

"Ah. Your engagement with the em-Bottho wasn't a bloodless victory after all, as I'd hoped. Regrettable but hardly surprising. Still, this won't do. Apply umbral cushions if you wish, but those duck-galoshes force you to waddle, old boy, and we should step more lively. You'll find your natural sole sufficient on firm sand."

"Ben, without this arrangement, I'd have trouble walking at all."

"A pain issue, is it? Sit for a moment and let's have a peek."

I sat, leaned back on my arms, lifted my feet a few inches off the ground, and withdrew my "galoshes." Ben touched the clear bandages and the microdocs pulled back. Exposed to air, my wounds began to sting. A lot.

"We needn't deal with your arm," he announced, "except perhaps to nudge recovery. But this presents a different matter. I wasn't expecting *all* the skin to be gone. Quite the problem for your taurei, I daresay: balancing support, healing, and protection, while allowing necessary movement."

"Taurei? Another name for a fourth skin?"

"Another name for sentient cells. Kindly give me a moment."

The magician sat very still. Nothing happened except the burning got worse and my abdominal muscles began quivering from keeping my feet suspended. Then Ben blinked rapidly a few times and looked at me. His eyes had taken on the colors and luster of peacock feathers.

He smiled. "Anticipating some business with mirrors, were you? My native energy isn't therapeutic, so I'm tapping reserves on loan from the Compassionate One. Keep those legs raised!"

Ben leaned over. A mist of turquoise droplets sprayed from his transformed eyes, raining down on my ankles and feet, spreading. The moisture stuck to my skinless flesh, bringing exquisite cooling relief. In moments, my feet had a new kind of skin, baby-blue with irregularities suggesting tiny, overlapping feathers.

"Should last until the real thing grows back," the magician said with a satisfied air. "Any better?"

I touched my right foot. "Doesn't hurt one bit! Ben, you're a wonder!"

"Not at all, my boy." He stood and stretched. "Not as a healer, that is. Ready?"

Jeeves flowed back to create sandals for me. I stood and took a few trial steps. "Lead on, DeHut."

Crossroad's sun poked blazing fingernails through low points in the high chasm walls; here and there, the sand sparkled like pulverized yellow diamonds. My stomach, finding such marvels inedible, growled. Our corridor of sand kept widening until the cliffs were miles apart.

My strange companion who was no stranger whistled a tune in an Arabic-sounding scale, lifting his legs higher than seemed necessary with every stride. His walk had always reminded me of some long-legged waterfowl. His whistle wasn't musical, more of a prolonged squeak.

Mercifully, the serenade ended. "Your stomach needn't grumble much longer, David. Just a trifle farther we'll stop and have a nibble."

"Good. I could eat. Ben, which is the real you? Bird or human?"

"I'll go into all that shortly. But I'm parched with curiosity: how did you defeat the em-Bottho? Touch and go for a while, I expect?"

"You mean that ... Easter Weeble?"

He chuckled. "I remember Weebles! A fair description, indeed. When I learned that it had reappeared to pursue you, I feared that all our plans—never mind about that right now. 'Em-Bottho' means unbreakable in CasCan, a Vyre dialect, and I confess to being jolly surprised to find the beast so very broken." He sighed. "The Vyre had the honor of naming it since they were its first victims here some twenty-seven cycles ago. You shouldn't have *had* to deal with it, David, but all your protectors had been called away. Upon learning the bloody thing was loose, I was sure I'd lost you."

I studied my old friend with x-road vision. How much could I trust this ... person? Should I try to minimize my new abilities?

Silly question. My attitude needed updating. Back in the meadow, my enemies had seen my talent in action, and Ben had claimed to know all about it. I was the one operating in the dark.

"Ben, do you understand what's been happening to me?"

"Better than you do, I daresay. Sticking to recent events, I know about the picture sent to the UN and how you were conscripted to come here."

"Wait. You *know* about that photo?"

"Certainly. I delivered it. Likewise, I wrote the message and provided the hidden map. Rather clever, if I say so myself. If you'll recall, I was on hand to provide you an illusion of privacy while you investigated that silly playground."

I nodded to avoid interrupting by unleashing the barrage of questions that filled my head.

He smiled. "And since I'm familiar both with your, ah, potentials and Scome enhancement machines, I felt no surprise when I rescued you earlier to find you dangling from your umbral force. However, *nothing* I know of explains a shattered em-Bottho."

"Okay. How about this? I'll demonstrate my egg-cracking technique if you'll tell me more about my 'potentials' and those machines."

He didn't respond for a long moment. "Yes, I suppose that time has come. I accept your proposal."

With a thought, a shadow lever and javelin appeared in my hand—this had gotten easy! I hurled a bolt of shadow ahead of us expecting a gasp of astonishment. But my friend was a tough audience.

"That's all you did?"

"No. I used hardened microdocs as a spear-tip. Hit *really* hard."

Ben shook his head. "You've developed this talent to remarkable degree in a short time, but you must've had phenomenal luck. Found a weak spot."

I thought it over. "Are you aware I had a ... an encounter with a Supernal, and afterward, my suit—"

"Any virtues the Dancer wove into your taurei would be inapt for destruction. That isn't Her nature. I admit that I'm baffled. How did you avoid this em-Bottho's primary weapon?"

"Which is?"

"Hydrofluoric acid."

"Oh. Right. It spat at me once, but I dodged."

"*Once*? Dear boy, you lead a charmed life. I wonder ..."

"Ben, I'm doing some heavy-duty wondering myself. What the hell is going on? Why did someone here want me, specifically me, on Crossroad? How did I wind up on some alien hit list? And, the biggie: what is *happening* to me? Aside from this shadow weirdness, look at me. Look at my head. Remember all the hair I didn't have?"

The magician nodded as he always had: four times in quick succession. So birdlike, I realized.

"We've much to discuss, David. But I must give fair warning. You will find certain revelations hurtful. I see shade and a place to park our fundaments not far ahead. There, we shall picnic, and I'll share some remarkable truths, some less than pleasing."

"I just want the truth," I said, although my strong preference was for the pleasant variety. "Hey! You said 'this' em-Bottho. There's more than one?"

"Not here."

"Best news I've heard all day." I hesitated. "Are they intelligent?"

"Less so than a jackal."

"Then how would a solitary specimen get here?"

"The answer is integral to the tale. Ah! Here we are, the perfect ledge to relax and chat. Any special lunch requests?"

"Yes. Please include food."

Ben laughed. "And so I shall."

An overhanging slab about thirty feet up shaded a flat natural stone bench. What a relief just to sit down! Then I learned how handy it is to have a mage around. Trays of hot foods appeared alongside frosty pitchers filled with intriguing liquids, crystal goblets and plates, cloth napkins, silverware, all laid out on a white tablecloth edged in blue ankhs.

"Wow!" I said sincerely. "All this out of thin air?"

"This air isn't thin, my boy, but its carbon inhabits an inconvenient form. Our modest repast owes its savory existence mainly to, ah, earthy elements."

"Is this sort of magic difficult?"

"Some skill and energy are involved, but healing your feet required more from me."

"Well, I definitely appreciate both efforts."

"Appreciation is always welcome. May I pour you a beverage? Fresh pineapple and cantaloupe juices with finely crushed ice may be a pleasant surprise."

He handed me a filled goblet. Right then, dishwater would've tasted sweet. "Ambrosia!" I meant it.

He nodded smugly. "Speaking of fluids, David, *never* wander out here alone. Sands appearing dry may hide deep pockets of an emulsion far more dangerous than Earth's quicksand."

"I'll remember."

"Then, as you Yanks say, dig in!"

I dug, postponing all questions. Ben also seemed content to dine in silence except for one critique aimed at me concerning "hasty savoring." When I finally slowed to nibbles, he put down his fork.

"This snack meets with your approval?"

"Sorry, should've told you. Everything's wonderful!"

"Including the butter?"

I gave him an appraising stare. "Sure. All right, what's up with Crossroad and milk products?"

"Nothing is 'up' as you so colloquially put it. But it seems that something here has boosted your olfactory sense as it has your eyesight. The butter I assembled lacks certain organic compounds." He glanced down at the footsteps we'd left behind us and sighed. "We'll likely be interrupted, but I can at least begin. Are you feeling ... strong?"

"Strong enough to listen."

The magician eyed me sympathetically. "This *will* be difficult. I'll just tell you straightaway. Ever since your brothers were murdered in that plane crash, I've been—"

I found myself standing, shaking a finger at Ben. "Hold on! That explosion was an *accident*! The investigators ruled out—"

"They were wrong. So sorry."

"My God! Three hundred sixty-five people died on that flight!"

That horrible morning began with a phone call from our fertility clinic. For eight months, my wife and I had been trying and failing to make a baby. On my end, so to speak, the sperm sample I'd provided had evidently been misplaced, and the lab needed a fresh supply. We were still waiting for Sara's results.

Sara took the call, did some yes-ing and un-huh-ing, and promised to come down to the clinic ASAP. I could tell from her lack of expression we had a problem. Some sharp-eyed medico, poring over her sonograms, had noticed a minuscule uterine "anomaly" best checked out pronto.

A bad start to the day made worse by a time crunch. We'd arranged to rendezvous with the twins and Josh's wife, Amber, in Boston to catch a late afternoon flight out of Logan. My parents' fiftieth anniversary was pending, and they were second-honeymooning in Spain. Josh, Amber, Michael, Sara, and I planned to surprise them in Madrid.

Over my protests, Sara insisted on driving herself to the clinic, citing my unwarranted reputation as a worrywart and overall fussbudget. Also, someone had to do the packing and I wasn't the one with the uterus issue. I stuffed suitcases, and waited.

At noon, my wife was on the line, telling me calmly that she'd had a small lump excised, said lump being rushed to the clinic's lab. She gave me permission to borrow a neighbor's car and get the hell down there, and she'd arrange for a later flight. Waiting for results could delay us and she knew we wouldn't willingly leave without those results. As long as our jet took off before midnight, we'd make the big party in time.

One nice thing about cyber-cytology: news comes quickly—when a technician's available. By the time I'd given the twins a heads-up, driven to Springfield and located Sara, she was smiling. "Benign" is such a lovely word. Relief made the transatlantic flight seem brief. We didn't learn that the earlier supersonic had exploded ten miles from Lisbon until we'd checked into our Madrid hotel.

By then, it was late and we decided not to break my parents' hearts until the morning. Sara cried herself to sleep, but after trying and failing to console her, I stayed up all night, feeling cold and numb, trying to imagine some soft way to break the news.

Happy anniversary.

"Ben," I said quietly, "a forensic team spent two years investigating that crash."

He made a small, apologetic noise that wasn't quite a word. "They lacked the technology to discover the truth. See here, dear boy, I warned you this would hurt."

"Yeah. Just didn't expect the pain to be so ... personal. So who blew up that jet?"

"I can't be specific."

"I don't get it. Who could've possibly wanted to kill my brothers?"

"Dear, dear. You've missed the point entirely. No one wanted *them* dead. You were the target. Sheer luck you weren't on that flight."

I stared at him. All those people incinerated, so much grief, because of *me*?

Ben gripped my shoulder. "Not in any way your fault."

I didn't believe him.

"Since becoming your protector," he continued, "I've foiled enough attempts on your life that I've bloody well lost count. On Earth *and* here."

"What?"

"Doubtless your enemies already have plotted their next attack. If we are not brilliant and lucky, I may survive but you will die. Happily —" he stood long enough to execute a flamboyant bow "—I specialize in both areas!"

"Ben. Who *are* these enemies?"

"In two words: Hhoymon rebels."

Images of a twisted, blackened fuselage haunted me. "Makes no sense."

"Why not?"

"Hhoymon could've smuggled themselves back here, I gather, but wouldn't they turn into Larry, Moe, or Curly on Earth?"

"I fear you've been misled. Hhoymon become diminished on Earth, but not to imbecility. In human terms, their IQ might fall a hundred points, still leaving them brighter than some of your American presidents. Unpleasant for them, but hardly crippling. Besides, they have allies."

"Oh."

"And I'll warrant only *loyal* Hhoymon departed Crossroad. We'd *intended* to thus separate emmer from chaff."

Emmer? Some form of wheat, I assumed. Then his words registered. "You wanted the rebels to return."

"You must consider a spot of tea, old boy. You've gone rather pale. Shall I pour?"

"Ben, what the hell could Hhoymon have against me?"

He frowned. "You mustn't condemn the species! Loyal Grays have deduced the culprits to be a faction within one subspecies."

"Which one?"

"That remains unknown."

"Terrific. Whoever they are, what's their beef?"

"Ah. I believe I can answer that, but you'll need some background."

"Still listening."

"Then bear with me. As a historian, you'll appreciate how the situation we're wading in flows from ancient tributaries. Are you comfortable? I could assemble a cushion."

"For God's sake, Ben! Just tell me."

He looked away. "Centuries prior to the founding of Old Egypt, another civilization flourished in the same region. Let's call it Eldest Egypt."

"*This* is relevant?"

"Very. You of all people must have some notion of human events ten millennia before the twenty-first century."

"Um, Jericho's walls were just going up."

"Quite. A century earlier, Eldest Egypt already had rather sophisticated arts. One example survives today, albeit in modified form: an impressive statue of their goddess, 'Stys. Considerably later, the Old Egyptians added a lion's body."

"The Sphinx, I assume."

"Indeed. I foresee a small difficulty. Did you recognize the name 'Stys' or J'st?"

"Neither."

"Then I'll alter the old names toward the Greek and Latin versions you'll find familiar. Ah, the persistent influence of empires! K'ung Ch'iu, later called K'ung Fu-tzu, has been branded Confucius so deeply, I've heard *Chinese* scholars refer to him as Confucius! How many people today recognize that Moses and Jesus weren't their actual—"

"Ben, please."

"Sorry. We'll leave my peeves to a brighter day! I'll call that goddess ... Astisis."

"Isis."

"Correct. To resume: seven major gods were worshipped in Eldest Egypt, chief among them, ah, Sed. To Sed's left, the Moon-goddess Astisis glowed; on his right, her Sun-god consort, Reh, blazed. Astisis bore twin sons in perpetual conflict, Ahorus and—let's call him Ankh-hi-phon. These two struggled for dominance, thus engendering the seasons."

I fidgeted. In lecture mode, Ben became a bulldozer.

"David, sunlight and moonlight barred all shadow from Sed save for the crown of his head. Eventually this shadow became Ahkhpu, judge of the dead. Are you following so far?"

"To where, exactly? And how did you learn all this forgotten mythology?"

"You'll know soon. But I said seven gods and named six. You must pay *attention*, dear boy."

"Uh huh."

Ben sniffed disapprovingly. "Do you see the connection between these original gods and the later Egyptian pantheon?"

"Sure, except the mythology changed. But Ahorus is Horus ... of course, of course—sorry, there was this old TV show about a talking—never mind. I assume Sed became Set?"

"The six original gods were preserved. Others were tacked on later, Khnum being the first of these, then Ptah, Nekhebet, Nepththys, and Khepri."

"Ben?"

"Patience! One thing set Eldest Egypt's theology apart, my unlisted god. O-shib-irus, or 'Wous-ibr' to render the name more authentically, lived among these people. Physically."

I started paying serious attention.

Ben nodded. "His home was a pyramid set near the main city, Nam'an Em-phis. In truth, the White Pyramid inspired Egyptian obsession with the form. O-shib-irus became a friend to mankind, exerting a direct influence on locals and telling stories widely circulated by travelers."

"Osiris."

"Quite. Wous-ibr to Wousir then Hellenized to Osiris. But after He went into seclusion, legends conflated. Greeks slipped Osiris into their own pantheon, hybridizing him with jackal-headed Ankhpu and renaming him Kerberis, visualized as a triple-headed dog, guarding the underworld gates."

"*Three* heads." Rider had even told me the Librarian lived on Earth.

Ben's eyes sparkled. "I take it that Arfaenn and Maanza aren't the only First Divisions you've learned of."

"And I take it these First Divisions are the Travelers and Wous-ibr is now called Chybris."

"You have it reversed. Woo-Chybris was the name given to Him by Gray Hhoymon *before* He came to Earth. He'd lived among Hhoymon for the previous two terrestrial millennia, adopting their conventions."

"That's why they know so much about Supernals!"

"Urien, too, lived with them for centuries. Hhoymon have been doubly blessed."

"So why do *you* know so much about Supernals?"

Ben gave me a strange look. "I've been rather close to one. In fact, you have the pleasure of admiring one of the Librarian's original Earth heads." He turned his profile toward me and struck a pose.

"I don't—what are you saying?"

"Thousands of years ago, David, I was quite attached to a Supernal. By the neck."

"Um. You'll probably laugh, but you're giving me this crazy impression that the Librarian's heads are ... detachable, and one Sunday morning one of them—you—just wandered off."

"Precisely. All heads leave eventually."

I blinked, but nothing came into focus. "I'm lost, Ben. The Mind of Triangle Four showed me Chybris having three heads: eagle, porpoise, and human. Are you saying He once had a *fourth*?"

"Never. Three at a time is the rule. You've described the latest triad."

I looked my friend over from shoes to silver hair. "How did you fit?"

"Not in this body, of course." He thumped his chest. "Even post Chybris, I didn't assemble a human appearance for decades. Pre-Chybris ... I was born a wader. Threskiornis aethiopicus. An ibis, in modern terms."

Goose bumps puckered my arms. "So you're a bird after all?"

"Not," he said quietly, "anymore."

I studied his face. "You sure look human."

He shrugged. "Practice."

"Exactly how does an ibis become a god's head?"

A deep, distant thump rattled dishes and silverware. Ben jumped up, gave me a don't-move gesture, and took several long strides away from our bench. His hair blazed in the sunlight as he looked around. Then he shook his head and rejoined me in the shade.

"What's happening?" I asked.

"Let's stick to our business and let others deal with theirs. Where were we?"

"You were about to explain how you, um, joined up with Chybris."

"Quite. David, the First Born work from the inside out. When I was young, the Librarian approached me on a ... in a way I can't explain. His offer wasn't expressed in words or concepts, but in a pure feeling of promise.

"Just being *near* a Supernal is elevating. I doubt any other waterfowl has experienced such feelings. I yearned to be part of the Librarian, part of something sacred."

"Then?"

"I found myself standing on a riverbank, a familiar place, yet I scarcely recognized it. My awareness had expanded a thousandfold and my form had altered equivalently. Looking down, I saw a long neck, flexible as an asp in sunlight. As it moved, so did I. Then I observed where the neck was connected to an enormous body with massive legs. When those legs took a step forward and I felt soil crumble beneath my feet, I understood the body was my own. Not *exclusively* mine. Two heads on long necks were observing me."

"You were the third." This reminded me of the triple reflections I'd seen in the Dancer's vision, and the memory gave me a shiver.

"The third, yes. As I discovered upon seeing myself in the amber eyes of my neighbor, the maned one."

I frowned. "A horse's head?"

"Lion, actually. Later, the Bloodmage. A sad story, but for another time."

"Good Lord. And the other?"

"A crocodile's, dear boy."

"A lion and a croc. Sounds like a risky combination for a bird."

Ben laughed. "Nonsense. We three made a team, sharing thoughts with each other and with our Supernal host."

"So where was Chybris?"

Ben pointed at his heart. "Always with us, inhabiting our common body. Through Chybris, we experienced a common identity while preserving our individuality. Such joy!"

"Hold on. You mean Chybris had no head of—no *brain* of His own?"

The Mirrormage stared at me, wide-eyed and unblinking. "My dear boy, that is the most erroneous idea I have encountered in ten thousand years of life. The Librarian's brain is unarguably the most important object in the Pan-Cosmos."

"Really? Why?"

Ben sighed. "At the risk of being diverted from the mainstream of relevance, I'll summarize. The Pan-Cosmos, as a whole, experiences an endless cycle of ultimate expansions and ultimate collapses over what you may think of as vast oceans of time."

"Rider-on-beauty mentioned that."

"Ah. Somewhat prematurely, I suspect."

"Well, go on."

"With each fresh expansion, the Supernals reappear. They are … useful habits, gradually formed countless Pan-Cosmic cycles ago on the manifold, the infinite potential, of that unchanging reality beyond all conception. The Supernals, reborn, are initially nothing more than abstractions, twelve fundamental principles of mind: memory, reasoning, communication, imagination, emotion, control, learning, creation, competition, responsibility, self-awareness, and awakening. At least, that's how I think of them."

"Wow."

"Indeed. In each Pan-Cosmic cycle, *long* before biological life appears, there occurs a form of … condensation: the Supernals, while retaining their essential diffuse aspects, develop personalities matching their intrinsic principles, focal points where physical bodies manifest. Alone in what the Common call the 'New Dawn,' they relearn to interact with each other, and reestablish their natural relationships."

"Incredible, Ben! I'd like you to repeat all of this at some point so more can sink in. Just incredible! But what does this have to do with Chybris's brain?"

"Everything. Chybris is, of course, the memory principle. Remember, every Supernal is an aspect of mind, and as a famous Neme once said: 'There is only One Mind.' Once Supernals obtain corporeal forms, they begin having experiences and those experiences are stored—where else?—in Chybris's memory. The process is innate. But so *much* information needs to be stored that the Librarian is soon forced to develop a storage method with near-infinite capacity. Every cycle, He grows a virtually indestructible brain for this purpose, the Emeron, in English, the 'Living Diamond.' The current version He keeps secure within His torso. That, my dear friend, is the Librarian's library."

"Fascinating." An understatement. The implications made my head spin. "But what makes this brain so important?"

Ben's eyes twinkled. "I'm delighted you asked. At the end of each Pan-Cosmic cycle, when time becomes timeless and space vanishes, the Living Diamond, like all things, merges into the undefined. But the information it contained merges as well, and as the next cycle begins, that information influences the great expansion, preserving the best of the previous cycle, including the Supernals themselves, and redacting the worst. In this way, each Pan-Cosmos improves on the last."

"Oh. Okay. Now I get why my question was so stupid."

"Not stupid, David. Merely uninformed to a near-terminal degree. At this moment, time exists, and we may have less of it than we'd wish. I must resume the story that will answer your less cosmic questions. But first—"

He jumped up again, walked to the edge of our mineral picnic spot, and shaded his eyes as he gazed upward. He made an annoyed sort of grunt and returned to sit by me.

"Where was I in the main stream?" he asked.

"Um. You'd just found yourself one head of three."

"Yes, thank you. To my dismay, I learned my condition would be temporary. After decades or perhaps centuries of such intensity, I'd inevitably become too self-directed for such mutuality, although the emotional bond would remain. When detachment day came, Chybris would provide me a body built to whatever, ah, specifications I wished."

Weirdness on top of weirdness. I shook my head, but it didn't help. "Hmm. If the Librarian always wears three heads, you must've replaced one who'd gone solo."

Ben patted my knee. "There's hope for you yet! Mind you, my predecessor hadn't begun life as anything terrestrial, but as a bear-like creature from Jaahnim. I believe you've met the Firemage."

"The *demon*?"

The magician waggled a finger. "I wouldn't call him that."

"Right. Go on."

"I was about to. After my adoption, I lived in glory. Can't convey the splendor of it. Imagine being in an ultimately closely-knit family while—while dancing with the cosmos, exploring endless knowledge, breathing miracles. The resources available to the First Born are constant wonders, and the river of experience pouring into the Emeron from every Supernal is engrossing beyond description."

His eyes no longer twinkled. Now they seemed to glow.

"I should say," he continued, "that I only refer to Chybris as male because I'm male. Talk to S'bek Lightmage and you'll hear a different pronoun."

"S'bek?"

"The croc head."

BOOM. The shockwave tipped a goblet over, cracking a plate. Ben frowned and the picnic flotsam became dust. "I'd best abridge the tale," he said. "The Spherecerers exist in trios called Orders. The higher Orders have more intense individual members. Chybris, Binae, and Maanza compose the first Order. Arfaenn, Seris, and Urien, in the next, work closely with the first triad."

"They're more powerful?"

"Only more concentrated. Simpler. First and second triad Supernals have weaker ties with those in the third. But fourth-Order Supernals: ShiwaKhali, Aduum Vesheru Mahrda, and Khunuum ae Hovv, are almost hermetically independent save, of course, for raw experience channeled to the Librarian. Communication with them is iffy. Understanding them, even more so.

"Hence, Chybris was astonished and failed to react quickly enough when ShiwaKhali, the Dissolver, appeared on Earth." Ben licked his lips. "You might describe ShiwaKhali's Sphere as 'useful destruction.' The Dissolver emits certain vibrations that attack erroneous perceptions and beliefs: spiritual sand, if I may wax poetic, in a wind tunnel of the soul."

"Why is this 'useful'?"

"The intended result is a ... streamlining process helpful for some particularly, ah, impenetrable species."

He took a deep breath. "ShiwaKhali's intensity is appropriate for the stalwart entities He-She normally influences but Earth's creatures are too delicate for such abrasion. In fact, life on our planet is so tenuous and feeble, the Dissolver seems unaware of it."

Ben turned his eyes away from mine.

"David, when ShiwaKhali arrived in Eldest Egypt, plant life liquefied and the fertile area rapidly became wasteland."

"That's—"

"Animals collapsed and died, bones turned to treacle. Humans ..." He paused, his face now mask-like while tears drizzled down his cheeks. "People were in *hell*, David, their minds burning. Humans live encased in false ideas, opinions, and perceptions. Some of these are necessary for survival. But ShiwaKhali's nature sprayed all illusion with acid. And then, people died, their brains melted."

"Dear God."

Ben looked a thousand years old. "Only a few hundred Egyptians survived, perhaps those with the strongest delusions. Desiring to save them, Chybris begged ShiwaKhali to leave immediately."

I could only nod.

"The Dissolver's fourth-Order awareness wasn't—wasn't linear enough to understand the request. Chybris cried out to the Messenger for help. You've heard of Urien?"

I nodded again.

"Fortunately, Urien had entered His self-aware phase, manifesting wherever any being is having an insight. In this case, the Dissolver's, ah, ferocious stimulation provided the Messenger with an ideal host. He appeared in one of the few living human bodies and managed to dismiss ShiwaKhali.

"Chybris and Urien labored to repair what they could. Sadly, their therapeutic powers are limited and, tragically, Seris had greater disasters to amend. The two healed some humans, but local plants and animals remained a loss.

"That didn't end the catastrophe! The abundant destruction of plant tissues released much moisture and heat, generating a fearful storm. The Nile overflowed as never before. When the sun finally reappeared, Nam'an Em-phis was a ruin, a great civilization obliterated. The biblical flood. Survivors spread the tale."

"The Hindu deities of destruction," I said slowly, "are Shiva and Kali."

Ben's face relaxed and his eyes cleared, but the rivulets on his cheeks glistened. "Quite. And when early Arabs made a caustic mud from saltwort ashes, they named it 'al-*qili*.' You'll find endless linguistic traces. Wous-ibr became Lucifer, also Prouseb and thus Prometheus."

I snapped my fingers. "'Wous' means 'light' in Simple!"

"Indeed."

"So this ... stone fell into the pond of history and the ripples kept spreading."

"A valid analogy. Urien remained with us for decades, helping rebuild the land and treating some rather grotesque cancers, which appeared as far away as Sumer and Akkad. Survivors thought the world of Urien. They learned of His Brown Hhoymon name, Hhurm, and His endless life-sequence, and declared Him 'Am'n,' the Hidden One."

Amon. Old Egypt's first god. "It all connects."

He nodded. "David, *most* terrestrial names for deities, from Mazda to Hermes to Kwan Yin to Oshun, are derived from Hhoymon titles."

"Hmm. What's Urien's—wait. This stuff has something to do with *me*?"

"Assuredly. ShiwaKhali's visit, the Hhoymon civil war, your predicament, and ... another extraordinary event are all linked."

"I'm listening. Really listening."

"Good. Millennia of living amongst Hhoymon had made Chybris so fond of them He had to relocate lest attachment bias His work, and He feared the Dissolver had visited Jaahnim while tracking the White Pyramid to Earth. Considering His-Her, ah, temporal uncertainly, ShiwaKhali might even blight it *later*."

"You've lost me."

"I fail to see why. Chybris worried that in seeking to find Him, the Dissolver had checked to see if He remained among the Hhoymon on their planet. But ShiwaKhali does not usually experience linear time, and might therefore manifest on Jaahnim after finding the Librarian on Earth."

"Okay, I get it now."

"I should think so! In any case, Chybris inspired His Jaahnim acolytes, warning them of danger. A mistake, I fear."

"Why a mistake?"

"The Dissolver hadn't yet troubled any Hhoymon, but one might say they are highly imaginative in matters of personal risk."

"Yeah. Hhoymon City's locked down pretty tight. So what happened?"

"The acolytes pleaded with Chybris for protection until He explained His limitations. But He put Urien on the line, as it were, and the Messenger promised to move to Jaahnim. This did little to ease Hhoymon fears. Thanks to Chybris, they knew Urien wouldn't undertake to live among a new species without understanding them, which meant decades of the Messenger's unique research before He'd be useful, even after He arrived."

I must've looked confused.

"Urien lives sequentially, David. His Sphere is communication, and to improve as a communicator, He periodically seeks out undiscovered species and incarnates among them as an infant, hiding from Himself all knowledge of His past or true identity. He then undergoes the indigenous versions of childhood and adolescence, *directly* experiencing being a member of his selected species."

"When does—"

"After reaching basic maturity—the human equivalent would be no more than thirty years—He regains full awareness. *If* he survives. Most of His mortal lives end, I gather, prematurely."

"He won't save Himself?"

"Not if it interferes with learning. Should he reach maturity, He usually acts, for a time, as an ombudsman for the species. Eventually, He releases His mortal body and spends a second or a millennium absorbing what He's learned and communing with fellow Supernals, particularly His mate, Arfaenn."

"Mate? Supernals, um, shack up?"

Ben laughed. "That would hardly describe the relationship. Communication and artistic creativity are naturally married."

"How long has Urien been at this species switching game?"

"Time measured by the lifespan of stars."

"Repeating the same cycle?"

"Quite."

I had to grin. "So you can only be positive you're not the Messenger yourself if you wake up, in human terms, on your thirty-first birthday. Then if you ain't Him, you ain't Him."

Ben chuckled. "That covers it nicely."

"Let's get back to Chybris after the flood."

No more chuckling. "As you wish. After the tragedy and its

aftermath, the Librarian became reclusive. He's a tenderhearted chap in His personal aspect, David. Desiring to spare humanity should ShiwaKhali return, He moved the White Pyramid to the Atlantic depths, far from cities. He still observes human events, but keeps His distance."

BOOM! This one put a crack in the ledge supporting us. The magician ignored it, so I did the same.

"Was it the … diluvian nightmare that made you go solo?"

He grimaced. "No, but after the Dissolver, life changed. We were still a family, Chybris and we three, still dancing with the universe, but often with … heavier feet. Chybris felt personally responsible. The First Born have vast abilities and equivalent capacities, David, and He suffered proportionately." Ben's voice grew tighter. "He *still* suffers. He is truly Prometheus, sorrow eating at Him daily, or perhaps Lucifer, fallen bringer of light, remembered as evil due to echoes of so much—oh, bloody hell. Such hard feelings after so many eons. Are *you* all right?"

The Librarian's voluntary exile had struck a chord in me, moved me more than I'd realized. I shrugged, not trusting my voice.

"It *is* a harsh story, my friend."

I swallowed hard. "Anyone figure out what the Dissolver was after?"

"Urien did. Has anyone told you of Maanza's Reward?"

"Where other Supernals try to destroy Maanza's body?"

"Precisely. Apparently, ShiwaKhali came to Chybris for strategic advice. The Dissolver owed Maanza and wanted to … pay up."

Ben stood up again to peer both ways down the chasm. "What can be delaying him?" he muttered.

"Who?"

"Patience. But I'm taking overlong to reach the crux. Are you prepared to jump ahead some ten thousand years?"

"Provided I can do it sitting down."

He smiled weakly. "After Crossroad was assembled, Binae had Her Common invite Hhoymon as colonists. They accepted on the condition that they'd be protected from dangerous First Born. After ten millennia, they hadn't forgotten ShiwaKhali and feared that the Diplomat's presence might draw other Supernals. A quite realistic fear, so Binae promised to keep them safe."

I shifted uneasily. "Sounds like a big promise."

"'Big' rather understates the case. The Diplomat took Her vow seriously, violating the spirit of the Reward by enlisting Maanza Himself. The Defender developed an energy, ah, prophylactic to protect Crossroad's vulnerable citizens, and installed other technological wards. Meanwhile, Binae and Urien strived to convince ShiwaKhali to keep away. In the end, Urien felt uncertain if the Dissolver comprehended the need, and warned that He-She still felt an obligation to Maanza and would likely act on it."

"And did He? Or She?"

"Both He and She. Twenty-seven cycles back—some eighty years ago—ShiwaKhali appeared here, but too briefly to corrode anything or activate Maanza's protections. However, the Dissolver left behind two dangerous animals, three appalling creatures, and two truly horrific monsters. Our unlamented Easter Weeble fit into the mildest category."

"Why would ShiwaKhali do such a thing?"

"I've no idea. Even the monsters couldn't damage Maanza's physical—hang on! Would you *look* at that?"

Ben scowled at the cliff across the sea of sand below our feet. From this distance, even the largest tunnel entrances in that cliff looked no bigger than pinpricks.

"What is it?" I asked.

"Are they insane? They know I'm with you; do they think so little of me? Must be some bloody *test*. Did you say something, David?"

"What's *happening*?"

"See for yourself." Ben stuck out a forefinger, whirling it around in a large vertical circle. The finger left behind a clean silver line as it moved. When the ring was complete, floating in midair, Ben breathed on it. Just like that, it framed a mirror. I briefly goggled at my own reflection until the surface misted and a new image appeared. The mirror had become a telescope.

What it revealed spoiled my admiration of Ben's latest magic. I saw Big Mouth emerging from a tunnel opening, tongue-tentacles glistening in the light, every tongue pointed my way. A huge chunk of stone beside the tunnel broke free to crash on the sand. A moment later I heard another of those terrifying booms. Another mystery solved?

If so, it brought me no joy.

CHAPTER 26
PUSHING AGAINST THE SKY

"Most vexing," Ben murmured.

The beast's body emerged like the endless scarf from a conjurer's sleeve, visibly accelerating as more of its bulk escaped the constricting tunnel. The entire entrance to the tunnel broke free and scattered into a million pieces.

Now, for the first time, I could see more than the thing's head as it moved directly toward us. Lovely. The segmented back appeared armored in corkscrew spikes.

"Shouldn't we get moving?" I asked in a parody of a calm voice.

"Steady. Our only concern is determining our enemies' purpose."

Not *my* only concern. The whole creature finally emerged, and it seemed longer than the Trenton Zipway, but even less aesthetic. Ben's mirror acted as a camera on dolly tracks, a viewpoint keeping abreast of the monster. Big Mouth's legs were massive curved pistons hammering the body along, leaving a sand-wake....

The Mirrormage pursed his lips.

"Ben, you're planning on doing something, aren't you?"

He seemed startled by the idea. "Me?"

I turned my head to stare at him. "That thing is moving fast! You *can't* think my shadowcasting is strong enough to—"

"Dear boy, don't let the worm concern you. The vital thing is to stay sharp; this shabby attack may mask a serious one."

In Ben's mirror, the "worm" seemed no closer. I looked past the telescope's edge....

"Hate to bother you," I hissed. "But at this rate, in a few seconds it'll be on top of us. Looks hungry *and* angry."

"I understand your concern, dear boy. Anger so spoils digestion."

"BEN!"

He laughed. "Honestly, we've nothing to—why, here's an ally now."

A paranoid's worst delusion, an arachnid scaled to hunt dinosaurs, jumped from the hidden top of our sheltering overhang, landing almost delicately in front of Big Mouth. Lord Loaban reared up on four bristly legs. The worm made him look tiny.

Horror faced horror. Then, bright enough to shame the sun, pink lightning burst from the sand and formed a blazing cyclone of energy between the god's extended front legs. Snaps, crackles, and a whole lot of pops.

A machine-gun spray of sizzling bolts discharged between hairy legs and tentacles. Tortured air rumbled as if acres of tin sheet were shaking and Big Mouth bellowed, slithering to a halt. I smelled burning rubber and noticed a long shadow drifting across the sand.

Ben glanced upward. "And here, I believe, comes our closer."

Savior two appeared overhead, perhaps seventy feet up, a four-armed creature in a golden outfit that made Jeeves, by comparison, seem drab enough to wear when applying for a bank loan.

I'd last seen this gravity-challenged alien in the Chean-shee restaurant, where he, she, or it had seemed a clumsy sort of flier. But now I got a different impression seeing the character soaring through the air, supporting by *one end only* a granite slab larger than the Washington Monument. Grit falling on my tongue interrupted my disbelief. Hadn't realized my mouth was open.

When slab overhung worm, Loaban stopped wasting electricity and leaped backward. With seven legs that size, that god could *jump*. I was sure he'd land on us.

He missed, but our hero didn't. The falling stone hit monster with a tremendous, sickening crunch. Orange-marmalade goo squirted out from under the slab. Gold Lamé hollered down to us in some alien language, waved, and then vanished into the blue distance.

I was the first to break the silence. "What did it say?"

"Erigner? Loosely, 'Sorry about the mess, boys.'"

"Oh."

The Apnoti shook himself, jerking his bulbous body up and down like some grotesque pump. Smoke rose from his front leg-hairs and his head drooped. Seems hurling thunderbolts takes something out of you.

Ben bowed. "Our gratitude for your timely actions, Lord. Have you seen me in this guise? Do I not make a handsome mammal? I believe you've met Professor Goldberg; heard no end about *that*."

The spider made unpleasant squeaking noises and a moment later, I heard what was obviously a translation. "Your appearance and beliefs do not interest me, magus." I didn't see any speechstaff around.

"Do you likewise discount my thanks?" Ben asked, grinning.

"I keep what I earn."

"You've earned them."

"Pah. The worm was soft compared to the Dissolver's other pets. Have you bothered to inform your charge of the full danger?"

"On his own, he destroyed an em-Bottho. He isn't helpless."

The hairy face turned my way. "You look helpless. What are your plans?"

"Plans? Well ... Ben here was telling me—"

"I'm a tolerant deity. Feel free to ignore your impending termination as you see fit. While you two fools spit at each other—"

"It's called 'talking,'" Ben injected.

"—I shall again petition the Watergod for some *practical* assistance."

The magician snorted. "And you think that will help, do you?"

"Someone must do *something*, Juggler. As usual, only I realize this. Be wary!" The god turned translucent, transparent, gone.

I looked at Ben. "Juggler? Meaning magician?"

He looked embarrassed. "Chybris gave me the nickname 'Saint Juggler' because for some time, I tried to ... assist the human race. Finally had to give it up as a bad job."

"Why?"

"Several reasons. For one, it's too easy, when taking up causes, to start feeling superior to those who don't share your beliefs. The worthier the cause, the greater the danger. One fine day in 1229, if memory serves, I looked in a mirror and saw an arse."

"So you went, um, cold turkey on trying to help?"

"Let's say I cut back. The main issue is that I've never been wise enough to know the *consequences* of my actions. The best of intentions may not yield useful results."

"1229. My God, Ben, it just dawned on me. The history you must've witnessed firsthand!"

His scowl squelched my enthusiasm. "Trivia later. For now, let's confine ourselves to the relevant."

"Then let's do that. What's the 'full danger' Loaban mentioned?"

The scowl deepened. "The Apnoti's a bloody alarmist. I can't control the two major beasties, but neither can our enemies. The others I can handle or avoid. Describing them would please neither of us right now."

"If you say so." I glanced at the dropped slab; the goop around its edges had darkened. "That rock bothers me."

"Not, I daresay, so much as it bothered the worm."

"I'm serious. Seems impossible for anyone, however strong, to lift it from one end. Without proper leverage and counterbalancing—"

"The river of your thoughts runs muddy, dear boy. Do you think Erigner flies by pushing the air with bulging muscles?"

"Oh."

"He's no stronger than you, just a clever chap who's learned to channel gravity." Ben stretched and peered upward. "Speaking of which, I should apply a similar technique and carry us to a safer location. Have you cause to remain in this canyon?"

"No," I said slowly, troubled by his words "carry us."

"Excellent. A certain someone is tardy, and we shall be less vulnerable watching for him elsewhere. You'll enjoy this sleight: I call it the 'escaladder.'"

He pressed his hands together. As he moved them apart, a silvery bar some two feet long appeared between his palms, hovering in midair. He casually slapped it aside then repeated the process three times before grabbing two of the levitating bars, arranging one at my chest-height and another directly beneath at ankle-level.

"Grab the upper rung, David, and grip tight. Ah, I would suggest *now* being the appropriate time. Well done. You'll notice that the rung remains stable no matter how hard you pull. Now place your feet on the lower one. Grip tight as you can!"

"I'm not sure this is a good—"

Before I could finish, the rungs yanked me upward hundreds of feet. "Damn it, Ben!" I yelled.

"Jolly sensible notion you've got there," he remarked a moment later, rising alongside me on his own two bars. "I expect that your Guardian friend would tell you that you're bound and determined not to fall off."

I was about to say what I thought of his "sleight," and not quietly, when I saw what he'd meant. Unconsciously, I'd tied myself to the ladder with bands of shadow.

"Hilarious. What now? I'm not all that comfortable up here."

"Now we'll do a bit of traveling. This shouldn't take overlong."

Our rungs lifted us higher, then abruptly shot sideways over jagged canyon walls, more and higher canyon walls, and finally downward to the littoral of a new ocean of sand, this one tinted pink. We drifted toward a solitary monolith sandblasted to smoothness, and landed near its base.

"Next time," I gritted, absorbing my safety-ropes and stepping unsteadily to the ground, "*warn* me first."

"So sorry. Before we rose, I imagined the disagreeable items our foes might drop on our heads on the way up. Perhaps I trod a bit heavily on the petrol. May I make it up to you with another beverage?"

"Not until my stomach has rappelled down where it belongs. Ben, once again, who are we expecting?"

"Ah," he said, "just *look* at that view!"

I looked. Ahead of us, the pink sand desert sloped slightly downward, stretching immensely far into the distance. The Mind had shown me a similar scene back in my Constructor apartment. Odd, though, seeing Crossroad's sun moving so relentlessly and noticeably across the sky. Unlike Ben, it seemed in a hurry to get somewhere. As for the Mirrormage, he apparently preferred fussing and fuming exactly where we were.

For the umpteenth time, Ben stood to turn around in a slow circle, muttering peevishly while nursing something smelling of rum. I sat, sipping hot cocoa. Now that the sun had set, night seemed uninterested in taking over. The desert had been glowing like red flame for what seemed hours. Finally, languorously, as if it had all day, the sky purpled until twilight extinguished the blaze and Crossroad's profuse stars appeared, the Pan-Cosmic pentimento.

I worked it out. Crossroad is nearly Jupiter-huge, yet a "turn" takes almost twenty-four Earth hours. That's lazy compared to Jupiter's insane twirl, but it means that Crossroad's surface keeps scooting along far faster than Earth terrain. Ergo, the sun here appears to whip across the sky. But this world is also *shiny*, putting Venus, the solar system's albedo champion, to shame. The prolonged twilight had to result from this sun's oblique rays reflecting on terrain beyond the horizon. Case closed. Maybe. But whatever the cause, that fantastic ruby glow had been beautiful. Titian would've wept.

We hadn't spoken for so long that Ben's soft voice startled me. "Loaban was right, David. I *should* inform you about ShiwaKhali's monsters. Wouldn't do to leave you ignorant if something happens to me."

"Do me a huge favor. Don't leave me at all."

He smiled. "I shall endeavor to give satisfaction."

"Thanks. Okay, what was in ShiwaKhali's don't-care package?"

"Nothing pleasant. The two minor terrors alone did terrible harm. The em-Bottho attacked the Vyre, killing hundreds with its noxious spit and perilous reservoir. I believe the elastic ones have some rudimentary mental discipline, but it failed against the ... unbreakable ovum. Vyre leaders called on the Common who had a Mind imprison the egg.

"Meanwhile, the worm appeared in Blenntown where it consumed dozens of warriors and damaged several nests—domes, that is. But the Blenn soon contained it and petitioned Binae to decide its fate."

"Hmm. And those two are the *least* dangerous of the collection?"

"I'm afraid so. Of the three middle-threat monsters, two attacked Common headquarters in Triangle One. These proved immune to the regional Mind but were destroyed by weapons provided by Maanza. Unfortunately, the third, the *Chhide*, something of an immense insect, forced its way into Hhoymon City." Ben paused. "Perhaps I'd best show you." He grabbed a fistful of sand.

That hand began glowing from within, trapped light turning the fingers translucently red. Radiant grains slowly trickled out, sand pixels, gradually forming a pattern in midair. Colors infused the design, producing a 3D image of Hhoymon City. But not as I'd last seen it.

"Lord," I whispered.

I stared at the ruined towers, some apparently pushed over, others cracked or mangled. Twisted bodies, and torn off heads and limbs lay in the streets. Various smears might have once been people. The great museum alone, the Heart of Art, appeared untouched.

"Two thousand Hhoymon," Ben stated quietly, "died that day. The survivors were further distraught because they hadn't defeated the atrocity themselves." He grimaced. "It's unclear precisely what happened. Hhoymon and Blenn investigators tentatively concluded that the Chhide had been using some extraneous, unknown power source to block Hhoymon weapons. When it failed—they offered no explanation for the failure—the monster fled." The picture dimmed, its pixel-sand fell.

I shivered. "Extraneous power?"

"Ah. Binae, for example, constantly sheds force just as you and I shed heat. Part of Her spiritual metabolism, as it were. You are familiar with the concept of darshan? Excellent! Attuned beings can tap into Her spare darshan to extend their native abilities. Truthfully, David, my own powers are modest without any First Born to draw on; that silver force I employ is more borrowed than earned."

"Then who or what do you think gave that monster the extra juice?"

"I fear ShiwaKhali made a ... deposit before departing."

I felt sick. "Hate to ask, but if this Chhide was only a 'middle-threat' monster ..." I left the question hanging.

"By luck or charity, the major terrors arrived in wilderness areas. These two, mind you, were of a different order altogether. Not really creatures but, ah, embodiments of destruction. The lesser, which Hhoymon have termed the *Nedleugch*, appeared in the form of a—a bloody, malicious vortex. Ghastly powerful thing."

"And the champion bad boy?"

"The *Aiforrak*, a word with no English equivalent. Rock Dragon? Too sweet. 'Lithic Shark' hits closer. Lithshark! An adequate label for a perfect horror. Of all the Dissolver's refuse, this alone might give Maanza a scratch."

"Description?"

Ben exhaled heavily; his breath smelled of rum. "A fish to dwarf mountains! But it can loosen its form to swim through stone."

"Lord. Seems a miracle the two biggies didn't do any harm."

"No harm? It took us ten cycles to restore Triangle Two to a semblance of normalcy. In places, even your weak eyes couldn't miss evidence of phenomenal mutilation."

I shivered again. "How did you deal with monsters that strong?"

"Binae asked the Firemage, the Lightmage, and me to study them. By the time we reached Triangle Two, the Lithshark's ... waveform had transformed, becoming too abstract to secure. With Binae's assistance, I applied a reflective sleight on the vortex, turning its power on itself. But then it, too, transformed. At least, the change rendered both harmless and ever since, they've remained neither here nor there. May they exist in that state forever!

"Meanwhile, separate teams dispatched to deal with the lesser brutes made a distressing discovery: the Chhide, em-Bottho, and worm had vanished. The major monsters continued to generate random harmonics, but the others were simply gone. We suspected these three had been placed in an encapsulating field of unknown type and tucked away. Perhaps for a very rainy day. It seems, my boy, that for two of them at least, that day arrived."

I nodded unhappily. "And without waiting for any rain."

When night fully ruled, Jeeves puffed up against the increasing cold. Ben had fallen silent and kept making brief forays out into the desert.

Six large luminous bubbles in various pastels emerged from the sand to stand around us on trios of wire-thin legs—ethereal Japanese lanterns. No moths around to cast shadows or batter them dusty. Ben ignored them so I assumed they were his doing. A green one raised a leg to rub against its own bubble like a dog scratching behind an ear.

I was the one to rupture the stillness. "So, the Hhoymon were promised safety and their city was almost destroyed."

He answered without looking at me. "They were angry indeed. Many felt Binae had broken her sacred vow. But they'd known all along She wasn't omniscient or an intrinsically protective Supernal. They hadn't come to Crossroad to get *Her* protection although they'd demanded it."

"No?"

"Only one Supernal could truly defend them."

"Oh. Maanza."

"Precisely. They'd hoped that by serving Binae faithfully, She'd be willing to implore Maanza to add Jaahnim to a very select list."

"Did it work?"

Ben glanced at the nearest lantern, which grew bright enough for me to see his grim expression with ordinary vision. "Binae can't be manipulated. But when Hhoymon learned how the Common had defended Triangle One—well, many felt it would be a jolly good thing if Hhoymon replaced Common as Binae's primary aides."

"Oh. They wanted Maanza's superweapons."

"Wouldn't you? Hence, a cabal of Hhoymon set out to convince Binae of their superiority for the job. Binae declined the proposal. And that, we believe, was when a rebel faction decided to take a ... different approach to supplanting the Guardians." Ben's dark eyes seemed to turn darker.

"What approach?"

"Bio-psychological warfare."

"What's that?"

"Organisms tailored to distort a Common's perceptions. Permanently."

"Nasty. I imagine Hhoymon are master biochemists?"

"Indeed, but such weapons are difficult to hone. The rebels, through channels that have proved untraceable so far, tried to enlist loyalists in their scheme. A cold civil war ensued that only turned white-hot recently."

"What turned up the heat?"

"About three Earth weeks ago, the conspirators found themselves facing an unexpected crisis."

Three weeks. "Tell me."

Ben lowered his voice. "You look as if you've already guessed. The fighting began when rebels learned you were coming here."

"But *why*?" More people died because of me.

"Again, not your fault. We'd been expected trouble, counting on it, actually."

The breeze shifted, carrying a faint howl. To my shock, Ben's ears momentarily stretched into something almost canine. "Nothing to fear, David, only the wind."

Right then I didn't care. "Ben. Are you saying you *wanted* Hhoymon to murder each other?"

"Certainly not! The degree of violence surprised even the Watergod. Our plan was to stimulate just enough trouble to either reveal the rebels or justify expelling all Hhoymon. That's why we'd asked them to put you up. We had to isolate the rebels somehow. So, we made sure they knew you were coming."

CHAPTER 27
SIBLING REVELRY

My jaw felt so tight it seemed my teeth would crack. "Damn it! We're back to square one. What do the rebels have against me? Why should my visit cause problems for anyone?"

"Easy, lad! I'm only certain about part of it."

"*What*?" I shouted in a whisper.

"Patience, patience. When he arrives, all shall fall into place."

"You still won't say who?"

"Consider it a—an unexpected counterweight to your many hard losses. Look! A meteorite. A rare sight in Crossroad's sky. An auspicious sign!"

My interest in meteorites had hit an all-time low. Guilt chewed my soul. So much death and grief; my own brothers ...

Ben patted my arm. "You mustn't take life so personally." He produced two fresh cups of cocoa and handed one over like an apology. The night went silent except for our sipping and occasional *plinks* from cooling rocks. The familiar drink steadied me, providing an emotional barrier against a chill I sensed more than felt.

"How much longer?" I finally asked.

Silence.

Me: "You say we don't know the rebels' racial type. Didn't loyal Hhoymon find rebel corpses after their war?"

"None."

More silence.

Me: "Was Loaban hiding on that overhang before we got there?"

"Certainly."

"You and the spider had it all worked out?"

Ben tilted his head to regard me. "Actually, the Watergod assigned us our roles."

"Oh. Did he tell you where to find me?"

"Good thing too, since you've become so elusive of late."

"I have?"

"Bit of an enigma there."

Apparently, my feelings showed.

"Steady, David."

"It's like fighting a—a damn super-Hydra," I groaned. "One question gets answered. Zap! Four more pop up."

"Indeed. When wind ruffles water it's hard to see reflections, but a picture *is* forming."

I stared hard at him, wondering if his *Ugly Duckling*-related metaphor had been coincidental. "I hope."

"I didn't require the Watergod's aid to find you in that underground meadow," he said thoughtfully. "Knew you'd pass through there eventually. But how our *enemies* keep managing to find you beggars imagination. You've become quite the phantom lately."

"Why? I haven't ... wait! Maybe I know why." I described my Neme disguise technique.

"Sorry, old boy. We wanted you to feel reasonably secure in a dreadfully insecure situation, so we had the Minds play along with your idea. Besides, we had something better than thought forms to track you with, something that solved multiple difficulties."

"Explain."

"Earth's universe makes a poor medium for telepathy." He waved a hand. "Here, resistance is minimal and mind-powers as commonplace as camels among Bedouins. Since the rebels might well have telepathic allies, we needed to mute your, ah, mental tannoy, thus also making it difficult for *us* to monitor you. A pretty problem."

"Rider claimed I'd been given a mental shield for privacy."

He chuckled. "Indeed. The instant you arrived on Crossroad, we infused your bloodstream with organisms specialized for mental phase-cancellation. I expect you felt some dizziness?"

I nodded.

"Initially, we were jolly pleased with ourselves. We had telepaths hidden within Great Hall Four and only those quite close to you could sense your surface thoughts. Meanwhile, the organisms carried a hidden, ah, signature that blazed on our instruments like Djer's pyre. Then it all went pear-shaped. The hardy organisms began dying off. We had to keep replenishing them and supply was limited. Much ado behind the scenes. In the end, only giving you a taurei stabilized the cells."

I took a slow breath. "So, I have to admit you were right: a picture is forming, but not a pretty one. Let's see if I've got everything straight, and you can check my deductions."

"Proceed. This should be interesting."

"Way, way, *way* back, the Hhoymon, already plenty paranoid, learned that at least one Supernal was the worst sort of news. My first deduction: the Librarian or maybe the Messenger, both of whom had hung out with them for centuries, had told them of another Supernal, Maanza, who protected entire species from pretty much any danger, once He became involved with that species. Am I on track so far?"

"Spot on, and I'm surprised. That's quite the deductive leap."

"Without it, none of this makes sense. To continue, when the Powers That Be—I'm thinking more the Power That Is—on Crossroad invited Hhoymon to establish an entire colony here, not just an Enclave, the Hhoymon agreed if the Diplomat promised to keep them safe. Clever plan. They knew that defense isn't in Binae's nature, and figured She'd be calling on Maanza to set up defenses for their colony. Once Maanza became involved in protecting them on Crossroad, they believed He'd automatically take on the job of defending their home planet, which made it worth the risks of coming here.

"Now here's where it gets dicey. Second deduction: rather than enlist Maanza on behalf of the Hhoymon, Binae and the Messenger simply tried to discourage the Dissolver from visiting Crossroad, and succeeded just enough to keep the Supernal from popping in for more than a few seconds.

"This didn't work out too well because ShiwaKhali happened to be playing a game of Injure Maanza, and dropped off a load of monsters here as part of the game for some reason we don't yet know.

"One such monster practically destroyed Hhoymon City, and some Hhoymon decided that the plan to cozy up to Maanza needed a major boost. These particular geniuses figured that if Hhoymon replaced the Common as Binae's chief assistants, they'd be in a better position to directly deal with the Defender. Still good?"

"Jolly good."

"But most of Crossroad's Hhoymon wouldn't go along with the plan, which required killing off the Common, and that's how matters stood for decades until very recently when a civil war broke out, which you claimed had been triggered for no reason I can imagine by my upcoming visit. The rebels lost, but blended into the general population so well that neither loyal Hhoymon or Crossroad authorities could identify them. So the Common kicked out all Hhoymon, believing that only rebels would sneak back still trying to implement their plan, and could then be exposed. Brilliant idea, except the rebels are too smart to be found.

"Now we come to me. Years ago, a team of rebels came to Earth, I have no idea why, to murder me. You took it on yourself, again I don't know why, to stop them. Years passed, and bad things happened to people I love. Then, with your help, I was drafted to come here as part of some new plan, which so far makes no sense to me but seems to have caused nothing but grief. Ever since then, I've been steered this way and that, including to a roomful of Scome machines, the whole time ... bugged."

He frowned. "'Bugged' only to protect you. But as I said, that signature has vanished. Your summary is masterful as far as it goes, and your pithiness puts my loquacity to shame." He shook his head. "I remain gobsmacked by your insight concerning Maanza."

"Which one?"

"His habit of assuming responsibility for an entire species once He feels responsible for any of its members. I'm astonished you'd managed to realize that with so little information. But I swear, David, lately the center can't even get a grip. It's as if some unknown force enjoys annulling our plans, and I'm not even certain our enemies are responsible."

"Why so much urgency to block my thoughts? What the hell were you trying to hide?"

He had the nerve to grin. "Almost everything about you: your background, your work, and your suspicions. Above all, we had to keep the photograph that brought you here an absolute secret."

"Why?"

"To prevent rebels deducing our basic plan."

"*What* plan? And if I'm such a liability, why drag me to Crossroad?"

"Surely, I'd already made this clear. This world really has dimmed your intellect! You were to be the bait to draw out our enemies."

I nodded firmly. "I did understand that much, but I wanted to know if you had enough raw chutzpah to come out and say the word 'bait.' My mom told me as a child: 'Son, learn to be bait, then you'll always have something to fall back on.'"

I regarded the ultra-alien stars, barely muted by our lanterns, and then turned to glare at my companion. "For God's sake, Ben."

He winced. Slightly. "Our intentions were impeccable, dear boy."

"Uh huh. Impeccable. Words fail. But the big question rolls around yet again: *why me*?"

"We know your enemies fear you. Why else would they have made such efforts to kill you on Earth?"

I could feel my teeth grinding. "And they fear me *because*...?"

"We're uncertain."

"Are you *kidding*?"

"Easy, dear boy. No sense in getting overwrought. I'll say this much. We believe the threat you pose involves your, ah, involvement with the Scome."

I blinked stupidly. "Involvement? The fact I've been studying—wait. You think I've stumbled onto something concerning the Scome that threatens the rebels?"

Ben looked uncomfortable. "I'll add something more: once you found where we'd hidden the Scome machines, we felt confident they'd reveal themselves."

I let the "we'd hidden" slide for the moment and didn't bother keeping my voice down. "WHY? The rebels are nuts! *All* of you are nuts!"

"Perhaps."

"Good God! No wonder Loaban thought Rider was being reckless with my health! If you expected me to get attacked, Ben, where the hell were you when that rock hit my arm?"

Without my Crossroad vision, his blush would've been too faint to see. "The rebels came up with, ah, a red herring that detained me. I am truly shamed."

I felt too upset to ease up. "So I was drafted because I pose some mysterious hazard to these rebels? Maybe they're allergic to bait."

"We were *also* attempting to salvage your life. For eight years I've warded you on Earth; you may recall recent events concerning an explosion in your office and a certain bus? Without my aid, these incidents would've gone far worse for you. Unless we identify your enemies, they *will* kill you eventually."

I felt my own face reddening. "Sorry. Good point."

"Dear boy, water under the bridge. Let's stop snapping at each other like old jackals and enjoy the night, which is getting a bit nippy itself." He stretched. "Here's where it's good to be the mage. Prepare to be astounded!"

Ben tilted his head back. Silvery lines sprouted from his jaw, lengthening. In seconds, he sported a long white beard. Despite everything, I laughed; with that buildup, I'd expected far more.

"Well, David? Does it make me appear antiquated? Rather matches my campus nickname, what?" At the university, no one had dreamed how old "Old Ben" really was.

"How were you protecting me on Earth?"

He grumbled deep in his throat. "With vigilance and effort."

"Magic works on Earth?"

He eyed me narrowly. "'Magic' is science based on principles you haven't yet discovered or fully explored. Take homeopathic pills, for example."

"C'mon. Those are just placebos."

"But why do placebos work? Almost everywhere, connections exist between mental and physical realms. If you—"

A sparkling blue light limned the horizon.

Ben turned toward the fading phenomena, eyes doubling in size. My back-of-the-neck hairs stirred. I started to speak but was shushed by a brusque gesture.

A silvery bead appeared on Ben's forehead, swelled dramatically, brightened, and burst from his brow Minerva-style—scrambled mythology since the object flattened into a mirror more evocative of Aphrodite. He closed his shrinking eyes and the mirror sped off, trailing light like a horizontal comet. I waited, brooding over Ben's revelations while trying not to anticipate ones to come. I didn't care for the trend.

He finally looked at me. "Can't see anything amiss. Still, at this point everything unexplained is worrisome."

"No wonder I'm so worried. Shouldn't we ... do something?"

"Indeed. We've tarried overlong. I'll be gone for a time. Stay near these lamps! Promise me you'll not wander."

"Where would I go?"

"I shan't be long."

Ben's face paled to white, matching his hair and beard. His entire form shimmered, turning glossy then fully reflective. This time he didn't change form or embed himself in a flaming sphere. Instead, a Ben-shaped mirror suddenly darted toward the nearest cliff. I caught one glimpse of him *running* up the vertical wall.

Then I was alone.

I sighed, gazing up at night's twinkling blanket. Stars directly overhead zipped by as if invoked by an anti-Joshua. On a world with mountain-sized monsters, that kind of speed seemed an excellent idea. Could I somehow use shadowcasting to match Ben's quickness?

Again, the notion of shadow wings crossed my mind and got crossed off. Too risky. Perhaps a hang-glider? Right. How would I get off the ground? Extrude an extra-tall dark ladder and jump off the top? *Hello*, I thought. *Would any ideas short of totally idiotic please cut ahead in line?*

I could move shadow damn fast. Should be some way to take advantage. High-speed land travel? What about shadow spider-god legs? I extended four long black limbs from my torso and cautiously used them to lever myself off the ground, got balanced, moved one dark leg forward, and began stumbling around like some horribly impaired arachnid.

Back on exo-terra firma—buggy legs dissolved, real ones shaky—I had an inspiration: *short* legs. Hundreds of 'em. I'd lie on my stomach, extend shadow threads beneath me, and centipede myself along.

Stretching out on the sand, I extruded filaments from chest to ankles. As threads lengthened, my body lifted. Two feet above the ground, almost floating, I willed my shadow carpet to move. The threads all jerked backward, hurling me forward. Onto my face.

Ouch.

But a shadow-pillow had formed so rapidly that my pride took the larger blow; even *Jeeves* had been caught with my pants down. Deciding to postpone further experiments in rapid transit, I stood, shadow and figurative egg dripping from my face. Pity my subconscious hadn't yet learned this cushioning trick back in the meadow. Or had some atavistic impulse made it reach for the nearest tree?

I frowned at my microdoc cast. As armor, Jeeves wasn't all that wonderful. Could shadow do a better job? It was certainly faster....

I wrapped myself in blackness and tried walking. Lovely. Enshrouded this way, I'd lose a race with a snow-suited toddler. And such thick darkness behaved capriciously; it kept sinking into my body. Still, in an emergency, some extra padding—whoa. *There* was a thought. Shadow could filter through Jeeves, but what if Jeeves didn't cooperate? Could microdocs block something so immaterial?

I maintained my attempt at shadow armor and ordered my suit to prevent any reabsorption. Just like that the darkness stabilized. Grinning, I patted myself on the back with four shadow-arms.

Question: was Jeeves acting as a physical barrier or somehow *relaying* my instructions? Both my personal allies responded to my thoughts, so a kind of telepathic chain might be possible. A lurking notion burst into center stage, bowing and hamming it up. Could my microdocs micromanage my shadow? Maybe I'd given up on rapid transit prematurely. I dissolved all blackness, lay down again, regenerated threads, and gave Jeeves literal marching orders.

Microdocs were to assign themselves to individual threads. Upon my command, 'docs would coordinate everything, making most threads act like tiny legs working in efficient sequence. Evenly distributed among these moving parts, other threads were to shorten themselves slightly and remain vertical to give me stability. I added refinements. When turning, microdocs would act as a telepathic differential, individualizing thread stride-length from one side of the shadow carpet to the other. I gave similar instructions for speed-control.

I extruded a shadow crash helmet, took a breath, gave the go command ... and shouted, "Stop!" I looked around. The lanterns had become distant glowing dots. Disbelieving, I tried to rub my eyes and rubbed microdoc goggles. Right. At that velocity, I'd needed them.

Well, I'd broken my promise to Ben, but hadn't done any other harm. Or had I? Conceivably, those lanterns did more than cast pretty lights. With a word to Jeeves, I returned to my post; the sheer speed of the piggyback ride made me laugh. And with the proved collaborative abilities of microdocs and shadow, I might pull off a stunt that would impress even the Mirrormage!

Preoccupied, I didn't notice Ben returning until he was close. He'd shed his reflective gloss and he wasn't alone. My heart started pounding; perhaps it knew something I didn't. The newcomer had to be either the bizarre Neme who'd hugged me in the Vyre village or an identical twin.

"Here he is," the magician chuckled. "He'd arrived early, found a nice comfy spot to wait, and our boy fell asleep! Can you—" He froze, sniffing the air. "You, ah, didn't leave the warded area, David?"

"I'm sorry, I did ... accidentally. Just for a moment."

Annoyance twisted his face then vanished. One thing I'd noticed about Ben: he laughed, got angry and sad, made mistakes, yet he never got *stuck* in any emotion. And he didn't waste time with recriminations. "No help for it, we'll leave straightaway. Why take risks? Move first, talk later, eh?"

The lanterns evaporated. Ben extended both hands and brightness sprayed fiercely from his palms. In seconds, the Neme and I wore glowing silver from our heads down to our feet. The mage then re-plated himself. From inside my new shell, the world remained perfectly visible, but blue-tinged.

"*Will* yourself forward, gentlemen, as you would on a Safe-road," Ben advised. "Keep upright and don't move your legs. I'll start slowly 'til you get the knack. David, follow me closely," he turned to the Neme, "Jacau, you'll follow David. Ready, gentlemen?"

For the second time in minutes, I zoomed along without any muscular effort, but unlike Safe-road travel, movement required continual intent. Whenever I lost focus, Ben sensed it and stopped long enough for me to catch up. The passing sand under my mirrored feet became a blur, faintly scored with endless straight lines.

A long cliff appeared in the distance; we reached it in seconds. Ben's quicksilver form led us through an opening and into a descending tunnel so dark my x-road vision had to take up the slack. Our pace here seemed suicidal but some guiding force intervened; didn't even stub a toe. I became more worried about getting left behind as Ben kept picking up speed.

We followed a twisty pathway, mostly angling downward, and emerged into brightness: a valley carpeted in golden sand and trimmed in mountains. Untimely daylight and a jade sky told me that some of this had to be illusion. Everything appeared dry enough to crackle. Ben brought us to a stop, de-plated us all, and flopped on the ground, panting as if he'd sprinted the whole way. His face was sweaty, hair beaded with droplets. No beard.

He sniffed. "Should be ... safe enough here. Wait ... 'til I ... catch my breath."

I wasn't tired, but might've done some flopping of my own if the sand hadn't felt so damn hot. An instant later, microdoc sandals solved that problem and I stopped hopping from foot to foot.

Strange place. Scattered, cactus-like plants crowned with ferny growths interrupted the desert monotony. I waited, trying not to stare too obviously at the stranger. I know what you *aren't*, I thought. Meanwhile, the stranger stared openly at me with all three eyes.

"Our temporarily furry friend here," Ben finally said, "has been studying English lately. I believe he might prefer to introduce himself."

"Such be true," the fake Neme said with an accent reminiscent of Bela Lugosi. "I *would* wish to introduce me. Did not know you would ever be allowed here or would have learned this language long ago. On Earth, they called you David Goldberg?"

"That's my name." My voice was a little unsteady. "I heard Ben call you 'Jacau.' I assume that's your name."

"One of them."

"Well ... I'm pleased to meet you, Jacau."

"You should be pleased to meet. I be only your *brother*!"

I stood for a minute, blinking. "Come again?"

"Be my fresh English so weak? I be Jacau Gothhowl, elder brother yours. I only *look* Neme. Truly—"

"Hang on, Jacau!" Ben interrupted. "David, my apologies. It occurs to me that I've been dreadfully overeager to keep this moment a surprise and haven't done a thing to prepare you for it."

I shrugged. "I've already guessed Jacau's a Scome."

"Well. Yes. But then, so are you. Brothers are usually the same species."

CHAPTER 28
LOCUTION, LOCUTION, LOCUTION

Is this why Sara and I couldn't have kids? I thought numbly.

"It's quite true," Ben said gently.

His obvious concern cracked my emotional ice. "It can't be! I'm *obese* compared to a Scome. My skin color's wrong. Hell, I've got hair everywhere!"

One of Jacau's speaking diaphragms expanded. "Be you ... shedding?"

That question, I slowly realized, must be a *joke*. The un-Neme-like stretched diaphragm had been meant to represent a smile. My so-called brother was grinning like a white sunrise....

Ben stood up. "Your original genetic structure has been altered appropriately." His eyes narrowed. "How did you determine Jacau's real nature?"

"Last week," I explained impatiently, "he argued with Sun-toch-sew in a strange language. When I asked what language it was, Rider got coy. Made me wonder. Also—no offense—Jacau makes a lousy Neme, so why bother disguising him at all? There's more. Should I continue?"

Ben sighed. "No. You are either unexpectedly perceptive, or we are bunglers. I'd prefer the issue remain unresolved. Come, let's find some shade and talk."

I followed him, thoughts spinning. I'd never imagined getting the chance to meet a Scome. Doing so should've been the highlight of my career. Now, the suggestion that I'd been so intimately acquainted with one my entire life spoiled the fun. But Ben's claim had to be wrong—of *course* I was human. I encouraged myself to fume. Better than whimpering.

The three of us plodded along, Jacau barely keeping up. Even for a

Neme he was slow. Ben stopped near a quartet of tall cacti, which cast the deepest shadow for miles. We sat down, Jacau last. "What be this place, Magus?" he asked.

"A touch of home for homesick Common."

I didn't give a damn. "Ben, Jacau can't *really* be my brother?"

"I promise you, he is. Unhappily, we couldn't let you remain with your birth family."

I just stared at him.

"Listen closely, David. As is required of non-parallel universes, the natural laws of the Scome native cosmos vary from the ones you and I are accustomed to. There, the interplay between mind and body can produce prodigies. You must understand that conditions on Muuti are bloody harsh, harsh that only such prodigies combined with Scome intelligence have allowed the species to survive."

"What are you—"

"Just listen. Every generation of Scome has a few members born with one or two extraordinary abilities that will emerge as the child develops. Most Scome have mere touches of these exotic talents. I'm sorry to report that you are a unique case, something of a ... freak jackpot on the genetic roulette wheel. Prenatal tests on *you* revealed dozens of potential Scome powers, several of astonishing intensity."

"*What?*"

"We knew you would quickly become a broadcasting telepath of unprecedented strength. If we hadn't relocated you early on, you couldn't have helped but reveal where your people were hiding."

"I don't—this is completely—"

"Those, ah, devices you recently encountered were designed to stimulate dormant Scome powers, each targeting a specific ability. Our plan was to awaken one of your powers."

"Wait! Now I'm sure of it. The Scome are hiding *here* on Crossroad."

Ben's eyes narrowed. "What makes you this sure?"

"For God's sake. Why stick those machines someplace where Jacau's people can't use them? Hey! I wondered if the Common had two secret Triangles tucked away. I'd bet one lies somewhere ... maybe directly below us."

"We are most fortunate," Ben sighed, "that you've become so hard to read."

Jacau watched me as if hypnotized. "Why under *this* Triangle?"

I turned to face him squarely. "Machines like that must be important and you'd want convenient access. Plus, the vegetation near

Oracle Waters and in the meadow below has this, um, super vitality. Reminded me of Muuti jungles I've seen in Neme holicons."

He made his white smile again. "Reminded you of *home*."

"Speaking of home, tell me, why did the Scome abandon Muuti?" I'd been seeking that answer for so many years....

Nemes don't growl, but Jacau did.

"They've been hiding," Ben interjected, "from Hhoymon rebels."

"Seriously? The damn rebels again? A billion people evacuated their *world* because of a few Hhoymon?"

"I should certify we're secure before I explain. Anyone care for a chilled beverage meanwhile?"

Ben released another flying mirror and closed his eyes for several minutes, occasionally frowning. I nursed iced tea, appreciating the coldness without noticing the taste, wondering what Ben saw through his traveling spyglass. Jacau struggled to sip a green liquid through his Neme feeding tubes. I struggled to cope.

"No immediate hazards," Ben finally announced. "But wisdom suggests pressing on."

"The Scome exodus *first*," I insisted.

"Very well. As I said, the rebels were developing biological agents to, ah, disable the Common. Some six Earth decades ago, Hhoymon Loyalists deduced that these agents were nearly perfected."

"Isn't that supposedly when the Common discovered the Scome?"

"Indeed, and they were impressed. Jacau's people possessed only fair mechanical technology, but their medical expertise dwarfed that of all other species living on Commonworld, even including the Blenn. The Common, as usual upon finding humanoid sentients, shared the information with Hhoymon. You've seen holicons of Muuti cities."

"Of course."

"Did you observe any barricades? So much as a moat?"

"Um ... no."

Ben raised a finger as though I'd conceded a point. "Life on Muuti is *competitive*, David, even plants can be aggressive. Still, if we were there this instant, we wouldn't find a spike-beast or whipping vine near any building."

"Why?"

"Biological wizardry. For centuries, no native life-form has attacked any Scome."

"Really? That is impressive."

"When it comes to biological sciences, Hhoymon are rank amateurs compared to Scome. Thus, the rebels found themselves facing a, ah, triple-barreled threat."

I glanced doubtfully at Jacau. "Go on."

"The Common were bound to invite such a remarkable species to set up an Enclave here, perhaps a city. Rebels feared the Scome would soon detect the bio-psychological weapon they planned to use against the Common, or provide a cure after the weapon was deployed."

"Okay, what's down barrel two?"

"Once the Common were, ah, decommissioned, Binae might choose Scome rather than Hhoymon for her new assistants. Blenn would never accept the honor."

I frowned. "If the Common were killed off, wouldn't Binae try to find out why? What if She learned Hhoymon were responsible?"

"Doubtless the rebels planned to immediately confess, leaving the Diplomat free to choose loyal Hhoymon. Our enemies are, I fear, the most ruthless of beings: idealists."

"There's a third barrel?"

"The largest, hollowed out by pure paranoia. The rebels feared that before their weapon was perfected, Scome scientists might already be living here. What if the newcomers desired the high office for *themselves*, discovered the Hhoymon weapon and modified it to use against all competitors? You see? The rebels had to resolve that issue straightaway."

I took a slow sip. "What happened?"

"Remember, they truly believed the long-term survival of their species depended on gaining Maanza's protection. In rebel hearts, David, the Hhoymon seed of paranoia had blossomed into something terrible."

He stopped talking. Under the fake sky, sadness added a decade to my friend's face—still a vast understatement. A thin chill, forerunner of a deeper cold, ran down my spine. Jacau growled again.

"Do Hhoymon weapons," I asked softly, "work in Muuti's universe?"

"Poorly, for the genocide the conspirators had in mind," Ben stated. "The rebels worked, ah, feverishly to adapt sapient cells into a deadly Scome-specific strain and released this pestilence all over Muuti."

"But if Jacau's people were so advanced ..."

"Doubtless the rebels felt that no species, however medically adroit, could survive an attack so brutal and sudden. Are you well, dear boy?"

"Just tell me the result."

"Our enemies were playing far above their class. Your ancestors had developed sapient cells of their own, even more adaptable and sophisticated."

I glanced down at Jeeves, now reduced to shorts, sandals, and a thin T-shirt. "More adaptable than *this*?"

Jacau made a barking sound and he and Ben swapped glances. The mage smiled as if he'd never been sad in his life. "Dear boy, what you are wearing *is* a taurei, the Scome version of a fourth skin."

I found myself half-chuckling, half sobbing. My companions stared at me.

"It's ... too much," I choked out. "I've tried to be ... so careful not to ... to take anyone's word for anything here. Turns out I pretty much believed *everything*."

Ben chuckled then turned serious. "We applied considerable misdirection, David. On Crossroad, your broadcasting talent began stirring. We couldn't risk telling you much until we were sure your mental camouflage was trustworthy."

"Finally makes sense!" I sighed. "Getting back to Muuti, I suppose Scome microdocs ate the rebel virus?"

"Eventually, but many Scome became ill. When tests proved that the pestilence was artificial, Jacau's people knew parties unknown had attacked them. But they trusted the Common and laid the problem before the chief Guardian."

"Who suggested they hide on Crossroad, lock, stock, and all three barrels."

"Indeed. By then, rebels were likely adapting large-scale energy weapons for Muuti's reality. Therefore, the Scome population was brought here and installed precisely where you suspected. We selected this Triangle because the iron-rich sands above us, beyond the faux sky, naturally block radio waves of all sorts."

"A billion people to move overnight. Quite the logistics problem."

"Oh, yes. The job required two of Maanza's star-fleets."

"Weren't you worried about hiding the Scome almost literally under the rebels' noses?"

"Aside from the natural barriers above us, Maanza installed a ... firewall to keep the refugees hidden. Meanwhile, we acted to safeguard Scome biotechnology, destroying every semi-organic 'machine' remaining on Muuti. But at Binae's request, we leaked the information that Nemes had found a forgotten cache of enhancement devices and hidden them in Triangle Six."

"Why?"

"We'd planned to arrange an enhancing room for surreptitious

Scome visits, so She thought the place would make a fine trap for the unauthorized."

Jacau was sitting very still now, staring downward.

"I've little to add," Ben continued softly. "After everything was settled, the Common proclaimed the Scome had mysteriously vanished."

"And a fake mystery was born. Tell me about ... my birth."

"Bit of strangeness there. After your parents were transplanted, they wanted no more children until the rebel threat was abated. You'd no business being conceived, yet you were born on Crossroad."

Home sweet home. "Accidents happen."

My brother looked at me. "*Our* birth control be sure."

"Jacau's right," Ben stated. "But, as I said, you're something of an arsenal of latent wild talents, some of which even your people can't identify."

I shook my head. "If it weren't for shadowcasting, I wouldn't—hey! Is my supposed *potential* why the rebels want me dead?"

"How would they know of your potential? Although once you used an enhancement machine, we were sure they'd find you even more threatening."

"Then what *is* your theory?"

Ben's expression was dead sober. "After Nemes contacted humanity, the insurgents apparently investigated and found you living on Earth."

"How?"

"I can only speculate. Consider how the Common search the universes for conscious beings by using a device sensitive to minuscule distortions in space and time."

"Yeah. The so-called intelliscope. And?"

"Perhaps the rebels, with superior technology, can identify precise species."

"Hmm. Okay. They find me on Earth. Then what?"

"Try to think as a paranoid, dear boy. They uncover a Scome on Earth. Only one. What does that suggest?"

"I don't know. Some kind of spy?"

He snorted. "Your psychosis is woefully deficient. I fancy they'd view you as a weapon."

"A *weapon*?"

"A biological one, of course. Sixty years ago, rebels had attempted genocide. For decades, they'd feared reprisal. Then they find you secreted among a species the Common would inevitably invite to join the Commonwealth."

I looked at Jacau. A Neme can't make a fist, but he came close.

"Why inevitably?" I asked.

"Because, as Hhoymon had known for millennia, *Chybris* lives on Earth, which implies that humanity is indeed worthy."

I nodded thoughtfully. "So the rebels would worry I'd get here one way or another and give them a taste of their own reverse medicine."

"Precisely."

Against my will, I was starting to believe. "All right, Ben. Even if I was doomed to become a telepathic loudmouth, couldn't I have stayed on the same *planet* as my Scome family? With all the ultra-tech and weird powers around here, surely ... *something* could've blocked my childhood thoughts."

His eyes softened. "You were fated to be too strong for us to take such a chance. We needed a new kind of thought screen, which would take years to develop. And what disguise would be certain proof against Hhoymon?"

"We hated this decision," Jacau added.

Ben's voice became incredibly gentle. "Your parents let me hold you in my arms an hour after your birth."

Jacau made a choked noise. "Truth be, you were funny-faced, but I loved you despite."

"You lived here," Ben continued, "until our telepaths heard your first mental whispers. We didn't dare wait for the shouting. I'm truly sorry."

"My parents?"

"Devastated. We were all devastated."

"Hell. Is Earth really—"

Jacau spun to face the open desert. "I hear scratching, magus. Far."

Ben's ears stretched into sails. "Likewise," he muttered, closing his eyes. A new mirror burst from his forehead and flew off.

We waited, listening. Suddenly the mage's ears snapped to normal. Something small and bright flashed toward us then orbited Ben's head so fast it seemed he'd sprouted a halo. Just as I realized the prodigal mirror had returned, it zipped away in a new direction.

Jacau moved closer to me. How would *I* have felt abandoning a baby brother in an alien universe? How my parents must've suffered! My parents. Yes, I was accepting it and all it implied. I stared at my brother's face, trying to imagine the Scome within the Neme facade.

"How old were you, Jacau," I asked softly, "when I was taken away?"

"Three cycles."

Not quite nine years old. "Can't imagine what you went through."

My brother grabbed my good arm below the shoulder, perhaps trying to make sure I was real. "Mother was ..." he lost control over his voice and his words became incomprehensible squeaks.

I clasped him the way he was clasping me. "I want you to know my life on Earth was *good*. My foster parents were wonderful."

A strange thought occurred to me. "Jacau, what's my real name?"

"Tuvid. Tuvid Gothhowl," he answered proudly.

I blinked. "Tuvid? That's ... quite a coincidence."

"By time you left, you could say Am-am, Bo-bo, and Tuvid."

Momma, poppa, and Tuvid. Jacau's pronunciation surprised me, but the Dhu-barot was too simple to misinterpret. I saw what he was driving at: my Earth parents had named me David after hearing me babble "Tuvid."

"Our parents' names?"

"Father be Beod, mother Aleen."

"Still alive?" Jacau was around eight years my senior, so Aleen and Beod were likely very senior citizens.

"Living strong."

Ben's eyes opened. "Scome are early bloomers, but they tend to last."

"Scratching stopped," said Jacau. "What found you, magus?"

"Only stirred-up sand, lad."

For no reason, I shivered. "Stirred from wind?"

"Can't say. But we should travel." We all stood, and Ben raised his hands.

"One second," I begged. My lips felt all rubbery. "Was ... my wife's aneurysm accidental?"

"My dear boy," he looked unhappy, "I doubt it. My deepest regrets. There, I failed you both."

God knows how many miles we traveled before Ben called a stop. Again, he was exhausted. The ersatz sun blasted directly above us, and shadows remained few and very far between. We sat on the hot sand in a strange triangle, two humans and a Neme, not one of us what we seemed.

"What galls me, David," Ben said, mounding sand into crude pyramids. "Is that after so much death and bother and risking your life, we *still* know so little about the bloody rebels and less concerning their allies."

Right. "Give me a moment and I may be able to help out in both departments."

His eyebrows rose. "Few things would astonish me more. Do you know what loyal Hhoymon most fear? That their rebels have made alliance with certain Crossroad demiurges. Some are quite formidable."

"Well, if my idea pans out, we might have some solid answers."

"What is this idea?"

"My brother," Jacau declared, "will surprise you."

I smiled. "We'll see. After the rebels broke my arm, I gave my suit some fancy orders. If I was attacked again, squads of microdocs were supposed to fly out on my command, invade the attackers, and then make themselves inconspicuous until any Common, Neme, or Blenn tested for them."

Ben shook his head. "An elaborate request!"

"That's just the prelude. I told the invading teams to be fruitful and multiply enough to send out new squads to infect any beings the attackers ... fraternized with. Eventually, I hoped, marking *every* conspirator."

"Heavens," he said mildly. "You have quite the high opinion of your taurei."

"You bet, although this pushes the limit. I stole the concept from a Hhoymon tract on using microdocs for medical imaging. Ironic, huh?"

"Clever, inventive, and splendidly absurd. Still, you've nothing more, ah, immediate in mind for revealing our enemies?"

"Au contraire! I ordered a separate crew of 'docs to go out and thinly cover my attackers. Each one was supposed to memorize its position relative to every other 'doc on the same body, and then return to me."

"David," Ben laughed, "sapient cells can fly but they do have limitations."

"I'm sure. But these little guys keep surprising me."

Jacau leaned forward. "How would your coming-back cells teach us anything?"

"I'd planned to have them create a microdoc framework in midair."

"I have doubt, brother. If cells ... stick together so much we can *see* them, they will be too heavy to float."

"Smart, but I may have a way to make the framework visible. Look, folks, we needn't debate this. When that fog appeared in the chasm, I gave the go command. We can find out *right now* if the imaging part of my plan worked."

No one objected, so I mentally ordered my returning micro-heroes, if any, to move out and assemble into their memorized positions, if they remembered. I waited a moment, sent out a stream of shadow, and asked the levitating 'docs to make the dark stuff conform to all assembled outlines.

Jacau reacted to my shadowcasting with obvious surprise, rattling off something in Dhu-barot. Then he fell silent because my crazy idea had born dark fruit. Five black, three-dimensional sculptures appeared before us.

Jacau and Ben both shouted wordlessly.

Four shapes resembled human children. The fifth shape was chilling: a tall thin biped with tentacle-like arms stretched out over six feet. One arm was curled up at the end as if grasping something. A rock perchance?

"Impossible," Ben breathed. "Taurei cells cannot do such things! David, allow me to be the first to invite you into our Council of Elders. Membership fees are due every twenty-two turns."

"Ben, what the hell is that hideous creature? And what are kids doing on Crossroad?"

"Hideous? My dear boy, your creature is merely a Vyre with extended arms. As to the 'kids' ..."

"Oh. I know what they are."

"I would expect so," said the Mirrormage. "Silver Hhoymon."

CHAPTER 29
THE TIDES THAT MARCH

The mage walked around, observing the shadow-forms from all angles.

"My dear boy," he said, "I withdraw all my previous remarks concerning your diminished mental capacities. You came up with this sleight while on the run, did you?"

"I didn't really expect it to work."

"Thus establishing you'd retained a spark of sanity in your madness. Gentlemen, we have witnessed the impossible."

Jacau studied my profile as I frowned at the largest statue. "Ben," I worried out loud, "do you think *all* Vyre are in on the plot?"

"Unlikely. But every Silver remaining here is surely a rebel."

The hot, dry air felt like sandpaper in my throat. I asked Jeeves to drop my Neme thought-form disguise; evidently, I'd never needed it. No noticeable change. I'd probably lost the disguise somewhere along the way.

"Why didn't Hhoymon records," I asked, "show that some Silvers had stayed behind? Wouldn't a simple headcount have done that?"

"You underestimate Hhoymon ability to obfuscate records, and you forget that the rebels may have departed but then returned."

"Then what about social connections? Exiled Silvers arrive on Jaahnim, look around, and Uncle Harry's suddenly gone missing. Seems a giveaway."

"Except relatives are informed, as all records show, that Harry is bound to another Hhoymon world on one of ten thousand spaceships. David, these people are bloody brilliant and have had decades to plan for contingencies." He finished his tour and sat near us. "Which is why I'm smiling. Your technique is precise enough to identify *individuals*!" He grabbed my hand and pumped it. "I wouldn't have credited it, but there they stand, plain as the beak on my face. Well done, you!"

"Aw shucks."

"I'm quite sincere. Perhaps your entire plan succeeded, and you've created the first spy pandemic in history! Should our allies learn to spot your, ah, secret mini-agents at a distance, you may have won our war."

"We can hope."

"Scome be good at hope," Jacau remarked.

Ben gave him a sympathetic glance. "So now, dear friends, we have vital news we mustn't keep to ourselves. If—*what was that*?"

I'd felt it too: a brief hollowness in my stomach as if we'd dropped an unexpected floor in an elevator. Suddenly, the air felt even drier and tasted ... strange. Ben sniffed and scowled. "Everyone stay quiet."

He sat utterly still, eyelids at half-mast. A breeze cooled my overheated face and I hoped Jacau wasn't sweltering under his fur. We both flinched when Ben suddenly growled, "What's the bloody *problem*? Can't reach even the Watergod! I'll try again. But first, David, kindly erase your charming tableau. No saying who might turn up without a by-your-leave, and we don't want our enemies knowing we've got their number."

"Good point."

"How do you make shadow so *strong*," Jacau demanded as I dissolved the sculptures.

"Don't you know? Your Shadowcaster nightmare grabbed me and—"

My brother waved an arm impatiently. "Yes, yes! I had such grabbings myself. When I used the Earth box to make eye record."

"*You* took the photograph Ben brought to Earth?"

"Magus said it could help you."

"Damn. It's a small Pan-Cosmos after all. Are your machines designed to be so aggressive?"

Ben snorted disapprovingly. "I already informed you that we'd rigged the enhancement room as a snare."

"Yeah, but I figured Scome would be exempt. And why set up a tourist trap with posted danger signs?"

"Signs wouldn't discourage rebel investigators. But someone, ah, innocent might stumble in."

"After accidentally picking the lock?"

He shrugged oddly, one shoulder at a time. "Some beings here can pass through solid walls. But I hadn't expected *Jacau* to be molested. I believe Maanza reprogrammed the machines to seize anyone bearing non-Scome technology and determine their species. A Scome would then receive enhancement; all others would be detained. I daresay the Common have means to retrieve such captives."

"Okay. So why did Jacau use a human camera?"

His eyes twinkled. "Because I owned one. No other kind for sale in London."

The breeze deserted us, and my brow beaded with sweat. "Another thing: what made the print ... irreproducible?"

"I applied Scome preservative oil, which blocks intense light. Didn't want the UN—"

"Hey! After Jacau was grabbed, you *knew* it would happen to me!"

"The Watergod said it was needful and you wouldn't be harmed." I lifted my cast and he looked embarrassed. "Not directly." He stood, glanced around, and lowered himself into a squat. "Any *other* itching issues?"

I eyed my brother and Ben understood. "He was so eager to see you I couldn't say no. I thought a Neme pattern would be least conspicuous."

"You can restore him?"

"He can do so himself." Ben frowned at Jacau. "Restructuring a body, not to mention installing the appropriate projective templates, is bloody byzantine work. To minimize my labors, I've provided this fool the ability to transform at will. A skill he immediately abused by seeking you out prematurely."

"I had to go!" Jacau protested. "But I be sorry to worry anyone."

Ben waved a dismissive hand. "I question your sincerity."

"At will?" I asked. "Did you give Strong the same ability?"

"Of course."

"Interesting. She never returned to her real form when I was around. Ben, why make her human in the first place? I never bought the idea it was to help me feel more comfortable."

"Ah." To my surprise, the magician flushed slightly. "That was my idea. We didn't want you noticing the many ways we were manipulating you. I thought giving her abundant ... pulchritude would rouse your hormones, and thereby distract you."

"Tuvid," Jacau said, interrupting my glare at Ben. "How do you make shadow so strong and do what it be not meant for? Look! If I push hard ..." He held out a hand and a pencil scribble of a shadow emerged from one finger, quickly dissipating.

I studied his now shadow-less finger. "Okay. What *is* shadow meant for?"

"Hiding," Jacau stated. "In dark. What you do—"

The freefall sensation lasted longer this time. When it ended, Ben looked grim. "Rested or not, I'd best call out again. The Watergod should be keeping, ah, a third ear turned toward me and if I still can't reach him something's catastrophically wrong. Keep quiet and alert."

Wasn't long before the veins in Ben's forehead throbbed from strain. "This is maddening!" he hissed. "Can't touch any of our allies!"

"Has something happened to them?" I asked.

"Ha. More likely, happened to *us*."

"Oh."

"I'd hazard the rebels have somehow swept me from the fray and you two were carried along." He sighed. "I need to travel a fair way, but if I go alone it shan't take long."

"To do what?" I hated the idea of Ben abandoning us, even briefly.

"Triangle Six's Mind is a passive monitor intended for species who'd find the active configuration intolerably invasive. A proper place to keep secrets. But a communication node is hidden just beyond this park. From there, I'll have a direct line to the Common." Tennis-ball-sized bubbles, transparent in the sunlight, rose from the sands to surround us. "I'll soon return. For Seris's sake, both of you *stay right here*. Can you manage that challenging task this time, David?"

"I promise."

Ben turned silver, but slowly. Then indigo lines appeared on his mirrored form, writhing and widening until his entire surface was blue. "By the Undivided!" his eyes glared like blue spotlights. "This is *beyond* aggravating. Has Binae departed Crossroad? Not bloody likely!"

Jacau asked something in Dhu-barot that only made Ben angrier.

"Because She's the *Diplomat*! She'd never leave in a crisis."

One of my brother's eyes began orbiting the others—typical for an upset Neme—but Jacau clapped a hand over the roving retina. "Then why say 'has Binae abandoned'?"

Ben visibly calmed himself. "Because I can no longer access Her energy, which manifests as an *argent* flux. This blue force is mine and far less potent. Now, completing a round trip of some two hundred kilometers will take me much longer."

"This desert," I blurted, "is that big?"

"It's a bloody huge room. You do realize that if you spread Earth out flat, it would easily fit into a single Triangle? As I was *saying*: I won't return so soon now. Nevertheless, stay put!"

Sheathed in blue mirror, the magician raced over the dunes and was gone in moments. He didn't look any slower to me.

Jacau managed to get all his eyes under control. He and I studied each other. "Be this the strangeness?" he asked.

I nodded. "Whatever you mean, I agree."

"I be hungry to speak English better. That way we ... we can ..."

"Get to know each other?"

"Yes! This I would like."

"Me too." In my chest, an emotional knot loosened, and a different one formed. Without my wife and family, I'd been so lonely that I hadn't dared admit it to myself. But now, in a situation that practically reeked of peril, I again had something precious to lose.

"Jacau, I thought I had no relatives left."

"I also have lost someone important: you! We Scome have big feelings for family."

"Tell you what, you fix my Dhu-barot, and I'll try not to ruin your English. Oddly enough, I can *read* your language even though I don't know how to speak it."

Then my own words rang in my ears: suspicion calling. I felt sure that Able Firsthouse hadn't taught me proper Dhu-barot pronunciation because he hadn't wanted my childhood memories stirred.

When Ben finally returned and de-mirrored, his face appeared calm, but he popped his protective bubbles by stomping on them. "The node failed."

"Which means?" I asked as he sat down.

"I've no idea. Everything feels ... blurry, but I can't put a claw on exactly why. Jolly good thing you've both got taurei protection, I expect."

Both? Only my taurei showed.

Jacau aimed an eye at Ben. "But you reached this node?"

"Certainly."

Jacau patted the ground. "Then we remain on Commonworld."

Ben nodded thoughtfully. "So I imagine."

I looked at each of my companions. "How could *that* issue be in doubt? We all felt some weird sensations, but the scenery didn't change."

"It's not that simple, David. Crossroad's reality is layered."

"So I've heard. But are you claiming we could be miraculously transported to another desert *visually identical* to this one?"

Ben shrugged. "I should make only one definite claim: we're in trouble."

"Orders?" Jacau asked.

"We'll dine, and then sleep right here. I'll need much rest before attempting to move three bodies at speed for any great distance.

Tomorrow, we'll aim for Triangle Two's security nexus and hope for the best. Unfortunately, said nexus is several thousand kilometers away; not a brisk trip with my present powers."

"Any Safe-roads around?" I asked.

Ben smiled sourly. "I'm ancient but not entirely senile, dear boy. On my recent expedition, I detoured to several Blenn highways. None seemed to, ah, recognize my presence."

"That sounds bad."

"At this moment, David, everything's bad."

I looked at Jacau. "Not everything."

"I meant involving our *situation*."

"Well, maybe I can solve our transportation problem."

Ben regarded me. "Oh? How?"

"By making a kind of ... running carpet using shadow threads. You can lower those eyebrows; I tried it. It's fast and can carry both Jacau and me."

"That *would* be helpful." He patted the sand. "Last time I was here, I rode on Maanza's shoulders."

"Big shoulders, I gather."

"The Defender has bodies for all occasions. Some are scarcely twice your size, others are vast."

"How vast? Hey! You were so sure Binae would never leave Crossroad. Is this entire *planet* one of Binae's bodies?"

"My dear fellow! You have the most extraordinary imagination. The concept 'fevered' springs to mind. Even a Supernal might find a planetary form a trifle bulky for convenience. You show up for a quiet dinner at a friend's house and cause bloody big tides! Speaking of food, who's hungry?"

I drew Dhu-barot glyphs in the sand, trying to associate them with Jacau's noises. My companions argued, Ben alone using English. Evidently, my brother wanted to dine in his natural form, which the mage vetoed, fearing we could be observed.

I coughed to get Ben's attention. "How 'bout making him invisible?"

"Invisible to whom? The problem with bending light—ah! I'd almost forgotten. Ages ago, the Lightmage discovered an interesting sleight with borrowed entropy, which may serve. She called it Ankhpu's Cloak. Very well, Jacau, I will accede to your desire to eat in comfort. Friends, prepare for a wonder! Assuming I recall the procedure."

I wondered if Ben was about to cover Jacau with a really *long* beard.

Standing, Ben scraped a circle around us using his foot. The resulting mark was oddly precise, seemingly carved with something sharp. He leaned close to the line, whispering to himself, breathing heavily. My arm hairs rose as if from static.

He reached with a fingertip and jabbed the line. Could've sworn it wiggled before collapsing into nothing.

"Nearly forgot the full mnemonic," he huffed.

"Are we invisible?"

That bought me a glower. "Do we *look* invisible? I haven't activated the bloody thing." He banged the ground with both hands; the sand around us hissed, releasing a fog of blue-black dust. "Don't fear to inhale the powder, chaps. This will clear momentarily."

Good to hear. By now, I couldn't see to the end of my nose and the dust blocked even my Crossroad vision. Instinct made me hold my breath, which was no strain with good old microdocs; but after a few minutes, not needing air felt a bit creepy.

The dust suddenly precipitated into a solid-looking dome enclosing us like an igloo and I unleashed my lungs. Although my x-road vision remained on the fritz, I could see thanks to a bizarre campfire burning on the sand between the three of us. The little fire, with lavender flames, emitted a blast so cold that Jeeves thickened in front. Hot desert breezes rushing through our dome fanned the arctic blaze higher.

"I've been stupid," I admitted, goggling at the icy flames. "All this time we've been broiling in the sun, I had a shadow umbrella at my fingertips. And making a shelter like this would've been, um, a snap."

Ben gave me a raised eyebrow. "And *your* shelter would've been undetectable from the outside?"

"Um."

He turned to my brother. "Feel free to revert."

Ben materialized a meal, but I couldn't take my eyes off Jacau who was suddenly taller and vastly thinner, garbed in brown fabric identical to Jeeves in its pre-Swan days. He bore only one ornament: a golden ring with a red stone.

He seemed almost skeletal, but on him, it looked as natural as it was. His muscles, clearly visible through the thin fabric, were slender but well defined. Evolution at work. Muuti, as I'd learned from Able Firsthouse, is a planet filthy rich in both danger and food, where speed and agility are crucial and stockpiling calories pointless.

Jacau was a biped greyhound. His exposed skin, reflecting the weird campfire light, appeared mottled in shades of purple. But I'd seen images the Neme had retrieved from Muuti, and knew his true skin colors were a mixture of green, tan, and brown. With every motion, his body proved itself a masterpiece of efficiency and precision. Watching Jacau manipulate the Scome cutlery Ben had reproduced, I saw a grace born from extreme physical competence, and a strange beauty.

Nothing was wrong with his appetite. "After this," he announced from behind a pile of food, "I want mores."

Ben winked at me. "Scome are grand on preemptive refills."

Jacau's eyes moved constantly; a world filled with quick teeth could make a species wary....

I snapped my fingers. "That's why!"

"Why what?" Ben prompted.

"Why the Scome never invented TV. Or movies. They don't like keeping their eyes still."

Ben nodded. "Moreover, they lack persistence of vision. But their eyesight is as keen as their reflexes. Observe." Without warning, he hurled a fork at Jacau's head. I didn't see my brother move until he handed the utensil back. He hadn't missed a bite.

"You were genetically, ah, tweaked to blend in with humanity, but I daresay *your* reflexes are adequate."

"True." People were often startled at my quickness, but compared to Jacau I moved like a snail with a bad back. *Wearing a Neme body*, I thought, *must be a real trial for him.*

"Tuvid?" Jacau said, spreading his arms wide. "How do I look?"

"No wonder you can't cast a proper shadow." I knew he'd heard a deeper message when he reached to squeeze my hand.

I didn't much notice the food, but I'm sure it was superb. Another convenience in accompanying a sorcerer: no dirty dishes, no leftovers. "Anyone fancy a pastry?" Ben asked after we'd eaten, but got no takers.

I felt too full and drowsy for dessert and Jacau must've felt similarly; we began a yawning contest. I was too tired to ask who was winning. Sand, Jeeves, and shadow made the best mattress money couldn't buy. We said our goodnights and the fire dwindled to cool violet embers.

Before drifting off, I glanced at Ben. He sat erect in the dimness, legs twisted into a full-lotus pretzel. An ultra-blue sun, small and faint, shimmered near his heart. A pale, almost silvery shade of ultra-blue radiated from his scalp, turning his hair cloud-wispy.

When, I wondered, did I learn to see exotic colors with my *eyes*?

CHAPTER 30
LESS THAN HEAVY

Dreams troubled my sleep. The Watergod spoke, but my ears were too stopped up for the words to get through. The lady with shoulder-wings appeared twice, in a misty, uncommitted fashion. She, too, had something to convey, but all I heard were squeaks.

When I awoke, the fire had been reenergized. My brother sat, brushing sand off his legs, and Ben now wore an ivory caftan. "Been awaiting your pleasure, old boy. Tea or coffee? Hot *duka*, Jacau?"

Jacau growled with such disgust I decided to forgo my morning duka, whatever it was, and settle for coffee. After a light breakfast, my brother converted to Neme-hood. Then Ben doused his contra-fire and dissolved our dome. Just like that, we were ready to go. None of us had a burning need for professional bathroom attendants.

My head seemed to expand; I could *see* again! I lay on my stomach, had Jacau stretch out on my back, and wrapped us both in stabilized shadow. The shadow-rug practically exploded from me, ready for its traveling orders.

"What *are* you?" Jacau murmured.

"Right now, your taxi. Hang on!"

Ben became a blue mirror. I gave the go-ahead, and we darted across real dunes beneath an artificial jade sky. When I proved capable of keeping up, Ben accelerated until he settled on a cruising speed. The ground rocketed by, and I appreciated Ben's skill at avoiding obstacles.

After twenty minutes, we reached a towering *trompe l'oeil* of distant mountains, pierced with a tunnel that led us up, and up, and outdoors to a barren land under a dawn sky. The real Crossroad sky.

Ben paused to utter dire warnings. This area appeared overendowed with boulders, but the chief danger was falling into a miles-deep vermiculite pit, a golfer's worst nightmare, that Ben called "vugs."

Ben insisted that I follow directly behind him, which sounded easy until he began swerving around at speed. Inspiration saved me from a mental hernia: let Jeeves do the driving. "Follow that mage!" I ordered. It worked, freeing me to notice how my neck felt after so many minutes of keeping my head tilted back so that I could see forward. Jacau's hidden taurei remained on duty. His microdoc goggles matched mine.

Sunrise struck rainbow glints from the sand. Jacau kept putting a furry finger before my eyes to point out interesting rock formations. I was too busy making sure Jeeves avoided said rock formations to appreciate them. Fortunately, Jacau made a smallish Neme. Even so, I felt squished.

I reduced neck-strain by resting my chin on my stacked hands, extruding threads to support my folded arms. Better, but minor bumps did bad things to my chin and occasionally my tongue. With the sun halfway up, we paused for lunch under another Cloak. Ben, bless him, massaged my cramped neck.

Jacau and I sampled each other's meal. He didn't rave and I decided Scome food must be an acquired taste.

That night, we talked for hours in our little fire-conditioned dome, and Jacau and I traded language lessons. For me, it seemed harder than learning Dhu-barot the first time; I'm a quick study, but a slow unlearner. Ben helped by clearing up small misunderstandings.

When my throat became too raw to practice bizarre noises, Ben asked how I was bearing up under the strain of carrying Jacau. "He's not heavy, he's my brother," I said, deadpan. "Got a question for you: what about Thoth?"

"What is your concern?"

"No mention when you were talking about the Egyptian pantheon."

A sly smile. "An understandable oversight. Do you happen to recall how the Old Egyptians represented Thoth?"

"A bird-headed man."

"Ah. Modesty forbids me to reveal which species of bird."

I stared at him. "They based Thoth on *you*?"

"As an aspect of Chybris."

"Wow. Any basis to the Book of Thoth?"

"Indeed. Chybris's brain: the Living Diamond."

I shook my head. "Scratch Egyptian mythology anywhere, and the Librarian keeps popping up."

"I, too, own a questioning, Magus," Jacau said. "Why be Tuvid's shadow so ... enduringable?"

Ben tilted his head. "You know what his prenatal tests revealed."

"Yes. But shadow can *never* be so firm."

"I would've thought the same, old boy."

"What," I asked, "*is* this shadow stuff?"

The mage hesitated. "I've no idea. Ectoplasm? Dark matter? Mental plasma?"

"No sale. But you said that a few Scome in each generation have other crazy abilities."

"In potential, yes. More so in the past, before the Scome had gained dominance over their world. Today, most such talents remain vestigial."

"Then I'm a throwback?"

"Perhaps a throw-forward. Your shadow *is* uniquely potent."

Ben gave Jacau a look I couldn't read. "I should reveal something else. The Nemes didn't tell humanity about the Scome for a lark."

"I'd wondered about that."

"Indeed. Nor was Able Firsthouse's attachment to your university a coincidence."

"What are you saying?"

"Your birth family and I pressured the Common into giving you an opportunity to learn about your heritage. That's the long and short of it."

I stared at him, dizzy from the way the universe seemed to be revolving around me....

Next morning, Ben and I gobbled piles of fluffy pancakes. Health food. Jacau munched on brown crackers with a cheesy smell and declined to try pancakes. Ben estimated we'd reach Triangle Two's border in six turns and the security post two turns later.

The next several days felt bittersweet. I couldn't have asked for better companions, although I missed Rider and Strong. And the journey never turned routine thanks to geological marvels such as a sparkling wonder Ben called "Amethyst Rising." Nights proved equally interesting. Our mage was a treasure trove of lost information; my sense of wonder kept expanding.

Occasionally, hills we passed rumbled. Not, I hoped, from hunger. Sometimes Ben would speak and echoes returned, minutes later, with astonishing clarity. I never adjusted to the terrain's gargantuan scale. Not just the distant, heaven-high mountains. Once, I dropped a rock in a chasm and listened for a full minute without hearing an impact.

Rarely, hoots or whistles resounded far away, but the only life we saw was a kind of brown moss. We did come across various peculiar tracks....

On the flip side, my neck ached constantly, and Ben grew too tired to summon a Cloak. At night, we sat under unnamed stars near the glow of a sensible fire: an orange-flamed furnace compensating for a new chill in the air. All my dreams were full of fear.

———

As Jacau's English improved, he asked more questions. Why was my taurei white? Why the cast? What was Earth like? And a real poser: why did I look so young?

"Our people know how to slow aging, Tuvid, but *you* might be my child's child."

"Could you whip up a small mirror?" I asked Ben.

"A novel endeavor," he remarked dryly as he obliged.

My face looked younger than ever; all signs of grief erased. The unlined skin seemed a betrayal of Sara's memory.

———

One evening, I recounted my experience with Arfaenn and the Swan, hoping my companions could shed some light. They were fascinated, but added no illumination although I suspected Ben knew something he didn't share.

Jacau, who appeared improbably young himself, opened up about his own life. He had a wife, Anvara, and two adult children: a female, Bel, and a male, Jasol. I was an *uncle*!

He missed Muuti keenly and claimed that constant worry about being discovered by rebels had kept any Scome from feeling at home here. Still, his people hadn't been wholly isolated; the Common, some trusted Nemes, and the Firemage visited frequently.

Room was no problem. The hidden Triangle comprised far more land area than Muuti's and Earth's continents combined. Pop math quiz: how many cardboard boxes do you need to move a billion people?

———

Third night out, during dinner, I grinned and put down my fork. "Ben, I've just had an insight."

"Concerning?"

"Insights. You said Urien ... appears when anyone has one. Couldn't we reach Him that way? He could tell our friends where we are. Maybe He *already knows* our situation, because of my insight!"

Ben shook his head as though dislodging a fly from an ear. "Without debating what constitutes an insight, David, your idea won't work. Sorry."

"Why not?"

"The part of Him that *is* insight can't be sent on errands. What we need is His persona, His locus, and adequate power to reach Him."

"Rats. Ben, where did the Supernals come from? Originally."

"Even they don't seem to know." He gave me a sly grin. "My notion is that some extra-bright species trillions of Pan-cycles back built the lot of them. And they've been improving themselves ever since."

Next morning, when I awoke, the air tasted different, staler somehow, unsatisfying to breathe. Jeeves appeared infested with nervous ripples.

My cast was gone, which seemed grossly premature, but when I had Jeeves retreat, my right arm looked and felt fine. On a hunch, I checked out my feet. Yep, I'd been fully reupholstered.

"Everything shipshape, old boy?" Ben asked.

"Must be rich. I seem to be well healed."

He looked pained. "Someone has spent excess time with a certain planetary security chief."

I let Jeeves flow where it would. "*That's* Rider's job?"

"Binae's right hand, ah, whatever."

After breakfast, we started off as usual. I'd gotten my traveling act together. My brother lay in a shadow sidecar next to me, with separate shadow threads and controlling microdocs. I'd tried riding upright, but at speed, air-resistance was brutal. Hence my perpetual neckache.

We stopped for lunch in a wide valley. Titanic mountains, bleached a pallid blue by distance, surrounded us, and gray ghosts suggesting even taller peaks loomed behind those. Underfoot, chatoyant minerals decorated taupe sand.

Ben scowled and sniffed the breeze. "Something smells ..."

"Bad," Jacau added.

Muttering to himself, the mage extended an index finger, which rapidly turned turquoise and shiny, and left a shimmering blue line behind as he traced a large oval in midair. An image appeared within this oval frame: a remote butte in close-up detail. Another magic telescope, I thought, but Ben added a wrinkle. He grabbed the frame with both hands and, visibly straining, pushed it in a wide circle around Jacau and me. When he let go, it kept circling us, gradually accelerating.

Soon, a wide blue band with a gauzy look surrounded us, whipping the sand below into an ankle-high cyclone. Distant objects came into focus as if we were inside a hollow cylinder made of telescopic lenses.

"Report anything suspicious," Ben ordered. The three of us studied the panorama, turning to take in all 360 degrees.

"By S'th," he finally groaned as the spinning lens evaporated. "I can bloody *feel* it, so where is it?" He glanced downward, his face instantly three shades paler. Crouching, he scribed an oval in the sand and muttered to himself again. This time, I could hear his words but didn't recognize the language. We all watched his new artwork fill with gray striations. An underground view, I guessed.

He switched to English and confirmed my suspicion.

"Pointless, gawking at rock formations. Only something moving signifies." He hammered a fist straight down and immediately shoved it into his armpit. "Hara! A chilling exchange." Then he leaned over, blowing into the oval as if making a birthday wish. A uniform pool of blueness replaced the grays.

An animated form appeared in the blueness, its outline suggesting a small alien fish with spiny fins, a corkscrew tail, and an elongated tube of a mouth. I smiled, seeing the fishy thing twist around, apparently chasing its own tail.

"Cute," I said. "What is it?"

Silence. Ben looked up at me, his face a mask of horror. Which unnerved me although I saw nothing bloodcurdling about the tiny animal. What in the Pan-Cosmos could scare the Mirrormage this badly? The miniature nemesis swam back and forth, doing laps. Then it changed shape. The fishy outline became a bumpy blob and expanded tenfold.

"It's ascending! Move out!" Ben yelled.

Unneeded advice; the desert *vibrated*. Jacau and I threw ourselves on our bellies, I rewove our shadow carpets, and off we sped.

"What the hell *was* it?" I called ahead.

"Lithshark," Ben shouted over his shoulder, setting an unbelievable pace. "I've badly ... underestimated ... our enemies."

My brother stared at me. "A powerful monster," I explained over the rushing wind. "The Dissolver's worst."

Ben skidded to a stop, hurled something downward, and took off again. After a moment, I noticed another oval video screen on the ground, this one accompanying us as we traveled. We darted into a boulder-strewn area, and I cursed my lack of foresight in not placing Jacau behind me; our extra width forced Ben to choose an inefficient route. Even so, we darted recklessly between stony pillars, driven by the increasing rumble from below.

When we emerged into the open, I glanced downward and got the scare of my life. Our screen had expanded radically to fit the lizard-fish, which now appeared larger than a battleship. The monster kept twisting and wriggling as it swam through the ground, easily matching our progress.

"BEN! It's right beneath us!"

"No! Still a good kilometer below. Bigger than you think!"

"Magus, *fly* us," Jacau demanded.

"Can't. Not all three, not high enough. I'll carry you both for a bit. Make some real headway. David. Cut the shadows binding you two. Everyone ... *hold on*."

Next instant, some force lifted me upright and pulled me close against Ben's left side while my brother wound up standing just as close to Ben's right. The mage put an arm around each of us. "Time to do a *real* runner, shall we?"

Our velocity became fantastic. Ben screamed something, but the wind shred his words to nonsense. I stared into the vast glowing oval under our speeding feet, watching the nightmare below, almost hypnotized. We weren't pulling ahead.

"It's too bloody quick!" Ben mage yelled in my ear. I noticed Jacau desperately tugging at his right hand, God knows why. Then it was too late. The Lithshark's outline changed again, expanding. Our screen also expanded, but not nearly enough to contain such a shape....

Ben's fresh burst of speed became so intense it blew my shadow armor off. The monster erupted barely behind our heels; we were thrown forward on a thundering wave of sand and rock. For a few crazy seconds, we surfed on a landslide. Then we slid to a stop.

Ben was spent, panting and trembling. He'd dropped his human form and all his feathers drooped.

I looked back, petrified. No living creature could be that big. Instant orogeny. A mountain had sprung up, which was only its *head*, waving like a buried Titan shaking a volcano at the sky.

The beast's skin was painful to look at, something like a super-potent black light glared behind the blotchy grays visible to the naked eye. Sullen red fire overwhelmed my Crossroad vision, and I felt blinded.

The Lithshark had no visible sensory organs, but it had a *voice*, a bass trumpeting loud enough to shake the stars.

"No bloody good," Ben gasped. "You two. Get away fast as you can. I'll give a shove to ... get you started. I love you both—don't be afraid! Avoid spots where sand lies flat. I'll catch up. When I'm able."

Before we could respond, Jacau and I were enveloped in cobalt flame. When it faded, we'd been thrown forward over a quarter mile. Together, we whirled around.

The monster, now horizontal, sped along like some giant half-submerged submarine. It left an astonishingly modest wake behind as it chased a bright blue ball that kept leading the monster away from us at an angle. The ball raced along, blue lightning with a tailwind, but the Lithshark was faster.

Then *three* spheres rolled off in different directions, but the beast seemed only interested in one.

I knew it had swallowed Ben when I saw an intense blue flash lighting up the vast mouth ... from the inside. The light grew dimmer as it moved further down the mouth, closer to some unimaginable destination. Finally, the blue fire died. I felt that I'd died myself.

The monster circled, turning in our direction.

"Tuvid! Help me!" Jacau yelled, tugging at a finger. "I can't feel it!"

"What?" I asked numbly.

"My ring! H'ap Shai's gift. Must use! When I take Neme form, it cannot be seen or felt."

I couldn't miss his urgency, although I didn't understand it. Then it dawned on me that he could've located his ring instantly if he'd been willing to expose his Scome form, but risk his species. His courage galvanized me out of complete paralysis.

"Tuvid!" Jacau urged.

I visualized the golden band, sent a "find this" command to my microdocs, and assigned them shadow stuff to make it visible. Seemed pointless, but if it was this important to my brother ...

My tiny friends were harder to fool than my senses. A shadow outline formed on Jacau's finger. He must've come very close to pulling it off and dropping it.

Relying on vision alone, I removed the insubstantial thing and carefully handed it to Jacau. He looked around wildly then placed the red stone against his middle speaking diaphragm. As with all Nemes, protective bones edged the diaphragm. Using these rock-hard "lips," he bit down violently. The only result I could see was a stream of blood dribbling down his chins.

"Get us gone, Tuvid!" He dove into his traveling position. "We must survive alone for a time."

I doubted survival would be an option; the monster was already too close. But I threw myself down and jetted us over the sands, attempting new speeds by increasing the length and number of shadow threads. To my surprise, we somehow kept ahead of the mile-long mouth. The combination of our outrageous speed and being half-blinded by the Lithshark's hellish energy gave me a severe case of tunnel vision.

Then our pursuer passed us by as if we stood still. The damn thing had been *playing* with us.

The fishy body seemed to stretch forever. I reversed directions, hoping the monstrosity was too big to notice. But as the gleaming tip of the corkscrew tail passed, I realized I'd made a good move in a losing game. If Jacau and I weren't going to join Ben, I'd have to come up with—

Too late, I noticed the area just ahead was utterly flat, unbroken by even a single rock.

Without our microdocs, we would've suffocated quickly and been crushed slowly. Ben had warned me that vugs were deep pits of something worse than quicksand, and if I fell in one, I should count myself dead.

Damp sand covered our heads before I could give Jeeves or shadow any orders, and the Lithshark's earthquake-rumble grew loud enough to drown out any scream. The blackness was absolute, my extra vision still blinded. Holding my breath, I drew my brother close. I'd never find him if we lost touch. Strong arms wrapped around me, and I shadow-roped us together.

Impossible to tell how fast we sank. I extruded shadow wings, hoping to slow our descent. My terrorized brain came up with an unlikely notion that we might even glide to the vug's edge and climb out ... somehow. I tried flapping the wings. Didn't seem to help.

The general noise level remained consistently brutal, but sporadic pressure waves battered us like pile drivers. Jeeves clearly took the brunt of the pressure; I prayed my brother's taurei was doing the same. Panic kept gaining on me. And it brought me a new fear: if my wings made our motion even partly horizontal, any moment now we could slam into something. In despair, I hurled out shadow tentacles, begging them to grab onto something solid. Anything. The rumble escalated unbearably....

Suddenly, we rocketed upward. Friction almost pulled my brother away from me, despite my bonds. Evidently, the tentacles had latched onto an *eruption*.

Daylight had never looked so dear.

Jacau and I were tugged high into the air. Now I understood. My shadow had hitched a ride on the Lithshark! When we'd vanished, the monster must've gone hunting. The creature's titanic mouth quested back and forth; we dangled from it like spiders on black silk lines. I told those lines to let the hell go.

While we fell, the monster dove beneath the surface. Its final headshake had thrown us well past the treacherous sand. Blackness billowed from me, but the ground came up fast and knocked my breath away. Again, Jeeves provided oxygen. All shadow dissipated, and Jacau and I sat up.

Stillness. Only a gentle vibration from below. Jacau looked a mess, shoulders bleeding where yellow pelt had been ripped away, face scraped raw. But his three button eyes shone like sunlight.

"Such events do not happen, Tuvid!" A microdoc surf washed over his wounds. "And look you ... there it be!" he cried. "Vulspoka. The midnight rainbow!"

A bizarrely horizontal cyclone seemed to be floating in the middle distance, zooming our way. Then one end touched down near us. A translucent bridge perhaps twenty feet across lay at our feet, glowing with ultra-red tints, arching away until it merged with the sky.

"Why 'midnight'?" I asked, staring.

Jacau sounded surprised. "Because it be black."

I didn't argue. Something was leaping along the span, approaching with unnatural speed, moving like a Harryhausen animation. The quivering from below intensified.

Jacau shouted something in Dhu-barot as the leaper drew close enough to recognize. The Firemage. Now what?

"Some call him a demon," I observed, almost calmly.

"Nice peoples can have wrong beliefs."

The bear-centaur finished his accelerated tour with a hundred-yard leap that almost brought him close enough to touch. While my heart scuttled back down my throat, he stared down at me, exhaling fire.

"Sorry," I said awkwardly, wondering if I still had eyebrows. "I don't understand, um ... combustion."

He glanced past us and roared flame and ash at the sky. I turned. Far away, but not far enough, miles of Lithshark had reappeared. The monster sped toward us as the demon kept roaring.

"H'ap Shai commands us," Jacau translated, "to ride his Rainbow.

He will remain here to slow the enemy. He promises to escape after we do. There be more, but he says we must leave. Now."

The demon made a shooing motion so commanding that we obeyed instantly. Underfoot, the bridge felt soft but solid. I took several almost involuntary strides and learned how the Firemage had reached us so quickly; this Rainbow was a super-Glideway. Jacau caught up with me a moment later. We'd already traveled over a quarter mile.

The world lit up. I turned and got a double shock. H'ap Shai had raised a staggering, white-hot wall of fire. And the Rainbow now ended in midair, only ten yards behind us.

The monster burst through the blaze, splashing the inferno aside, galaxies of flame shooting everywhere. The colossal mouth gaped, dripping incandescence, but the morsel it tried to snap up was gone.

We stood still but the bridge kept carrying us away from the battle. Already, distance rendered the Firemage invisible, but I saw a line of brightness swing around and strike the monster's head. Thunder resounded seconds later. The Lithshark didn't appear to feel a thing.

By unspoken agreement, Jacau and I resumed walking. Kept my pace Neme-slow and clamped my teeth against the question foremost in my heart.

"On Muuti," Jacau said, perhaps also postponing the inevitable, "not even ... vegetables grow so big."

"I think you mean trees. Same on Earth. Do we ... know where we're going?"

"Yes. H'ap Shai said he was in Triangle the Tenth when he heard my cry. We will finish near Hhoymon City."

"Cry? Oh, your ring. How's that eye you used to break the stone?"

"My taurei has already fixed. And look, our faces stop bleeding."

Hadn't even realized I'd *been* bleeding. I brushed a hand across my forehead; it felt oddly slick.

"What *was* that ring?"

"A ... loadstar. H'ap Shai, who helps Scome, gave me that to call him but warned he would not hear unless I truly feared. He said break stone between rocks. We had no time so I bit without teeth. Now the ring be gone."

"A one-shot deal." I had to lead up to my real question. "Jacau, do you think the Firemage survived?"

"Of that, I am sureness."

I braced myself. "*Any* chance for Ben?"

"Lord Djehuti was a brave and wise being," he said softly.

Djehuti: Egyptian name for Thoth. Ben DeHut. I hadn't made the connection. My eyes filled with acid tears, for Ben and all the wonderful, irreplaceable people I'd lost. I walked the magical highway in the air with grief a steel band squeezing all hope from my chest.

CHAPTER 31
TRICYCLE BLITZ FOR TWO

The Vulspoka proved even faster than a Safe-road but equally breezeless. Mere minutes later we crossed into cloudy night and began slowing and descending. A spot of gold lay at the Rainbow's end.

Hhoymon City's crystal dome lay below us to our left. Seen from above, the canopy appeared almost transparent, its yellow tint adding a warm glow to the illuminated buildings beneath. The taller structures displayed an exaggerated perspective, appearing absurdly small near ground level. Something strange and ugly dominated an area just beyond the city's center, but I couldn't tell what it was.

The crisis caught me by surprise.

We'd decelerated to a mere sprinting pace and might've been about fifteen hundred feet up when the bridge before us flickered and vanished. By the time we managed to stop, our toes hung over the edge of a very fatal drop. We backed off and turned around. Perhaps the bridge had been vanishing behind us all along. Jacau and I stood on an unsupported, tiny slice of Rainbow. A short walk anywhere would guarantee one hell of a fall.

The golden dome remained a quarter mile away or so, and at least three hundred feet down—too far for a shadow-ladder. I had a bad feeling our patch of Rainbow wouldn't last long. And to crank my anxiety dial a final notch, Jeeves began roiling. Terrific. An enemy attack would make a nice distraction as we were plummeting.

Unfortunately for my nerves, a shadow-parachute seemed the best way down. My brother, Michael, had gone through a skydiving phase, and I'd watched him exercise this insanity using what he called a "ram-air canopy." For our purposes, an old-fashioned chute seemed easiest to construct.

I told Jacau my plan. He wasn't enthusiastic.

The bigger the better, I thought, sending out clouds of darkness to congeal overhead into an immense umbrella with a central vent for stability. My brother muttered a Dhu-barot phrase I didn't recognize. "You can make so much!" he added.

"Keeps getting easier." Which I demonstrated by generating enough extra shadow to wrap harnesses around each of us plus ropes attaching our harnesses to the canopy edges.

Stabilize this mess, I told Jeeves.

Two nice things about shadow-parachuting: the chute weighs virtually nothing, and starts out pre-opened so it can't get jammed. Two nasty things: it requires occupying a high place, and the jump can be accidentally initiated by the tiniest gust. Such as the one that pulled us into emptiness.

The canopy's edge caught on the bridge above us, leaving us dangling from the Rainbow like a bad mobile. A fresh wind sprang up, the chute pulled free, and we were falling ... but slowly, thank God!

After a long moment of pure terror, I looked around. Where my harness didn't obscure it, Jeeves displayed its normal placidity. What danger had threatened us before?

"I'm getting the hang of my power," I remarked, forgetting the classic connection between "pride" and "fall."

"Hanging from it be what we do," Jacau growled. Perhaps acrophobia runs in the family.

Our angle of descent carried us toward the shining dome. As we drew closer, the air warmed.

"Tuvid, this chuting be a way of going *down*?"

Yep, we were rising. "Must be the hot air. The city radiates heat; we're in an updraft. I just need to widen the vent in our ... well, I suppose it's a balloon now."

"Okay." He'd picked up the word from me.

I enlarged our canopy's central gap until we were again falling, albeit with the death-defying abandon of pennies in honey. A light rain began pattering on the taut shadow above; I searched for a good landing spot.

"What be wrong with your taurei?" Jacau snapped. He'd noticed it first: Jeeves had assumed its armored form.

"Damn! This started on the bridge; it means we're in—doesn't *your* suit warn you of danger?"

"Taurei does no such thing! What danger?"

"Don't know, but let's get down fast!"

I widened the hole above just in time to let in a sudden downpour. We plummeted, angling away from the dome, sheets of rain keeping us company. Just before we hit the ground, I repaired the chute. The resultant upward tug on my harness squeezed my torso with sickening force.

I landed badly, slamming into wet dirt, thrown forward onto my face. Shadow and microdoc padding helped, but my knees hurt, and the world seemed to spin around me for a moment. I sat up and regained just enough sense to dissolve the chute before it could drag us along.

Jacau's fur dripped. "We will arrange an arrangement," he said quietly. "No more chuting. Are we still in danger?"

"Yeah, but I guess it's no longer so close." Jeeves kept twitching between smooth and partially armored.

My brother watched, fascinated. "Whatever that white bird did, your taurei be something new in the worlds."

I didn't contradict him, but I remembered Jeeves acting as my early-warning system pre-Swan. "How do we get into the city?"

Jacau looked around. "We follow you. You said you knew this place."

"Not from *outside*. Let's explore."

My brother, I learned, had excellent night vision, and I had something even better. Even so, it took us three soggy hours to find an entrance. Once within the city's upper tunnels, we headed toward the domed-in area, now several miles away. As we trudged along empty, echoing passageways, I kept trying to contact the local Mind. No luck, but I figured we'd run across allies eventually.

Jeeves remained moody, but whatever meant us ill stayed hidden.

Then I noticed a patch of fog far behind us. My suit thickened, forcing me to slow, but the fog only matched our pace. Soon, a second misty patch joined the first. When a third, then a fourth perambulating fog appeared, I decided to forgo their company, although it meant revealing my exotic power.

I assembled my magic carpet, shadow-strapped Jacau and I to the top, and we flew along as fast as I dared in this unfamiliar environment. I looked back and wasn't delighted to notice the fog banks keeping up, and that their ranks had doubled.

When we passed a row of parked tricycles, I had a vision of mist-concealed Silver Hhoymon behind us, pedaling along with some fiendishly efficient gearing system. We flew down a long ramp, slid onto the purple surface of an open Glideway, and the sudden extra speed turned the view around us into a special effect blur.

In seconds, the Glideway ended, and then it seemed we moved in slow motion. Buildings lay ahead, outskirts of the downtown area. I blessed everyone who'd arranged for me to study Hhoymon City maps.

The misty spots were closing in. I pushed my carpet faster and sprayed out a shadow-smokescreen behind us. We zigzagged our way through the clean streets and our pursuers finally fell behind.

Some high-speed chase this was: heroes on their stomachs, scooting along on a fuzzy black carpet, child-sized villains probably pursuing on toy tricycles. All we needed to meet Hollywood standards would be a fruit-cart to smash.

I was terrified, mostly for Jacau. Jeeves had proved immune to the rebels' energy weapons, but my brother's suit was a fabric of a different color. I ordered Jeeves to armor him too. Nothing doing. Evidently, it wouldn't defend anyone but me. I *had* to reach Rider, but the local Mind still ignored my shouts.

We were well under the dome now, shooting toward the narrowest street I recalled from the maps. I hoped our enemies would get in each other's way.

Hhoymon City seemed depressingly uninhabited, lacking in amenities such as Nemes and Common. Truly, this was a poor day for sightseeing. The park was beautiful, the buildings graceful, slabs of semi-precious stone glowed marvelously. But the ugly thing I'd glimpsed from above spoiled the picture.

Near the city's center, I finally saw it clearly. Some colossal, sadistic entomologist had found four Airbus-sized wasps and glued their heads and abdomens together. The monster's body segments blazed vivid yellow with orange and black stripes. It squatted across the tops of two skyscrapers. I twisted my head and used x-road vision to get a different perspective.

"What the hell," I muttered, "is it?"

"A monster," Jacau suggested.

"If not, I'd hate to see one."

Huge yellow drops of some volatile fluid dripped from the body segments in an insult to the concept of rain. Halfway down, these dispersed into brownish-yellow smog, giving the air an ugly mustard tint. The stretch of road directly beneath hissed and eroded.

Good thing, I told myself, that I'm wearing a Scome gas mask. It's so vital to select the proper wardrobe for the occasion.

Hhoymon architecture is lovely, and I'm sure incredibly strong. The creature proved itself stronger by tearing off the top of a skyscraper and flinging it down at us.

I begged my carpet to forget running and start jumping. We started bounding along in thirty-foot leaps, hitting hard enough each time to rattle my back teeth. The largest chunks of the artificial avalanche missed us with a comfortable micron to spare, but small debris pelted us until I raised a shadow umbrella. The umbrella then shielded us from a new hail of pieces rebounding from the pavement. But it also blocked my view above, so I dissolved it the instant I dared, just in time to catch one heart-stopping glimpse of something enormous ... falling.

The monster hit the pavement. The impact produced the loudest, most horrendous sound I'd ever heard. The entire city lurched, throwing us into the air. At least, I thought, *that* horror is dead.

Then the damn thing stretched itself to better fit the street and began lurching toward us in *spasms*. It appeared slow, but I could barely stay ahead. And I made another charming discovery. Our enemies had arrived. With reinforcements. At least fifty patches of mist closed in fast.

My mind raced fast enough for escape velocity. "Jacau. I know a possible hiding place. But if we can get in, we'll probably be stuck there."

"Act as you should."

"Then hold on, this is going to be close!"

To reach my goal, we'd have to beat the monster to the intersection behind us. I reversed direction and without thinking used a shadow-arm to pluck a large moonstone boulder from a patch of greenery.

Jacau gasped, and I knew why. That rock had to weigh over three hundred pounds. I couldn't even feel any strain! When had my shadow gotten so strong?

Boulder hoisted overhead, I flew us directly toward the wasp-thing to simulate an attack, a joke considering relative sizes. But for a wonder, our pursuer slowed. Why rush when dinner is running toward your mouth?

The top of the thing's head opened into a vast and appalling maw. Four pairs of dripping mandibles separated, behind them, a steaming lake of slime. Mere yards from this hideous orifice, I hurled the moonstone with all my will.

The boulder half-melted before it splashed inside, which hardly mattered—any creature that could survive such a fall wouldn't be bothered by a pebble upside the head. Meanwhile, I made the sharpest and fastest left turn in history. We entered a new street, rocketing toward the city's very center. Braking hard, I flew us up a long ramp until we'd reached the top. There, we stopped and I dissolved the carpet.

We stood together, facing the magnificent entryway to the tallest structure in Hhoymon City, a tower capped with a fluted crystal spire smoothly melding into the milky dome a thousand feet above. In this building, Hhoymon displayed art and artifacts from hundreds of universes.

"The Heart of Art," I announced.

The two matching doors ahead appeared to be polished crystal slabs, forty feet high, and might've been a menace to birds or delicate flying heroes without their metallic inclusions. Golden, mineral stars floating in a crystal sky ...

"Tuvid," Jacau growled, pushing hard against one of the giant slabs. "This will not moves. How do we get in?"

REVELATION FOUR
THE GOLDBERG VARIATIONS

Be still, my soul, my journey is my native land.
—AFTER NIKOS KAZANTZAKIS

CHAPTER 32
A CROOKED HOUSE

The day before Able Firsthouse had gone on his recent vacation, he just happened to bend my ear about Hhoymon Tower. Able went into so much detail about how these specific doors were secured after visiting hours that even at the time, I thought it odd.

Now I just happened to be uniquely equipped, in theory anyway, to open them. Coincidence? Not a chance. I knew, down to my bone marrow, that some heavy-duty Crossroad figure, maybe the Watergod or Binae, had sneaked a peek into the future and asked Ben to make sure I had all the information I needed at the appropriate time.

I had the information, and this was definitely the time to use it, and fast. My problem was figuring out how, but I already had an idea.

Boiling it down, the nearly indestructible double doors weren't locked, barred, or bolted, but *bonded* to each other, and could only be freed from within the building. According to Ben, the bonding process included the enormous, hidden opening mechanism.

He described the only two ways to gain entrance.

One: a docent stationed in the lobby could depress a wall-mounted diamond plate, sending a coded light beam through a central optical conduit to the de-bonding system. Two: with no watchperson on duty, a sophisticated scanning device would admit the approved visitor by directly activating the light beam. In both cases, coded light had to pass through the main conduit.

Jacau shoved again with no better result. This, I approved of. I didn't know how Rider had gotten investigators inside, but if the security system admitted *us*, we'd almost certainly be stepping into an ambush.

My task would be simple. I only had to press one unreachable button.

The street behind us had turned to pea-soup fog, but only its tendrils touched the ramp. It troubled me that our attackers seemed to be hanging back, but our only way out was forward.

I raised a hand, placing it on the glassy surface before us. If light could pass through ...

Breathing a silent prayer, I pushed an arm of darkness into the thick quartz-like material. I felt a mild sense of resistance, then the blurry limb was through, reaching toward a pressure plate on an inside wall. I narrowed my shadow's tip, placed it on the plate, and told the shadow-finger to push.

The great crystal rectangles slid apart with no more sound than hands stroking silk. Jacau shouted Dhu-barot praise as we ran into the wide lobby.

My next fear had ripened: would the doors *close*? Able had mentioned a safety protocol, a concession to the Heart's public nature: once open, this entrance would remain open if anyone was nearby. Few things would offend visitors so much as being cut in half.

Were any enemies within this safety zone?

I tugged on Jacau's arm, and we ran ten yards down the lobby before turning around. Black marble lined the walls, a galaxy of small lights twinkled overhead. I watched the entrance.

The sound of giant doors whispering closed was the best music to my ears. I ran back to the doors. The world outside had darkened with fog; thick mist flowed leisurely up the ramp. No wasp-monsters in sight.

The rebels could've easily kept the entrance ajar, but hadn't bothered. Clearly, these doors would open for *them*. But the Silver geniuses hadn't foreseen everything. I tried out an evil chuckle that might have sounded less amateurish if I weren't so scared. I glanced around the lobby. All seemed well so far.

"Did the enemies want us here?" Jacau asked.

I tried to shrug but Jeeves had become too stiff. "If so, they probably figured they'd have us cornered either inside or out. But let's surprise 'em."

The pressure-plates appeared lucid as tap water, some set low for White Hhoymon. Choosing one at random, I pushed a stream of shadow against the diamond octagon. For one awful moment, it couldn't get through. Then it rushed in, and I kept adding more until I felt the central conduit had to be filled. I assigned microdocs to stabilize the arrangement.

"What did you do?" Jacau asked quietly.

"The doors won't open unless a light beam reaches a hidden sensor. With any justice, I just blocked the beam."

"Can we test your success?" My brother was a practical fellow.

I exhaled noisily. "Let's find out." This time using my hand like a normal person, I pressed a different plate than the one I'd just used. The doors didn't budge.

"Goods for you!"

"No champagne yet, Jacau. If our Silvers can access a Mind, they could possibly undo my trick. But for now," I grinned, "I pronounce this museum closed until further notice."

I took a final look at the foggy view. "Come on." As we walked down the lobby, I sprayed darkness in our wake.

"If enemies enter, will shadow block them?" Jacau posed when I stopped.

"I doubt it. But they've got ... ray-guns. Once they realize they're locked out, they might try shooting through the doors. We don't want them seeing we haven't gone farther into the building."

"I have a better idea: going farther into the building."

"Sorry, Jacau, I'd better tell you. Sun-toch-sew warned me this place has gotten weird. Apparently the evicted Hhoymon messed up the—the *geometry* in here to discourage looters in their absence. Two Blenn came to investigate, got lost, then some goddess with a super sense of direction went in after them."

"And?"

"Got lost herself."

"Okay. So we be careful. How did these Blenn open doors?"

"I wondered about that. I suppose Hhoymon loyalists gave the Common—"

"I have a bigger thought! Our enemies need a place of operation. Best would be someplace no one would *dare* enter. Why would loyal Hhoymon twist space when their doors be easily locked?"

His logic made sense. "Damn! We'd better assume the worst: the *rebels* screwed with local reality, they control this building and know how to navigate here. Which implies they're not necessarily all outside. Which implies, damn it, that we can't count on being safe right here. Okay. I suppose a place this confusing would be a good place to hide. I hope." Not that we had a choice.

"In every case, Tuvid, we must seek refuge. Quickly."

"Right. But before we rush in like fools, we'll need some way to survive."

"What be the danger?"

"I'm not sure. But the Blenn were supposedly wearing ..." after drawing a blank, I managed to recall Rider's phrase "... macroquantum-reality suits, whatever they are, so—"

Jacau looked around wildly. "*Why?*"

"I gather," I said slowly, thinking it out, "Crossroad is something of a ... composite from many universes. I'd guess it was tailored for the Common, and the Minds were created to accommodate guests with other requirements."

"So?"

"Assume the rebels have somehow, um, delaminated reality in this building and insulated us from the local Mind. A casual stroll here might carry us into *all* sorts of universes."

He went silent for a moment. "How can we predict?"

"There's our problem."

"Solve, please. With hurry!"

The doomed Blenn had reported this tower had "mirrored" itself in many directions, becoming an unpredictable maze. And Jacau's logic suggested that an unwelcoming committee might suddenly appear. So, we had three things to avoid: getting lost, lethal environments, and enemies. I saw possible solutions for the first two, but only luck and stealth could save us from the third.

A dull boom shook the soundproofed building.

"*Tuvid?*" my brother urged.

Problem two seemed easy. Drop enough breadcrumbs and we could retrace our route no matter how disoriented we felt.

"I think we'd better go on foot and take it slow," I said. "Give me a moment to get a few things set up, and then we'll get moving."

Working quickly, I ordered Jeeves to dispatch a squad of microdocs to remain behind whenever I took a step, remaining inert until I sent other soldiers to find them. But not knowing how few 'docs would remain findable, or how many would deplete my taurei faster than the organisms could reproduce, I let Jeeves decide how big each squad would be. From the surprise success of my enemy-outline experiment, I wasn't worried about how long my microdocs could live independent of me.

No, my main worry centered on running into fatal universes.

Without reality-stabilizing gear, we'd need a damn good warning system. I had something crazy in mind.

I emitted an arrow-shaped shadow and ordered microdocs to stabilize it and keep it floating upright six feet directly in front of us. Then I gave Jeeves detailed instructions: constantly send scouts exploring ahead of us, and have them return to report to those operating the arrow. If they'd found conditions ahead benign, 'docs were to keep the arrow turning clockwise. If questionable, counterclockwise. If conditions were dangerous or no scouts returned, the arrow operators would dissipate the arrow. Jacau and I would then immediately change course, I'd make a new arrow, and we'd restart the entire routine.

By now, Jacau would've been hissing through his teeth if Nemes had any. I explained my plan to him, ignored his un-Neme-like snort of disbelief, thought "start," and the arrow began twirling. Clockwise! I blessed my little buddies for being so very understanding. But how were they at grading universes?

Jacau muttered something in Dhu-barot, and I only caught a word that meant "unreal."

"Here we go," I muttered. "Slowly."

We dawdled along a corridor leading straight into the tower. Jacau kept a general lookout while I concentrated on the arrow. But after twenty yards, the passageway opened onto what Able had called the "atrium," a vast open shaft piercing every floor of the tower. We both stopped as if our feet had been nailed down. Able's description had been comically inadequate.

A specimen from God's own mineral collection dominated the space: a black opal-like pillar a thousand feet tall containing enough polychromatic fire to reignite Chicago a thousand times over. *Jeeves*, I thought, *you've been seriously out-opaled.*

"I have never," Jacau whispered.

"Me neither."

We took a step forward. Suddenly, the pillar appeared to extend downward as far as it went up, surrounded by a hole so wide that we seemed to be standing only a few yards away. The hole clearly echoed the atrium above, but none of this could be reflection, not from such a sandstone-rough floor. Besides, the lower half of the doubled pillar and the floors the hole exposed below had a tentative, vaporous quality.

Freaky, I thought, but hardly disorienting. Maybe this wouldn't be so bad after all.

I gritted my teeth, told myself the hole couldn't suck us in, and took another step. Phantom versions of the pillar, atrium, and countless floors shot in all directions. Some versions of the tower seemed to stretch indefinitely. Another small step and several phantoms appeared solid.

Jacau and I looked at each other, shuffled forward again, and the original column became one ray of an intricate opal star. Pillars and copies of the tower's interior reached in a thousand directions. I could see it all, which seemed absurd; everything stood in the way of everything else! Yet pillars shone through walls shining through pillars. And the colors! This had become a misty paradise, sparkling with a million tints and intensities of mineral fire.

A baffling scene, stunning in every sense, but finding our way back should be easy, even without my micro-breadcrumbs.

The big drop lay just ahead so we turned to move around the central structure rather than toward it. Suddenly, a pillar-spoke blocked our way, just past my floating arrow.

I took an experimental shuffle toward it and the entire opal star appeared to rotate like a cosmic turnstile, leaving the obstacle ahead in the same relative position.

More confident, I took a full step and Jacau joined me. And I felt as if someone had just spun me around a dozen times....

I couldn't reorient myself. Various float-tube entrances, dimly visible through the confusion, glowed along a curving wall ahead. Most were set at crazy angles and some in unexpected colors.

If green was up and violet was down, what was orange? Or yellow?

"We have moved strangely, Tuvid."

"Yeah. I noticed."

"This be what the Guardian warned of?"

Jacau sounded so tense that I turned and really looked at him for the first time in hours. His fur was bedraggled, and his paws twitched. We'd been through a lot since we'd stopped for lunch halfway around this world, and hadn't even gotten the lunch.

"Don't worry," I said, trying to mean it. "I bet our rescuers are on the way."

"This be a terrible and beautiful place."

"Definitely. Never thought we'd end up here."

"End?"

"Sorry. Poor word choice."

He waved a stubby finger around. "All these copies be from different realties?"

"Hadn't thought of that, but you may be right. I wonder if their alignments match their underlying superspacial orientations."

"Tuvid, you ask a very mind-heavy question. But now, this is more important: I no longer know which way be where."

"Likewise, I'm afraid. And if you want more bad news, the tower may be getting more complex while we wait. The Blenn that came here reported that copies were copying themselves."

"In such case," Jacau snapped, "we must stop waiting."

"Right. Let's try to reach a green float-tube and see what happens when we go up a floor."

Running, or rather staggering through, a gauntlet of centrifuges, we found we could lessen the spinning sensation by angling toward the hole, but I didn't dare get too close. And we kept getting nowhere, slowly. Maddening to see a tube a few yards away, only to have it vanish after the smallest step.

More alarming, some external changes became unpleasantly melodramatic. One moment everything turned grainy, the next, everything was painted in shades of pink.

My brother grabbed my arm. The black arrow had vanished. Poisonous universe dead ahead. "Well," I said, "now we know our warning system's doing something. Let's try another slant."

I produced another arrow. We took a few cautious steps in a different direction, and the new arrow took to spinning clockwise.

Step, whirl. Step, whirl. Then, by sheer luck, a green tube appeared right next to us. I hesitated, afraid our final step would chase the thing away.

"Hurry, Tuvid. We may never reach another."

The tube stayed put, and we jumped in. But on our way up my nerves got a workout. I'd positioned the arrow overhead and the damn thing reversed directions six times. Fortunately, the trip was brief and the worst part only a momentary burning in my throat.

It occurred to me, way too late, that the green light might've indicated "down" if this shaft were one of the mirrored sort. We could find ourselves strolling along some ceiling on a sublevel that shouldn't even exist.

When we stepped out, shockingly frigid air gave me an instant faceache. Jacau's fur fluffed, Jeeves inflated airbed-style, and my breath became a foggy speech-balloon. The local Mind? Definitely snubbing us. I studied the frost-plated corridor through a microdoc ski mask and goggles, and did some goggling myself.

I would've expected a hallway abutting the atrium would have a view overlooking said atrium, or at least curved around it. Instead this hall ran dead straight, appeared endless, and lacked any openings overlooking anything. Rime-coated doorways and widely spaced float-tube duos syncopated the high walls. No visible ceiling. Far, far above us, pink clouds rushed past.

All of this seemed perfectly normal compared to all the haphazard sheets of nearly transparent colors hanging in midair, wavering like Mylar strips over a lamp. Spaced at irregular intervals, cross-corridors intersected this one.

Jacau turned toward me. "You said you be leaving a trail behind us?"

I nodded.

"How can we follow this trail *down* an up tube?"

I'd worried about that. "I figure that since tubes are always paired and close together, we'll backtrack by following my trail to whatever shaft we've used, take the one alongside, then pick up the, um, scent at the bottom."

"You hoping." He shivered and hopped from foot to foot. Perhaps his taurei had more limitations while he was in Neme form.

"Speaking of elevators, Jacau, let's find another. It's too cold here and we shouldn't hide anywhere near ground level."

"You have done well this far, Tuvid. I be proud you be my brother."

"Thanks. Feel the same about you." Was I *blushing* in this icebox? "C'mon, I think my teeth are starting to freeze."

Again, the building pirouetted as we walked, and I doubted we were traversing a single hallway. Still, the route ahead stayed straight. Just before we reached the nearest set of float-tubes, warmth wafted from an open doorway, and I peeked inside. Bones. An immense horde, some elaborately carved or painted, some plain. Huge ones, tiny ones, weird ones but mostly broken ones. An open graveyard. Jacau detoured to pick up several nearby fragments and examine them.

I was more interested in how the room appeared to stretch back forever with repeating patterns of the same bones.

In the new float-tube, our arrow oscillated again, but again we rose too quickly to die. I prayed our ride wouldn't *end* in a bad spot. The temperature soared and Jeeves thinned to summer gear.

The third floor had thick pink clouds for walls. Sweltering now, we splashed along a shallow stream under a sky in swirling shades of brown. We'd just passed a cross-corridor when my arrow started wobbling. I hadn't included wobbling in my instructions to Jeeves.

"Maybe a warning message," I guessed. "Let's take it real slow and single file. Me first."

Five steps later, the world seemed to twist ninety degrees. Suddenly, I was falling—sideways! I hit with a thud, contradicting the wall's puffy appearance. Unlike me, Jacau landed on his feet.

"Be you hurt?" he asked.

"No, but ..."

The wall formerly on our right had become our floor. Its cloudy opposite made a respectably high ceiling. To our left, the stream defied the new gravity by running parallel with the roiling brownness to our distant right. Unfortunately, the corridor ahead was now an open shaft, tremendously deep and tall. How the hell were we supposed to get across?

"Maybe the down-force will change back," Jacau suggested.

That thought didn't delight me. With gravity subject to whims, our hallway might suddenly become a vertical drop, or we could be flung into the distasteful sky.

I kept these fears private as we approached the intersection. At the drop-off's edge, I lay on my stomach, peering downward. Far, far below, the shaft curved.

"Ideas?" I asked, inching backward before standing up. "We can't trust a shadow-bridge to stretch that far and support our weight. We *could* parachute."

"I say never to chutes! We should learn more."

Jacau still held the bone chips he'd picked up. He threw one several feet straight ahead. I leaned closer to watch it fall. He tossed the next a bit farther, which dropped just as willingly. He put more juice into the last throw, and the chip sailed about seven feet beyond our edge. As if swatted by an invisible hand, it darted horizontally to splash into water. Okay. If we could reach that point, the streambed would resume floor duty.

"Hide me with shadow, Tuvid. Keep it with me."

I obeyed, realizing he wanted to convert to his Scome body. He leapt without hesitation. My x-road vision, piercing my shadow, showed him safe and re-transformed before I could even swear.

"Jacau! Don't move an *inch*; you're ahead of our warning system!"

"Yes. And I cannot see. Remove darkness, please."

I did so and stared at the Neme standing sideways on a wet wall.

"Tuvid. Come to me."

"Will do." According to my eyes, I was about to jump into a bottomless pit. For a moment I just stood, breathing hard. With Jacau calling out encouragement, I backed several yards down the hall, got a running start, and took off. He caught me before I could fall into the river. "So easy," he said.

We reached some new tubes and floated upward.

The fourth floor struck me as gothic, its murkiness strangely viscous and my warning arrow nearly invisible to normal vision. Progress became slow because the arrow couldn't decide which way to spin. Sporadic flashes blinded us, revealing nothing, closely stalked by deep thunder with overtones of insane laughter. And the place was inhabited.

Colorless beings followed us, only visible, as Jacau put it, from the "edges" of our eyes as they matched our pace with relentless patience.

Extra insecurities I didn't need; the treacherous gravity had already met my full daily requirement. My skin crawled as I passed close to a semi-seen figure towering over the rest.

"This tower be not much improving," Jacau grumbled when we reached the next set of tubes.

The next few floors offered bizarre variations but no serious challenges. Level seven's floor was a spongy fog, and its ceiling was a flowing river punctuated by moving negative spaces, waves in intaglio. We stopped at a new set of tubes, yellow and blue.

"What could *these* colors mean?" I asked.

Jacau hesitated. "Soaring or dropping more than one floor?"

"Of course! Take forever to get around in here otherwise. Good thing I brought along a functioning brain: yours."

"But how *many* floors will these go?"

"Pick a number from two on up."

He grunted. "Then answer this: which soars?"

"I'd assume the left one as usual. Let's—" I'd suddenly caught a faint melody, sonic equivalent to the hazy beings we'd encountered below, only detectable from the edges of my ears. "That's beautiful."

"What is?"

Surprised, I looked at him. "Music. Your ears are better than mine; don't you hear it?"

"No."

"Like ... underwater violins. Coming from somewhere above. I have a feeling we should go there."

"Be you sure this isn't noise from a—a—"

"An exhibit? Could be."

"Why should we follow this noise?"

Why indeed? "I can't explain it. Just a hunch."

"Then we follow."

We stepped into the yellow shaft and began rising. Fast. By now, I expected the arrow to vacillate, but didn't appreciate it when the backspin became rapid enough to *whistle*.

We'd ascended perhaps twenty stories, give or take fifteen. The new corridor was a floor-to-ceiling orange lawn. I spurned some pink and white elevators, seeking a green one. The song seemed louder, and I didn't want to overshoot. I tried to speak.

Rather than my voice, circular ripples in the air emerged from my mouth, spread across the hallway, rebounded from the verdant surfaces. As returning waves collided and re-collided with each other, they created patterns that grew progressively fancier while the individual ripples grew smaller.

Jacau was sharp. He simply pointed at the arrow quivering uneasily at two o'clock. We traded glances and kept our mouths shut until we entered a green up-shaft.

According to my uneducated guess, our next stop wound up somewhere around level twenty-eight. Compared to the bizarre corridors we'd found below, this one seemed almost plain, entirely paneled in something resembling New England quilted maple. A series of widely spaced closed doors lined both walls. The hallway stretched indefinitely before and behind us as if time itself had been veneered with wood. I turned in place, slowly, listening.

"Lost our homing signal," I sighed. "Might as well stay on this floor."

"Good. I be weary."

"Me, too. Let's find a room to hole up, but farther from these tubes just in case someone we wouldn't like visits this floor."

After a modest hike, I stopped. "Okay, Jacau. Let's say Camp Gothhowl lies behind ... *that* door."

He shoved the featureless rectangle then tried sliding it aside. "How do we enter? It be lock-ed. We shall try another?"

I grinned. "No need, assuming these have the special, extra-secure Heart of Art locks, which might as well be custom-designed for someone like me. Here's the picture as I understand it: doors open from the outside with voice commands, but only from authorized voices. From inside ... you'll see."

"How do you know this? How did you know how to open the front doors?"

"A friend, a *real* Neme, practically talked my ear off about this place." I chuckled, noticing three Neme eyes suddenly aimed at my head. "Yes, Jacau, I still have both ears. I meant that he talked a *lot* about the museum, mostly about how clever the locks were."

"How very lucky!"

"I doubt luck had anything to do with it. Now, watch this."

I sent a flat band of darkness—for once truly resembling a shadow—through a slim gap under the door and ordered it to rise up inside the room. Feeling terrifically sly, I sent micro-supervisors along to guide the blackness to find and push any pressure plate. The gap abruptly filled with light. Whoops. So the room had more than one kind of switch. A bit deflated, I dispatched new 'docs to choose a different plate and was rewarded by the door gliding open.

We entered cautiously and the door closed automatically. The room was unoccupied. I spotted two wall-plates and quickly forced enough shadow inside the clear one to choke its optical conduit. Entrance thus secured, I studied our refuge: an office, medium-sized and windowless. Century lamps in the high wooden ceiling glinted off a ruby-red desk, and four chairs had enough cushions to make two impromptu mattresses. Everything seemed a comfortable height and size, scaled for Grays.

Five MARBLEs and a sleek MARBLE reader with a blinking ready light lay on the desk—someone must've left in a hurry. Excellent! We had a comfortable place to hide *and* free entertainment. Which left two trivial issues: food and water.

CHAPTER 33
CROCODILE TIER

Pacing all around the room, I watched my arrow spin clockwise. No dizziness. This office probably lay within a single reality. But something felt ... off.

I dissolved my warning system, flopped into the desk chair, and tried to figure out why walking had felt so awkward. Each individual step had been easy enough, and I didn't feel an ounce heavier.

Reaching for a MARBLE, I felt the same kind of awkwardness and clumsily knocked the little sphere off the desk. Jacau put out a blocking foot, but the MARBLE stopped on its own. He stared at it a moment before handing it to me.

In my mind, I replayed the incident and shivered. MARBLEs are hard, perfectly round, and surprisingly heavy for their size. Yet, this one had hit a wooden floor with only a faint tap and had barely rolled.

Its weight felt right. I put it on the smooth tabletop and nudged with a finger; the damn thing rolled twice then seemed to get stuck. Was this place ... magnetic in some weird way? Or ...

"Jacau, know what inertia is? The tendency for moving things to stay in motion?"

"Surely."

"I'm guessing this room is somewhat lacking in that amenity."

"Yes! We be ... en-cubed by hard surfaces, but all sound be dulled. Will this damage us?"

"Don't see how."

"Okay. You rest; I survey." He went exploring, and I grabbed the sphere and turned it in my hands, admiring its beauty.

These things really did resemble big marbles, which is why some witty engineer had forced the "backronym" by naming these devices

"Memory And Recall Block-Loading Elements." Their colors, internal patterns, and degrees of transparency changed as information was added or altered, but they were always pretty.

On Earth, MARBLEs, MARBLE-writers, and MARBLE-readers functioned perfectly to store and retrieve any kind of information, and so far, no one had found a limit to how much information could be stored on a single sphere. But Able Firsthouse had told me that in the Hhoymon universe, storing data was the least of what MARBLEs could do.

I stuffed the one in my hand inside the reader and, remembering the funky inertia here, carefully grabbed two more. For the sake of efficiency, most MARBLEs were assigned information on a single topic.

Above the desktop, a 3D animation demonstrated the use of highly pressurized water as a cutting tool. A Gray Hhoymon voice added laconic commentary.

The second MARBLE displayed specialized techniques for erecting White Hhoymon-style skyscrapers. I watched a construction team, shown in ultra fast-forward, raising such a miniature tower. I shook my head at seeing background glimpses of the Heart of Art.

The third MARBLE contained an animated diorama and a revelation.

An alien desert appeared, seen from perhaps twenty feet above golden sands. A tribe of primitives feasted nearby, clearly on their way to becoming Nemes, but needing a few eons of buckling down to the business of evolution. Several females had bumpy, furry growths on their backs.

"Look at this!" I called out and Jacau hurried over to stand beside me.

The ur-Nemes surrounded an immense cactus topped with colored ferns. Three natives were using flat stones to scrape away thorns; others had sunk their feeding tendrils into already cleared areas. The soundtrack: an orchestra of cheery tri-toned voices. A very old Common stood near the cactus, looking as unfinished as the Nemes, holding a long, pointed spear in one palsied hand.

Then a large low-slung animal with yellow fur, one hell of a mouth, and a sneaky way of moving entered the scene, approaching the tribe as smoothly and quietly as a fluid. Silent as it was, and noisy as the Nemes were, the Common hooted, spun around, and ran toward the animal. The viewpoint panned in closer.

The beast sprang, dodged the Common's spear-thrust, and bowled over a female Neme. Horrendous jaws ripped off her left arm along with much of her chest, bones snapping like firecrackers. She screamed in three pitiful voices, furry legs kicking while her tribe-mates stared in horror. Neme blood, I learned, spurts in brown and pink.

The ancient Common leaped and speared the carnivore's back, but the wound only seemed to enrage it. It whirled and caught one of the Common's legs in hooked teeth. As the two massive figures struggled, the Nemes joined their voices into a low-pitched rumble.

I assumed they were trying to scare the beast away until blood burst from the creature's eyes. Seconds later, it died, evidently killed by focused sound alone. So much for Neme harmlessness.

But the Common was dead, the female as well. The tribe burst into a heartbreaking symphony of lamentations. I shuddered.

Jacau put a warm paw on my back. "How did Hhoymon get this picture?" The images fast-forwarded as blurry Nemes dug an improbably huge pit in the sand with flat stones and bare hands.

"I don't know. Could be a clever reconstruction. Or with their technology, they—what's going on?"

Normal speed had resumed as the entire tribe gathered around one mature female. She extended her feeding tubes. One at time, with great formality, four other Nemes squirted a pale green liquid from their tubes into hers. She swayed, fell, then tribe-mates caught her and placed her tenderly in the pit. Suddenly, I *knew* what would follow. Just didn't believe it.

Six Nemes ceremoniously placed the Common over their sleeping companion. Next, they added the dead female. Almost casually, they threw in the predator's carcass and overfilled the pit with sand.

Finally, they used the Common's bloody spear to pull down some cactus ferns, and placed these on the new dune as if putting flowers on an unmarked grave. The whole tribe sat down and waited.

"They be the same," Jacau whispered. I understood him because I'd jumped to the same absurd conclusion.

The image shifted to a cross section of the burial dune. Everything appeared insubstantial except for the sleeping figure. In accelerated time, we watched her feeding tubes extending into the ghostly bodies above. Then she began changing.

Her body thickened and elongated. Breathing slits developed on both sides of her newly massive chest. The three "mouths" drifted and merged, nostril-slits vanishing. A head-crest sprouted. Her paw-like hand lengthened and grew extra digits. The eyes mutated; her fur fell out and leaf-like projections burst from her body like weeds while her feet ballooned into large pads. I blinked when the feeding tubes separated, wriggling toward the surface, a herd of thin worms.

The viewpoint followed the worms. They broke though the dune's summit, pushing aside the fern memorial. The tribe shouted a great chord of thanksgiving, swiftly excavated the dune, and pulled out their transformed companion. The corpses had become mummies and the Neme rose to her feet, now a Common.

"No wonder they trust each other," I said softly.

The remaining MARBLEs weren't nearly as interesting or disturbing. The last, judging by format, seemed to contain Hhoymon poetry. Impulsively, I had Jeeves make a pocket and stowed the sphere inside.

"I could eat," I confessed. "How about you?"

Jacau glanced down at his stomach. "This form has a slow speed to starve. It be you I fear for."

"Don't. By now, I should be ravenous not just hungry." I yawned. "My taurei must be keeping up the old blood sugar. Hope it found food around somewhere; otherwise it'll kill itself feeding me." I felt too tired to worry.

We placed two rows of cushions on the floor and lay down side by side. I switched off the light with shadow and Jacau seemed to fall instantly asleep. The fact of Ben's death, almost forgotten in the last stressful hours, hit me hard. I hurriedly shoved my thoughts elsewhere.

One thing I hadn't had recently: solitude. For me, seclusion provides a northern light of the soul, shedding no warmth but plenty of cold steady light. This semi-private moment was close enough for two things to come into focus.

Biology be damned, I was *human*. Humans in a human society had raised me. In my case, nurture not only trumped nature, it tromped it with both feet. I accepted Jacau as my brother and already loved him, but we would always be different species. My Scome family would have to accept that.

And I'd been so focused on asking why *me* that I hadn't spent enough energy asking why *now*.

"Jacau?" I whispered too quietly to wake him.

"Yes?"

"Why did I get drafted for bait duty after all these years?"

He was silent so long, I figured he'd spoken in his sleep until he said, "Tuvid, I only know two parts of it. For one, you were in danger."

"That much I already know, but I have a feeling there's more to it."

"Yes. For two, our people be tired of fear. Many have run dry of patience. One clan warned the Common they would wait not much longer."

"To do what?"
"Strike back."
"How could they tell loyal Hhoymon from rebels?"
"They could not. All Hhoymon were in danger."
"Oh. I see."
"Sleep my brother. This day has been large and sad."
He turned his back to me and settled down.
I stared up into darkness and kept seeing Ben's face....

———

I jerked awake, pulse hammering, disoriented, searching with my Crossroad vision. Then I remembered the dream. My subconscious had blended the wasp-bodied monster and Lithshark into something too loathsome to sleep through.

We lay with our feet toward the door. The office seemed unchanged. Then I glanced the opposite way and sat up so fast my brother was startled awake.

"Quelta?" he croaked in sleep-drugged Dhu-barot, unable to see the three eerie figures standing behind us.

"Were we," I asked very quietly, "expecting company?"

"Someone be here?" Already, he sounded calm and alert.

"Three someones. Wait."

Keeping my attention on the motionless newcomers, I slowly stood, eased over to the light switch, and pressed it. I didn't want our guests to know about my shadow abilities.

Jacau spun around. Now he could share my heart attack. The illumination revealed a pair of bulky silver-gray creatures with opaque helmets flanking someone extraordinary even by Crossroad standards.

With a Velcro-releasing sizzle, one gray figure wrenched its backpack off, reached inside, and began pulling out and fitting together thin pieces. I watched grimly, considering defenses against unknown weapons. Then I caught on.

"They're okay, Jacau! Just two Blenn in reality-stabilizing suits. I think the industrious one's assembling a translating rod."

"And the middle?"

"Must be the lost goddess." I stared at her, puzzled by a sense of familiarity.

She seemed about my height, slender, with a long head whose bare skull had the color and luster of burnished bronze. Her wide, protruding mouth was equipped with impressive chompers. A short blue shift left her coppery, almost flat chest bare, and left exposed humanoid legs shading from dark bronze at her wide feet to golden near her knees. Her bronze arm ended in delicate black human hands. Ultra-red energy flowed like blood throughout her body, even shining through her shift.

Her eyes were enormous, slanted, and bluer than sapphires; cheeks high and catlike. Conch ears, nose a mere bump with violin f-hole nostrils. Her skin was reticulated with large but faint scales.

I looked at her shoulders and finally understood.

On each shoulder, a tiny wing fluttered—transparent, prismatic, and delicate as a soap bubble in sunlight, swiftly accelerating to an iridescent blur. Music from a duet of ethereal violins filled the room.

Jacau and I traded glances. The gorgeous sound seemed to carve out its own reality, and I recognized the music I'd followed earlier. But this time I heard it with my ears. The Blenn speechstaff, a song-staff I suppose, began translating—two voices singing mostly in unison with occasional word variations. And *this* translating rod conveyed emotion.

"I regret to cause you alarm," sang the voices. "Our purpose/desire was guarding you as you slept."

"I've seen you," I said, "in my dreams." *Where you looked a lot more human.*

"And there, I have seen you. I am S'bek. My companions/wards are (buzzing sound) and (buzzing sound). I know your names."

"You were Chybris's crocodile head."

"And did She not make of/for me a body splendid?"

"It's ... amazing." *Why would an ex-croc request wings?*

"I see the direction/question in your gaze." The music seemed to laugh. "I desired a voice without sacrificing a sensibly rigid mouth. My kind has long befriended birds who sing to us and clean our fangs. Thus, my plumes."

Jacau stood. "You be the goddess who cannot get lost?"

"*Some* might declare me a goddess. I am only titled Lightmage."

"But you be lost now?"

"Not so! The paths for leaving are clear. Yet on all tiers much below this, paradox holds me in thrall: any step in an exiting direction changes the direction for exiting. I am not lost, but helpless."

I nodded. "So you couldn't approach us until we reached this floor. I heard you calling, but how could you tell we were in the tower?"

"I have warded your dreams. Our deeper minds have grown an affinity/attachment. I sensed your nearness and sang out to you."

While I sorted that out, Jacau studied the closed door. "How did you enter?" he asked.

"Most walls become porous with proper lore."

"Oh?" I said thoughtfully. "But not the tower's *outer* walls?"

"Fortified against intrusion/penetration. David of Goldberg, you have ears for nuance."

"S'bek," I hesitated. "Do these Blenn know about my ... companion?"

"Both work intimately with Guardians and share their secrets. But you must not *express* secrets. These halls may have ears/sonic sensors."

"I'll remember. Any way to get a message out?"

"Our efforts have failed thus far. What message would you sing?"

"A warning: the insurgents are Silvers with Vyre allies, and they seem to control ShiwaKhali's monsters. Also, *help*."

Her huge eyes narrowed. "I have not seen monsters, but we have avoided Silver Hhoymon and elastic persons for many tiresome turns. They will soon threaten us here, so we must all—"

"How could they find us?" Jacau demanded.

"I am not privy to their methods, but I tracked you here by following your spoor."

Betrayed by my own breadcrumbs. "My fault, S'bek. I marked our route to this room with, um, taurei cells."

"Those, I have not perceived. But adaptive garments shed excretions of their own."

"Damn!" And gross. "I've been leaving behind an obvious trail?"

"Very subtle. But the enemies may have machines to detect/follow it. I notice my comrades now desire to join our dialog/harmony." The Blenn were rocking slightly on their single legs.

"Please forgive me," I said to them. "Your translator didn't translate your names, and my mouth can't make the sounds I heard. Would you mind terribly if I call you, um, Pro and Con for now?" I'd pointed to each in turn.

Pro holstered her speechstaff, both ultra-aliens removed their helmets and performed a bobbing sort of bow. Con, the shorter Blenn, answered first.

"How grateful we are for this splendid opportunity! Our embarrassingly primitive machine failed because our names are meaningless noises, barely suitable as identifiers. The names 'Pro' and 'Con' are vastly superior to our original designations, and I will proudly adopt 'Con' permanently. We have only met and already I am far in your debt." Then Pro gave a crib notes version of the same speech. Should've suggested "Verbose" and "Terse."

Both Blenn gazed at me, waiting like disciples for further words of wisdom. I had to say *something*. All that expectation ...

"I visited Blenntown and was surprised to see so many Vyre. Are you worried that some are working with Hhoymon rebels?"

Con raised several pinchers. "Your conception of us does you credit! Clearly, you are too greathearted to suspect we Blenn of the low duplicity that often makes us hang our heads in shame, even in the privacy of our own domes." I doubted the Blenn physique permitted head hanging, however private.

"When we first met the Vyre," Con continued, "we were ungenerous enough not to extend our fullest confidence. Thus, we encouraged some to live amongst us."

I frowned. "You felt they bore watching?"

"Your succinctness puts me to shame!" I winced internally, remembering Ben saying something similar. "I would gladly study at your bottom ... your *feet*, I should say. I need detailed instruction in being pithy. Everyone says so."

"I've gotten similar complaints. How far did your, um, lack of confidence extend?"

"We are not an intelligent species, but should any Vyre in Blenntown turn on us, they may find us not utterly unprepared."

Jacau said something I didn't catch because the goddess's built-in violins began playing again, adagio.

"I am curious, David of Goldberg, about your taurei trail. How did you intend to follow this?"

"I'll demonstrate."

I coached my personal staff then released some microdocs and shadow. The 'docs were commanded to detect their fellows on the floor and daub them with darkness. A heartbeat later, black footprints virtually covered the floor.

"A rare talent," S'bek conceded, "but surely this leads nowhere."

"I blew it." How had "blew it" been translated? "I forgot to *stop* leaving breadcrumbs, which I've just fixed, and I've tromped all around here. But if we start in the hallway—wait! Got an idea." Were microdocs sensitive to time and order?

I erased the floor shadows and gave Jeeves new instructions. One by one, black footsteps formed, evaporated, and reappeared. We watched the progress of an invisible man walking backward, leaving briefly visible tracks. The show ended when the shadow-tracks, toes pointed toward us, reached the door.

"Well?" I asked with a touch of pride.

S'bek's eyes glowed like bright blue excitement. "Did that display match your *speed* as you roamed this space?"

I glanced at Jacau who nodded. "I think so," I said. "It slowed toward the end, and when we first entered here, I didn't just rush in."

"Lovely/wonderful! I can follow such a dance, match it tread for tread."

"Why can't you simply follow my, um, spoor?"

"For the reason I cannot follow my own scent to escape. On all lower levels, I believe velocity defines/creates one's route through superspace. If we fail to return at that precise rate, any trail will soon end."

When Hhoymon set a trap, they set a trap. But by sheer dumb luck, my backtracking system might work, although how we could follow it at a "precise rate" escaped me. Maybe she had a perfect sense of rhythm to match her directional talent, but that gravity twist on the third floor would pose—

"Voices in hallway," Jacau announced quietly.

"Rebel patrols approach," S'bek confirmed. "Slowly."

I glared at the doorway. "I think they've got some way to keep tabs on me that doesn't involve either microdocs or spoor."

The goddess played a soothing melody. "It matters not. We have time for a graceful exit, and by the unexpected route."

"Good to hear! I've got a way to transport people fast, but I sure wish we *all* had reality-stabilizing gear."

"How have you avoided deadly realms thus far?"

The floorboards groaned. Rippling waves of ultra-red rose from the polished wood like visible heat.

"What's happening?" I cried.

"I know not!" S'bek sang. "We must leave immediately. Ah, my vanity!"

Con hopped forward. "Pro and I can extend our reality fields enough to include these noble friends."

"Do so," the Lightmage ordered. "Afterward, David, you must carry my comrades/wards quickly, as you offered. I can transport only myself at speed."

I snapped out orders of my own. A wholesale exchange of what were probably dubious glances ensued, but nobody protested. Jacau and I lay on the floor facedown. To keep our group compact, the Blenn, re-helmeted, sat on our backs.

For a moment, the only thing oppressing me was Con's surprisingly heavy weight. Then her protective field expanded, and I felt positively suffocated. I shifted to a slightly less uncomfortable position, and the field resisted my movement, I suppose countering subtle changes in reality status. Gritting my teeth, I lifted all four of us on a shadow carpet. The field made balancing tricky.

"A marvelous talent," the Lightmage sang, streaking past us. "Now, follow." By the time I got the mini-circus turned around, she had her head pressed against the rear wall, green light pouring from her mouth.

Suddenly the green light died and S'bek snatched her head back as if she'd been burned. "I now comprehend our peril; our enemies are conducting/conveying energies from this structure's outer shell into this room."

"You mean we're *stuck* here?" My voice squeaked.

"Can your talent lift the four of you high?"

"How high?"

She pointed to the wooden ceiling.

"I'll try."

Turning my head sideway to see upward with x-road vision, I gradually extended all shadow threads. We seemed to float on a rising black column. Near the ceiling, the carpet got wobbly.

The goddess drifted up to join the flock. "My winged brother, Djehuti," she remarked, "taught me the skill/art of floating."

She doesn't know Ben died, I thought miserably as she placed her mouth on a wooden plank above. This time, her green light spread across the ceiling into a halo large enough to contain our entire group.

S'bek pointed upward, floated higher, and vanished into the halo. I thickened my shadow threads and kept extending them, holding my breath as we passed smoothly through the wood into an enormous new room. The emerald radiance faded and the ceiling that was now our floor solidified.

Unfortunately, that floor began emitting the nasty shade of ultra-red permeating the office below. As did the distant walls and ceiling. No oozing through the wainscoting for us, it seemed.

I couldn't breathe but not because of Con's reality field. Jeeves had plugged my mouth and nostrils. And turned to shining armor.

My carpet fell apart, likely because I'd completely lost focus, and we all stood up uncertainly, like survivors after a train wreck. I didn't need any warning arrow to know this place was irredeemably lethal. Jacau and I should've died instantly; nothing humanoid belonged in such a universe. Everything looked and felt *wrong*.

But the Blenn maintained our protective field as S'bek radiated stability and strength, blowing a bubble of livable reality into an ocean of disruption and death. Her wings fluttered. The sound warbled, but the translation came through. "Do not inhale yet!"

Right. The atmosphere had an odd murkiness that suggested it wasn't springtime fresh. I could tell that my microdocs were feeding me oxygen from somewhere, and assumed Jacau's taurei was doing the same, but I worried about the Blenn.

I looked around at what had to be the Oversize Glass Sculpture Exhibit. The room held dozens of huge sculptures without crowding. These glowing, multicolored constructions, some easily over sixty feet tall, provided the only illumination. Local physics twisted all colors and forms into something fevered and perverse, but I wasn't much in the mood for art appreciation.

A malevolent atmosphere, I thought, *with equally malevolent occupants.*

We were surrounded at a respectful distance by a dense ring of Silvers and Vyre, all wearing reality-stabilizing gear. The Vyre appeared unarmed, discounting their arms, but their partners held an arsenal of evil-looking weapons. Massive pieces of machinery squatted among the sculptures.

At first, I thought S'bek was sticking out a luminous tongue at our enemies. But the "tongue" kept expanding and becoming more tenuous until we stood within a ghostly sphere of light.

"Breathe now, should you desire," she said. "I have purified/clarified the air around us! And be of tenacious heart!"

"We've been *aimed* here," Jacau whispered in my ear.

I imagined Rider's voice: Who ever said you only herd the ones you love?

CHAPTER 34
SMOKE SIGNALS

The virulent atmosphere conducted sound with the efficiency of steel. Squeaks from tiny shoes against the polished floor burst like bombs; murmurs of high-pitched voices rang triumphantly.

The rebels had maneuvered us with cruel competence. Lower stories probably had rooms this big, but there, a single step might have carried us to a far better place. I wondered what kind of hellhole universe polluted this place. Even the massive artifacts appeared ill, as if leaking invisible vital fluids.

Two sculptures kept us company within the circle formed by our enemies. They seemed resentful. One was merely Pro's height excepting a long spike on top, and vaguely ovoid with a flat base. A spiral nebula of blazing specks filled the clear interior. The other suggested a giant hawk with turquoise wings folded against a cloudy aquamarine body. A beaked, eyeless head stared blindly down from a good twenty feet off the floor.

S'bek's hyper-sapphire eyes glittered, and I felt waves of intense energy radiating from her. But if she struggled to reopen the floor, she failed. Without a word, the Blenn hopped in opposite directions to stand on either side of our little group, and S'bek produced an angry-sounding squeak with her wings and moved to occupy the central position.

For almost a minute, no one in the room moved or spoke. My skin prickled with eeriness and tension, and my mouth felt drier than dust. My heart pounded as if the ultimate finish line was just ahead. It probably was.

I did what I could by wrapping all five of us, individually, in the densest shadow I could muster, articulating it to allow some range of movement. I left our eyes unprotected so we could see, but the Blenn wore helmets and Jacau and I could count on microdoc goggles if needed. If my unilateral actions distressed anyone, they were too polite to complain.

After asking Jeeves to stabilize the shadow-work, I couldn't think of anything to do except wait.

Our enemies had watched my performance with interest. One Silver uttered a short remark, which the local acoustics amplified painfully, and then dozens of soprano voices began yelling. Disappointingly, the Blenn speechstaff didn't translate. The Vyre remained as taciturn as the sculptures.

I could guess why the shooting hadn't started. While our group was vastly outnumbered and outgunned, our side had a goddess-mage and a peculiar fellow with peculiar powers. This hardly equalized matters, but it made our enemies wary.

I wondered what kind of weapons we faced and what threat the Vyre posed.

Perhaps the goddess anticipated my question. Her wings hummed. "Fear not the stretching ones. They will not dare employ/throw magic or missiles against *me*! Their task will be defense. Look to the Silvers for danger."

New, surplus worry: the Vyre used *magic*?

The Hhoymon squabble finally died. Everyone waded through another oddly viscous moment. Then one little warrior uttered a single word.

Next instant, scores of dazzling rays focused on S'bek. The rebels must've declared her private enemy number one. Despite my layers of protection, I felt the implications of horrific heat....

I heard a horrendous sizzle and smelled acrid smoke. Incense from a burning goddess? Every ray winked out, and I gazed anxiously at the graceful figure by my side.

"Fear not, David of Goldberg." Her music became shrill. "No form of light can harm/burn me or any flesh I shield. But my smock has suffered. Alas, my favorite!"

While the goddess reassured me, sharp Hhoymon voices scraped my eardrums. Rebels studied readouts from handheld devices; others leveled weapons at us: rifle-length, streamlined cones, whining as they powered up. I started thinking about relatively low-tech projectiles.

Then our entire group was blasted, not by bullets, but multiple colored rays blending into a quivering whiteness. S'bek raised her arms, and the energy weapons might as well have been flashlights with dead batteries. When they fizzled out, she lowered her arms and stepped forward. Without my permission, her shadow armor turned transparent—she *wanted* to be seen.

Her wings revved; amber light coruscated from her skull, pulsing hypnotically, reflecting brightly from sculptures and dimly from Hhoymon and Vyre helmets. Abruptly, her body blazed, sending coppery flames shooting up a hundred feet. Her right hand ignited into a flare fiercer than an arc-welder's torch. The Vyre bellowed a phrase in unison, and the air around them shimmered.

With a startling hiss, sun-bright light leapt from S'bek's glowing hand to play over our enemies. And bounce off harmlessly. But then she waved her *left* hand; fountains of lime sparks sprang up directly under a cluster of rebels.

Jacau shouted a word of Dhu-barot praise.

It took me another second to get it. S'bek's lightshow had been a theatrical feint, and she'd used the floor to both conduct and disguise her real attack. Which was ... what? Nothing seemed to be happening.

Then five little Hhoymon and two Vyre screamed and exploded into a shower of smoking blood and dismembered limbs. The Blenn buzzed as though moaning, and I had to breathe in gasps. S'bek dimmed, her shadow armor reappearing. Her body swayed, but she stayed on her feet.

Before the first whiff of carbonized flesh hit my nostrils, Silvers had doused their dead in some brown liquid. Teams hauled away steaming bodies and body parts while others sprayed more gunk around. Unoccupied rebels stood and made furious noises at us. Swearing, I assumed.

Jacau turned toward me. "Tuvid, you must be strong. We need you. We will kill or be killed here."

He was right, and I hated it.

"My deceit will not work/succeed twice," S'bek warned. "The Vyre already extend protections."

I forced my mouth to move. "How can I help?"

"I require some rest. How much mass will your talent lift?"

"Not sure."

She pointed to the glass ovoid. "Can you hurl that?"

The sculpture wasn't large, but it probably outweighed a Mercedes. Still, I'd hoisted that heavy boulder yesterday without strain....

"I'll try." I wrapped thick shadow-cables around the artifact while keeping my side-vision on a group of rebels pushing a massive machine toward us. I didn't like the looks of this machine, especially its huge obsidian lens and central mirror.

I put my whole heart into trying to lift the statue. The damn thing merely wiggled. I attached more darkness to the spike and tugged. If I could get the bastard on its side, maybe I could *roll* it at—

SNAP! The spike cracked off and the sculpture went dark. I stared at the object dangling in midair: a glass spear that must've weighed two hundred pounds. *By God,* I thought idiotically, *the curator's gonna be pissed.*

Exerting my will, I hurled the spike fifty feet straight up—every rebel head lifted to watch it rise—and casually let it drop into a huge shadow glove. I tried to catch eyes, but they were indistinct behind enemy helmets. "Truce?" I hollered, and the roar of my voice frightened even me.

"No truce," one Hhoymon replied in perfect English.

I'd never worked faster, remolding the shadow glove into a colossal hurling stick, commanding this lever to whirl around, and ordering my shadow-clamps to release the glass javelin.

Almost caught them napping. The spike shrieked through the air, but just before it struck the ultra-alien lens, dozens of Vyre arms stretched to intercept it. The glass shattered on the floor, and I decided Balanced Clearhouse had overlooked a practical aphorism: art makes a lousy weapon.

Our enemies cheered, and I whispered "sorry" to my companions. Jacau reached across S'bek to pat my shadow-padded shoulder. The goddess stood more erect now.

The big lens flashed like a supernova. For a terrible moment, I couldn't see a thing. I heard popping sounds and felt a sudden pressure on my back.

My senses cleared. The blast had missed us, striking the beaked sculpture, now largely a puddle of lava. It seemed the Hhoymon had decided to murder us via a bank shot. Molten glass, furred with sparks, was spreading fast, about to bury us knee-deep then burn off our knees.

I turned my head. Whatever kept trying to shove me toward the glass lava wasn't visible, but the force kept getting stronger. I built a shadow-levee against the pressure and another to block the glass. Neither one held.

Could S'bek still levitate? Just as I decided to weave a *family*-sized shadow carpet, she whirled around. Something long and thick whipped through the air, vanished, but left a startling afterimage: a shining reptilian tail. Suddenly, the push from behind vanished and the molten silica began oozing *outwards*, leaving a few boiling puddles behind.

Grateful as I was for the rescue, I felt horrified to see scores of small shadow-paddles directing the glass with a flurry of little shoves. The deadly pool moved like something alive. Was my shadow acting on its own? Had Jeeves taken command? Then I felt my power flowing. Some hidden, ruthless part of my mind had bypassed my conscious control.

The Vyre chanted together, but either molten silica was immune, or the paddles were too relentless. Our enemies had a serious problem on their hands. Rather, their feet. Rebels in a wide arc backed up, a few too slowly. I winced at the screaming....

"We make a fine team," S'bek sang. "We must keep wreaking harm before they sound our limitations." *She* didn't regret inflicting death and pain.

Ten Hhoymon in reflective garments rushed up to spray white foam along the floor. Foam hit lava and the room filled with fog, crunching noises, and slowly dying whistles. Gradually, the air cleared to its former murk, revealing five Silvers consulting while the rest watched us with total attention.

The lava had congealed into a most impractical paperweight.

Hoping to interrupt enemy planning, I scooped up one of the remaining puddles on a shadow-shovel and waved it menacingly. Ten blazing rays converged on my load, vaporizing it to an empty threat. Meanwhile, the five strategists continued arguing; judging by voice-tone, attempting murder could be a frustrating business.

I could almost sympathize. We were proving to be unpredictable, dangerous, and hard to kill. I knew why the rebels weren't simply throwing everything they had at us. Attacking the Lightmage, they couldn't trust their technology; any weapon might develop an extra edge turned against them.

"S'bek?" I whispered. "Can you—"

"BEWARE!" Her wings shrilled.

The ranks of our enemies opened. Something huge and dark rolled through. For one ghastly second, I thought my own blackness was attacking us. Then I noticed the many smoldering eyes amid a spherical forest of hooks, claws, jaws, and spiral teeth. Steam and a sullen glow gushed from a dozen open mouths.

This rolling nightmare seemed unaware that the largest remaining lava pool smoldered directly in its path. I got ready to shift the pool for best effect if the monster veered off course. *That*, I thought, *should solve this problem.*

It approached the deathtrap, slowed, and sent out five rough, purple tongues to lap up the molten glass.

"What be this roundness?" Jacau asked calmly.

Con answered. "In my youth, my teacher spoke of a fiery world of rolling giants, predators of vast cravings with furnaces of unstable elements at their cores. But I was a poor student, so my conclusion we face such a predator is likely erroneous."

Terrific. A rolling *nuclear-powered* nightmare. I shadow-cast a blockade and the monster burst right through.

"Can you stop it?" I asked S'bek.

"We shall learn," she responded with a grim little melody. She reached into her mouth and extracted a tooth while her wings revved to a shriek. Next instant, the tooth expanded and stretched out to become a white sword that practically screamed sharpness. She jumped forward already swinging the weapon. I saw it ignite with blue fire just before it struck the beast. Blue sparks flew everywhere and a concussion like a hundred-cannon discharge shook the room.

But as S'bek returned to us, the monster kept coming, apparently unhurt. It approached us with the barely constrained excitement of a stalking animal and stopped about twenty feet away. Perhaps deciding which morsel appeared tastiest.

Con tugged at my shadow-sleeve. "Kindly remove your protective material from Pro and me. This is a threat we may be lucky enough to manage."

Trusting her, I dissolved their armor. They threw down their backpacks, withdrew some black rods, and quickly assembled them into a long pole. Pro held one end of this against her suit and the other to the floor. While Con adjusted tiny controls on one rod-section, the beast rolled toward us like a spherical juggernaut. The closer it got, the uglier it looked....

The monstrosity slowed. Then stopped, rocking back and forth, quivering.

Con pulled several small brown cubes from her pack, hopped close to the beast, and held her cubes near one vertically-fanged mouth. The grotesque orifice kept snapping, but Con's timing was perfect. The brown objects arced past sets of incandescent fangs. The monster shuddered and went still. Steaming, mustard-colored froth began pouring from every mouth.

I looked around at the rebels. They were silent, staring at the corpse. I couldn't believe it either.

"What did you *do*?" I asked Con as she hopped back.

"Almost nothing. We merely borrowed the subdued inertia from that reality where we found you, channeled it up through this floor, concentrated the effect and sent it ahead in the predator's path. I regret how slow we were to comprehend the obvious fact that such a creature requires a wholesome inertia to roll and continue to roll. A simple plan from our simple minds."

A squadron of Hhoymon left their circle, heading away from us.

"What kind of poison was that?"

"Lunch," stated Pro.

Con, of course, had more to say. "Our food contains considerable amounts of lead, and I suspected that a creature with such a metabolism might find the snack unsettling. The experiment seemed worthwhile and proved more successful than I deserved."

Rebels were returning, carrying large thin sheets of something brighter than tinfoil.

"If we live through this," I remarked absently, "remind me not to accept any dining engagements in Blenntown."

Con hurried to reassure me. "Despite our inferior intellects, we will learn what humans cannot eat before we offer you a meal!"

"I'm sure. You Blenn are ... impressive." Her dark chitin seemed to go a bit paler. Alien blushes?

That's when it happened. One instant, Con rocked by my side, then she was gone, leaving behind only a wet droplet and a long green smear. Horrified, I sighted along this bloody exclamation mark, but saw no sign of her. Hadn't even seen what hit her.

Pro buzzed a terrible wordless grief and S'bek's wings fell silent. Jacau pointed at a squat, unimportant-looking machine.

Pro still held the conducting pole. Her pinchers became a blur as she adjusted the controls. Without speaking, she threw the pole to the Lightmage who seemed to give it a gentle tap. Suddenly, the thing whistled through the air as it zipped toward the machine Jacau had indicated. Several Vyre raised their hands, bathing the long missile in shimmering light. But the pole only *sped up*, slamming into its mark with preposterous force. A huge fireball erupted, incinerating the machine and four nearby rebels.

I stared at Pro. In a split second, she'd evidently set her device to reverse any impeding influence and to explode on impact. My knees buckled....

Jacau leaped and caught me. "We will sorrow later, Tuvid," he said. "Look what they be doing!"

A diamond-hard resolve to protect him and my surviving friends lifted me to my feet. Hhoymon had begun spreading metallic sheets on the floor followed by other Silvers placing self-supporting posts on the sheets. A third team strung thick wires from post to post.

"What be this?" Jacau asked.

No one answered.

S'bek and I looked at each other and then did our damnedest to ruin all this unnecessary construction; I tugged posts sideways with shadow-ropes while the goddess toyed with sheets and wires. But the Vyre stepped forward, hummed some alien Gregorian chant, and a vague, brown barrier sprang up to protect the workers, and then our efforts only bought us dirty looks.

When the miniature power lines made a complete circuit around us, rebels ran new cables from the wires to the room's largest machine: a massive double cylinder. The arrangement reminded me of an electric fence.

One Silver Hhoymon waved bye-bye to me, but I didn't wave back.

With a sound like God's own bug-zapper, a storm of violet sparks sprayed up from the foil sheets to orbit the wires. The sparks accelerated until every wire appeared encased in neon tubes. Then a cancerous-purple disk formed high over our heads, its circumference fitting neatly inside the ring of our enemies. Instant migraine. All my muscles started aching. The enemies' reality-gear began flashing with green scintillations. Pro buzzed, and I heard the music of S'bek's wings, but the translator staff had stopped working.

I set a shadow-wall above us. The disk's unholy light intensified, glaring through my shadow. Even with microdoc goggles, I had to turn my eyes away. I thanked God for my Crossroad sight and kept thickening my barrier.

Then the purple threat descended, and my power couldn't touch it. Desperate, I swung a shadow-mace with microdoc spikes at one cable. Nothing doing. The rebels merely watched. *Maybe*, I thought, *we could charge them and break through....*

A malignant purple hoop materialized around us, slowly contracting.

While I attacked the hoop, S'bek blasted the disk with laser-like beams of light. Neither of us accomplished a thing. Then Pro's stabilizing gear emitted a blinding green flash, and I felt a subtle change for the worse as her reality field failed. Pro seemed unhurt, but I didn't like the way she kept rocking so hard on her leg.

This had become a nightmare's nightmare. I noticed S'bek's protective bubble shrinking and knew the goddess had to be near exhaustion. Maybe Pro noticed the same thing; she steadied herself and rooted through her backpack, but seemed to come up empty. I didn't know what to do.

"Tuvid," my brother murmured. "It has been a great joy to find you at last. Such great joy in being with you for this small time."

His self-possession restored some of mine. "Same here. I'm so sorry you got involved in this."

"As always, I choose my own path."

The air smelled horribly stale. "Jacau, I *know* our friends are searching for us. I just wish we could ... send up a flare."

He snorted. "See colors here? See how they ... melt at the edges? We be in a very bad place. Who would look here to see our signal?"

Death was our ceiling—now ten feet over my head—and our wall, just a few yards away. I didn't know how we'd die when either menace reached us, but didn't doubt the result. My entire body had filled with pain; I knew we were all suffering. But we had no way to escape. Sometimes there's only one thing to do and you do it. Even if it's pointless.

I took a slow, deep breath and began to discharge clouds of shadow, going strictly for quantity. I kept pushing the stuff out until the entire vast room with its hulking artifacts and enemy army became foggy with my special darkness. Hhoymon voices yelled uneasily.

And I'd just begun. Concentrating harder, I sped up my emission rate and ordered microdocs to spread the stuff throughout the tower as far as possible.

"What be you doing?" Jacau asked quietly.

My efforts took a lot out of me in every sense, and I was already panting, but he deserved an answer. "If anyone's ... looking. They'll need. Something ... to see."

We were running out of time and room, but I focused on pouring out blackness. My stomach hurt as if I hadn't eaten for days. My vision went blurry. Along with the others, I lay flat when the nearness and harm of the disk made standing impossible. Spewing shadow, I ignored the horror descending toward our horizontal forms.

The goddess's wings played a dirge. I released shadow.

The hoop and disk touched, passed through each other. My bones were burning.

Felt as though I was pumping out the raw material of my flesh, bones, and guts. Streaks of darkness and light shot back and forth behind my eyes. The shadow armor I'd wrapped around us dissolved like tissue paper in water. The air went very bad; S'bek, too, was spent.

Obviously, I was dying, but I kept working in the faint chance of saving my companions. Sara, Michael, Josh, Amber, Con, Kind, Ben—their names gave me strength. I pushed out shadow, too committed for regrets....

"Stop, Tuvid! *Stop!*" I could barely hear Jacau's voice.

I tried to ignore him. But an unexpected sensation, like ascending in a supercharged elevator, distracted me. Too weak to move, I was slow to understand....

The disk and ring were gone.

Normal, healthy reality poured into the room like sunlight, bringing air refreshing as new love. My shadow-fog dissipated, revealing Blenn by the dozens and not the small variety. Blenn warriors, limned with the chrome fire of Binae's energy signature. They stood around us, glowering at our attackers as if daring them to try anything. One giant snatched Pro up off the floor and kissed her on the top of her ugly head. The Blenn army buzzed deeply in continual thunder.

Jacau helped me sit up. "Hey," I croaked, "we're saved." The din almost drowned my voice. The Lightmage danced joyfully, her music now an ode to life.

H'ap Shai appeared, bellowing a red tower of flame, nearly scorching the ceiling to modestly announce his presence. And then my eyes brimmed over. The *Mirrormage* stood by my side, wearing his natural form, dripping a final vestige of chrome energy! Most of his feathers were gone or mutilated, and the skin beneath was red and raw, but Ben had never looked better to me. I couldn't speak.

He patted my hand until something scooped me off the floor. As if repeating the scene with Pro and the Blenn warrior, someone seemed to be kissing *me* on the scalp.

I felt an itching vibration and heard a voice in my head. "Ayn-Seris! Glad I am to find you."

I twisted my neck to enjoy Rider's familiar features. The Guardian —now I understood the term!—had placed its speech diaphragm against my skull to conduct sound.

"What kept you?" I whispered, trusting my friend's ears.

Rider held me at arm's length, regarded me with concern, then pulled me close, gave me a quick hug, and returned to talking to me through my skull.

"Cataclysms we have battled, and you were truly hidden. Details later. For now, David, I am saddened to report you sound unwell. Perhaps worse than usual! We must get you repaired."

"Okay. Can we take my ... friends along?" I waved a finger in a vague arc toward Ben, Jacau, S'bek, and Pro.

"So be it. How nice when siblings can be friends!" Rider's slurping laughter was a pure comfort. "Finally, we can dispense with fictions."

"Does that—"

"Yes, all Scome can stop hiding. Or return to Muuti should they desire. We have collected all enemies save those here. As to these remainders, would *you* care to dispute with Blenn fighters?"

I stared at a warrior, pretended for a moment the hulking thing was an enemy, and shuddered.

"As you hear, David, the rebels dare not apply weapons. Our war is silenced."

"Wonderful." Colored sparkles flickered behind my eyes. "But what kept you? Or did I ask that?"

"You did. We've been crest-deep in monsters while you were out hearing the sounds. Your eyes are closing. Do you require sleep?"

I couldn't answer, but felt a profound gratitude. I recognized that Con's death, added to the death of so many that I love, had just written an indelible command on my soul: treasure life and those you care for while you can.

I faded out like a pleasant dream evaporating at the dawn....

CHAPTER 35
CEREMONIAL

Luxurious softness beneath me, something puffy under my head, and a feathery warmth over my body. My extra vision cleared enough for a groggy peek. My eyes snapped open. Somehow, I'd expected to find myself in my Chean-shee apartment.

Instead, I lay on a classic four-poster bed within a stupendous cavern. The rough walls shimmered with peaceful aqua ripples. Strands of ultra-red floated by like levitating cotton candy. The colors reflected from a silver swan embroidered on my coverlet, Ben's touch, I imagined. I knew where I was even before turning my head toward the tank suitable for leviathans.

"You," I mumbled in drowsy accusation, uncertain what I meant. Poseidon bobbed gently in his illuminated water, apparently asleep.

Rider spoke up from behind me. "Do humans not say let sleeping gods lie? Here, sleep *is* the lie."

I sat up and turned around to find Rider, Strong, and Swift sprawled in chairs behind the bed, accompanied by an assortment of empty chairs. Perhaps Poseidon was planning to show home movies. Strong, still in human form, got up to give me a kiss on my forehead. Swift also rose long enough to shake hands with me, Neme-style.

It occurred to me the gesture lacked the measuring-up quality of a human handshake. Instead, the touching hands became allies, back-to-back, ready to defend each other. Why hadn't I realized that before?

"How long have I been out?" I croaked.

"Three twists and a turn," Rider said cheerfully. "How are you?"

"Ask me when I wake up." I studied the trio and cleared my throat. "I learned something about you people."

"Learned what, comrade?" Swift asked suspiciously.

I had Jeeves release the stored MARBLE and held it up. "Found some of these in the museum." I frowned at the sphere. "I seem to have stolen this one. Anyway, another MARBLE showed how to ... recycle a Neme into a Common."

My listeners traded glances. "Unfortunate," Rider admitted. "Binae asked of us long ago to hide our connection, but Hhoymon will be Hhoymon. Speak of this not to anyone else, present company excepted." Rider's crest tilted in the Watergod's direction.

"Jacau knows."

"Him, I shall caution later. Soon, your family will arrive. Others, also. I desired to ask you for something beforehand."

"For what?" Good God. My biological parents were coming! My hands turned sweaty, and the room felt hotter. Here was my chance to earn gold in the Olympic Awkwardness Medley.

"Your forgiveness. You were my responsibility during your visit. Yet not since I became Binae's security chief has there been such unnatural disasters."

I grinned. "On Earth, a politician said something similar after a flood: 'This is the worst disaster to hit California since I was elected.'"

Strong giggled but Swift had harsh words for Governor Pat Brown. "Careless bracketing," he remarked primly.

"Anyway, California survived. And so did I, because you came through when it counted."

Rider gazed at me. "Perhaps. You are a fount of surprises."

"You mean the shadowcasting? I thought—"

"That power, the Watergod *told* us you would find. But earlier, you betrayed a talent most unexpected."

"I did?"

"Seeing," Swift explained, "without eyes."

"*What*? Rider, you told me that developing new senses here wasn't unusual!"

Slurp. "Deceitful me. Truth is that youthful conditioning makes a strict mental filter."

"Then why should I be different?"

"Because you are. No better answer do I hold."

Strong leaned toward me. "We all felt awful keepin' you in the dark. But we're still huntin' down some answers ourselves."

I heard a soft splash, but Poseidon's eyes remained closed. Do gods dream?

"Speaking of hunting, how did you find us in that ... tower of universes?"

She smiled. "Well, the rebs had done some job of hidin' you. Even

Binae was scratchin' Her head! Then, the Firemage allowed he'd sent you to Hhoymon City and She figured you'd hole up in the museum, which was too dangerous and chockfull of realities to search. So, She asked the Dancer for help. When you got *real* creative, Arfaenn spotted you. I hear that cloud you made was really somethin'."

"So my smoke signal actually worked. In a way." I'd never considered using my talent a creative act.

"You cast a large shadow," Rider said.

I tried to look modest. "Well, you know what Balanced Clearhouse says about practice."

My visitors stiffened. Had I committed a faux pas?

Swift's eyes did something odd: crossed until they touched. "You allude to Second Aphorism," he grunted. "Cousin Able's translation, yes? How did he phrase?"

His formality increased my uneasiness. "Um, 'Individuals improve at whatever they practice including love, hate, and understanding.'" Except for faint sloshings from the tank, the cavern became dead silent. I'd offended everyone for sure.

Swift produced a choked hum and a loud slurp escaped Rider's speech diaphragm. Then three ultra-aliens burst into three versions of guffaws.

"What," I asked, "is so damn funny?"

Rider regained control enough to answer. "Since the underlying secret you already own, David, I'll tell you why Binae drafted me to lead Crossroad security. I was the *only* Neme all families agreed on. Balanced Clearhouse, in your service! Maxims compiled as you wait."

"You! *You're* Balanced Clearhouse?"

"No longer."

Learning that my friend was a three-hundred-year-old legend must've done hilarious things to my face, judging by everyone's reaction.

"We are having great bliss startling you," Rider said after the tumult and slurping had died. "Since you know what you know, can you guess the literal meaning of our word 'O-gen-ai'?"

"I—not really."

"It translates *from the ground*. Is not 'common' another term for 'ground' in human electronics? Neme ambassadors honored our connection but obscured it by pulling a slow one."

"I see."

Swift pointed to my MARBLE. "You found that ball near one holding Neme secret?"

"Practically touching."

"May I examine?"

He took the sphere and studied it. "Antique formatting. You saw contents, comrade?"

I shrugged. "Hhoymon poetry, I think." Strong's eyes widened, and I remembered she was a poet.

Swift pointed an eye at me. "Why did you take?"

The question made me uncomfortable. "Beats me."

"I must learn if this, too, concerns Nemes. You wish I bring English rendition?"

"Yes. That'd be great."

Swift turned to Rider. "Permission, Guardian?"

Rider waved an arm. "Get to the top of it, yes. Just return before the ceremony."

Ceremony?

Swift waddled to the great doors, which swung open and closed quietly behind him. I shot the Watergod a suspicious glance then turned back toward ... *Balanced Clearhouse*. Unbelievable.

"Rider, you've got *every* rebel in custody?"

"So we believe."

"How did you find them all?"

"You will be smug to know. Your plan to infect them with taurei moles succeeded."

"Really?" I felt a warm glow of pride, certainly not smugness. "I didn't really believe it would work. But how'd you spot my little spies?"

"A machine we have for sifting the Pan-Cosmic desert for sands of consciousness. I hear impatience in your nodding. Not feeding you fresh enough information, am I? So what? I say it never hurts to waste words. We always have excess."

"A growing surplus," I agreed, smiling. "Please go on."

"After the Mirrormage sang of your plan, we sensitized our machine to any whisper of Seris's energies. Then easy it was to locate our enemies."

"*Seris?*"

Rider pointed at my chest. "Djehuti thought She'd blessed your taurei making every cell resonate to Her love."

I looked down at Jeeves with awe. "I ... only saw a swan."

"Compassion has many aspects."

"Hey! Maybe that's how the Silvers kept track of *me*."

Strong frowned. "Not likely, darlin'. We're sure Her perfume's there, but on *you* our machine can't get a whiff. We don't know why."

The doors began to open. "Ayn Hovv," Rider said, "here's—no. Wrong person, not the one I expected."

I didn't care. Ben strode into the room like a wingless ostrich enhanced with arms, hands, and joy. He bounded to the bed and after a dramatic flourish held a silver tray supporting a mug of coffee. I grinned at the cloth napkin, spoon, cream, and bowl of sugar cubes. With tongs.

"You see, dear boy, how barbaric aliens can be?" Ben turned a twinkling eye on Rider. "Civilized folk would've offered you java straightaway."

"Bless you, Ben!" I said, reaching for the tray and placing it on the coverlet beside me. The aroma alone gave me new energy. "Rider just accused you of being the wrong person. I beg to differ." I sipped. "Ah. Just what I needed!"

"I'm pleased to see you pleased."

"What pleases me most is seeing you alive. You look great."

No lie. He exuded humor and health. Even in this dim light, his restored feathers appeared burnished. His head flicked sideways, birdlike, for an instant and my Crossroad vision caught one of Poseidon's eyes just closing ponderously.

"Ben, I've been dying to find out, um, why you didn't. I saw that … thing swallow you."

"You'll recall the cold fire we enjoyed in the desert?"

"Sure."

"As the Lithshark swallowed me, I used what remained of my power to raise enough cold flame to freeze my body solid. That protected me for long enough."

"But how did you escape?"

"My survival, dear boy, resulted from cleverness and skill. Luckily for me, Chybris is clever, and Seris so skillful. The Librarian, I've learned, apparently had … bookmarked me when I went off on my own. If my life fades, He knows. He pulled me out rather *after* the nick of time, but rumor has it I'm a tough old bird, and Seris healed me enough to—ah, look who Ra's ship has carried in!"

He hopped over to hug the Lightmage just now stepping through the doors, literally, dressed in a sari as dark and star-filled as a tropical night. Arm in arm with Ben, she walked over to the bed and favored me with a smile of notable toothiness.

"S'bek," I said. "I thank you from the bottom of my tired heart."

Her wings played a brief duet, which didn't contribute to the word-glut Rider had mentioned since no speechstaff was around. Then she patted my head, nodded to Rider and Strong, and made herself comfortable in midair.

"Ben," I said, trying not to stare at S'bek. "What did the rebels *do* to us in the desert? How could they isolate you from Binae's power?"

"A new technique." He pulled up an odd little chair and perched on it. "The question," he said, bowing toward Strong, "may lie nearer your field than mine, dear."

To my surprise, Strong reached over to ruffle his feathers affectionately. "Somewhere in the middle, I expect," she said.

"David," she continued, "you remember me sayin' this world has all sorts of realities folded together?"

"Absolutely."

She tapped her head. "Brainy rebel scientists analyzed the forces unitin' the works so they could use the same forces to put people or whatever *between* folds."

"A single trick," Ben amplified, "applied to conceal us from our allies, screen themselves at will, hide monsters, and inverted to lessen Crossroad's binding power within their museum. Bloody clever. In the desert, we were re-laminated, as it were, in a paper-thin shell."

I nodded. "Makes sense. I even felt something tear when we were rescued."

"Certainly. When we deduced the rebel technique, Blenn engineers developed a counter. But it was jolly incredible anyone could hide us, ah, just below Binae's sight."

"How did the rebels control the Dissolver's monsters?"

"They left that part, dear boy, up to the Vyre. And didn't we just underrate *them*!"

"I'm short on admiration for insurgents today, but surprised you can hide anything from Supernals."

"That depends on the Supernal. Our Diplomat lacks aptitude for *hunting*."

"Well, one thing I do admire is your recuperative powers, Ben. You look offensively healthy."

He bobbed his head. "Again, thanks to Seris. When Chybris retrieved me, I was all mess."

I shuddered. "Must've been horrible."

"Being half digested wasn't my cheeriest hour, but I'd suffer it again to spend time with the Pure Heart."

"And the Lithshark?"

"The monster has resumed formlessness."

"Let's hope it stays formless. Hmm. When Chybris was saving you, I wonder if He noticed anyone else nearby that might need rescuing."

Ben raised a palm. "The Librarian observes me from *within*. He wouldn't have been aware of your predicament."

"A heads-up He needed," Rider put in.

The Mirrormage muttered something like "born iconoclast."

With my final sip, all coffee paraphernalia vanished, tray included. My fingers traced the remaining rectangular indentation in the coverlet.

"With their great disappearing act," I said, "why did the conspirators stay in the museum after the cavalry arrived?"

Ben honked more than laughed. "Irony there. That particular reality was *too* separated from Crossroad. They had no binding force to work with. A pity, what?"

"Damn shame."

"Perhaps they couldn't have ducked out anyway. By then, the Diplomat was watching. The Vyre are skillful, but Binae is Binae. I doubt She would've let such bloody killers get away."

I thought about Con. "Ben, I'll never forget how you sacrificed yourself to save us."

His beak defied its avian nature and twisted into a smile. "Thanks to Chybris, I can savor your appreciation. By the bye, you'll be pleased to learn that the Heart of Art has been restored—re-merged, I should say—to normalcy. Care for more coffee?"

As I took sip one of cup two, Rider and Ben began chattering with each other like politicians at a convention when someone else is giving a speech. Meanwhile, I agonized over meeting my parents. What the hell should I say? Perhaps Strong sensed my nervousness. She moved to sit next to me on the bed and described some of what I'd missed. Most of it sounded worth missing. Rebels had ravaged Common headquarters in Triangle One using horrific new weapons, my least favorite giant mutant wasp, and something even more devastating: the Nedleugch, one of ShiwaKhali's two major pets, an enormous and ultra-violent tornado-like force as powerful as the Lithshark.

Maanza's superweapons permanently swatted the giant bug, but couldn't harm the vortex or break through the latest Hhoymon energy shields. The Common begged Binae to recruit Maanza, but with major abominations loose, She wouldn't, fearing the Dissolver's trap—whatever it was—would finally be sprung.

Instead, She enlisted Chybris. Although neither Supernal is natively aggressive, they acted as colossal energy sponges, draining power from monsters and enemy weapons. Facing defeat, the rebels vanished en masse along with the hostile tornado.

Then Strong's tale took another upturn. Ben returned terribly injured, but he managed to tell Binae about my attempt to infect our enemies with a microdoc plague. Binae then had the Common reprogram their sentient-life-detector to spot what Strong called "compassionate anomalies" based on the silly idea that my plague had, well, gone viral. The device looked for Seris-infused sapient cells, and being a *very* broadband detector capable of dredging simultaneously through sheaves of realities, the rebel roundup was quick.

"We lost a lot of good folks in this fight," Strong said. "Sorry to burden you with sad tidings, darlin', but I thought you ought to know. The ceremony comin' up is partly to honor them."

"Glad you told me. What will happen to the conspirators now?"

Strong rose to her feet. "Probably exiled to a 'trap' universe, a one-way trip for sure. Back to my chair before I plumb tire you out. Try to rest."

Nice thought, but no rest for me. Being in bed felt ridiculous in this situation; more so as the gang swelled. The doors opened to reveal Pro and a taller Blenn standing calmly under Lord Loaban's abdomen as though waiting out a rainstorm under an awning. Pro gripped her fancy song-staff.

Loaban strode in. His bearing spoke volumes and the first title was *I Told You So*. After waving a hairy leg at our group, he bypassed us to climb the ramp abutting Poseidon's tank, reared up to place four clawed feet respectfully against the glass, then lay down and appeared to join the Watergod in naptime. Fresh scars on his head glistened in the dim light. I figured he'd earned the nap.

Rider, jabbering with Ben, made an eloquent arm gesture both calling the two Blenn over and inviting them to make themselves at home. They levered across the room but then just milled around, bowing repeatedly. When everyone in sight had been bowed to, Pro spun to face me.

"My inferior, the Least whom you once honored by visiting, sends her admiration and best wishes."

Her buzzing had dropped in pitch just as I'd heard the word "inferior." A clue about Blenn languages? Here was a case where etymology, etiology, and entomology connected....

"Please thank her for her courteous message," I replied. "I'm honored to have met her. And it's great to see you again."

"All honor is ours," she responded, predictably.

"How are you feeling?"

"Ashamed due to being so proud to know you, wise sir. You have not only supplied me with a glorious new name, I understand you are responsible for saving my life." She moved closer to me. "In Con's name," she said confidentially, "I am endeavoring to be more prolix."

"Good work," I murmured back. "Keep it up."

Pro spun away to address Rider. The Blenn, it developed, were unsure where to sit, afraid of blocking someone's view of the guest of honor, *me*.

"A Blenn in the way," I said, "would only enhance the view."

The remark seemed to baffle Pro, but Ben and Rider laughed. Strong appraised me as if she'd heard a deeper meaning in the remark. Finally, both Blenn resolved the issue by lying on the floor in swimming position.

"What *is* this all about?" I asked nervously.

Ben cleared his throat. "Prepare for a unique tribute, Professor," he said in a stuffy voice. "You're to receive official commendations, which demands an official ceremony."

Clearly, he shared my attitude about such events. Never attended one that wasn't morbidly dull. Would it be different here?

Then my family arrived, and I pried myself out of bed. My legs felt weak, but I hobbled to the doorway.

Empty fears. We all cried a little, but the meeting wasn't at all awkward because my parents, Aleen and Beod, were so damn happy. Like Jacau, they were all whipcord and sinews, but improbably youthful. Beod, my father, seemed scarcely older than my brother who stood in his natural form with a wiry arm around his wife, Anvara. Jacau radiated pride, as if I were his exclusive discovery.

Between my faltering Dhu-barot and Jacau's emergency corrections, the five of us managed a very personal conversation, rudely ignoring everyone else for a time. I doubt anyone cared.

Beod informed me we'd all be spending the evening together, and I'd meet more relatives, but immediately post-ceremony every mortal except me had been instructed to leave the cavern. Apparently, several gods with nothing better to do intended to conduct *another* ceremony. I don't think I groaned out loud.

Then I confessed to Aleen that I still considered myself human.

"Who claimed you weren't human?" she asked via Jacau.

"Uh ... your interpreter for one. And the Mirrormage."

She patted my brother's arm. "Djehuti may not know the full truth, but Jacau be young, and young tend to oversimplify."

"You mean I *am* human?"

"In part. What better way to make you look the part, Tuvid? So with Binae's help, we borrowed genetic material from a nice human couple."

I stared at her. "Who?"

"Arthur and Susan Goldberg, my child. Who else?"

"Wait. Wait! My adoptive parents are also partly my *real* parents?"

"Does Earth lack reflectors? Isn't the truth be written on your face? Hadn't you noticed any family resemblance?"

Well damn, no wonder why I'd turned out looking so much like Arthur.

"You have four sets of parents, dear."

I was stunned. If only my Earth kin could've known....

But Rider called my name so I led my family across the room. The bed had been replaced by an embarrassingly throne-like chair that Ben pulled out for me with an exaggerated flourish. I gave him a dirty look and sat.

The Chean-shee Administrator appeared; right on her tails was my friend and tutor Able Firsthouse. Again, I tottered to the doorway where both people greeted me warmly. Able promised we'd get together soon, and the pair walked me back to what was becoming a crowd.

The little fellow dressed in gold flew in, only flipping upside down once.

Then a ruby inferno blazed up near the great tank. H'ap Shai emerged from the fire, his skin a shag rug of flames. He crossed the room to stand behind Beod. A droplet of water spilled over the tank's rim and dowsed the remaining conflagration.

My father grinned up at the Firemage while S'bek blew the demon a toothy kiss. H'ap Shai fired back some kind of acknowledgment, then turned his balefire eyes on me.

When I tore mine away, I found a contingent of Hhoymon in four sizes and colors walking toward me. The loyalists had returned. In perfect English, a Silver spokesperson lamented the grief their outlaws had caused. Strange, meeting Silvers who weren't enemies.

Rider greeted the next arrivals: four Common. I only recognized Collector-of-fine-moments, the crestfallen Common. Then five Vyre showed up, and Rider quietly told me how some of the best Vyre magicians had been blackmailed into the conspiracy. Rebels had secretly approached them, threatening to unleash the em-Bottho on their Village.

When Swift reappeared with a package tucked under one arm, my chair mutated into something even more rococo and conspicuous. I glared at Ben, who gazed back with a newborn's innocence.

The ceremony began with several touching speeches praising and mourning those who'd given their lives in the recent battle. Then it was time for the All-Crossroad Apology Marathon, and I soon realized that

Poseidon and Loaban were feigning sleep to hide falling asleep. Everyone seemed bent on apologizing to everyone else, at length. Afterward, the orations focused on me.

I was granted honorary citizenship with the Hhoymon, had my Scome citizenship acknowledged, was offered an ambassadorship to Crossroad, and shanghaied into the "Deep of Demons," as the speechstaff translated H'ap Shai's phrase. Time passed. More time passed. And still the ceremony droned on.

By then, I was basically comatose, staring at the watery light-patterns on the walls.

At exceedingly long last, it was over and people began filing out, a process slowed by an epidemic of congratulations, too many aimed at me, perhaps for my role in ending the rebellion, more likely for having outlived the ceremony.

Before a parting kiss, Aleen spoke of tests she wanted to run later to explain my rejuvenation. Strong, Beod, Jacau, and Ben each hugged me before they left, and Rider said we'd be hearing each other soon. Ben threatened to keep in close touch and S'bek played a cheerful farewell melody and departed through a wall. I felt surprised the two mages weren't invited to the god session since both seemed to make the cut.

On his way out, Swift detoured to hand me the package he'd been holding. "You were correct, comrade," he admitted. "MARBLE you took holds only old poems. Here is simplified translation. Return MARBLE to museum?"

"Please do."

"Demon is sending me evil eye; I must go."

Hoi polloi finally gone, the Apnoti jumped from ramp to floor in one bound. Poseidon opened his huge eyes. H'ap Shai tilted his head to shout flame at the ceiling then scooped up Pro's fancy speechstaff, which doubtless hadn't remained by accident. Loaban chittered and in my head, I heard, "Are we private?"

"Private indeed," answered a voice like modulated surf, "with Djehuti and S'bek standing guard. Don't worry, David," the Watergod continued. "We are not so cruel as to inflict a second such ritual on you."

"That's a relief," I confessed, with a nervous glance at the powerful company I was keeping. "What's going on?"

Poseidon lifted a flipper from the water. "Binae has asked us to clarify some obscurities."

"Good. I was—"

"We begin," H'ap Shai fired, "with you explaining why you and Jacau foolishly abandoned the Rainbow."

I blinked. "Your bridge was shrinking! And my taurei started warning me of danger, which—"

"Nonsense! We intentionally trapped you to keep you safe."

I wondered if H'ap Shai referring to himself in the third person might be an artifact of once belonging to a three-headed four-brained community.

I didn't hear Poseidon speak, but the demon whirled to face the tank. "It is not trivial to *us*, Swimmer. I will not have anyone think us negligent."

"Then the issue," Poseidon offered, "should be resolved. David, do you consider dropping from great heights dangerous?"

"Of course!"

"Then perhaps your taurei simply responded to your intent to jump. You understand the Firemage only attempted to protect you?"

"I do *now*."

"Excellent. Then shall we all move on?" He paused, but no one objected. "Excellent again. David, Binae wants you to know that both the distinction and conflict between Crossroad's so-called gods and demons are crafted deceptions. We are all allied."

I frowned up at H'ap Shai. "You sure seemed mad at the Watergod in the Hall of Games."

"We are adroit at acting hot-blooded."

"World class, but why fake anger?"

Poseidon answered. "Except in the most secure environments, my fiery partner acts to preserve our illusion of disunity should his interactions be observed by hostile beings. In this way, Binae hopes to tempt any such enemies to recruit 'demons' against Her Common and their overt allies, the 'gods,' before attacking Crossroad."

"Huh. Sneaky."

"That's part of Binae's nature, David. Diplomacy includes mediatory elements but also drier, and often clandestine activities. Our Diplomat has described diplomacy's deceitful side as the art of manipulating others into manipulating you to your benefit."

"Do you have enemies aside from the rebels?"

"I cannot say."

"After all this, *more* secrets?" *David*, I told myself, *try not to shout at gods*.

"I cannot reveal, dear friend," said Poseidon, "what I don't know."

"Oh. Sorry."

"Have you other questions?"

I nodded. "You bet. I don't suppose that glowing juice you gave me was hair tonic?"

The breakers laughed. "After you reported being stung, we feared you'd been poisoned. My elixir was analeptic and a general anti-toxin."

I touched my neck.

Poseidon rotated to another facet. "As to your hair, you have many dormant abilities. Perhaps Crossroad's ambience awakened a talent for regeneration."

I shifted nervously. "Don't like the idea of secret 'talents' with their own agendas. I'd much prefer ... wearing the pants in my own body."

H'ap Shai reached down to nudge my arm. His finger blazed, but didn't burn. "We, too, fortified both you and your taurei when we first met," he said via speechstaff. "For this reason alone, we approached you in the Hall."

I remembered him grasping my shoulder. "To protect me against poison?"

The demon chuckled a long flame. "Certainly not! We warded you against *heat*."

"You have another question," Poseidon stated confidently.

I gazed into the immense eye gazing down at me. "Right. Why are you VIPs bothering with me? I've served your purpose, so why am I still on your radar?"

"There's a saying on Crossroad, youngster," the Apnoti said. "Gods care for their own."

"I don't understand."

"We believe," Poseidon offered, "you are becoming one of us."

"*Me?*"

"Perhaps your unique heredity is responsible. But such things do rarely occur, sometimes through intercession or technology, but on occasion—"

Loaban growled. "Get on with it, Swimmer."

The surf-voice swelled. "You are a proto-god, if you will, and deserve to share in our secrets along with our responsibilities."

I gaped at the three deities in turn. "I—I don't *feel* like a god."

Two great flippers stretched over the tank's rim. Poseidon pushed himself up far enough to lean mountainously over the side; water cascaded to the floor. "Neither do we. That feeling would be an immature delusion."

"Explain. Please."

"Observe the ocean without following the waves. I'm speaking of individual reality, David. The only thing even gods can *ever* perceive is perception itself, the inseparable blend of perceiver and what is perceived. All titles, names, and concepts including self-image lie in the domain of relationships."

H'ap Shai laughed, showering the floor with sparks. "The Swimmer spits truth! Talk to Binae; ask if *She* feels like a goddess."

"I'd like to meet Binae." Would I really? So far, meeting Supernals hadn't exactly been soothing.

Poseidon slid backward; for a moment he was completely submerged, which didn't dampen his "voice."

"In truth, you have. She desired to observe you closely."

"*What*? You mean someone I already know is really a Supernal in a ... fake mustache?"

"Turn and see."

The stupendous doors sprang fully open and the silver-eyed waiter from the Chean-shee restaurant strolled through.

CHAPTER 36
ASCENT

I stared harder than I'd ever stared at anything, but all I saw was a typical male Constructor. Well, not quite typical. Unlike every other Chean-shee I'd seen, this one's eyes had never changed color. The Goddess had been hinting all along....

The Diplomat projected no great sense of presence. She lacked even a fraction of Loaban's charisma, and Poseidon dwarfed the Trapper in every way. Nevertheless, the three gods paid homage in their individual fashions. Then the Firemage and spider vanished.

My head throbbed with each beat of my heart as the pseudo-Constructor sauntered toward me and stopped a few feet away.

The raccoon face seemed to smile. A sparkling wheel of purest ultra-blue emerged from Her forehead, spun like a baby hurricane, and expanded. As it spread, the ape-like form faded, transmuting smoothly into a silvery cloud, not quite obscuring a central, lightning-sheathed sun.

In that terrible room in the Tower, I'd sensed the inpouring of healthy reality when I'd been rescued. This felt similar but infinitely more intense.

Power inundated the room like ocean bursting into a cracked submarine.

I felt lightheaded in both senses; the air suddenly smelled painfully fresh. My fingertips dripped silver fire....

"At last," a voiceless voice spoke from the center of my own chest.

Did I say She lacked presence? An elephant could *stand* on Her force.

I levered my mouth open; my vocal cords seemed very distant. "Binae, I assume?" I wasn't trying to be funny, that's what came out.

"You don't remember me even yet."

"We've met before? I mean, with you ... revealed?"

"We have met and met. You have been my friend and wisdom throughout innumerable Pan-Cosmic cycles."

Again, I had to search to find a voice. "How—how is that possible?"

"Know yourself. You are the tender In-dweller whose Sphere contains self-discovery, communication, and heart-knowledge. You delight in endlessly playing hide-and-seek with your final identity. I've called you here because I need your guidance."

I could only whisper. "Who do you think I am?"

"Hhoymon called you 'Messenger' when you lived as one of them."

"You think I'm *Urien*? Ben told me—specifically!—that Urien's more regular than Old Faithful." Now I couldn't stop talking. "Supposedly, He gets Himself born in some new body, and when maturity hits—pow! He wakes up. Every blessed time, for *billions* of years! Ben said if Urien wore a human body, he'd snap awake in thirty years. At the *outside*!"

The cloud brightened. "Dear one, even we, most ancient of ancients, can learn and change from the learning. In your previous life, I believe you used the high native intelligence of your current species to help leverage some great insight. You haven't shared that insight with me, so I know it has no relevance to me. Yet here is the result: you have remained submerged in this incarnation longer than you ever have. I did not wish to wake you before you were ready, but when Arfaenn danced that you'd begun to awaken on your own, I dared wait no longer.

"I brought you here expecting you to soon emerge in Crossroad's perilous winds, and so you have. I see you floating just beneath your conscious mind like my beloved disciple in his tank."

"If this is true," I said very carefully, "I'm unaware of it."

"Fear not. I will help you."

A silvery arm and hand formed, reaching toward me. I tried to step back, but my legs wouldn't move. Binae's foggy fingers sank into my chest. I felt a sharp tug and a brief, satisfying pain. Then I began expanding, rising high into the air like a seated Blenn untwisting her leg.

I allowed my true nature to come upon me.

Now.

My laughter is music and thunder. What most tickles the spirit isn't higher consciousness itself, but a rapid increase of consciousness....

With my human conditioning in abeyance, my Truesight fully

opens; I see in all directions at once. As I expand, so do my perceptions. I look both outwards and inwards to enjoy the One playing at being matter, energy, and time, creating its ever-shifting symphony of elegant interacting patterns.

Gravity's minute attenuation makes a delicate spectrum shift from the room's floor to ceiling. Subtle. Beautiful.

I hear the stars singing and the same ecstatic melody inherent in the dance of electrons.

I regard the Watergod and appreciate the wealth of his hard-earned wisdom; an instant later, I've grown so much that the god is revealed as a beautiful and talented infant. His eyes shine with reflected glory and watch me with awe. The water around him churns with waves crowned with golden fire.

I remember that eternity does not involve duration and infinity is independent of measurement.

I laugh again, remembering what it means to be a god.

No great power is required. Godhood is consciously playing whatever role has arisen for us to play while simultaneously recognizing ourselves as the Pan-Cosmos experiencing itself. That is the apex of existence. No more can be achieved, and it matters not how low or high the prominence we occupy.

My role and therefore my desire is to act as a bridge of understanding between conscious beings. Yet the Pan-Cosmos keeps expanding, expressing itself as new species and in the evolution of established species. Thus, I need an ever-increasing personal understanding that in turn demands constant learning and exploration.

Here is the first paradox: I am *made* of understanding, and exploration requires separation between explorer and that which is explored.

Here is the second paradox: I am insight itself, and wherever insight occurs, I am there. But I do not experience these insights because they are not separate from me.

To fulfill my role, I cannot exist entirely as a pure principle, but must manifest myself, in part, as a person. Therefore, with each Pan-Cosmic Unfurling, I reinvent my special way to limit myself: living in a series of forms, beginning each life as a mortal, complete with ignorance, pains, risks, and the shifting rainbow of emotion. Learning and exploring.

Before being David, I'd been a Silver Hhoymon. When I finally awoke to my Supernal identity, I assessed the meager profits from that lifetime and recognized that my unvarying routine had brought me to a dead end. To keep learning, I needed a new pattern. Guided by my own nature, I searched the Pan-Cosmos and upon discovering the Scome, I *knew*.

Drawn to one mating Scome couple, I ensured the union would bear fruit, assembled specific genes, and entered the newly fertilized egg. I always begin from the beginning and truly let go....

Between the Hhoymon threat and the results of Scome prenatal testing, my Scome parents felt the need to perform genetic modifications of their own to my developing embryo, splicing human genes to produce a hybrid form that I hadn't consciously anticipated. I became Scome, human, and hidden Supernal.

Below me, Poseidon expresses delight in a thousand-wave choir. I add a note of harmony and stretch my senses....

Chybris waits on Earth, experiencing us all from the White Pyramid. Maanza trains troops on Ramdajulad; he feels my attention and bows. I bow in return and brush my mind gently across the great skein until it touches my mate through the countless millennia: Arfaenn.

Even in our personal aspects, relationships between Supernals are based on the relationships of our Spheres. As Sara Goldberg had once observed, true art rides on compassion. But its power comes from communication and insight. Thus, Arfaenn, Seris, and I maintain our eternal connection.

Naturally, Sara understood art! My dancer had done me an astonishing honor: incarnating herself as human just to keep me company on Earth for a few precious moments. When she could no longer postpone her own work, she'd had to release her humanity.

My smile, another thing David's life has taught me, reflects off the damp walls. How well I understand his recent attraction to Strong! As a poet, Strong has long been a part of the Dancer. But ever since Strong's direct encounter with Arfaenn, some part of my mate constantly dances within her. I send Arfaenn my love and thanks, and receive a soul-warming response.

Even in human form, she'd protected me. Her harmless tumor had prevented us from boarding a doomed jet.

Enough play! Diplomacy, too, needs her insight.

I focus on Binae. She knows something is horribly wrong on Crossroad, associated with ShiwaKhali's monsters, but is unable to clarify the threat. As we communicate, I keep my sensations and comprehension restricted; too much glory, and I will unfold into a state too expanded for usefulness. In this timeless moment, Binae and I consider how to resolve the current crisis and how to approach some likely challenges ahead. Even Supernals have limitations, and reality has a way of bypassing the clearest precognition.

She and I inspect Crossroad in tandem. I adjust our mutual perceptions to different frequencies until we observe two large and complex waveforms oscillating from pole to pole. Binae is baffled, but I have an insight of my own and ShiwaKhali's plot is revealed to me.

These two monsters alone are involved, the others mere distractions. Perhaps as soon as Maanza's next visit, the monstrous waveforms will coalesce into something exponentially dangerous. The Warrior's current body might not perish, but Crossroad's mortal denizens certainly would. As David, I'd dreamt of monsters merging....

With the problem identified, a solution is obvious. I reveal my insight to Binae who shines brighter with gratitude and relief. I assemble my aspect as Messenger and call out to Maanza, Aduum, and Chybris. They respond and send us the energy we need.

Binae supplies finesse while I supply guidance, and with our borrowed power we weave the two ghastly patterns into a knot even ShiwaKhali couldn't dissolve. Our combined strength transports the attached numinous entities to an empty universe.

Should the Dissolver attempt to retrieve them, our knot will tighten, flattening both waveforms, releasing energy pungent as a nova. This would scarcely faze ShiwaKhali, but perhaps He-She might detect a gentle hint. Binae is satisfied.

Responsibilities temporarily discharged, I examine my latest life, assessing what it has taught me so far.

Until David, I'd always allowed myself to awaken before facing those childhood problems that greatly outlive childhood. I'd never been a middle-aged member of any species, never faced the challenges of being a fully adult mortal.

Emotional growth requires resistance, and my lives have always become easy just when most beings must struggle if they wish to advance in their personal development. Adventures are no substitute for obstacles. As David Goldberg, I am finally confronting *consequences*, dealing with adult loss and childhood wounds.

My Dancer, knowing my desire, had come to Crossroad to provide a clarifying lesson, sending me into a realm of symbolic manifestations. No wonder the Ugly Duckling story had affected me so! All my Earthly life I've misunderstood my nature, despised my appearance, and forgotten my mother.

Yet the story also concerns *growth*. Before this life, I couldn't have seen it. I'd never glimpsed childhood from a mature perspective. My powers have blocked my vision.

What I'd missed isn't trivial. *All* children of sentient species are potential gods who become, almost invariably, stunted through the gravity of brutal experience. Tragically, the greater an individual's capacity for conscious existence, the more delicate and easily injured the evolving spirit.

How can childhood go so wrong? This has become clear to me, and the revelation has brought me a delightful surprise.

Human infants aren't born experiencing any separation between themselves and what they experience. In truth, such separation is only a mental construct. But the illusion of a perceiver separate from what it perceives is a practical tool, helping a body survive the dangers inherent in mortal life. Informed by a billion years of evolution, parental influence and embedded instincts operate to provide a human child some sense of identity.

But that sense is hollow. Seeking within for a self to grip, a child can find only emptiness. To perceive what they've been taught is themselves, children must use the world as a mirror.

On Earth and elsewhere, parents, caretakers, teachers, and society itself can be a harsh looking glass for a sensitive child. What happens to the developing personality when what appears to be its own reflection is distorted into ugliness?

In their sufferings, Ugly Ducklings everywhere seek their true selves, sense only emptiness, and misinterpret emptiness as worthlessness....

Mortal sensitivity can bring lasting pain and crippling limitations; but now I know what such sensitivity is *for*: not for self-protection through pain avoidance as I'd believed, but for experiencing the suffering of others, to develop truly conscious compassion.

With such compassion, a mortal or even an eternal fool like me can share Seris's wings.

Even now, I peer into Arfaenn's luminous metaphor; the Lake's soft waves lapping the shores of prosaic reality, the Swan watching us all with love and, above all, patience.

I observe my physical vessel, which Binae gently supports. Time to return to my role, yet the Goldberg persona will never again forget our deeper nature. And all my abilities will slowly become available to him; Shadowcaster merely provided an excuse for one specific power to emerge.

Arfaenn was right. I *have* been awakening, and my mortal body gradually regenerating for months now. As David, I hadn't believed anyone who'd remarked on the change. And to counter the rebels' unfair advantages, I'd done something unprecedented: interceded in my mortal life.

I'd caused the hardy organisms for shielding David's thoughts to begin dying off to indirectly procure a taurei, which intuition told me would be needed. The stinging sensations in David's neck were my doing: skin cells briefly turning rock-hard, which caused minor bleeding. As my earnest but inadequate defenders had suspected, Hhoymon assassins hidden by Vyre skills had experimented with invisible darts.

I'd been the one alerting my microdocs to approaching dangers. Later, my will had rendered my body untraceable so that David could face some challenges unassisted. For me, growth and learning far surpass safety and comfort.

When a Vyre had hurled a rock at David's head, I'd applied shadow to pull my body aside, but had allowed the missile to strike my arm, using shock and pain to cover my moment of conscious intent. Against the em-Bottho, I'd had time to apply more subtlety, disabling its spitting ability and placing a destructive force inside my shadow spear.

David nearly caught on after sinking into the vug. I called the Lithshark to us, affixed shadow tentacles to its mouth, and kept them attached despite overwhelming friction. Fear had provided just enough distraction to obscure my blatant breach of physics.

In the tower of confusion, I'd reluctantly swept molten glass toward our enemies at a crucial time. The twisted Heart of Art ...

When the fearful silver ones had seen how effectively I'd begun to use my shadow powers, they became convinced I was near full awakening. Thus, they'd manipulated me into their museum, hoping that by destroying my body in some far-flung reality, I'd be delayed finding my way back to Commonworld, at least long enough for their plans to mature. I used their ploy to educate my human self, transporting some specific MARBLES and a reader to a high office and steering myself to that office. I'd wanted David aware that O-gen-ai and Nemes were one so they'd allow him fully into the circle of their secrets. And I planned for him to read what was stored on the one MARBLE I had him steal—*my* poetry from my life as a Silver Hhoymon.

For centuries, I'd lived amongst Silvers as a conscious avatar of myself where the Hhoymon had loved me, studied me, and discovered my innate energy signature. Just as the Common had identified Crossroad's enemies by searching for microdocs infused with Seris's hallmark, the rebels had stumbled upon my signature when, investigating the potential threat of a new species invited into the Commonwealth, they'd scanned Earth.

The rebels knew me and feared me. Should I ever visit Crossroad, I might awaken, see into their hearts, and expose their plot. If the scan had revealed my current genetics, their concern would have multiplied; being part Scome, I might side with Scome interests.

So they'd attempted to destroy my body with a series of what would seem like accidents. They didn't dare operate blatantly lest it force my awakening, and hoped I'd die ignorant and then waste decades in starting a new life. And they'd panicked upon learning I'd been invited here.

All so foolish. Deprived of physical form, I would have exposed them immediately.

The Watergod's palpable happiness as he gazes up at me reminds me that I, too, am happy. More than that, I am content. I bless Poseidon and gaze fondly into the simple magnificence of ultraspace, and beyond and within to the Real, that ultimate mystery that cannot be grasped or understood, but provides all things including space a place to be.

I am always home. I belong in and to the Pan-Cosmos. I am what I want to be, and I flow with the moment as naturally as an albatross rides the wind. Even for Supernals the self is empty, wonderfully empty. Otherwise, eternity's weight would crush even us.

Awakening is a joy. Forgetting myself in a new form is a joy. Hearing the heart sing as if for the first time is an incomparable joy. As I live, my spirit grows deeper and richer and I am blessed in countless ways. A sapphire blaze of gratitude radiates from me.

Binae bids me a loving farewell, and I shrink down, putting on the Goldberg body and mind as if it were a beloved and familiar garment. I still have much to learn from this marvelous incarnation....

The Diplomat vanishes and, for a moment, the cavern is still.

At first, all I saw were the shadows of exaltation. Then my mind filled with the glare of a thousand insights, a brightness that threatened to carry me away again.

Just breathe, David, I told myself. *Slow and easy.*

A breath stagnates if you cling to it. Eventually you must let go and trust new air to flow in. Could there be a more blatant message about excessive clinging to people, to things, to life? We can't really hold firm to *anything*, yet we break our hearts trying....

Stop. No more! Not yet!

Gradually, my inner light dimmed. The cavern seemed to darken in response. I sighed, turned, and stared up at Poseidon. "You never know," I said in a small voice.

"Never," he agreed cheerfully.

Impulsively, I trudged up the ramp and sat down at the top, leaning one shoulder against a wall, appreciating the support. I was tired and cold with a chill alien to the cavern's tropical heat.

After my meeting with the Swan, I found my nervous system unready for such intense energy levels. This was much worse. A warm and miraculously dry flipper reached out to drape over my shoulders like a giant shawl. Its weight should've crushed me, but it felt lighter than a feather and tremendously reassuring.

After a few minutes, I noticed Swift's poetry translation still in my hand and unwrapped it. The bottom page escaped, and I retrieved it with shadow-tongs. Turned out to be the title page. I'd opened the package upside down.

The smooth paper had been illustrated with a stylized figure: a Silver Hhoymon with two arms but seven hands. Five hands orbited the body, each a different color, each making a different mystical-looking gesture. Below it, I found this first stanza:

I traveled the space within space,
In lonely, lovely hours
I followed the ways of the wandering rays
In the grasp of celestial powers.

I read no further, put the page where it belonged, and put the manuscript on the platform beside me. Couldn't quite remember what Binae and Urien had discussed but sensed that was a good thing for my peace of mind. I let my tired eyes fall to my taurei. Could Jeeves survive Earth's physics? Hated the idea of abandoning my faithful microdocs. Would my shadowcasting function on Earth? Or my enhanced vision?

For that matter, did I even *want* to live on Earth, returning to my former life? Most of my friends were here now and I'd been redundantly bequeathed with Crossroad citizenship....

Strange how little I could recall of Urien's thoughts. But a few concepts had stuck. Apparently, weird talents would be finding excuses to pop out of me, one by one, like patient measles. Hell, one excuse already existed.

After Shadowcaster had grabbed me, I'd stumbled and fallen victim to the next monster in line. Hadn't gotten a good look, and the photo I'd taken was gone, but I could describe its location. Perhaps someone in my Scome family would tell me what power it was intended to stimulate.

Something else. Now that I'd proven to be my own Deus ex Machina, my life was *not* going to be smooth sailing. Urien planned to milk my humanity for new insights and that meant trouble—severe challenges made harsher to compensate for increasing abilities. Sure, I'd survive as a Supernal, but my body and personality weren't under any kind of warranty.

No sense in worrying. Right now, I needed rest and more rest. I leaned against the glass, let myself relax, and perhaps as a gift from someone gifted, suddenly felt completely at peace.

As I drifted off, I sensed my body being gently lifted. Fine with me. Knowing I was in safe flippers, I gratefully accepted the blissful gift of sleep.

GLOSSARY

The Pan-Cosmos

The entirety of all non-parallel universes. Truly parallel universes can't exist for more than an instant because the similarities between them create an attraction that forces them to merge. However, there are countless numbers of non-parallel universes where some altered, important aspect of native physics creates a permanent separation. The Pan-Cosmos goes through cycles of expansion and slow contraction analogous to the concept of the Big Bang and the Big Crunch. During the final contraction before the next "Pan-Cosmic Unfurling," every universe is absorbed into something indescribable, and cosmic time ceases until the expansion.

Planets

Earth: Not particularly harmless.

Jaaynim: The Hhoymon home world (see Hhoymon below).

Muuti: The abandoned Scome (see Scome below) home world. A somewhat warmer planet than Earth with continents largely covered by lush jungles and rain forests.

Ot-u-klin (English translation is "Meeting of Roads" or "Crossroad World") and often referred to as "Commonworld": This world is the unique junction of all non-parallel universes, the one place where all forms of science and magic operate as they would in their native universes.

Ramdagulad: Maanza's (see Maanza below) artificial fortress planet.

Species

The Blenn: If otters had evolved from insects that hopped around

GLOSSARY

on a single leg, they might resemble the Blenn. This species is one of several on Crossroad with technology at least centuries ahead of human technology, but perhaps the Blenn's most salient feature is humility that reaches so far into the realm of self-deprecation, it practically touches the bottom.

The Chean-shee: With both monkey-like and raccoon-like physical characteristics, the Chean-shee have no sense of hearing, but are sensitive to the faintest vibrations. They are telepathic and also communicate through gestures and changes in eye-color.

The Common: Known by the Nemes as "Guardians," the Common are humanoids almost covered in hearing organs that resemble leaves, stand over eight feet tall or taller, and manage affairs on Crossroad.

The Hhoymon: This species has four distinct major races, each race typically exhibiting a different color and size range. The Grays are a bit taller than the average size of human adults, the Browns shorter but usually heavier and stronger, the shiny-skinned Silvers typically less than five feet in height, and the Whites at least a foot smaller than the Silvers. All four races are equally brilliant, super-geniuses who may be even more technologically advanced than the Blenn in certain ways.

The Nemes: Somewhat resembling teddy bears with sparkly fur, they are the Common's primary assistants who use their phenomenal language skills to engage in first-contact missions to species the Common are interested in as potential members of a Pan-Cosmic community.

The Scome: This is the species that for no apparent reason abandoned their home world, Muuti, and destroyed all their advanced technology while leaving behind most of their literature, art, and architecture.

The Vyre: This mysterious and rather spooky species can radically alter their body-shapes, making their forms follow whatever function they need. They possess magical abilities, and live in villages that would be ideal for filming horror movies.

Crossroad's Supernaturals

The Apnoti: A powerful deity the size of a small truck and whose body is similar in shape to a tarantula.

H'ap Shai, the Firemage: This powerful being appears modeled on a centaur variation with the body of a huge equine and the head of a bear. The Firemage communicates by emitting flames, sparks, and smoke from his mouth, depending on translation devices for those who don't speak the language of fire. Rather than relying on hooves, he flies on powerful jets.

GLOSSARY

The Mirrormage: the Mirrormage began life as an ordinary ibis until becoming, by invitation, part of the Chybris. The Egyptian god Thoth was based on the Mirrormage, partly due to the ancient Egyptians conflating the Mirrormage with Chybris.

S'bek, the Lightmage: Originally a crocodile uplifted by the Librarian during the reign of the Egyptian pharaoh Neheb. When S'bek earned her independence from the Librarian, Chybris gave her three gifts, the ability to enter other being's dreams, a perfect sense of direction, and a potent power of illumination.

The Watergod (known under many other names): Somewhat resembling a triple-sided walrus at least as large as a blue whale, the Watergod appears on Crossroad within a giant tank.

The Supernals

These are the Firstborn, the twelve Principals, who reappear as each refreshed Pan-Cosmos explodes into new existence. Each expresses a major aspect of the mind, a "Sphere," which is why they are also referred to as "Spherecerers."

Aduum Vesheru Mahrda the Preserver: Vesheru is the Supernal of Continuity.

Arfaenn the Dancer, also known as Athfaenn: Arfaenn is the Supernal of Art and usually appears as a series of flowing and graceful images not limited to any specific location.

Binae the Diplomat: Binae usually manifests as a glowing cloud, but can and will change form depending on circumstances. Binae's Sphere includes generating mutual understanding between opposing forces, creating compromise, treaties, and collecting deliberately hidden information.

Chybris the Librarian: In general, the Librarian has three heads (which are replaced from time to time) but four brains, the central brain being the Living Diamond, which acts as a storage unit for the experiences of all Supernals during each Pan-Cosmic cycle, and releases the stored information when the next cycle begins.

Khunuum ae Hovv the Awake: Khunuum is the Supernal of Wisdom and is strongly connected to ShiwaKhali. This Supernal links all Spherecerers in their primary aspects as the fundamental Principles of Mind with that ultimate mystery beyond the mind.

Koreosai the Organizer: Koreosai is the Supernal of leadership and wise management. This Spherecerer seldom manifests a body, but occasionally makes exceptions and then usually appears as a spiral galaxy.

Maanza the Protector: Maanza's Sphere of protection and defense

GLOSSARY

includes weapons, battle skills, tactics, and technological sciences including medical science. The Protector designs and occasionally upgrades the physical forms of other Supernals, and has developed several nearly indestructible forms for His own use.

Seris the Compassionate, also known as Quanen: Seris is the Supernal of empathy, love, emotion, and healing who can appear in many forms, but the forms usually include wings on which images of suffering beings appear.

ShiwaKhali the Dissolver: ShiwaKhali is the Supernal of Clarity whose intrinsic energy strips away false thinking, false images, and illusion. Most creatures are far too fragile to withstand this Supernal's erosion, but the Dissolver works with beings durable enough to survive and profit from this influence.

Urien the Messenger, also known as Hhurm: Urien is the Supernal of Communication including communication with deeper levels of understanding, which allows the Messenger to act as the Supernal of Insight.

Zelud: No human concepts can describe or fit this Supernal, but Zelud's Sphere involves pure creation.

ABOUT THE AUTHOR

Rajnar Vajra was born in the year that Chuck Yeager broke the sound barrier and something mysterious happened in Roswell, New Mexico. Coincidence? Perhaps.

Aside from writing, he is a professional musician, songwriter, music teacher, a practitioner of Zen and other contemplative disciplines, and has been a jeweler, a painter, a recording engineer, and more. He follows developments in science, health, and understanding the mind's nature with the closest attention. Not, perish the thought, partly to mine human progress for story ideas.

He has appeared more than thirty times in the pages of Analog Science Fiction and Fact and has also appeared in the online stories at Tor.com, and in Absolute Magnitude. His novel *Dr. Alien* has been published by WordFire Press, which now presents *Opening Wonders*.

twitter.com/RajnarVajra

amazon.com/Dr-Alien-Rajnar-Vajra-ebook/dp/B0B5GC2YKF

YOU MIGHT ALSO ENJOY ...

Dr. Alien by Rajnar Vajra
Rambunctious by Rick Wilber
Selected Stories: Science Fiction volume 1 by Kevin J. Anderson

Our list of other WordFire Press authors and titles is always growing. To find out more and to shop our selection of titles, visit us at: wordfirepress.com

facebook.com/WordfireIncWordfirePress
twitter.com/WordFirePress
instagram.com/WordFirePress
bookbub.com/profile/4109784512

CPSIA information can be obtained
at www.ICGtesting.com
Printed in the USA
LVHW031200270423
744075LV00012B/121

9 781680 574654